Maslow's Hourglass

Maslow's Hourglass

HATTIE BRANTWOOD

Swift Publishing Ltd,
145-157, St John Street,
London,
EC1V 4PW

This book is a work of fiction. People, places, events and situations are the product of the author's imagination. Any resemblance to actual persons, living or dead, or historical events, is purely coincidental.

© Copyright Hattie Brantwood, 2015. All rights reserved.

No part of this book may be reproduced, stored in a retrieval system, or transmitted by any means without the written permission of the author.

First published by Swift Publishing in March 2015

ISBN: 978-0-9927154-4-1
ebook ISBN: 978-0-9927154-5-8

Meetings and Making a Start

They met, as arranged, under John Betjeman. Celia arrived first, naturally, striding along the upper floor with her wheeled Samsonite rigidly clattering behind her. She wore a pale green linen suit; a nearly ankle length skirt and a semi fitted jacket reaching to the hips. Celia is a striking woman for sixty-six - tall, slim, a confidence in her stance which prompts people to pay attention and give her the respect which she is used to. Her hair is pure white, wiry curls, cut short. Grey eyes behind wire framed glasses that seem to pierce and analyse everything they see; the subtle sheen of expensive skin care giving her a polished, pearly appearance.

Fetching up within two feet of Sir John's slate setting she stood her case to attention beside her and used both hands to flick through the file she was carrying. A slight smile seemed to confirm that everything was as it should be, so she closed the file and swung on one heel to take in the bronze figure with its head tilted back and its hand on the hat to stop it falling off. 'Lovely' mouthed Celia. She wondered why it had caused such a furore when it was installed. Utterly JB as far as she was concerned, perfectly capturing his boyish enthusiasm and wonder at the world.

Eventually she changed position and scanned the crowds in the distance. She checked her watch and her lips thinned. Nobody was late, yet, but they probably would be. Such an echoing place; chimes and announcements all the time, and the sounds of lifts going up and down, the constant drumming of feet. Everyone purposeful, knowing where they were going. She looked up again and spotted two familiar figures fifty yards away, walking towards her but not hurrying. One was taller than the other; she was in casual slacks and a fleece gilet, navy and cream. The shorter one was a little fuller figured, in pale chinos with a pink cotton jacket. Gwen and Gerrie, the sisters. Good. Ah, and some way further back, the limping figure of Linda with her walking stick in one hand as she, like everyone else, hauled her suitcase behind her with the other.

Celia stood still and watched. Gwen and Gerrie were stopping every few moments and looking back, to make sure that Linda was not being left behind. They waved at her in encouragement. Once Gerrie pointed across the concourse to something, and Gwen followed her gaze before touching her shoulder and laughing with her at whatever they had seen. Eventually they ambled up and stood looking at Sir John, crooking their necks. 'Hello, Celia!' said Gwen. 'I'm so glad you suggested meeting here. I've always wanted to see this. It's quite impressive, isn't it?'

'Yes, indeed. And without him, this whole place would have been flattened and something ghastly put in its place. He only just saved it in time. Have you seen the hotel? It's open now – stunning.'

'No, we haven't' Gerrie shook her blonde head. 'Perhaps there'll be time when we come back, before we go home.'

'Isn't there another statue?' asked Gwen, turning in a slow circle. Gwen is stringy, lean, faded. Pepper and salt.

Celia nodded, once. 'Yes – quite different. Almost brutalist, prewar; two lovers, but a bit disturbing. There's no time to look at it now.' She looked at her watch. 'Anyone know what's happened to Mags?'

Linda arrived looking a little strained. 'She's here – I've seen her. I spoke to her.' She pulled her case round in front of her, let go of it and leaned on her stick, her breathing slightly laboured. 'Hi, Celia. I shouldn't worry, there's plenty of time.'

'Yes, but there's no need for it. If Mags is here we should all be together. What's she doing?'

Linda rubbed her forehead under its straight auburn fringe. 'Buying a magazine and some water. And something to eat for the journey, I think.'

'Well' retorted Celia. 'That's silly. Once we're with Making Tracks we're completely catered for. We get food and wine – even champagne if we want it – on Eurostar.'

'It's all right, I can see her' Gwen was standing on tiptoe in her canvas Land's End shoes. 'She's there – look. Mags!' she waved and smiled broadly.

Mags walked up briskly carrying a suitcase without wheels; it looked heavy. She dropped it thankfully on the platform and flicked her fingers. 'Ow. I should have left this at the Making Tracks check in. I passed it down there. Now I've got to carry it all the way back.'

'No, it's much better that we all check in our luggage together' Celia said firmly. 'Right – everyone's here, so let's start our holiday! Sometimes I wondered if we'd ever make it, but we were determined, weren't we?' Her smile was bracing.

'I knew I would have to go all the way back again' remarked Mags to Linda as they made their way to the big glass sided lifts. 'I might buy a better case when we're on the continent. One with wheels.'

'It would have been easier if we'd met at the Making Tracks rendezvous point, but Celia wanted to start off on the right foot I suppose.'

'In control?'

'Well, it's her baby, this holiday really, isn't it? We'll have to see whether she lets go once the tour manager takes over.'

The other three had gone ahead and Mags and Linda had to wait for the next lift. 'You know what I'm looking forward to most?' asked Mags 'Being able to talk Woman for the whole five days.'

Linda heaved herself and her case into the lift and pressed the button. 'Ah. Yes. I know what you mean. No men to worry about. Do you think they'll cope?'

'They've got no choice!' smiled Mags, and the lift began to move, taking them down to the ground floor.

★ ★ ★

Celia reached the check-in with Gwen and Gerrie ahead of the other two. As they walked from the lift Gwen asked 'Any idea who our tour leader is? Did they send details?'

'Alex somebody or other.' Celia didn't slow her pace. 'There's a not very good photo, taken in Salzburg I think. Not sure if it's Alexander or Alexandra. There'll be a Making Tracks sign at the meeting point, though.'

Gerrie, trailing slightly behind, pointed and said 'There it is. And that must be Alex – black tee shirt and jeans, with the Making Tracks umbrella....'

A gaggle of other travellers were gathered round, like a Wild West wagon convoy in a protective circle with the suitcases in the middle.

'Honestly.' Celia shook her head. 'Do they think their cases are going to be whipped from under their noses? There are plenty of police around. It's perfectly safe – there's no need for it.'

Gerrie caught up with them and rested her case beside her, lifting the strap of her large bag over her shoulder so that it was safely across her chest. She kept one hand on the clasp. 'It's the English abroad' she smiled. 'Especially the older ones. We're amongst the youngest, by the looks of it.'

'They're not abroad yet!' retorted Celia. 'Heaven knows what they'll be like in Cologne, or Munich'.

'They'll probably have gone native by then. Or died of a heart attack.' Gwen craned her neck and caught Alex's eye. A hand was raised in response. Several members of the party turned to look at the newcomers, smiling warily.

Linda and Mags joined the group, Mags breathless and muttering 'I was ten feet away, look – in Marks and Spencer, buying some water, and then I had to struggle up to Betjeman and back again.... bloody ridiculous....'

'Right - are we all here?' Celia counted heads. She reached into the outer flap of her shoulder bag. 'Four envelopes, one each – all the details as far as I know them. Train times and so on, but Alex will tell us which platforms, and which carriages, and we have reserved seats so we'll be told those as well. We may not be put together.'

'No problem' Mags smiled. 'It's always interesting to meet other people and chat to them. We'll be with them for a week – it'll be fun!'

'I wonder how many of us there are?' mused Gwen.

'Twenty five' a hand was thrust towards each of them in turn from under the umbrella. 'You're the group of five, booked in by Mrs Hennessey? Great, everyone's here. I'm Alex, according to the information sheets, but I'm always called Sandy. Now, I'll tell you what I've just told the others.....'

A few minutes later they all had their tickets and information about the platform, carriage and seat numbers, and were at the back of a fairly orderly queue waiting for their tickets to be slipped into the slot to let them through to the Eurostar lounge. It was at least twenty minutes before Mags, who found herself at the back, was safely through the passport check and the baggage search and could spot the others on a bench with a space saved at the end with a coat on it.

She sat down and passed the coat back to Gwen, positioning her case between her feet but leaving the strap of her bag across her chest. 'Well!' she remarked brightly. 'So far so good!'

'What do we think of Sandy, then?' Mags leaned across Gwen to speak to the other three. 'Are you thinking what I'm thinking?'

'No idea what to think' said Linda. 'Is it a boy or a girl?'

Silence.

'Difficult' frowned Celia 'When the name is androgynous as well. How old do you think he or she is?'

'Mmmm – late forties? Early fifties?' Gwen hazarded. 'I looked at the arms; quite muscular, slim though, fine hairs but quite a lot of them.'

'Goes with the freckles and mousy hair. Any evidence of shaving, or stubble?'

Linda's voice was loud enough for Celia to put a finger to her lips. 'Really!' she said, shocked. 'That's going a bit far. We'll soon find out. I think it's a woman.'

'Nice voice' put in Gerrie 'but again, could be either. And black tee shirt and jeans and trainers – doesn't give anything away, does it?'

'It'll be the hands' Linda decided firmly. 'That's what'll tell us'.

'No, it'll be the shape. Shoulders and hips. And the walk.' Mags pulled out her newspaper and began to read.

The departure lounge was packed with people; some obviously on business, with a minimum amount of smart luggage and an air of blasé resignation, leaving their seats and ascending the correct escalator just before the information was given out. Others were travellers making their own way, couples and families checking their documents and looking wildly about them for notices and directions to toilets and coffee outlets.

'We're a pretty disjointed bunch' commented Linda, gazing over the crowds.

Gwen followed her eyes 'I can see some people who are obviously part of our group' she said 'because of the labels. I don't expect we'll get to know them much, especially as the five of us are going together.'

'Oh, I don't know about that' objected Mags 'I think once we're all together in the same hotel, and meeting up on excursions and for meals, we might get quite friendly with some of them.'

'Huh.' Linda was dismissive. 'I haven't seen anyone yet that I would want to make a closer acquaintance of.'

'They might not be our type' Celia added primly 'but I think we can make the effort to be civil, at least.'

Linda's lips were pressed in an uncompromising line.

There is always a period at the start of a holiday when time seems to change gear; it takes a little while to get used to, out of routine, and things seem to drag or rush by until a new rhythm establishes itself. Sandy had begun a brisk round of the dispersed Making Tracks passengers to say that their train would be boarding next, when the co-ordinated rising and grabbing of luggage made it unnecessary.

Speaking simultaneously, Mags said 'Already? That was nearly an hour, and it went by in a flash' and Celia commented as she slipped her paperback into her pocket 'At last. I find these enforced waiting periods very tedious....'

Brussels: time to talk

The group assembled outside their prebooked carriage, and Sandy gave out tickets, issuing Celia with all five of her party's. She made sure that her little band each had their own. 'You need to hang on to this; it's got your seat number on it.'

A tall man with unnaturally red hair said loudly 'We're not trusted to look after our own tickets, then? I said, we don't get them till the last minute?' but nobody encouraged him with a response. Cases were loaded into racks at the end of the carriages, and Sandy shepherded everyone patiently into their correct places as the train began to move away exactly on time.

'Don't people look fresh and scrubbed up?' said Mags to Gerrie. 'Hair neat and tidy, pressed shirts and trousers and clean jackets. Can't see a single laddered pair of tights!'

'Well, you make an effort, don't you? Beforehand. It might be a different story when we're on the way back after more than a week.'

Mags and Gerrie had been put in neighbouring seats; Celia and Linda were together, and Gwen was with people who were not on the Making Tracks holiday, although she struck up a conversation with them.

The train didn't stop at Ashford; meals were served, and by the time eyes were raised to look out of the carriage rural France was passing by the window at an increasingly fast rate. There was a short stop at Lille, then coffee was served as they accelerated towards Brussels.

There was quite a wait between trains; most of the Making Tracks travellers ventured out into the street, found it uninteresting, and came back into the station again.

Linda and Gerrie had been wandering aimlessly round the concourse for a quarter of an hour when they came to a halt.

'I don't think those chairs and things belong to anyone' Linda pointed with her stick. 'Let's sit down for a bit.'

They made their way towards an old brown leather sofa, pushed against a wall, and three club chairs. On each side was a coffee outlet with aluminium patio furniture, but this tatty corner, including one chair with a broken leg which leant over at forty five degrees, looked unconnected with anything else.

They sat down on the sofa. Two of the chairs were pulled away at an angle with the other one facing them; they were occupied by two African men in immaculate suits and a girl of about eight, who was sitting opposite them with an open book on her lap. One of the men had a black toddler asleep in his arms, a little boy with thick curly hair. The girl's face was wary, closed; her eyes darted from one man's face to the other as they spoke. She didn't read her book.

'I hope Gwen and Mags know what they're doing' said Gerrie as she sat down. 'Three and a half hours between trains sounds an awful long time, but with ours being late in and all the business with the cases, it's only just over two now.'

'I thought this station would be in Brussels; in the centre' Linda unzipped her fleece. 'I didn't realise you had to take the local train into town in order to see anything'.

'Or walk'.

'Well, I couldn't walk that far, anyway, and Sandy said it took forty minutes. Supposing you got lost? I think it's too much of a risk.'

'Gwen wanted to see the Grande Place. She likes a brisk walk, and she's got a map. I just hope they'll keep an eye on the time. They can always come back on the train. Or take a taxi if they're pushed.'

Maslow's Hourglass

'She's quite an open air type, isn't she?' Linda had been taking in the crowds; now she turned her head towards Gerrie.

'Mmm. Roy's a vet – well, he was. He's retired now, almost. They've always had animals and they've got quite a bit of land. Gwen's not a chintzy type, never has been. She likes to be out and about. We grew up on a farm....'

'Did you?' Linda raised her eyebrows. 'So you haven't always lived in Canterbury?'

'Oh, I don't live in Canterbury. I live in Winchester. Gwen and I grew up in Devon.' Gerrie bent her blonde head and examined her varnished nails. They were a delicate pearly pink.

'That must have been an idyllic childhood. What sort of farm was it?'

'Sheep; and a few milk cattle. We grew a couple of fields of grain. Chickens, as well – I've never tasted eggs as good as those, ever.'

A girl in an overall appeared from nowhere, with a small notepad. 'Coffee? Cappuccino?' she demanded. 'For the sitting.'

Gerrie and Linda looked at each other. 'Two cappuccinos' Linda said. 'Is that all right, Gerrie?'

Gerrie nodded.

'How much?' Linda moved towards her purse.

The girl shook her head sharply. 'No. With coffee'. She vanished.

'Well!' breathed Linda. 'So much for this sofa being for poor weary travellers.' She looked at her watch. 'We'll have to make the coffee last for about an hour, if we can.'

'I tell you what' Gerrie leant forward 'it always beats me how they know we're English. You don't have to open your mouth, anywhere – any other country – and they know you are, straight away. How does that work?'

'Practice, I suppose. They see so many tourists from all countries, they know how we do our hair and what sort of clothes we wear, they can tell a mile off.'

'That girl sounded eastern European. There seem to be people here from everywhere. I wonder how much they'll rip us off for the coffee?' Gerrie took out a square red purse. 'You can pay for the next one, it's all right. I use this purse for Euros when I'm in Italy,

13

and my proper one for back home. Otherwise I get in a terrible muddle.'

'Well, I've got to get used to Euros and cents. I think some have got milled edges and some have grooves – I'll sit and look at them properly tonight so I know which is which. Don't want to give them a one Euro instead of twenty cents....'

The girl reappeared with a tray and two cappuccinos 'Five fifteen' she said. 'Five Euro fifteen cent'.

Gerrie gave her a note and a coin. 'Here's six'.

The girl frowned. She took the money and said 'I have to come back. I have to find coin'.

Gerrie waved a hand. 'Don't worry about it. Keep the change.'

With a mechanical smile the girl was gone.

'That's quite a big tip' mused Linda. 'Eighty five cents. Ten per cent would have been fifty cents, or a tiny bit more....'

'Oh well' Gerrie sat back. 'Too bad. I can't be bothered. I expect she needs it.'

Linda had picked up her cup and saucer. She took a sip. 'This is actually very good coffee' she said 'a nice little doily thing, and a miniature biscuit in cellophane – I'll keep that for the hotel room'. She slipped it into her pocket.

'Good.' Gerrie tried hers. 'You're right. Lovely – I needed this!'

'So tell me more about you and Gwen. Have you still got the farm?'

'No. There were three of us children; we had an elder brother and he took over and farmed for – oh, forty years or more – till long after Dad and Mum had gone. He never married. He only died about five years ago, from an aneurism, just like Dad. The lease on the farm had to be sold.' She looked thoughtful.

'So that's where Gwen gets her enthusiasm for the great outdoors. She could have stayed there, I suppose.'

After a short pause, Gerrie said 'Yes. She could have. She married the vet, of course, that's what happened, but she was in her late twenties by then; she and Dad and Robert had been doing all the physical work between them. Gwen and Dad were very close....' Gerrie sipped her coffee.

Linda nudged Gerrie 'Look!' she said 'Over there! You watch, that girl's doing exactly the same thing with that couple!'

'I think they're on our trip....'

'Yes, they are. It's the man with the dyed hair and his complaining wife.'

'Pat'.

'Is that her name? What's he called?'

'Don't know yet; but he's always going "Pat, where's this? and Pat, did you pack that?" – it would drive me mad if he was –'

'But look – Pat's given her a note - and the girl's shrugging – and Pat's waving her away – I bet she makes stacks of money with that trick.'

Gerrie sniffed. 'She might not get any wages, you know. She might have to live on the tips...'

Linda shook her auburn head. 'Don't be silly. This is Brussels, the heart of European government. They'd have to be above board here. When I worked in finance, I had to deal with people here and in Strasbourg a lot, to do with regulations and interpretation of the law about investments and pensions.....'

Gerrie's jaw had tightened. 'Hm. Well, I think you should use your eyes. Just look around you for a minute. How long have we been here – a quarter of an hour?'

'I should think so. And another quarter walking around first, probably.'

'So, have you spotted that tall woman – with all that bling – approaching the men in the queue for the bureau de change?'

'No. I hadn't noticed.....she's gone to one side now. She's on her mobile. Oh, she's back, simpering and shaking her hair at that man in the overcoat....'

'She's on the game. That's what that is.'

Linda was wide eyed. 'You reckon?'

'Of course! Absolutely!'

'Crikey.'

'See that Asian woman in the long skirt? Over there on the other side of the concourse?'

'The one with the baby. Very tiny baby.'

'She's begging up and down the shops and the coffee areas. Look.'
'Oh, yes....'
'Probably not even her baby. My son Steven said that in Romania women beg through bus windows; they bang the baby's head on the side of the bus until you give them something.'
'This isn't Romania, this is Brussels.'
Gerrie snorted. 'I don't see there's any difference! Global village, these days. Same continent.'
'But when you think; we were joking, weren't we, that this is where the Gravy Train comes in. Mags was laughing about that – she said "so this is the famous MEP Gravy Train we keep reading about!" I mean, all the politicians and bureaucrats from all the member states must come through here. They would see all this going on.'
'Yes, but they wouldn't. One, they don't come through this part, they all have chauffeur driven cars waiting for them; they get whisked straight off to their posh hotels. And two, they don't care about the little people, the small fry getting trodden on at the bottom of the ladder. And three, actually, there's not much you can do about it. Mainline stations are always magnets for down and outs, prostitutes, con men, they always have been. And drug dealers – look at those men on the corner, by the burger joint.'
'What about them?'
'They've been there all the time we have. Africans, again. There's a briefcase on the floor between them. They're waiting for someone; they're not catching a train, that's for sure.'
'How do you know it's drugs?'
'I don't. It might be anything – money laundering, proceeds of crime –'
Linda stared hard at Gerrie. 'You have an incredibly lurid imagination. No, really. I'm quite shocked.'
Gerrie shrugged. 'Just look around you and see what I see. Maybe I'm wrong about it all.'
'Quite honestly, I'd be appalled if you're right and shocked if you're wrong.' Linda gave a short laugh. 'I thought Gwen was bringing her fluffy little widowed sister along on this holiday and it turns out to be Miss Marple!'

Gerrie sipped some more coffee. She wrinkled her nose. 'Gone cold' she said. 'I hope I'm a lot tougher than Miss Marple. I'd rather be Cagney or Makepeace, someone like that.'

'Lacey'.

'Whatever.'

After a pause, Linda said 'I've just realised why Gwen and Gerrie have been bothering my head. It makes me think of Ben and Jerry. Ice cream.'

Gerrie sighed heavily. 'Yes. It's not as if I haven't heard that before.'

'But they weren't around in the late forties, nineteen fifty – so it's just coincidence, then.'

'My mother was Welsh'.

'Oh. Hence the Gwen.'

'Gwenyth. Yes.'

'Pretty name.'

'It means happiness.' Gerrie's voice held no emotion.

'That's nice.'

Gerrie took a little while to reply. 'My mother was terribly homesick. She had Robert first. He was a little man, for my father to raise on the farm. I don't think she ever felt he was really hers. It was when my sister was born that she truly had someone to love. But...'

'What?'

'Oh, it's a long story.'

Linda looked at her watch. 'And Gerrie is Geraldine, I suppose.'

'No, Gaerwen.' Gerrie pronounced it in all its lilting, rolling Welshness. 'You won't have heard of it.'

'I haven't –'

'I couldn't pronounce it as a little girl. The nearest I could get was Gerrie.' She smiled at the memory. 'My mother used to tease me. We were very close. I was the youngest, of course. I loved her dearly.'

Linda cleared her throat. 'We'll have to make tracks soon. No pun intended. I can't get anywhere fast. Oh look – over there, outside Carrefour – '

'It's Celia. I don't like the way she's carrying her bag so loosely on one shoulder. She ought to put it across; it would only take a moment for someone to pull it away....'

'There you go again. You really do have a dim view of the world.'

'She's got her passport and money in there, and all our tickets. Bonanza.'

'Nobody would dare rob Celia!' Linda laughed.

'Oh dear. Another example of the British abroad; arrogance. Some of these types would make mincemeat of her. Now - those four boys on bikes; have you been watching them?'

'They're just riding up and down; they're only youngsters. Give them a break.'

'They're what – ten, eleven, twelve years old?'

'No idea' said Linda shortly.

'And they've been in the station for at least an hour, riding around groups of people. Bag snatchers.'

'Don't be silly.'

'Then why aren't they in school?'

'That much I can tell you. School is only in the mornings on the continent. They start early and finish at lunch time.'

Gerrie shrugged. 'Have it your own way. Celia's going into Carrefour; oh good, she's put her bag on properly with her hand on the clasp.'

'Feel better now?'

'Yes'.

'Good' Linda began to sort out her belongings, zipping up her fleece and reaching for her stick.

'Except for those men.' Gerrie looked towards the two Africans on the chairs with the silent girl and the sleeping toddler. 'I think that child is drugged. And have you seen the terror on the girl's face?'

Linda craned her neck. 'I expect there's a simple explanation.'

'As to why they've been there so long? No mother? Child sleeping unnaturally? Eight year old girl absolutely silent, not reading, too scared to talk to the men, watching their faces all the time? You can't tell me that's Dad and Uncle. Impeccable suits, no luggage. That's trafficking, and I fear for the future of both of them but especially the girl. Come on, we ought to think about moving. It's none of our business and I can't bear to think about it any more.'

They both stood up; Linda stiffly, grimacing as she moved one leg forward and leant on her stick. 'Good thing we haven't got our cases' she said. 'That's one advantage of these holidays; it's really helpful sometimes when they hold them while we wait - between trains.'

'We'll find our luggage in a cage up on the platform' Celia had seen them and come up to join them. 'Sandy's responsibility. I've bought some Belgian chocolate to take home to Kenneth.'

'If I were you I would have waited till the return journey' remarked Gerrie. 'You've got to carry it for a week now, and stop it melting. We're back here on our way home – you could have got it then.'

'Ah but there's only fifty minutes between trains on the way back, and if our incoming one is late...' Celia, as usual, had an answer.

Observations: some questions answered, others arise

'Tell you one thing' said Linda 'I can't wait to get to Cologne and book into the hotel. I want a shower and a hot meal. There is a lift, isn't there Celia?'

Celia eased the strap of her bag on her shoulder and then changed the Carrefour carrier to the other hand. She smiled. 'Absolutely. Don't worry, it's been my top priority to make sure your room will be accessible, in both hotels.'

'And the room sharing?' Gerrie asked as they walked. 'I'm with Gwen, I know.'

'Five is an odd number' responded Celia 'so I'm on my own, and Mags and Linda will be sharing.'

'That's all right' Linda nodded. 'I know Mags quite well and we get on; well, we have up to now!'

Celia smiled. 'It's all been thought through. Nothing to worry about.'

They made their way up the escalator to the platform for the Munich train. 'Far too early' commented Gerrie. 'It's forty minutes yet'.

But at least half the party were already on the platform, some of the women sitting on seats while their menfolk chatted to each other and wandered up and down.

'There's Duracell' Gerrie giggled.

'Who?' Linda frowned and looked about her.

'Chap with the dyed hair and the complaining wife. What is it with these men? Either they wear toupees that look like a squirrel's nesting on their head, or they dye their hair like Donald Trump. Whatever happened to growing old gracefully?'

Linda fingered the artificially auburn curls above her ears; Gerrie noticed, not for the first time, that her hands were very arthritic, several twisted fingers and large knuckle joints.

'I suppose if we women like to look our best, we can't blame the men for doing the same' Celia's cut glass accent made her sound prim. 'We're all children of the sixties, after all. Perhaps he was a real swinger in his day.'

Gerrie giggled again. 'Swinger!'

She earned herself a sharp look from Celia.

'Reg! Reg!' his wife called from the bench.

'Ah!' grinned Linda 'Now we know it's......'

'Reg and Pat!' Gerrie and Linda spoke in unison.

'We'll soon get them sorted out' nodded Gerrie. 'Who's the woman with the huge arse?'

'Sh!' Celia was scandalised. 'I hope you're not going to make personal comments about everyone –'

'There's no need for it' muttered Linda under her breath to a rubbish bin.

'I'm quite worried about Gwen and Mags' Celia craned her neck along the platform, and went to squint down the staircase to the concourse below.

She came back within a minute, and Linda soothed 'There's still half an hour. Stop fretting.'

'But they should be back. I hope they've remembered the platform number. And we'll be in carriage number twenty two, so we have to be on the F part of the platform otherwise we'll be opposite the wrong section of the train. I hope our cases arrive soon...'

'Now look!' Linda stood like a rock in front of Celia. 'We're all grown ups; if Gwen and Mags miss the train, it's not your fault, it's theirs. And the cases are Sandy's responsibility. You're on holiday – come on, enjoy yourself! I dare you!'

Celia didn't smile. 'We have to have time to load our own cases. They don't do that for you.'

Linda breathed out heavily. She turned to Gerrie who was hissing 'Listen! Listen to Duracell!'

'How old do you think I am, then?' Reg was leaning down over the woman seated next to Pat. 'Go on! Have a guess! I bet you're wrong!'

'You don't have to answer him, June' Pat sighed to her companion.

Gerrie and Linda exchanged a triumphant look. 'June!' they said together.

'Do you think her husband is called Terry?' asked Linda.

'He's already told me how old he is' nodded the man standing next to Reg. 'I must say, I was surprised.'

'You were, weren't you Mike?' Reg straightened up. 'You said you were! I play golf five days a week, and tennis twice a week in the summer and I swim twenty lengths every Sunday morning. Don't I, Pat? That's what keeps me young. Go on, June – how old do you think I am?'

June pursed her lips; she was an angular woman, pale, with wispy brown hair. 'Well. I don't know.'

Pat shot her husband a look. 'You don't have to, June. Stop it, Reg, you embarrass people.'

'Seventy?' ventured June.

'Oh.' Reg looked irritated. 'Most people say sixty or sixty five. I'm going to be seventy two on this holiday." He recovered himself. 'It's because I keep myself so fit. I play golf five days a week, you know. We always have a good holiday round about my birthday, don't we Pat?'

'Yes'. Pat was eating a sandwich. 'Want one, June?'

'Oh, here they are. Thank goodness.' Celia had spotted the two brisk figures of Gwen and Mags striding up the platform towards them.

At the same time a lift door opened and two wire cages of cases were wheeled along to a space near the large 'F' hanging above them. All the luggage had the fluorescent orange labels with black numbers which denoted Making Tracks passengers.

A scrum followed in which the male members of the group tried to pull their cases off, even if they were several layers down, and the porters shouted 'Attendez! Attendez! Wait, Wait!'

Sandy stood in the middle of the melee, deftly removing people and getting between the cages and the passengers. 'If you'll stand back, please, back behind the benches, let the porters unload – we can take our cases then. Back please!'

The empty cages were clattered away and the men dived on the luggage again, tripping over each other and calling out 'Colin! Colin! This one's yours!' and 'Iris – take this, love.....'

'Sandy! Sandy! Our cases aren't here! They've lost our cases!' This was Duracell in full panic mode.

Sandy's hands rose in appeasement. 'It's all right Reg – there's one more cage to come. They can only get two in the lift at a time. Let the others take theirs. Yours will be here in a minute.'

Celia had got hers, and so had Mags and Linda, but Gwen's and Gerrie's were still to come.

'Whew!' breathed Mags. 'I was thinking what a nice job it must be, leading a tour like this one. Sensible older people, nothing to worry about with all the trains and the hotels booked. But that was a nightmare – you need to be a special constable and nursery teacher all at the same time. Sandy's welcome to it.'

'And this is only the first day' agreed Gwen. 'Wait till they get their collective danders up over something else – the food, or the weather –'

'Oh, they will!' Celia was confident. 'Some people only go on holiday in order to have a good moan. You wonder why they bother to go away at all.'

Linda and Gerrie mouthed 'There's no need for it' at each other and shook a little.

Eventually everybody was on the train. Seats were all numbered, but whichever end of the carriage they clambered into, up very high steps and straight into the back of the person in front who was stuck, they found their seats were in the middle or at the other end, and most of the luggage had to be heaved up on to overhead racks. So a ten minute struggle took place while cases were manhandled through the narrow gap between the seats, people tried to back into seats to let others past, and found they were occupying the space someone else and his case were trying to get into. The train manager was exasperatedly trying to get through and keep some kind of order, and refreshments were being loaded into the storage areas between the carriages. Tempers became very frayed; Pat could be heard complaining loudly and at length. 'Reg! This is not what we paid for. You need to say something. Tell Sandy. Fill in one of their forms. This is great, I must say. You and your ideas...'

Linda nudged Gerrie 'Listen! Listen to Duracell!'

'Could you – ever so sorry. I've got a torn ligament in my shoulder...I play tennis twice a week, you know, but I think I've – would you? Thanks – ta – thanks!'

A small, wiry man festooned in cameras and binoculars and with only a backpack was gamely trying to force two red tartan cases up onto the rack above the seats. Just as he began to wedge the second one into a small space the train moved off and there was a scurry as the remaining members of the group staggered against each other and found their spouses and seats. As the train picked up speed order began to be restored, and smiles of relief spread along the carriage.

Gwen and Gerrie were sitting together, Mags and Linda were in single seats one behind the other, and Celia was in a group of four, next to the wiry man with the binoculars, and opposite Mike and June Finch. Mike immediately set the table up between them all – 'Do you mind? Thanks. I want to spread my map out' – and Celia took out her book, smoothed the spine out, and began to read.

Linda squirmed round in her seat to talk to Mags behind her; she grimaced at the pain in her hip. 'Did you get to the Grande Place?' she asked.

'No, we didn't, but we did see the Mannequin Pis! By mistake.'

'What do you mean, by mistake?'

'We got caught up looking at the architecture – some of it's lovely – and the main road was very noisy, so we went off piste – sorry, unintentional pun – and found some other things. We had to keep an eye on the time so we realised we had gone the wrong way for the Grande Place and had to head back to the station. What did you do?'

'Stayed in the station. Sat and had a coffee with Gerrie, did lots of people watching.'

'That's always fun.'

'Scary...'

'Why?'

The train entered a tunnel.

'Scary people. Tell you later.' Linda turned painfully back to face forwards and tried to get comfortable.

Gwen was talking to Gerrie. 'I hadn't realised quite how bad Linda's getting.'

'She couldn't have gone into Brussels, seen any of the sights. Unless she'd taken a taxi, I suppose.'

'You have to be quite fit for these holidays. I don't think people realise.'

'Sandy got her case into the train, did you see? And put in on the rack. You're supposed to be able to do that for yourself.'

'We've got a couple of boat trips, on the lakes; she ought to be able to manage that.'

'Oh, that'll be all right. And apart from Cologne at the beginning and the end, we're in the hotel for six nights, no more moving about for a bit. That's good.'

'Salzburg.'

'Hope she'll be okay there.'

'Hallstadt.'

'Train and boat.'

'But the salt mine?'

'Oh, she'll never manage that. That's out.'

'I don't know much about her' mused Gwen. 'Celia seems to know her somehow; I think she worked for a firm of financial advisers.'

'She's got a husband.'

'Stuart.'

'What does he do? Financial?'

'No idea. I don't think they've got any children.'

'She had a car accident when she was forty, that much I do know. Celia told me. She was very badly injured – that's why she's in such a state.'

'Poor woman.'

'Yes. Oh good – they're bringing something to eat....'

Sandy, who had been doing paperwork, sprang up and went from seat to seat, leaning on the headrests and explaining that there would be hot and cold drinks, including wine or beer, and sandwiches and sweet snacks, but they would be charged for. There was a menu in the stretchy magazine nets on the backs of the seats, with prices.

After their mini-briefing Gwen asked Gerrie 'So what do you think? We must decide. Male or female?'

'Mmm. Still not sure.'

'Female, I reckon.'

'Probably. Let's see which loo she uses!'

'Ah, but the ones on the train are unisex.'

'True.'

Properly abroad, now, and acclimatising

Mags was looking out of the window. Amazing; the countryside was lovely, immaculately farmed, with pretty little villages. So clean. She began to notice the roads, even the narrow ones through woods or along the sides of fields; all completely free of potholes and well metalled. Not a bit like England, she thought. And no rubbish, no flytipping. They were in Germany now. Even where the houses backed on to the railway the tiny gardens were ordered, organised; little plots of vegetables and flowers, tidy sheds, strips of well maintained allotments, colourful and carefully kept.

We could learn a lot, she mused, as she chose a coffee and a ham roll from the trolley. She smiled at the attendant, a slim, tanned metrosexual with an earring and perfectly groomed hair. 'Thank you madam' he nodded smoothly 'I will take payment on my return. Enjoy your snack.' He moved on.

Mags thought of Dudley, alone at home. He would have bridled at the obviously gay attendant, and said something aloud. She wondered if she ought to feel guilty at being released from his prejudices; but what was the point of going off with the girls if she wasn't free to take in the extraordinary world around her? She felt an almost physical switch operate in her brain, an opening to experiences. It was pleasant. She wanted travel to literally broaden her mind – wasn't that what it was for? She bit into her roll and took a sip of coffee, turning to look out of the window again.

The couple behind her were chatting quietly; it was impossible not to tune into their conversation – American accents, but refined; educated. Mags had glanced at them once or twice, in the Eurostar lounge and on the platform. Both tall, slim; he a silvery man with frameless glasses and a pale jacket and chinos, she willowy and blonde, six feet tall with a contralto speaking voice which Mags found soothing. Not at all the brash, nasal tones she associated with American tourists. They seemed cultured, well travelled. She caught the words 'Sacher torte.' 'In Salzburg' replied the husband. 'I think you can get it anywhere, but the best is from the Sacher hotel. They've got the secret recipe'. 'I want some of that, Donald.' 'We'll make sure, dear. There'll be time.' 'Good. Good.'

The attendant came back, deftly collecting the cash and picking out change from a leather purse attached to his belt. Another attendant was striding down the central gap, looking a bit like Robbie Williams, thought Mags, with short gelled hair, surprisingly wide blue eyes and dark brows and lashes. He reached his colleague and put a hand on his waist to gain his attention. A happy smile passed between them, hands touched. Robbie walked on, still smiling. Interesting, thought Mags; the travel industry seems very popular with the gay community. You hear about trolley dollies on aeroplanes, but it seems to be true on the trains as well, at least the European ones. And there was still the Sandy question to resolve.

Germany was streaking past the window at a racing speed; sometimes the train ran parallel with an Autobahn for a while, and it was easy to see how much faster they were going than the fastest cars. Mags nodded off from time to time, her head cushioned on a rolled up cardigan against the window. Linda had borrowed her newspaper and was reading. Celia read her book and looked up sometimes to see what was outside. Gwen, also next to the window, dropped off or chatted to Gerrie, who was keeping an ear on everyone else's conversations when she could.

The countryside changed to long, open plains, then to woods and villages, to vineyards and maize fields. On one side there were solar farms; acre upon acre of rectangular solar panels covering an astonishing area of land. The women noticed it first. 'Colin – look! All those out there! I've never seen so many!' Then the men began to point it out to each other and debate it between themselves. 'That's all part of the German plan to be completely carbon neutral by twenty twenty. I read about it. Look, there's a small factory over there, only one storey, but there must be thirty panels on the roof. Another field full, see? And the end of those rows of vines – must be at least a hundred. We should do that.'

'Haven't got the sun. Haven't got the climate.'

'Haven't got the room, either. Those fields are as big as some of our towns.'

'You'd think they'd have more wind turbines. Haven't seen many of those.'

'It must be windy across all this open land, surely?'

'You've got to store the power, that's the problem they've got. Doesn't matter how much sun there is, what happens at night?'

'Must make a dent in their bills though, must make a difference.'

'Costs millions to do it all. Where does the money come from?'

'Huh! All our taxes. The money we pay into Europe. We've paid for this!'

Interesting how the men take over conversations, thought Mags. It will be a real treat to be free of that for a week. She drifted off again.

Sandy made another trip up the central gap, swaying from side to side to talk to the Making Tracks group. 'Here is a list of all the people on our holiday. I wanted to make sure that nobody objected before I gave it out, but it's nice sometimes to have the names in front of you, isn't it?'

Couples were given one sheet each, but the Hennessey party had five, all issued to Celia. Linda twisted round to talk to Mags behind her 'This is good, isn't it? Now we can work out who's who.'

'I bet there's nobody down here as Duracell, though' thought Mags.

Gradually everyone began to realise that they were nearing the end of the first day's journey; Cologne was just over half an hour away. The indication lights over the toilets at the end of the carriage glowed red as small groups of people waited to use them, chatting quietly and bracing themselves against the compartment wall. The evening closed in and there were yawns and a general casting around for coats and jackets. Eventually one or two of the men began to heave down cases from the racks, and to pack up books and newspapers into hand luggage. The women combed their hair, touched up their makeup, tidied their bags. The train began to slow down, a subtle but unmistakeable shift to a suburban speed; neat houses gave way to office blocks and car parks, and as they entered the Koln Hauptbahnhof they experienced the staggering lilt of a long train in the process of arriving at its platform. The two attendants passed through at speed, looking businesslike, all banter and familiarity gone. The train manager stopped one of them and barked something; the attendant shrugged and strode on.

At last they stopped, and the next ten minutes were taken up with an ungainly struggle with luggage, blocked doorways and impatient regular passengers who were burdened with nothing more than a laptop or a small briefcase. Sandy was marshalling the Making Tracks passengers on the platform, as usual looking like a character from a Western film with the suitcases firmly in a circle and the people ranged round them ready to fight off any marauders.

'Stay here. Stay with your luggage' Sandy had to shout over the hubbub. 'The cages will be here in a minute, and they'll be loaded up and taken to the hotel. You can follow me then; the hotel is very close to the station, across a main road and one block down the side street. Stay with me, and remember the traffic flows the other way. Be careful as you cross. And watch for pickpockets.'

Cologne station was in the process of renovation; there were wooden walkways and sloping paths, scaffolding and temporary notices everywhere; but eventually they were through the concourse, past the shops and bakery outlets and following Sandy's Making Tracks umbrella as it forged its way through the crowds.

The foyer of the hotel was not large, and Celia's party found themselves squashed against a service door. The routine was clearly familiar to the staff and to Sandy, and access cards were quickly handed out, room numbers memorised and once the cases had arrived and been claimed, it was a matter of waiting for the one lift to take six people at a time to their floors.

'We could use the stairs' suggested Mags.

'Bit difficult with a heavy case' demurred Celia. 'And we've only one card per room. Better stay together.'

They managed to cram themselves into the lift's third ascent and staggered out on the second floor. 'See you downstairs for the buffet supper. Shall we say half an hour?' Celia pulled up the handle of her case and stalked down the corridor.

Gwen and Gerrie collected themselves and their cases and went off to their room, and Mags and Linda looked at the room signs on the wall and headed in the opposite direction. 'See you in half an hour!' 'See you! I'm starving!' 'It smells lovely, I must say...'

Travel weary

Mags opened the door, leaving her case in the corridor, and held it open for Linda. Then she picked the case up and followed, dumping it near the wardrobe as the door banged shut.

Linda sat down heavily on the edge of the bed by the window. 'Oh God, I'm tired' she breathed. 'I need to take some tablets before we eat.'

'I'll get you a glass from the bathroom' volunteered Mags. 'Do you need some water? Sandy assured us that we could drink tap water anywhere we're going.'

'It's all right, I've got some bottled.' Linda eased her jacket off and bent to remove her shoes. She lay back on the bed and closed her eyes.

Mags brought the glass round to the side of the bed and opened the window. 'No view' she said. 'Nothing out there, just a flat roof down below and a wall.' She drew the curtains.

'Well that's all right. We're only here for one night. This room doesn't look too bad....' Linda struggled to a sitting position and dug into her bag for a pill box.

'No it doesn't' agreed Mags. She opened the wardrobe. 'Oh, a mini fridge. What's in it? Quite a lot – fruit juice, nuts, brandy, couple of miniature bottles of wine....'

'Tea making stuff?' Linda swallowed some water, tipping her head back to get the tablets down.

'Yes, the usual – tea, coffee, sugar, hot chocolate.'
'Milk?'
'No milk, but I brought some.'
'Wow! Well done!'
'I always do. I pack a small travelling kettle, an adaptor, tea bags and milk whenever I go anywhere. You can always take it home again if you don't need it. I did ask Celia on the phone, and she said she'd check what was supplied. I don't think she did though. But anyway, I've come prepared.'

'Are you going to unpack? I'm not.'

'No' replied Mags. 'Not for one night. I'm not going to change for supper, either.' She unzipped her case and took out a nightdress and a sponge bag. She threw the nightdress on the other bed. 'I'll go in the bathroom first, quick wash and brush up. Won't be a minute.'

When she emerged Linda was on her phone. 'All right. Long as you're okay. Are you sure? Fine. We're just going down to have something to eat. No idea; I think it's hot, though. Tomorrow, when we get there. It'll be lateish, I think. Don't know, seven o'clock? Something like that. One hour ahead. Take care then. Bye.'

Mags had left the bathroom light on and the door open. 'All yours' she said. 'Been talking to your husband?'

'Yes. Stuart. Are you going to ring yours?'

Mags pursed her lips. 'I don't think so. Not tonight. Maybe tomorrow after we've settled in.' She looked at her watch. 'Ten minutes. We'd better get a move on.'

Linda clambered painfully off the bed and lurched towards the bathroom, steadying herself on a chair and the cupboard under the television, finally leaning on the bathroom door jamb.

'Do you want your stick?'

'No. I'll cope. I think I'm getting worse, though.'

Mags laughed. 'I think we're all pretty stiff after the day we've had, with all the climbing in and out of trains and hauling our luggage around everywhere. Don't forget we're all over sixty!'

Linda didn't smile. 'Maybe I shouldn't have done this. I wanted to prove something to myself....I think it'll be my last trip abroad.' She struggled into the bathroom and closed the door.

Mags picked up the TV handset and clicked the set on; it was tuned to the BBC news channel. She turned the sound up so it was just loud enough to hear, and sat on the end of her bed staring at the full length mirror on the opposite wall. She saw a slimmish, dark haired woman with a very pale face; looking tired, pasty. Neck sagging a little. shoulders not as well set as they used to be – drooping a bit. She sat up straighter. Smart jeans, tailored, and a white top. A small Swarovski crystal on a silver chain round her neck. A present from Dudley. Technically. Actually she had bought it herself. He hated Christmas. Do you want something? he'd asked. What do you want? It's no good me getting it – I don't know what you want. I'd get it wrong. You buy it. Whatever you like. I'll pay you for it. So she had bought the necklace on a shopping trip with her daughter. Then there had been trouble about wrapping it up; she'd left the box out on the kitchen table for a couple of days, but he'd said nothing about it. In the end, she'd picked it up and showed it to him. Do you like it? he'd asked. Yes, she'd said. Yes, it's lovely. Good, good – and he'd gone back to reading the paper. Will you wrap it? she'd asked him. He'd looked up. Why? Well, presents are usually wrapped. You can have it wrapped if you like, he'd answered, rubbing his nose. Whatever you want. I'm no good at wrapping things, you know that – if you want it wrapped, you'd better do it yourself. I'll pay for the paper. The familiar sensation of being in a bizarre drama enveloped her. He didn't mention paying for the necklace. She decided not to wrap it up; instead, she wore it on Christmas Day. He said nothing. At teatime she went and sat next to him on the sofa, fingering the chain at her throat; thank you for this, she said, smiling warmly at him. Is that the necklace I bought you? Yes, I love it! Good, good. She simply couldn't bring herself to ask for the money. But in January when he was checking his credit card bill, he'd come along the passage from the study and asked her – did I ever pay you for that necklace? No, she said. No, you didn't. Dudley looked cross. Why didn't you ask me? I said I'd buy it for you. Why didn't you remind me? Mags had shrugged. Slipped my mind, she said. I want to pay for it, Dudley had insisted, a little peevishly. Shall I give you a cheque? That would be fine, thanks.

But he never did. Mags knew where he kept some cash, and for several weeks she had tormented herself with indecision, wondering whether to confront him and ask for the cheque, or whether to forget all about it, or whether to help herself to the money he kept in a shoebox at the bottom of his wardrobe. The whole question took on ridiculous proportions as these things always did; if she took the money, would he notice? Should she take it all at once or quietly siphon off a twenty pound note three times? But he should notice! He owed it to her! The horrible atmosphere which would ensue, though, would sour their relationship for ages. Why did you have to take it? He would round on her. It's not as if I mind you having it; what I'm angry about is that you didn't feel you could simply ask me. I've told you I want you to remind me, and now you've gone about it in an underhand way; what sort of message are you giving me? That you think I'll lose my temper? Or that you don't trust me to keep my word? This is very serious, Mags. I don't like the way you seem to think of me. She had heard it all before; it always ended in misery.

When Linda emerged from the bathroom Mags was rubbing her temples.

'Headache?'

'Yes; just a slight one.'

'Hunger, I expect. Could you hand me my stick? And my handbag? I've just had a lick and a promise with the soap in there and a towel. I'll quickly comb my hair and put on some lippy – there – now I'm ready.'

Mags turned off the TV and went to the door, letting Linda out before turning out the lights and closing up. Linda turned to her and said 'Pretty necklace. I do like that – it's so delicate, and it goes with anything. Present from your husband?'

'Mmmm.'

Getting to know the others; and a revelation

Downstairs they found a surprisingly large dining room, with plenty of room between the tables. Celia and Gwen and Gerrie were tucking in to smoked fish and a pasta salad with crusty bread and butter; a waitress was whisking away three empty soup bowls. It was a table for six, but Duracell and his wife were also seated there, so Mags and Linda passed by and made for an empty table further along. Pat was having a moan. 'I said to Reg, didn't I Reg, this is far too long for a first day. They ought to have thought about that. I'm going to tell somebody. And our room is much too small, we're not used to that. The bed's quite big, I grant you, being two pushed together, but there's hardly any room by the window. I've had to move the easy chair.'

Celia spotted Mags and looked up with a grateful smile. 'Are you all right? Yes? And Linda, I hope today wasn't too much for you?'

'I'll live' responded Linda, limping her way to a free table and sitting down heavily.

'That list of names, Celia' Mags leant over 'could we have our copies? I'd like to have a look tonight, to get to know people a bit.'

Celia rummaged in her bag and passed over two pieces of folded yellow paper. 'The food's good' she said. 'Lovely soup; a bit like leek and potato, but I don't think it is. The fish is super; and there's chafing dish of pork slices in gravy – you had that, didn't you Reg?'

Reg grimaced. 'I'll pay for it' he said, rubbing his stomach. 'Never was much good with pork; indigestion. Wind.'

'I did tell you, Reg.' Pat was cutting into a slice of cheesecake with a fork. 'Good job I brought the Gaviscon...'

Gwen and Gerrie tried not to look at each other; Gerrie pinched her lips together with pearly fingers.

'See you at breakfast, then, if not before' Mags waved in a general way at the table.

'Ten to eight' said Celia, crisply, before taking a sip of orange juice.

'Breakfast time?'

'No – meeting in the foyer to walk to the station. Didn't you hear what Sandy said when we got our keys?'

'Crikey. Good heavens. So we need to have breakfast at seven, or not much after.'

Duracell scratched his head with a thumbnail; Mags thought it was a practised gesture to prevent people seeing his grey roots. 'It's no problem for me' he grinned. 'I'm fit. I'm always up early, aren't I Pat? I say, I'm always up early. With the lark.'

Pat scraped the last bit of cheesecake off her plate and sucked the fork. 'He's fit, you see, Reg is. Plays tennis twice a week. Golf nearly every day. He's on the Neighbourhood Watch.'

Gerrie whispered to Gwen 'what is he, the second hand?' and they both exploded into fits of artificial coughing, managing to disguise it by wiping their mouths with paper serviettes.

They earned a glare from Celia.

Mags and Linda perused their lists over supper.

'Right' said Linda 'So here we are. There's Reg and Pat Cooper. That's Mr and Mrs Duracell. And Mike and June Finch.'

Linda put down her knife and fork. 'It says at the bottom that people are listed as they would like to be called by fellow members of the group. They've been asked.'

'Were you asked?' frowned Mags. 'I wasn't. I'm sure I wasn't. I might want to be called Margaret – how do they know?'

'They'll have asked Celia.'

'Ah, of course. Oh well; I'm always called Mags. I don't mind. What about Gwen and Gerrie?'

Linda peered at the paper. 'They're down as Gwen and Gerrie. Mrs Gwen Williams and Mrs Gerrie Wolfe.'

'I didn't know Gerrie's surname. How odd that they have the same initials as each other.'

'Gosh - Yes, it is. I didn't notice that. Mrs Celia Hennessey. Mrs Linda Jeffs. Here's you – Mrs Mags Furnival. Who's Donald and Maewin Chisholm?'

'Ah, they'll be the tall Americans. Unless there's another Donald.'

'No, there isn't'.

'Right, well they were behind me on the train. He was Donald. She wants Sacher torte.'

'Done her homework.'

'Yes, she sure has' smiled Mags. 'They seem very cultured and well travelled. I wish I had their cool.'

'What about the woman with the big arse?' Linda looked up.

'No idea. You mean that woman over there?' Mags pointed to a floral splodge at the food counter, spooning fruit salad into a small white bowl.

'Yes.'

'We'll have to wait till tomorrow to spot the others. There's a couple from Devon, I think, travelling with the small leathery chap festooned with binoculars. Haven't had a chance yet to pick out anyone else – I think there's a widow on her own. From Ipswich. Or Islington. Can't remember, I heard her talking to someone.'

'Tell you what' Linda had put her paper down and was dabbing her mouth with a serviette. 'One funny thing – there are two Pats and a Patricia. I wonder if we can guess those.'

'We know one Pat – Mrs Duracell.'

'I bet you anything the one with the big arse is a Patricia.'

'Bet me an apfelstrudel?'

'You're on.'

'With cream?'

'Don't push your luck!'

By half past nine Rooms 207, 208 and 215 were all occupied.

In 207 Mags and Linda were getting ready for bed. Mags moved deftly and found herself automatically in charge of checking that the door was locked, the lights out, the TV switched off. She asked Linda:

'I can set my mobile for an alarm. What time do you think? Working backwards from ten to eight in the reception area.'

Linda was in bed, propped up on pillows. 'Breakfast at seven then; get up at – quarter past six?'

Mags grimaced and fiddled with her phone. 'I suppose you're right. It sounds awfully early, and we're supposed to be on holiday…'

'Well, we've both got to use the bathroom and get ready. I'll have to have a strip wash; I can't use that bath, or the shower. That'll take me twenty minutes or so.'

'Mmmm.' Mags set the phone and put it on her bedside table. She slipped her nightdress on over her head and peeled off her jeans and top, folding them and laying them on her suitcase. Then she shrugged off her underwear and put them on top. It's like being at Guide camp, she thought; I can't remember when I last shared a room with anyone except Dudley or the children. Children! Both nearly forty now….

She got into bed. 'I think I'll settle down' she said. 'I don't mind if you read, Linda – do you want the paper?'

'Got it. Took it out of your bag. I'll just read for a few minutes.'

Mags switched off her light and lay on her back. She glanced at Linda, in profile as she read in the other bed. It may have been the unforgiving bedside light, or the angle of the pillows, but she suddenly felt shocked by how drawn and ill Linda looked. Sallow, sunken cheeks, stringy neck. And the incongruous purple-copper curls above her ears and at the back of her neck – her own hair, but strongly coloured and permed. The long, straight fringe brushing the grey eyebrows; Linda's habitual gesture of smoothing the fringe down with her crooked fingers.

I know so little about her, she thought. I wonder what her life has been like? I wonder what her worries are? I expect I'll find out in the next few days. I'm lucky that as far as I know I'm pretty fit, physically. At the moment. For my age. And then she slept.

In Room 208 Gwen and Gerrie were sitting on the separate beds brushing their hair and chatting. Gwen wore Marks and

Spencer pyjamas, Gerrie had a long satin nightdress and a matching robe with the sash left untied and hanging from its loops.

'So how is Roy, really?' Gerrie put her hairbrush down and opened a pot of face cream. She began to smooth it over her cheeks in an upward movement.

Gwen sighed. 'Oh, he's all right. You know Roy. As long as he's got his golf, he's perfectly happy, I think. He does a bit of locum work with small animals – he can't do equine any more. He loves horses, of course; he still goes racing with his friends and his golf club buddies. But he's had to give up treating horses, hasn't got the strength now, and he can't get the insurance. It's a shame, because that's where the money is.'

'Well, he doesn't need the money, does he?' Gerrie put the lid back on the face cream and shot her sister a penetrating look. 'The mortgage was paid off years ago, and you've always told me he had a good pension set up.'

Gwen sat back against her pillows. 'That's what I thought. That's what he told me.'

Gerrie waited, but there was silence. After a while she asked:
'You're not worried, are you?'
'What about?'
'Money.'
'I don't ... I don't think I'd better talk about it.'
'Why not?'
Gwen said nothing and turned her head towards the window.
Gerrie persisted 'Why not?'
'Oh ... there's nothing I can put my finger on. And loyalty.'
'Loyalty? But I'm your sister!'
'I know. I know. But Roy ...'
'What?'
'There can't be anything really wrong. He must know what he's doing.'
'What is he doing?'
'I'm not sure.' Gwen got off the bed and went over to the dressing table. She stooped to look in the mirror and wiped her finger over an eyebrow. Then she straightened up and turned round, leaning her back against the dressing table. She folded her arms.

Gerrie's voice hardened. 'Come on, what's going on?'

'I – I don't think we've got much behind us, after all. It's a bit worrying.'

'Why not? Don't tell me Roy's got a fancy woman?' Gerrie wasn't smiling.

'No, it's not that. I really don't think it's that. The family means a lot to Roy, he wouldn't do anything to upset Gavin or Jenny, never mind being fond of me.'

'Fond? Is that all?'

'Well, you know what I mean. It's nearly our Ruby Wedding.'

'Anyway' said Gerrie, unscrewing a pot of nail varnish 'Gavin's in Dubai, isn't he, with his family? From what you said, he's showing no signs of coming back? His firm's got a lot of business there.'

'Oh yes, Gavin and Ruth and the kids get a paid-for trip home every year, but they're very well settled out there. Jenny's only in the next village, though, so she'd be devastated if Roy and I – if anything happened to us.'

Gerrie finished repainting the tips of her fingernails and started on her toes, resting each leg in turn on a stool. 'So what's wrong, then? You must have some reason for worrying?'

'I honestly don't know. I have suspicions, that's all.'

'What suspicions?'

'I think Roy may be gambling.' Gwen's voice was emotionless.

'God.' Gerrie put the lid back on the bottle. 'God. I hope not. Why?'

'I wasn't going to tell you this. We ought to be going to sleep, we've got to get up really early tomorrow....'

'You can't just say something like that, and leave it there! Come on! For heaven's sake, why do you think he's gambling?'

Gwen sighed and got back into bed.

'I don't know what's happened to the deeds of our house. He said he'd decided to lodge them at the bank instead of keeping them in our safe.'

'Perhaps that's what he did.'

'Well, no, he didn't. But that's only one thing. You know when lots of little things happen and on their own they seem very minor?

But suddenly there's a sort of critical mass moment, and you get a shock and you see the whole picture? He never shows me bank statements any more; we used to pay off the credit cards by direct debit every month, but we don't now. One of them has been withdrawn; Roy said he had cancelled it because they had reduced his credit limit, but they phoned several times while he was out and wanted to speak to him.'

'That doesn't sound too suspicious to me.'

'Oh, there've been so many odd things. You know I worked for Social Services for twelve years? Only part time, but I paid into a pension. Well, Roy asked me to write to them for a valuation and to see what a lump sum would be compared to drawing an income from it. We decided that the lump sum was the best bet, so I drew that to invest in ISA's and things and Roy took the cheque to pay into our joint account while we thought about it. But he kept prevaricating and it's been nearly a year now, and whenever I ask about it he says he's getting advice, and there's a chap at the golf club who's looking into it, and he's ill at the moment, and the bank are getting a financial adviser to contact us, but they've restructured the office – there's always an excuse.'

'That does sound a bit concerning.'

'I know. And I was supposed to be having a new car; my Clio is nine years old and the garage says it won't get through the next MOT. Roy has always insisted that we each have a car. We need to, with me going over to Jenny's to collect little Rosie after school, or to sit with her if she's poorly when Jenny's at work. And half term. And doing my hospital car run. We've got more than enough money for a newer one; or I thought we had. But Roy got really nasty last time I mentioned it, and said surely one car was enough for both of us – we're retired, after all, he said.'

'Oh.'

'And things have gone missing.'

'You're joking! What things?'

'You remember the collection of brass things from the farm, that we had? Horse brasses, those antique ones, and the copper kettle, and the weights and those pewter measuring jugs? And the pictures.'

'Of course I do. Leo always said those were worth quite a lot. And he would know.'

'Missing.'

'Where from? You didn't have them out, did you?'

'They were in the loft, in a couple of big boxes. Labelled. I saw them there when Gavin took some stuff after he got married, and when the plumber came a few months ago he needed to move them out of the way, so they came out and went into the spare room.'

'Perhaps the plumber took them?'

'No, I was there when he and his mate passed them back up the ladder into the loft. I was bringing them some tea.'

'How do you know they've gone?'

'I went to get my case' Gwen pointed to the corner of the room. 'Roy was out and I knew I could get it down by myself, so I undid the ladder and climbed up. The loft isn't huge and only half of it has flooring in, and the only things up there now are three suitcases and the Christmas decorations. No boxes from the farm. Gone.'

There was silence.

'And' Gwen turned her light out 'I think he's had my Premium Bonds.'

'He'd have to forge your name for that.'

'I think he did. And most of my jewellery has gone' Gwen sounded as if she might be crying.

'Have you tackled him? You must! You've got to!' Gerrie turned her light out, too.

'He was up front about the jewellery' Gwen said quietly. 'He said it ought to be in the bank, it wasn't safe in the house. But after I had my critical mass moment, I went to the bank. I took ID to prove who I was. And I asked to see my jewellery. But they knew nothing about it. And they hadn't got the deeds, either.'

'You need to tackle him about it.'

'I need to do lots of things. Night, Gerrie.' She turned over and snuggled under the bedclothes.

Gerrie breathed out sharply though her teeth. 'I think it's just as well we've got this week away.' She lay down and stared into the darkness. 'Night Night.'

In Room 215 Celia sat in the chair by the curtained window, massaging Bronnley lotion into her hands. Her linen suit was hanging up in the wardrobe, her leather shoes paired properly next to her suitcase, her toiletries neatly laid out in the bathroom. A David Nieper cotton nightdress lay crisply folded on her pillow. She still wore a silk full length slip; her face was cleansed and toned, her white hair brushed and forming a silvery halo in the soft light. Her file was on her lap. And on the bedside table was a framed photograph of a distinguished man of around fifty in the uniform of a General in the Royal Green Jackets.

More is revealed

The journey from Cologne to Munich was testingly long. After the scramble in the morning for breakfast, getting cases down ready for the cages to take them to the station, and the straggly walk across the roads and through the concourse up to the platform via the temporary walkways, there was a respite while cases were claimed and heads were counted yet again. Another scramble into the carriage, finding seats, loading luggage into racks. But then the pace changed, and time seemed to take another shape as the day stretched ahead. People who had begun to get to know each other started conversations and discovered common interests. Mags found herself sitting next to Gerrie, with the other three members of the group a little further down the carriage making up a foursome with the woman travelling on her own.

'Winifred Burns' Mags read from her list of names. 'I think it must be her; she's the only one who seems to be travelling alone.'

'Yes' agreed Gerrie 'she's got a woven strap on her case with W BURNS on it, so I think we've crossed her off. I've worked out some of the others, too. That couple with the leathery man with the binoculars; they're Monty and Helen Bewley, and Monty's Uncle Alan.'

'Gosh!' smiled Mags 'You've done well! Fancy knowing he's an uncle.'

Gerrie put a hand near her mouth and whispered theatrically 'I earwigged when they were talking to the Ryecarts.' She grinned.

'All right then, who are the Ryecarts?'

'Simon and Patricia – she's the large woman who likes her floral smocks.'

'That's brilliant! Linda owes me an apfelstrudel.'

'What on earth are you talking about?'

Mags leant towards Gerrie with her list. 'See? There are two Pats and a Patricia. I bet Linda an apfelstrudel that the floral circular person was the Patricia.'

'Patricia-never-Pat. She says that a lot. Firmly. Even if someone doesn't call her Pat in the first place.'

'Isn't it funny how people are so sensitive about things like that?' mused Mags. 'I suppose they have an image of themselves which wouldn't stand up if a detail was altered, like a name.'

'A chip on the shoulder, you mean?'

'Not exactly – it just shows a certain fragility about them. About their personality. I don't care whether I'm called Margaret or Mags. But I know several Sues who don't think Susan suits them at all, and one Susan who loathes being called Sue. And now I think about it, I know a Susie who is over seventy.'

'Probably dates from school days, when teachers called you by your proper name. Or your parents, when you'd done something wrong.'

'Celia would know.'

'Would she?' Gerrie's eyes widened. 'Why?'

'She's done a basic psychology course. She wants to go further, maybe do an Open University one.'

'What for?'

'I think she's just interested. She's very bright, you know.'

'I don't know much about any of you, actually. I didn't even know I was coming on this holiday until three weeks ago.'

'I don't suppose you did' nodded Mags. 'Tell me your life story!'

'Gosh, I can't do that! Anyway, you'd be bored stiff.'

Mags settled back in her seat. 'Go on. Tell me a bit about yourself. We've got hours and hours on this train. I'll tell you a bit about me, and then we'll be evens. All I know is that you're Gwen's younger sister – that's it! Off you go.'

Gerrie patted her hair and then dropped her hands into her lap.

'All right. Well, I'm a widow.'

'Oh, I'm sorry' Mags cut in quickly. 'I didn't mean to open any wounds –'

'No, It's all right. It's more than two years now, I should be moving on. And I am. It was a shock, though.'

'It must have been.'

'No, it was a shock how it happened. Leo was an antique dealer, he had three shops actually. In Hampshire. We lived – I live in Winchester. I thought he'd gone to work. He'd said goodbye and kissed me and gone into the garage to get the car out as usual. He still ran the shop in Winchester but he had managers in the other two, and he usually visited them several times a week, plus there were auctions and viewings to go to and customers to see – he had no plans to retire. He loved it all. Anyway, off he'd gone, I thought, and I spent the morning doing some housework and baking and putting washing out, and I thought I would do a bit of gardening after lunch. So I went into the garage to get a rake, and his car was still there.' Her voice quavered just a little as she went on 'he'd – he'd got into the car and closed the door, and just had a heart attack. He was in the driver's seat, dead. It was awful.'

Mags stared at her. 'What on earth did you do?'

Gerrie blew her nose on a tissue. 'I really don't know. I can't remember. I opened the car door and there – there he was. I do remember that. I remember the ambulance people bending over me as I was sitting on a kitchen chair. I think somebody gave me a cup of tea. It's all a blur, really. I went to stay with Gwen and Roy for a month or so after the funeral. Gwen came back with me then, just for the weekend, it was so odd to be back in the house on my own. It still is sometimes.'

'Have you got any children?'

'We've got a son, Steven. He lives in Quebec.'

'Is he married?'

Gerrie pursed her lips. 'He was married. It's all a bit sad, really. They had a little boy, Anton – she was French, you see. She's gone back to Limoges and I don't suppose I'll see Anton again. He's six. I send him something every birthday and Christmas, but his mother is with someone else now and she's got a little girl, a toddler, and she's having another one. There's no point in trying to keep things going, if I'm honest. Anton has his own family, he doesn't need me. Maybe one day, when he's grown up, he might ... but I'll probably be dead by then. Or off my head!'

'So Steven is single again.'

'He has a partner.'

'Oh good! Perhaps they'll get married.'

'A male partner. He's a journalist and photographer.'

'Oh'.

People are full of surprises, thought Mags.

'How do you know Gwen?' asked Gerrie.

'Good question' Mags was relieved to be on firmer ground. 'It's quite convoluted. I used to run a business, a dress shop, in Canterbury. I got to know Linda, because she worked for the firm of financial advisers I used. And I had a widowed mother – she only died last year. I still don't know whether I'm relieved, or whether I'm missing her.'

'Did you get on?'

'No. I can honestly say we didn't. We never did; I wasn't what she wanted, I suppose. But - if I say that I miss, terribly, the chance that we might get on, would you understand? Does that make sense?'

'I suppose you feel bereaved of the possibility of a good relationship. That's still a bereavement.'

'But I'm relieved, too – enormously.'

'Bereaved and relieved.'

'Exactly! She was suffering in all sorts of ways, heart trouble and she was almost blind; she had terrible cellulitis, it kept recurring. She had to go to hospital with it two or three times, it never seemed to go away. We had to have nurses in nearly every day changing her dressings. She suffered with her teeth, as well, but she couldn't bear dentists. Everything I cooked for her was wrong, it tasted awful or she couldn't chew it. She was incredibly thin, in the end, she hardly had the strength to stand. We had to get carers to get her up in the morning and put her to bed at night, and they were constantly worrying about bedsores. You don't want to hear all this, sorry – '

'Did she live with you?'

'No. She lived in Faversham.'

'That must have been awkward.'

'It was.' Mags sighed and looked out of the window. 'I was trying to run the shop, and if I was there I felt guilty that I should be keeping an eye on Mum, and if I was in Faversham I felt guilty that I wasn't looking after Dudley...'

'I'm sure he understood.'

Mags turned back to look at Gerrie. 'That's a whole other story. We'd only recently got married.'

'Oh, I see.' But Gerrie looked puzzled.

'It doesn't matter' continued Mags dully. 'Where were we? Oh yes, how did I meet Gwen – well, as I say, I knew Linda from Sadler Samuel. They did my accounts and looked after my investments and my pension. Linda knew Gwen because they also did the accounts for Roy's vet surgery. One day when Gwen was in with some paperwork she mentioned to Linda that they had a litter of puppies, and did she know anyone who would like one? So of course Linda was telling everyone, and I was on my own at the time. The children had left home. I'd been aching for another dog – I've pretty well always had one.'

'I'm the same about cats. We've always had two at a time. Do you know, the day Leo died Spode disappeared and I never saw her again. Isn't that weird? I didn't think about it for a week or so, but it's true – she just vanished. None of the neighbours had seen her. I don't think she was run over. I often wonder what happened – or did she go off up to the woods to die of a broken heart? You hear of things like that, don't you?'

'That's very odd. I've no idea. Dogs don't do things like that – they're too worried about the next mealtime or a walk! Spode – what a lovely name.'

'I've still got Derby. Two sorts of china, you see – Leo was like that, he had a way with words, and a good sense of humour. We'd had Grinling and Gibbons before, and when we first got together he already had Hogarth and Cruikshank, two jet black brothers who never liked me much.' Gerrie gave a rueful smile. 'Leo had been married before, and I inherited them. I don't think they liked the change in regime. Anyway – go on –'

'Dogs. Yes. So I went out to Gwen's to see the puppies – it was about ten years ago, I suppose – and of course that's where Maisie came from and we've still got her. She's getting very elderly now.'

'What is she?'

'No idea! Gwen doesn't know. The bitch was brought in to Roy's surgery very pregnant, she'd been found somewhere, and he took her home to Gwen to look after.'

'That's Gwen all over. Their house is always full of odd animals and birds, and wire netting runs dotted over that field next to them. If you look in her fridge you'll find maggots and dog food and boiled fish heads – all sorts of rubbish, don't go putting anything you don't recognise in a sandwich!'

'Talking of which, here comes a trolley. That's good – I bought a roll and some water at the station, but I think I'll hang on to them. We've still got a long way to go.'

Gerrie, on the inside seat, had spotted Celia with a hot chocolate, so they both ordered those and a savoury pastry that looked like a small quiche.

As they ate, the conversations around them took their attention. A group of four behind them were roaring with laughter. They were exchanging chatter about grandchildren and things they had said.

'So Titus said to Ruby –'

'Titus!' Gerrie choked on her pastry. 'Pity this is cold. Just listen to them!'

'But Gerald, Gerald, remember that time at MacDonalds –'

Mags got her list out. 'Gerald and Iris Harper'.

'I remember Gerald Harper' nodded Gerrie. 'I thought he was dead. Adam Adamant'.

'Oh, yes!' Mags strained to look backwards between the seats. 'It just might be him! Oh no it isn't'. She made herself comfortable again. 'Not unless Adam Adamant is now bald and fat with a hearing aid and a stain on his shirt.'

'He might be! Who knows?'

'Would he have a wife called Iris, though?'

'Iris Adamant. Doesn't sound right, does it?' They both giggled helplessly.

'Oh, this is great!' Mags drained her hot chocolate. 'I feel so liberated – it's wonderful just to have a laugh! If Dudley – well anyway, it's just us girls and I'm going to make the most of it.'

'So what about Celia?' Gerrie brushed some crumbs off her lap and crumpled a paper napkin into a ball.

'There's a bin between these seats in front – look, if you pull the lid up...'

'Oh, so there is! I hadn't spotted that. They're very well designed in some ways, these trains.'

'Celia?'

'Yes, how do you know her, then?'

'You know how it is in a town. I've come across her in several ways – she used to buy clothes from my shop. She likes independent retailers. You could never describe Celia as a chain store customer.'

'No, that's true. You said she used to buy – '

'I sold the lease. I always knew I would when I got to sixty, but there were more reasons than retirement, when it came to the crunch. Business was down; partly the economic situation, partly just lower footfall in our part of the town. I wasn't the only one. It's been taken over by a pizza chain. But anyway, it was getting harder and harder with looking after Mum, and then there was Dudley. I'd had the good times with the shop and put some money away, but you know when something is on a downward spiral. Everything has its arc. Everything.'

Gerrie absorbed this. 'Yes, you're right. I'm in the middle of negotiating the sale of our antiques business. It's not the right time. But then, it never is. I think Leo hoped that Steven – well, you have to deal with things as they are, not as you want them to be. So, Celia – '

'The Hennesseys use Pierce Wiggin Fry.'
'Who are they?'
'Solicitors. They have a main office in London for the more complicated stuff, but the Canterbury branch deals with conveyancing and leases and things. I went to them when I was taking on the lease of the shop. They dealt with Mum's estate as well. And that's where I met Dudley.'
'Oh, so he's a solicitor?'
'He's a legal executive. He's been there for more than thirty years. He knows so much about the town, and how it used to be, and how all the businesses were connected and the history of them. He's a real fund of information, but the powers that be don't seem to appreciate him.'

Gerrie got up and looked down the carriage. 'The WC light's on, but there's only one person waiting.' She smoothed her Dash trousers down and set off.

Mags moved away from the window and sat in Gerrie's seat ready to make her way to the WC when Gerrie came back. Meanwhile the trolley made its return journey with a black plastic sack for the Styrofoam cups and other rubbish.

Journeys are never wasted

Mags and Gerrie settled down for a nap; Sandy went from seat to seat with details of the next train, which would go from Munich to Salzburg. There would be a wait of forty minutes at Munich, but the journey would not be very long – just over two hours. No help with luggage this time. Mags calculated that it would be after five when they reached Salzburg. Sandy warned everyone that the Munich train went on to Vienna and they needed to get off as quickly as possible.

 They passed through Frankfurt, where there was a lot of coming and going in the other carriages as people connected with the service to the airport. Mags thought, again, that it was bliss to be in first class. All you had to do was make yourself comfortable and watch while the crowds ebbed and flowed on the platform. There were designated places for smokers, inside marked lines on the concrete with large ashtrays installed in posts. Plenty of people were using them; there seemed to be more smokers on the continent than there were in England. Or maybe Canterbury was not representative, but all the same, it was noticeable how many people still lit up as she watched. And yet, there appeared to be more awareness of green issues; there were all the solar farms, and on the stations there were rubbish bins in three sections, for glass, newspapers, and other waste. People apparently obeyed the rules without question, smoking where they should and putting rubbish in the right place, and there was no litter to be seen. England is totally scruffy, she thought; it's embarrassing.

Mags drifted into a nap, and was woken by the raucous conversation behind her; Adam Adamant and the other man were telling jokes, and the women were laughing and joining in. 'I don't know about you, Colin, but I can't stand these young comedians nowadays' Adam Adamant was saying. 'Not funny, and it's all filth. Iris likes that Michael Macintosh – can't see it myself.....'

Ah. We can cross some more off, thought Mags, and took the folded list out of her handbag. Colin. Here we are – Colin and Wendy Harbottle. She listened carefully. A North Eastern accent – they must be from somewhere around Newcastle. He had a nasal, complaining tone which seemed to carry; they'll be the ones who came a day early and stayed the night in London before meeting up in St Pancras. She smiled. Almost everyone accounted for.

As the day wore on they stopped in Stuttgart, and then Ulm. Mags heard Celia saying to Gwen 'Ulm is simply beautiful, medieval origins. Look – no, this side – you can't see much, but it's well worth a proper visit. I was there when I was fifteen, as a schoolgirl, and Kenneth and I went later on. I would recommend it.'

There was more desultory conversation, and Mags could hear a man further back in the carriage talking about the technical and design differences between the trains they had travelled on so far, and the ones they would see on the holiday. His voice had a droning tone which irritated her. Must check who he is, she thought, and steer clear of him. I expect he's the sort who latches on to men, though, rather than women. At least I hope so.

The train began to move again. Gerrie roused and took a puzzle magazine out of her bag, and rummaged for a pen. She settled down with a frown on her forehead and began marking off a wordsearch.

There was a longer stop at Augsburg. There seemed to be a changeover of train staff, and loaded trays and refreshment trolleys were heaved on board. Mags looked down at the platform where a young family were reuniting with embraces and tearful kisses. It looked as if Dad, a young man with long hair tied in a pony tail and wearing shorts, had been looking after a child of about eighteen months who was strapped in a buggy, and they were meeting Mum who had got off the train with a holdall. When the greetings and hugs were over, they walked off arm in arm with Dad still pushing the buggy and Mum periodically resting her head on his shoulder for a moment. There must be a story there. It's Friday; does the mother work somewhere else, and she comes home for the weekend? Or had she been forced to go away for some reason? A sick relative? Who knows? Such human stories going on, in a station. Or not going on, that's the point – just a snapshot and then they melt away and merge into the general melee of humanity.

Mags slowly moved her attention to what was happening in the carriage as the train gathered speed out of Augsberg and into the last leg of this part of the journey. Rhythmic. Soporific. The quiet buzz of talk, the stuffy atmosphere. On the older trains you could open a window; these seemed to be hermetically sealed. That could give you a panic attack if you thought about it. So she wouldn't. She watched as a train attendant passed from the next carriage into theirs; there was a button in the ceiling which he pressed four times, and the glass door seemed to stay open. He manoeuvred a laden trolley through the gap; something dropped off it, and he stooped to pick it up. He pushed the trolley a little further, and reached back to press the button once. The door closed. Ah. Mags nodded to herself. Useful thing to know when they were all struggling with cases and trying to keep the doors open for each other. She let her thoughts wander on, to the week they would have in the hotel by the lake. Six nights. Celia had told them that she had asked for a table for five in the restaurant so that they could all eat together. That's a good thing, in a way, especially if they don't all do the same things during the daytime. It will be easier to catch up and compare notes. Five days. Five friends. What shall we find to talk about? An idea came to her and she smiled and looked out of the window again.

Munich was another station undergoing renovation. Here, though, there was a huge mock up picture on the platform where they were waiting, and the end result looked as if it would be spectacular.

Colin Harbottle and Adam Adamant stood in front of it, and were soon joined by the droning train enthusiast and Uncle Alan who had made a break for freedom from his nephew Monty. His cameras and binoculars jiggled enthusiastically as he pointed out the progress further along, and how it compared to the picture.

Gwen and Mags stood a little way away, amused at the back view of four elderly men gesticulating and explaining things to each other.

'Last of the summer wine' commented Gwen.

'Yes, absolutely!' Mags was delighted by this. 'I wonder who the chap is with the boring voice?'

'Gordon Garside. His wife is the other Pat.'

'I think Gordon Garside is really Foggy, don't you? Or Seymour Utterthwaite, the inventor....'

'No, he's Foggy. He's got the right build and the glasses. Gerald is Compo, I think – horrible shape, and stains down his front.'

'Yes!' Mags punched the air. 'All right then, Uncle Alan? Who's he?'

'Not sure it altogether works, but I think he might be Clegg. He's got the raincoat.'

'Yes, he's Clegg then. Which leaves Colin, with the nasal Geordie accent.'

'Oh, he's Howard. Of course he is. He whines and he's got a wife with a face like a slapped backside.'

'Wendy'.

'Yes, Wendy. So do you think there's a Marina, for Colin to have an affair with?'

'Celia' grinned Mags.

'Oooh, you ARE awful' said Gwen, giving her a push on the shoulder.

'Why is she awful?' Celia joined them at that moment.

Unabashed, Mags said 'We thought you might like the look of one of those chaps looking at the picture of the new station. Which one do you fancy? Gwen and I can't decide.'

Celia sniffed and surveyed the backs on offer. 'I'm sure their wives will keep them on a tight rein' she replied.

Mags stifled a giggle. 'Uncle Alan is here on his own, though. He might run amok.'

'Uncle Alan?' Celia's brow creased.

'Monty Bewley's Uncle; the chap with all the cameras. He's here with Monty and his wife. Do you know, it's their fifth holiday with Making Tracks? They always come together. They live in Devon. I don't know if Uncle Alan is a bachelor or a widower.' Mags looked at Gwen.

'It's none of our business' Celia said primly. 'I'm amazed at how much you find out about people.'

'Here's the train. We'd better help Linda – she's suffering rather.' Gwen moved down the platform with Mags and Celia just behind.

The Munich to Salzburg train had monitors high up in each carriage with maps and descriptions and the speed the train was achieving, each on the screen for about five minutes at a time. This was interesting and helped the time to pass; it showed the rivers being crossed and the towns they were passing through. The men were particularly fascinated, and said very little as they sat back and watched the train's progress. When it came to the speed, there were several gasps. At one stage it recorded 259 kilometers per hour; Mags happened to be looking up at that point and decided that this would be a suitable fact to remember and tell Dudley about when she got home.

There was a commotion a little further along the carriage, and then the comments spread like a ripple in a pond 'Mountains! Look, mountains! Gordon, look! Austria! Patricia! Look over there – what a sight!'

'I will lift up mine eyes unto the hills' thought Mags. What is it about mountains that give you a new lease of life? We've all been feeling travel weary and jaded and a bit ratty, but the sight of those majestic peaks – it's partly because we must be getting towards our destination, but there's more to it than that.

Celia, in front of her, turned round with a happy smile and said 'Have you seen the view, Mags? Isn't it wonderful – this is what we've come for. This will do us all good.'

Mags smiled and nodded, and suddenly felt emotional. She turned to her newspaper crossword to settle her mood. It wasn't long before Sandy was swinging from side to side up the carriage to say it was fifteen minutes to the Salzburg station, and there would be a coach waiting for the journey to Ischlkirchen.

Floral Patricia asked how long the coach would take, and when Sandy replied 'About an hour and a quarter, depending on traffic' she shouted 'No! No! Nobody said it would be that long! Simon, that's ridiculous. It can't be, after all the travelling yesterday, and today – I can't stand it!'

Simon Ryecart, a mild, stooped, academic looking individual, took her hand. 'It's all right dear; it did say so in the brochure. We did know. It won't be long now.' Patricia blew her cheeks out and stared scarlet faced out of the window.

The Making Tracks group were getting better at negotiating train stops. They all managed to get out, with their cases, without too much difficulty. Sandy took Linda's again, dropping it without a word in a space on the platform and turning to shepherd the stragglers into their wagon train formation as usual.

Having got everyone more or less together, Sandy raised the furled black and orange umbrella and started to lead the untidy crocodile out of the station to the coach, which was waiting with the storage doors up ready for the cases to be stowed underneath.

'Stay on the pavement' ordered Sandy 'while the luggage is stowed in the hold'.

Mags giggled. 'What's funny?' asked Linda beside her.

'One of two things. Either this coach is from Stowed in the Hold, or we've got stowed in the hold for supper tonight. Sorry – I'm getting weak minded.'

Linda made no reply.

Mags recovered herself. 'We can get on now' she said. Linda was ahead of her, but the coach steps were steeper than any others they had encountered in the last two days, and she faltered and couldn't move. It was Donald Chisholm, the elegant American, who came to her rescue and pulled her up to the top by her elbows, while Mags pushed her indelicately from the rear.

Another headcount, and they set off; Salzburg at rush hour time on a Friday is the same as any other major city, and the streets were clogged with traffic. There seemed to be a complex one way system; Mags thought they had been past the same church twice, in different lanes, but she wasn't sure. At last they were on their way, out of town and towards Ischlkirchen.

Settling in

'It'll be lovely to have a day in Salzburg' said Gwen, across the aisle. 'I liked the look of what we saw.' And as they passed through other places, she sat up straighter and said 'A sign to St Wolfgang! That's supposed to be gorgeous. They filmed White Horse Inn there. I wish we were going there this time, but it's not on this trip, is it? Oh, it says Hallstadt that way! Mondsee. That's the Sound of Music church – I think we're going there on Monday...'

Celia was by the window. 'It's going to be a busy week' she said.

Suddenly they were passing through a tunnel, and at the other side they could see a lake, blue grey in the evening sun, surrounded by huge mountains, and with a promontory reaching out into the still water with an onion-domed church on a crag, and a cluster of attractive houses round the foot of it.

'Ischlkirchen! Oh, look!' Nudges and pointing fingers. 'I wondered if we'd ever, ever get here...' Patricia-never-Pat looked like a deflated balloon; Simon patted her hand and murmured 'It's all right, dear. We're nearly there.'

As they pulled into the village square, the sun dipped behind a peak and it was as if lights had been turned down. It reappeared once or twice, ever weaker, but what took everybody's attention was the appearance on the coach of a fair haired, cheerful looking middle aged man in the Austrian traditional jacket and lederhosen, who said in practised English:

'Welcome to your hotel at Ischlkirchen. We hope you will be very comfortable during your stay – I am the owner, and my staff are waiting outside the entrance, in the square, to welcome you with a glass of wine. Your evening meal will be served in one hour, and if there is anything you need, please inform one of my staff immediately. Please. Enjoy yourselves.' And with a nod and a smile he was gone.

The hotel was five floors high, built like an enormous chalet, with balconies and flowered window boxes on almost every level. In the early evening light it looked magical, not least because the exhaustion and disorientation of two days' travel added to one's susceptibilities. Tables had been set out in the square with wine and glasses, and small snacks, and four waitresses dressed in traditional bodices and long flower-sprigged dirndls made sure everyone was catered for.

By the time the travellers had lingered with a drink, and looked at the quickly darkening lake just across the road, and the pretty church on the rock with its lights twinkling, the mood had changed to one of exhilaration and relief. In the cheerfully lit reception area proper keys were issued on brass plaques with the room number; the cases had been spirited upstairs and left neatly outside the correct doors.

The Hennessey party were on the second floor, with rooms looking out over the square and part of the lake, with the church on the promontory just within sight. Three rooms, each with a balcony; large and well furnished with a clean, modern bathroom. Celia reached her room first, closely followed by Gwen and Gerrie. Linda had to take the lift, and Mags didn't feel she could just leave her to it. So a little belatedly Linda and Mags sank into easy chairs and said to each other: 'It's only half an hour, now. We need to get ready and go down.'

'Well, I'm sorry, but I'm going to have a very quick shower.' Mags got up and went to her case, heaving it up on to the stand. 'I need one, I want to get changed, and I'll be ten minutes, no more.' She pulled out a top and skirt, a pair of court shoes and her spongebag, and vanished.

Linda sat very still. It was dark outside; night falls very suddenly in the mountains. The curtains should be drawn, but she felt she couldn't move. She leant her head back and shut her eyes, not to sleep, but to deal with the thoughts that crept up and frightened her when she was particularly tired, or in pain, or in a strange situation.

Mags reappeared combing her hair and smartly dressed for dinner. 'You go – I'll do my makeup. Your towels are on the left, the right hand ones are the ones I used. There aren't any toiletries, you'll need your own. They said that in the brochure.' She put both hands behind her neck to fasten the Swarovski on its chain. Then she checked her watch.

'I don't think I'll go down' said Linda in a dull voice, opening her eyes. 'I can't really face it. You go – I'll slowly unpack and sort myself out.'

Mags had started to blend foundation over her chin in front of the wardrobe mirror; she turned sharply and replied 'That's ridiculous! Of course you're coming down! It's our first meal of the proper holiday and Celia's got a special table for us. You need to eat. Come on – I'll help you. You don't need to change.'

'Yes I do.'

'All right, you do. I'll wait for you; get a move on, though.' She sat on the edge of one of the beds and applied her lipstick. She snapped her mirror shut and put it and the lipstick in her bag, and then got up again to move her case on to the bed and put Linda's in its place.

'I'll do the curtains' she said. 'Come on Linda, this isn't like you. Off you go.' She put out both hands and Linda allowed herself to be hauled upright. 'Here's your stick – yes, yes, take it, you'll be quicker. The light's on in there, now go and have a wash and get changed. I'll give you fifteen minutes – that's your limit.'

Linda winced and made her way to her case; she fumbled with the key of the padlock, and then unzipped it and rummaged for a pair of purple cotton slacks and a cream linen tunic. Mags had closed the curtains; now she crossed the room and took the clothes out of Linda's hands. 'Here we are' she said 'I'll put them in the bathroom. Find your washing stuff. Don't be long – I'm starving, and the others will be waiting for us.'

Mags busied herself with her own unpacking, carefully shaking and hanging her clothes in one half of the sliding wardrobe, folding clean underwear and small things and putting them on the shelves. Spare shoes went on the floor underneath the dresses and skirts. She closed her suitcase and stood it behind the door. 'I really must try and get a better one somewhere, with wheels' she thought. 'Maybe in Salzburg. I absolutely do not want to carry this all the way home again.'

She heard Linda use the shower, and eventually the door opened. Mags smiled 'Ready? Good – come on, before the others eat everything!'

Downstairs the dining room was a hive of activity. 'Gosh, it's much bigger than I thought!' said Mags. People were queuing up at a long salad bar, waiters and waitresses were threading their way expertly between the tables, and she could see Monty and Helen and Uncle Alan sitting with Floral Patricia. No Simon, but there was a space. The Bewleys were tucking in to a main course, but Patricia had nothing in front of her, so Simon must have been getting something from the salad bar for them. Further on, as the room opened out, Duracell and his wife and the Garsides were together, eating their salads with two bottles of wine on the table. Winifred Burns was with the Quiet Americans, as Mags was starting to think of them, and two tall grey haired women who had kept themselves to themselves, not joining in any conversations up till now. Mags thought they might be sisters.

Round a corner was an extension of the dining room, and there was a round table set for five, with two empty places. 'Come on!' Celia gesticulated from her place facing the room. 'We've been waiting for you! We've saved the seats on that side, so you can get out easily, Linda. My goodness, don't you both look smart!'

Mags sat down, and looked round at the others. Amazing what half an hour of freshening up can do; Celia had black slacks and a crisp Liberty blouse patterned with flowers, with the collar turned up at the back, which accentuated her elegance and good deportment. She wore a necklace of small pearls and pearl stud earrings. Gwen was in a striped cotton top and chinos. Gerrie also wore chinos with an emerald green blouse; Mags realised that the person Gerrie had reminded her of, ever since yesterday morning, was June Whitfield. The same sort of fluffy blonde appearance but with a core of steel.

For a while the conversation was about menu choices, what wine to order, and what the queue was like at the salad bar. Mags automatically suggested that she fetch some for Linda. Eventually there was a lull as their salad plates were removed and they waited for the main course, and a second glass of wine was poured.

'I've had an idea' said Mags.

There was an expectant pause.

'Go on, then' said Gwen. 'Don't leave us in suspense – what idea?'

'After tonight there are five nights, and five of us, so why don't we have a topic of conversation at dinner each night, chosen by each one of us in turn?'

Nobody said anything.

'No holds barred. We can talk about life, death, politics, husbands, children, jobs, money – there's no-one to stop us. Take the brakes off, let our hair down. We could make a pact that we can discuss anything at all during this holiday, but nothing is said after that. Completely confidential, never mentioned again.'

Linda sniffed. 'Is that all right with you, Celia? Or had you organised for us to be spontaneous in the evenings?'

Celia's laugh was just a little too artificial. 'I wouldn't dream of trying to organise anybody. Not at all. I hope you don't think that. It was just - someone had to get to grips with things, with Jane having to cry off.....'

'Awful' nodded Mags. 'I don't know how she's coping. Such a shock. They think she won't even see Christmas.'

'Don't' Gwen shuddered. 'I saw her husband in Boots.'

'Did you talk to him?' asked Mags.

'No. He looked anguished. Haunted. If you see what I mean. Sorry.'

Celia shook her head. 'I know. And then Rachel's mother dying, and her father having to sell up and move nearer – such bad timing. I think she's moving him in the day after tomorrow.'

'None of us know her, do we?' Gwen looked round the table. 'She's your friend, Celia.'

'That's true.'

'Anyway, we're nearly back up to a full team' continued Gwen, tackling her wine. 'Thanks to Gerrie stepping in at short notice.'

'Delighted' said Gerrie, inclining her head. 'I'd like to thank you all for letting me muscle in on your party. Whatever I hear will be treated as Top Secret, I assure you, so don't hold back.'

Linda's stick slid along the back of her chair and on to the floor. She bent awkwardly sideways to pick it up and stowed it under the table instead. As she sat up again she said 'Well I think it's a really good idea. And as Mags thought of it, she ought to be the first to choose a subject. Go on Mags – what shall we talk about tomorrow night?'

'I won't choose a subject, I'll choose a person' Mags answered firmly. 'I'll pick the first, and then they will have a day to think about a subject for discussion.'

'Oh, that's rather good' Celia clapped her hands together. 'That's quite clever.'

'Here's our main course.' Mags moved her glass out of the way of a smiling waitress. 'Right then. I'll choose Gwen. Gwen – you decide what you would like us to talk about tomorrow night. We'll all be refreshed; there are no trips tomorrow, we just have the day to wander round the village and find our feet, so we should be ready for some cut and thrust. Think up a challenging topic for us. Cheers, everyone! Happy hols!'

Little by little....

Although they were on the second floor the rooms were numbered 308, 311 and 315. In Number 308 Celia had everything unpacked and put away neatly. She watched the news on the TV and then switched it off. The photo was in its place on the bedside table, she had positioned a little travelling alarm clock beside it, and she spent fifteen minutes in the armchair, reading her book before going to sleep.

In 311 Linda and Mags got ready for bed in near silence, tired out. Linda switched off her light immediately; Mags finished her crossword and then settled down. They both lay awake in the dark for a surprisingly long time, breathing quietly and thinking their own thoughts.

Gwen and Gerrie, in 315, chattered desultorily as they undressed and washed.

'How's the sale going?' asked Gwen.

'The shops? Nothing at the moment. Well, no offers. One chap has been back twice and asked to see the books, but I'm not holding out any hopes.'

'What sort of chap?'

'Italian. He says he has shops in Florence and Lucca. Maybe he has. He says the market for antiques is very strong in Italy at the moment, and he wants to link in to the holiday trade as well. His wife is English and they're thinking of starting antique themed holidays for Italians to come to England and Brits to go there. He would bring them to Cambridge, Oxford, Bath and Winchester, with Winchester as their base.'

'Sounds as if he's thought it through. You'd be loaded.'

'Mmm. There's a bit more I haven't told you, though.'

'What?'

'I've got my house on the market.'

Gwen was wide-eyed. 'Oh. So – so where are you moving to?'

'It may not sell, in the current climate.'

'But if it does….are you thinking of Italy?'

'I've got so many friends there. And going down for a month or more at a time is getting a bit much. When I'm there I worry about the house. There's nothing to keep me in the UK now, is there?' Gerrie shot her sister a sideways glance.

Gwen made no comment.

'I might sell the Italian flat and buy something bigger, a villa.' Gerrie went on.

'Wouldn't you need a base here, in case you get ill and have to come home? And isn't there something about tax reasons?'

Gerrie was in her nightclothes. She sat down on one of the easy chairs and crossed her legs. 'I've thought long and hard' she said. 'Before we spoke last night, I had wondered about – possibly – asking you and Roy about moving in with you at some stage. You've got lots of room.'

'Well, we have, that's true. Are you lonely?'

'Yes. Honestly, I am. Leo's been gone two years now; to begin with everyone's all over you – the wives from the Rotary and people we both knew. But the water closes over them somehow, and you're left paddling your own canoe with nobody in sight. Married women are terrified of widows, especially if you've got a bit of money. And I've got no other family but you and Roy.'

'You've got Steven….'

Gerrie didn't reply.

'It's an idea' said Gwen thoughtfully. She sat on the edge of her bed and brushed her faded mousy-ginger hair. It's thinning, thought Gerrie. And her neck is getting stringy. We're all getting on, whether we like it or not.

'I wouldn't want to impose' Gerrie continued 'and from what you've just told me things are not as solid as they might be. I've stopped worrying about me and started worrying about you, now.'

'Oh, don't be silly. We'll be all right.'

'It doesn't sound as if you will, though, does it? If it really is as bad as you say, there must be a lot more you don't know about. Gamblers are like alcoholics, they hide their tracks and by the time you are aware of the problem it's far, far worse than you think.'

'Don't say that.'

'At your age you should be able to relax, with the house paid off and savings behind you and pensions built up – not watching it all slip away from you. You really must talk to Roy.'

Gwen was doubtful. 'It sounds so silly. I keep thinking about bringing it up, but the opportunity doesn't arise. One of us is just going out, or there's someone else there, or – it just sounds so lame. What do I say? Roy, I want to talk to you because I'm worried that we haven't any money?'

'Exactly that. Word for word.'

'But he'll brush it aside. Rationalise everything. Tell me not to be so melodramatic. He'll reassure me that I've got it all wrong.'

'Then don't be reassured.' Gerrie was firm.

'What do you mean? It would provoke a real row.'

'It will be a very uncomfortable conversation, I grant you. But I don't think you've got any choice. I think you need to go through all the family finances with Roy and ask for proof of everything. You can always apologise if it's all hunky dory, can't you?'

Gwen got into bed and lay down, pulling the duvet up to her chin.

'It's all awful' she mumbled. 'Good night.'

Although the next day was free of excursions, there was a guided walking tour of the village at ten o'clock, led by the hotel's proprietor. Most of the group assembled for it in the square, but one or two were missing including Linda and Floral Patricia. Sandy, smartly dressed in black jeans and a short sleeved black polo shirt, stood on a stone kerb to gain a little height, and reminded them about the free boat trip a little later before introducing their guide and melting away.

'Hmm' commented Mags to Gwen. 'I was hoping Sandy would be wearing a shirt or a jacket, so I could see which way the buttons went.'

'Still say it's an effeminate man' Gwen whispered.

Mags grinned and whispered back 'Still say it's a masculine woman!'

The walking tour was full of interest; they went round the promontory and looked up at the church, high up a winding path. In their own time it would be intriguing to climb there and get a better view, and in the monastery below, to inspect the unique pulpit which was in the shape of a fishing vessel with nets and fish carved underneath it, as if it were a working boat on a lake with the preacher in the middle of the deck. 'I will make you fishers of men.' An emotionally moving concept, thought Mags, deciding to investigate as soon as she could.

They were shown old buildings and the ancient monastery by the water's edge with a beautiful graveyard, lovingly tended as all Austrian ones are, full of wrought iron and enamelled pictures of the dead, and each resting-place a riot of colourful begonias and marigolds. More like flowerbeds than graves, and candles everywhere with glass shades to protect them from the wind. There was a wide wooden jetty and a second hotel on the water's edge facing the other way up Ischlsee, with a wonderful vista of still blue water and mountains, and a little red train on the railway threading its way along the side of the lake.

'Don't be deceived by the water,' warned their guide. 'There are terrible floods, but not when you think. In the winter the rain falls as snow on the mountains and it melts slowly. We can manage that; the lake's surface rises by many, many metres but we have systems of locks and sluices on the incoming rivers and mostly it is all right. But the summer – the rain falls huge in the mountains, and runs and runs. You see those clefts, the cliffs – there, and there, and there...... they are torrents. Waterfalls, thousands, millions of litres in the hour.

This is why we all have stone floors at the ground level. When I was twelve years old I remember the floods were at a record height – look here, you see the marks on this stone wall by the monastery gate? With the years of the levels? This high one here – I swam in our cellar and then I swam in the whole ground floor and my father was not pleased! He was not pleased!'

'Did your family own the hotel then?' asked a Patricia-free Simon.

'Oh yes. Yes. We have the hotel in four generations. Five now, in fact, my son is taking from me.'

The party walked on, learning about the village and its history and the fact that the main road along the lake had passed right through it until recently, until the tunnels had been built so that the traffic now used a bypass and the village was so quiet that you could walk in the road and hardly see a car.

'It must have made such a difference' said Celia. 'Imagine! All those lorries and coaches....'

'Fourteen thousand every day. The average. Fourteen thousand.' Their guide insisted. 'You cannot imagine. Only three years ago. What relief, and now we can have tables in the square!'

Afterwards some people went back to the hotel, some stayed in the square and had coffee. Celia and Mags sat on a bench overlooking the lake and waited for the boat trip.

'How's Kenneth?' asked Mags. 'I don't think I've ever met him.'

'He's staying with his younger brother and his wife, in Norfolk.'

'That's nice. Are they near the coast?'

'Burnham Staithe. Do you know Norfolk?'

'No. I have a feeling I've been there, perhaps as a child. But mostly I've been in Kent and Sussex, and the south west a bit. For holidays.'

'It's quite a way; both directions in a day is exhausting. Too much now, really.'

'It'll be nice for Kenneth, though, won't it? Seeing his brother and being by the sea. Is Burnham Staithe by the sea?'

'Yes. Kenneth's family always had a holiday home there. Since long before it was fashionable. He remembered – remembers going there as a boy, to a rambling old house without proper running water and no heating. People didn't think twice about that sort of thing in those days.'

'Is that where he's staying now?'

'Oh, no, the house is long gone. Sold several times since then. Alistair and Kate live in a barn conversion; a lovely house, partly local flint and partly wood. Lots of glass – there's a wonderful double height atrium affair with a gallery landing – it's amazing how big these barns are when they're turned into houses.'

'So what does Kenneth do – swimming? Fishing? Is there a golf course?'

Celia considered her answer. 'Alistair is sixteen years younger than Kenneth.'

'Goodness, that's a lot. Are they half brothers?'

'No, real brothers. Their mother lost three in between. I think two were girls. It must have been awful for her.'

'That's unusual…'

'It would be now, but I think it was a rhesus negative thing, and they know about that nowadays.'

'Oh, I see. I knew someone who had that. But – sixteen years; almost like being an only child. My husband is an only child.'

'Yes; they don't have much in common.' Celia shivered a little. 'I can't see the boat coming yet, can you?'

'No. Tell me more about Kenneth. If you want to.'

'The gap between us is even bigger.' Celia was gazing into the distance. 'Eighteen years.'

'Good heavens. So he must be – '

'Eighty four. It's hard to believe.'

'I had no idea. But he's still fit.'

'In some ways.'

'Slowing up a bit, I suppose. He must be.'

'He's not very well.' Celia sighed and looked at her hands. 'He's beginning to suffer from dementia.'

'That's sad. I'm so sorry. Are you sure, though? Sometimes it's something else, like a urine infection or a lack of iodine…'

'No, it's Alzheimer's.' Celia said the word clearly and deliberately, as if careful pronunciation of the word might subdue the horror of its meaning.

'He's been diagnosed, then.'

'That's at the top of my list when we get back. Well. Almost. I'm not looking forward to it.'

'It might be something else, though – you've got to keep your hopes up...'

'We've got a family friend who's a consultant psychiatrist, and also a professor of age related disorders. He says there's no doubt about the symptoms.'

'Short term memory loss, confusion, that sort of thing?'

'Well, all of those, and other things that are more disturbing. He gets up in the night and thinks the time is twelve hours different. Not long ago while I was asleep he got dressed and went down to the village to buy a paper. He came back and shook me awake; he wanted to know why the shop hadn't opened after lunch, it was well after two o'clock. And why was it dark?'

'My mother had an aunt who did something like that.'

'And Kenneth's becoming very anxious and distressed. He's frightened of odd things, like window catches. They terrify him – it's awful to see. And watch straps.'

'That's strange.'

'Not exactly watch straps, but if you leave your watch undone on a table, as you do – with the face lying flat, and the strap arching up each side of it, he thinks it's huge spider. He shakes and cries for hours. And he repeatedly wants to know what's for supper; he thinks the CGS is coming and he trots into the kitchen and demands to know what we're having and have we got plenty of brandy!' Celia was laughing, but her eyes glistened.

'Oh. You've got some difficult days ahead, haven't you?'

'Yes. I know.' Celia sighed.

Mags said nothing, digesting what she had heard.

'The thing is, Alistair didn't believe it.'

'Why not?'

'No idea. Well, I expect he didn't want to admit it, even to himself, for lots of reasons. In denial. But I spoke to him on the phone several times, trying to convince him; after all, it's his brother. He ought to take some responsibility, I suppose. But he said I must be exaggerating. He said their father had gone the same way, but it wasn't any great drama. Their mother had coped perfectly well. But – I mean, you can't compare it, can you? Their father was a judge, a law lord. A very prominent man. Their mother was a minor aristocrat. They had plenty of money, plenty of servants to take the edge off things. And quite honestly, the doctors were freer in those days to do things which might not be – well – approved of now. Unconventional. I think they drugged him up and stuck him in the library in the winter and in the orangery in the summer.'

'Heavens'.

'Well, you could get away with things like that in days gone by. Anyway, not long ago we had our Glyndebourne tickets and I decided it was no good, Kenneth was beyond that now. So I rang Alistair and Kate and offered to put them up and let them use our tickets. Which they did; they had a grand weekend and unfortunately Kenneth was not too bad for those few days. I think something in his brain went into overdrive, putting on a front so that Alistair and Kate couldn't see anything was wrong. He relapsed after they went home and he's been quite a bit worse ever since.' Celia pressed her lips together. 'So I thought – right; I've got to make you see this somehow. I need to find a reason for Kenneth to come and stay with you, and then you'll understand that the situation is getting critical.'

'I sort of wondered why you planned this holiday. The others were puzzled too – it seemed a bit....if I say out of character, I don't want you to take that the wrong way....'

'No, no, it's all right. It was out of character, I suppose, though I'm not sure what that is any more. We're at a funny age, aren't we?' she ended obliquely, as they stood up to move nearer the jetty; someone had spotted the boat coming across the lake.

....there are revelations....

Celia, a little chilly, sat inside the boat in the cabin area, with most of the others. But Mags felt she wanted to be outside, so she sat on the curved bench area in the stern, open to the elements. She was wearing a lightweight fleece, and had a much thicker one with her which she pulled on over the top. It was supposed to be windproof; she hadn't worn it before, but it seemed to do the trick. With the sun on the water there was something of a glare, so she put her sunglasses on as well and simply enjoyed the physical feeling of the wind in her hair, and the sound of the engine. Looking up she saw two huge birds of prey – some sort of eagle, probably – a good way apart from each other, gliding on the air currents and motionless with their huge wingspans very impressive even at this distance. Her gaze moved on, up and up to the tops of the mountains. Letting it slowly fall back, she noticed a square marked out in the water, some way into the centre of the lake. The water inside it had a different texture from the rest; a square that glistened, completely immobile, like a sheet of glass. Fish, she thought. A hatchery, perhaps. The proprietor of the hotel told us all about that, earlier; when they serve fish in the restaurant it's straight from the lake, as fresh as you could imagine. That's why you have to choose your supper menu at breakfast time, so they know how many to buy from the fishermen.

She gradually became aware that one of the two crew members was sitting in the body of the boat with the other passengers, explaining things about their surroundings. He was gesticulating as he struggled for the right English words, being helped by some of the tourists. From time to time he pointed at things on the left or the right, and twenty pairs of eyes turned to follow his finger. Mags slid along her bench until she was able to lean over the steps and listen.

'That mountain, that mountain over there?' the man was saying. 'That is Ischlstein. The same name as the lake. It is popular. Popular. For – er – the climb. Many peoples climb each summer. Three hundred, they climb each summer. There is a small restaurant up there – you see? You see? But there are many – ' his hands tumbled over themselves from his shoulder height to the floor. 'They fall. They die, it is very sad. Every year, many peoples. I am rescue man. I see many of this.'

There was silence. Then Duracell said 'Not exactly the East Anglian Mountain Rescue, is it, eh? Eh?' He was rewarded by laughter. 'You couldn't pay me to go up there. They must be mad, eh, Mike? They must be mad.'

June said mildly 'If you're young, though, and the view must be absolutely amazing....'

'Mad'. Duracell folded his arms, having voiced the definitive opinion.

Mags gazed at the mountain. She felt tears pricking her eyelids. Why? It's only a pile of stone, she told herself, rummaging for a tissue. I need to rationalise this. Why do mountains move me so much? It's a well known effect; it's not just me. They are so big, unimaginably big; what do they weigh? You can't even start to guess. And they're immobile. Solid. We are fragile and small and destructible. And then there is their age; they were formed hundreds of millions of years ago, we can't get our heads round that timescale. It's impossible. We're only here for the blink of an eye, a nanosecond. All the things we fight and worry and cry about – nothing. It's all nothing. We should look at mountains and get a sense of proportion. We're like ants running around the feet of giants. If only ants stopped for a minute and looked up, they might get an idea of their miniscule place in the world.

But then, we look at tiny things and get emotional, too. Young things, little things, we feel their vulnerability and helplessness. Awe and emotion at the vast and incalculable, and pity and emotion at the small and powerless. Perhaps that's what makes us human, or part of it. After all, a jaguar, for instance, wouldn't notice a mountain and would eat a mouse.

The rest of the day after the boat trip was 'at leisure to explore the village.' The first thing Mags did was to go back to the hotel room to see if Linda was all right and tell her about the boat trip and the landmarks in the village. But the room was empty, although it wasn't locked. The chambermaids hadn't been in yet and it smelled stale and looked a little chaotic. Mags opened the balcony doors to let in fresh air, and superficially tidied the pillows and smoothed the sheets on the two beds. She loosely folded her nightie and put it on her pillow. Linda's pyjamas weren't there; she went into the bathroom where the lights had been left on and found them thrown carelessly on the loo seat. She picked them up and came out, turning off the light, and put them on Linda's bed. If Dudley was here, she thought, he'd be telling me off for doing the chambermaids' job for them. What do you think we're on holiday for? He never thinks twice about the fact that I do all this at home, and I'm not a chambermaid. And about the matter of pride; you don't want the staff thinking that you're a slob. Men don't think like we do, though. In so many ways.

She made sure the door was locked as she left; if she couldn't find Linda she could always get Reception to give her a spare key – in fact, it would be a good idea to have one anyway if Linda was going to wander off. On her way back downstairs she slowed her step and began to look around her; there were archways and corridors in several directions which would repay exploration. Going in one direction she found a whole suite of conference rooms, some of which were occupied with the names of the organisations and the delegates pinned to notice boards outside. She went into one empty room and found a semicircle of chairs, a flip chart, and large notepads and pencils with the hotel's name on them stacked neatly on a side table.

Beyond the rooms was a small catering area, with seats along a window which looked out on to the lake. A dining section and kitchen contained large bowls of fresh fruit, baskets of cakes and rolls, and gleaming coffee machines, kettles and water coolers. How organised, Mags thought. How clean. How efficient. How inviting. How very unEnglish.

She retraced her steps and found herself back at the top of the stairs; on the other side of the landing was another room, and in it she found a computer on a desk, and Linda busy emailing.

'Hi!' Mags smiled and stood behind Linda's chair. 'This is useful; it's for the guests, is it?'

'Yes. I've been emailing Stuart; he'll probably reply this evening. He's got a hospital appointment this morning but he's going into work afterwards. I want to find out how he got on.' She signed off and looked round for her stick. 'How have you been doing?'

'Had an interesting time; do you know, it's after twelve already. Shall we go down and have a snack? I can tell you all about it.'

Linda was mobile enough to get across the square and the road and sit at a cafe by the lake, so Mags got her settled and then went to order coffee and Panini. As she sat down again she asked: 'So how is Stuart? Nothing too awful, I hope?'

Linda smoothed her auburn fringe. 'Diabetes' she said. 'We've known it for ages, or at least I have. Stuart wouldn't listen, he wouldn't go to the doctor's.'

'Oh, they're all like that.'

'He's been getting worse and worse; no energy, always falling asleep. Incredibly irritable. Very thirsty. That makes him get up in the night, and then he's even worse. His balance has been a bit dodgy. Things on his feet that won't heal – he's had a corn for two years. He went to the chiropodist twice but he's still got it.'

'Oh dear.'

'So now it's all come home to roost. He's got his first appointment at the diabetes clinic today, and he's got to have a prostate biopsy, and a few other things which sound horrible.'

'And he's still working. Is he still at Routledge?'

'Oh God, yes. He's been there for twenty six years. He's the assistant manager, has been for twenty years, I should think. He doesn't know anything else. Thank goodness the town still needs an ironmongers; all the time we think it'll close, but it staggers on. A bit like us.'

The coffee arrived, with hot cheese and sausage Panini.

Mags cut hers in half. 'We're always really pleased it's there. Where else would we go for a hinge for the garden gate or a peculiar sized jubilee clip?' she laughed.

Linda didn't. 'You'd go to B&Q. And while you were there you would buy some paint and brushes and a lampshade.'

'Routledge has those as well. Good old Routledge.'

'And you'd buy some plants and a watering can and a garden hose and some fertiliser, and some matching bedding and cushions for the bedroom. While you were about it you'd get some scented candles and towels, and if it was any time after the end of September you'd buy Christmas decorations and strings of lights and some crackers. You'd park for free and stay for a drink and a bun, and then you'd walk next door to Dorothy Perkins to look at clothes or go further on to the carpet shop. You'd call in at Boots and Next and then get your food shopping down the end at Asda....'

'Well. But it's much better at Routledge; somebody proper to ask about things, people who have been there for years....'

'Like Stuart. Oh, I forgot to mention his varicose veins. All the standing.'

'Exactly. Does Robin Routledge still own it? He must do.'

'There were two boys and a girl. Old grandfather Ralph Routledge started it, of course, after world war one. He had two sons, Robert and Richard. Robert was the older one, but he went into the RAF and was killed during the Battle of Britain. So Richard took it over in forty-five, at the end of the second war. Richard had Robin, Raymond and Rebecca. Raymond is rather a weak character; he's on the board, but he's pretty ineffectual.'

'What about Rebecca? We need a strong woman in this saga!'

'Oh, she fell off a horse and died when she was fifteen.'

'How sad. So Robin is still running the business.'

'A bit half heartedly. He's nearly eighty now, and I think he knows the time is almost up. They've been offered huge sums of money for the site. It's prime real estate, in the middle of the town. There have been lots of quiet conversations with the council about redevelopment, and approaches from businesses and McCarthy and Stone and those sorts of people about turning the building into characterful retirement flats. They've tried to talk old Robin into going out of town and moving Routledge into one of the units they can't let on the Greenhills industrial estate, but Robin's still got enough marbles to know that would be suicide, and they would lose shedloads of money before it went bust. Stuart thinks if the right sum was offered he would take it and say goodbye to the family firm. It's like haberdashers and all those other shops we used to go to when we were young – '

'Woolworths.'

'Exactly, and Dewhursts and Liptons and MacFisheries, all those – they've had their time. The world has moved on.'

'I'm beginning to feel like that.'

Linda flashed Mags a look. 'Don't be daft. You're all right, there's nothing wrong with you. You've got years left to enjoy life.'

'Enjoy life'. Mags wiped some crumbs from her mouth and scrunched up the paper napkin. She swigged the last of her coffee.

'Yes – enjoy life!' Linda was so vehement that her curls shook over her ears. 'for God's sake, Mags, what else is it for?'

Mags shrugged. 'The older I get, the less I'm sure about that.'

'Well at least you are getting older. Be grateful.'

Linda wanted a quiet afternoon; she seemed to have little interest in exploring the village. 'We've got nearly a week' she said. 'You go and have a wander round, and tell me what's worth looking at. I'm going up on my bed. I'll either read or go to sleep. I need to take some tablets in any case.'

So Mags walked slowly round the promontory, stopping every few yards to see the lake from a different angle. The afternoon sun was quite strong, although there was a wind. September was almost three quarters gone, and there was a hint of more uncertain weather to come. Some pleasure boats were on the water, and three sailboarders had got themselves out in the middle, harnessing the wind currents and zigzagging across the surface. Mags walked round a little further and found the two tall grey sisters sitting on a bench. They waved and greeted Mags, nodding their heads before continuing their conversation. Looking up, she saw the gleaming onion dome high above her and realised that she was at the beginning of the twisting path which would take her up through the trees to the church. She began the climb, and found it steeper than she had expected, but on almost every hairpin bend was a bench, placed perfectly to rest the weary traveller and give a view of Ischlstein or the lake or the village. She passed one which was empty, and one which was occupied by Winifred Burns, sitting alone. Mags slowed to a halt and moved towards the seat.

'No! Please don't!' Winifred's palm was held up immediately. 'Everyone thinks I want them to keep me company. I can assure you, I am quite all right on my own. I'm reading my book. This is my eleventh trip with Making Tracks. I wouldn't come if I was going to impose myself.'

'Well, my legs are aching. It's much more of a climb than I had thought. Would you mind if I joined you just for a few minutes until I get my breath back?'

Winifred's face barely softened. 'Do whatever you like. I don't own this bench.'

Mags sat down, not too close, and smilingly inclined her head a little. 'I'm Mags' she said. 'I think you're Winifred, is that right?'

'Win. I'm always called Win. It makes me very cross, they seem to have asked everyone else what they want to be called, but they've put me down as Winifred. It makes me cross.'

'You don't like Winifred?'

'My husband called me Winifred – he was the only one who did. It's special to me; when other people use it I feel insulted somehow. Affronted. Giles called me Winifred, nobody else. Nobody else has the right.' She shut her mouth like a trap.

'I can quite understand that.' Mags commented seriously. 'You're absolutely right to explain. I'm sure we'll all be careful, once we know how you feel.'

Win was staring out at the lake, and did not respond.
'Did you lose your husband a long time ago?' Mags ventured.
'Ten years on September the 7th.'
'I'm sorry. So you don't go away on the anniversary, you leave it....'
'Of course not. I was away when he died. I should never have been away. I will never forgive myself, never.'
'But you...'
'He had been ill for many years. Motor Neurone. Brutal. Savage. I wouldn't let anyone else look after him. Absolutely not.' Win banged her fists on her lap rhythmically as she spoke. 'He wanted nobody but me, I wanted nobody but him. And then the doctor persuaded me – ' she paused.
'They thought you needed a holiday?' suggested Mags softly.
'They said I was heading for a breakdown. A breakdown! As if I would have a breakdown! I was there to look after Giles, not to have a breakdown!' Win's jaw was as tight as a cheesewire. 'They made me send him to a hospice, so that I could get away. Get away – from my own husband!'

Mags began to feel as if she were being assaulted. She moved slightly further away.

After a little while, Win went on 'He died on the last day, the day I got back. They tried to get in touch with me, so they said. I will never believe anybody, ever again, about anything, so I don't know. They let him die, that's all that matters. I wouldn't have let him die. My job was to look after him, and that's what I did. He didn't die while I was looking after him, did he? What else did they do to him while I wasn't there? Did they starve him? Did they shout at him? I'll never know. But when I got back, he was dead.'

Mags thought of several things to say, but decided against all of them.

Eventually she asked 'Where's your home? Where do you live?'
'Impington.'
'Ah. Impington.'
'You won't know it; it's near Cambridge'.
'No, I don't, I'm afraid. I know Cambridge, of course.'
'Don't let me hold you up.'

Mags got to her feet. 'No. And you can get back to your book.'

Win did not reply; Mags continued up the path, but didn't look behind her.

Through the trees she sometimes lost her sense of direction as the path wove and zigzagged, every now and then coming out into a clear view which kept taking her by surprise. She thought she was facing towards the lake, but found the church dome way up in front of her; a few minutes later she expected to see the village and found she was looking at the lake again, but from higher up. At last she reached the top and found the church in an open area with chalky paths all around, with its western door open. Inside was Celia, standing stock still, looking through the wired screen which separated the porch from the body of the church.

....and conversations are struck up

'Hello, Celia! Can we go in?'

'No – it's padlocked. We can see it all, and the light coming in is beautiful. But we can't go any further.'

'I want to see this wonderful fishing pulpit...'

'Oh, that's in the monastery, not in this church. I want to see it, too.'

They stood side by side, taking in the peaceful interior of the church with the sunlight already striking the far wall at an angle, as the year was rolling on. Then they both turned, and went back outside. They leant against a rustic wooden balustrade, and gazed at the little boat jetty below.

'Did you come up the path, or the steps?' asked Celia.

'Path. I thought that was the only way.'

'No, the steps lead directly into the village, by the monastery. We can go down that way. I spoke to Teresa and Tabitha; they were sitting on a bench.'

'The tall grey sisters?'

'Well, yes. They're very interesting, actually. I had quite a conversation with them on the train. One of the trains. Can't remember which, now.'

'They look like two spinster school teachers.'

'Oh, no!' Celia laughed. 'Fancy you thinking that! One's had three husbands; the current one is away on his own holiday –

he's keen on archaeology and he's gone off somewhere, South America I think, on a historical dig sort of jaunt. That's Tabitha Amherst-Smith. Teresa Wolstencroft used to be something high up in the stock exchange, on some monetary committee. She has four children of her own and has adopted three others, two from Romania and one Downs syndrome who was her cousin's child, but the cousin was killed in a car accident. Her husband is a senior civil servant, something to do with MI5 or 6 or something. He's holding the fort at home. Although I think all but two of the children have flown the nest. But they also have his father living with them.'

Mags was silent.

Celia commented 'People aren't always what you think, are they?'

'No'. Mags said nothing for a moment, and then: 'I spoke to Win, a bit further up.'

'Ha!' Celia snorted. 'Nightmare, that woman. She ought to carry a health warning.'

'That's not like you!' Mags looked shocked. 'She lost her husband, and she can't get over it. I would have thought you'd be sympathetic – '

'Look' Celia turned away from the railing and they began to walk towards the steps. 'I have every sympathy for somebody's misfortune. We all have things to cope with. But that woman is stuck; she hasn't moved on.'

Mags suddenly realised why she had felt so much under attack; it was a feeling that was too close to home, that's why it had sneaked under the wire and upset her.

'There's no need for it' insisted Celia, tight lipped. 'Once it turns into self pity, it becomes an indulgence. Nobody wants to hear you feeling sorry for yourself all the time. Get over it. Somebody ought to tell her.'

'Perennial victim.'

'Exactly' nodded Celia. 'A self proclaimed martyr. That's your mindset, and everything that happens to you is used to feed that appetite – it's never satisfied. Poor you. Yuk! Somebody needs to tell that woman, before she spoils everyone else's holiday.'

They found the series of steps that led down to the village, Mags musing about what she had just heard, and still a little taken aback by the strength of Celia's reactions.

Passing down the landward side of the promontory they found a bright blue nylon rope slung between the trees, with a metal slider attached.

'Odd' commented Mags, frowning.

'I expect they use it to bring things up to the church' remarked Celia. 'Watch out, these steps are a bit slippery as well as being steep. I should go slowly.'

'Yet another place that Linda can't get to' Mags responded 'unless we could strap her into a chair and get her up on this pulley!'

Celia shot her a glance. 'You wouldn't think it was funny if it was you' she said.

No, thought Mags. I wouldn't, actually.

They arrived at the foot of the promontory and found themselves in a small courtyard with a boat repair workshop on the waterside, but they could see the centre of the village through an arch and walked forward on to the pavement. To the right was the monastery, but the road curved invitingly out of sight so they continued on their way.

'I do want to go into the monastery' remarked Mags 'but it might be better to save it for another time. It's nearly five o'clock.'

'Good heavens!' Celia peered at her watch. 'So it is! Let's just have a little look round the next bend, and then we ought to go back, I suppose.'

'There's no reason to just yet – at least, not for you. I should check on Linda, really.'

'No, I'll come back with you. There are one or two things I want to do, and I want to look in the little grocery by the hotel. I don't think they open late.'

'Oh, look!' Mags pointed to a little group of people outside what looked like another hotel. 'There's Duracell and Pat, and the Garsides, and Monty and Helen Bewley! They're looking at the menu, I think.'

'If it wasn't for the Edinburgh Woollen Mill and Cotton Traders, most of our group would be naked....' muttered Celia.

'Really!' Mags pretended to be shocked. Then she giggled. 'I wish you hadn't said that – I'm getting mental pictures that it'll be hard to get rid of.'

They joined the others. Duracell poked Celia on the shoulder: 'We've found another hotel' he grinned, as she moved backwards abruptly into the road. Mags steered her hurriedly back on to the pavement a little further away.

'So I see' Celia was frosty. 'It doesn't look as nice as ours.'

Monty nodded towards the framed menu beside the door. 'Our meals are included on excursion days' he said 'but not today. We can eat where we like in the evening. We're coming here tonight, to see if the food is any better.'

'Don't you like the food in our hotel?' Mags raised her eyebrows.

'Not impressed so far' droned Gordon Garside. 'I don't like salad. You don't, do you Pat?'

Both Pats shook their heads. Duracell's Pat pursed her lips. 'And we had that pork last night, in a sort of gravy. I didn't go for that. And the ice cream selection is not what we're used to. At the golf club – '

'– Golf club,' Duracell took over 'they have a proper chef. Good bloke. Trained by Gordon Ramsey!' he rocked back on his heels, watching their faces for the impressed expressions which failed to materialise. 'He makes his own ice cream. Can't beat it. Can't beat it. You like the Choc Chip Champion, don't you, Pat?'

She nodded vigorously. 'And the Forest Fruits. Really good, the Forest Fruits. We're used to quite a good standard of eating out.'

To change the subject, Mags caught Monty Bewley's eye and asked 'Have you mislaid Uncle Alan? Where's he?'

'Very energetic, is Monty's Uncle Alan' Helen had several chins, which didn't always act in unison. He's gone walking to the next village. You go on round this bend, then it opens out and goes along the edge of the lake. It's a couple of miles, but you can turn off up the mountain then. Uncle Alan wanted to see if he could get some good photos. He really wants birds, but he'll have to wait his moment for them.'

'There were two beautiful birds of prey over the lake this morning' enthused Mags. 'I think they were some sort of eagle; huge wingspans, and they hovered, a few hundred yards apart, for ages. They must have been resting on the air currents. I suppose they dive for fish – '

'Uncle Alan will find them!' beamed Monty, and winked. 'He's got a good eye!'

'Well, I hope he starts back in good time' Celia said crisply, turning to go. 'These nights fall very quickly. There's hardly any dusk. You wouldn't want him to get lost.'

Helen told her retreating back 'He's getting the train. There's a station in the next village as well as this one.'

'Bye' smiled Mags, following Celia down the road. 'Hope you enjoy your dinner tonight!'

They marched in unison back into the village, past the monastery and the church on the hill, through the square by the boats and back to the hotel.

Feeling more at home

'Bother' said Celia. 'The shop's shut.' She went to peer at the notice on the glass door. 'Ten in the morning to five at night, weekdays. Ten till one on Saturdays. Closed Sundays. Oh well. If we wanted Waitrose, we'd have stayed at home.'

'Quite' replied Mags. 'I'm really enjoying being where there's no supermarket, very little traffic, a language I have to make an effort with, and no chores to do! See you at dinner – and we'll see what Gwen's thought up for us to talk about.'

She had asked for her own key to the room, so she checked in the box at Reception and collected it, but it was the only one. Linda must be up there, then.

The room was locked; she let herself in, and found the curtains drawn and Linda, fully clothed except for her shoes, asleep on her bed. She woke up as Mags came in.

'Sorry to wake you' Mags smiled. 'Would you mind if I just draw the curtains and open the balcony door a little? To freshen the room up before it gets dark.'

'No, no, you go ahead.' Linda sat up with difficulty, and swung her legs over the edge of the bed. 'Had a good afternoon?'

Mags crossed the room to where she had set up her travelling kettle and two plastic mugs on a table under a power socket. She took the kettle into the bathroom and drew some cold water.

Maslow's Hourglass

'Really good. Smashing.' she said, plugging in the kettle and dropping two teabags into the mugs. 'I went up to the church on the promontory; it was terribly steep.'

'I couldn't have done it.'

'No. It was a steep zigzag path one way, and almost vertical sets of slippery steps on the other side.'

Linda sniffed. Mags thought she wouldn't mention the rope and pulley.

'Worth it, though?'

'Yes. It's beautiful, and the afternoon sun was pouring in through the windows; it's very unadorned and light and spiritual – liberating. Not like some of those dark ornate heavily Catholic places.'

'I was brought up Catholic' commented Linda.

The kettle boiled and Mags made the two mugs of tea, stirring with a spoon she had borrowed at breakfast time from the dining room. She added sugar for Linda, sachets also from the dining room.

'I didn't know that.'

'I don't go now. Not much, anyway.'

Mags got a small plastic bottle of milk out of the minifridge.

'Did you bring that?' Linda was curious.

'Yes. There's not all that much – I'll need to go to the shop for some more, but it's got funny opening hours.'

'I can offer you a little biscuit' Linda reached for her bag. 'I saved it from a cup of coffee I had with Gerrie in Brussels station.'

Mags brought the tea to her. She gave a rueful grimace 'You'll think I'm really anal, or mad; but I brought biscuits too. They're only digestives, but it's a bit of a ritual of mine – I always bring the ingredients for tea and biscuits when Dudley and I go away. Have one of these, and save yours in case you need it on one of our trips.'

She took a packet of McVitie's out of her bedside drawer.

As Linda sat on the edge of her bed, and Mags sat down in a chair by the window, Mags said:

'So you were brought up Roman Catholic?'

Linda nodded.

'Were you a large family, then – lots of brothers and sisters and cousins....'

Linda laughed, without humour.

'Certainly not. I was brought up by my aunt and my grandmother. They were incredibly repressed and buttoned up; always worried about what the neighbours thought, and trying to impress the Parish Priests.'

Mags waited.

'Even as a child, I had to go to confession. It's supposed to kick in after you're confirmed, but my grandmother said Satan liked to gain control as early in your life as he could, and you must be aware of your sins and confess them – well, almost from babyhood.'

'That's hard.' Mags drank some of her tea. 'That must affect you.'

Linda said nothing.

'So you lost your parents.....'

'My father was killed at the end of the war, when I was two months old. August forty-five. Terrible, really – just chance; another month and he would have survived, I suppose. My mother married an American and went to live in South Carolina, so her sister and mother brought me up. Her sister was the older one, actually. Anyway, she was my aunt, and the two of them ruled the house with a rod of iron. My aunt got married in the end, very late – about forty, she was – I was a teenager, and then after that it was just me and Grandma.'

'Where did you grow up?'

'Near Nottingham. I went to the girls' grammar school – scholarship, of course. I liked school, is some ways. At least I was with my own age group; at home it was all doom and gloom and older people. And I was good at maths and science. I wanted to be a meteorologist.' Linda smiled slightly. 'I don't know where I got that from. I was good at geography. I still love maps.'

'So do I' agreed Mags. 'I get really depressed sometimes in the late autumn, when it's so dark and miserable. I said so to a friend last year, and she said as soon as you get that dragging feeling, get the maps out. Mind you, she's a keen cyclist. She spends the winter planning her trips – she thinks nothing of going off all over Sussex and Kent on her bike, and if it's miles and miles, she just comes back on the train.'

'Ah, I expect she's young and fit. Or fit, anyway.'

'She's turning seventy soon.'

Linda didn't reply.

'So your Grandma was the only really stable person in your life while you were growing up' pursued Mags. 'Apart from your aunt.'

'Beryl worked. My aunt. She was out all day; secretary to a bank manager. Grandma ran the house.'

'When did your Grandma die? Were you grown up?'

'Oh, God, yes. She lived to be ninety one. She always wore black, I never remember her in anything else. She had dementia for a long time.'

'Horrible. I don't know if we're seeing more of it these days, or if people are just less hung up about talking about it. Did she go into a home?'

Linda sighed. 'No, not till the last year or so' she said. 'I looked after her. I wasn't very good at it. It's left what I suppose you'd call a legacy. Mentally. I'm terrified of developing dementia myself.'

'Oh, I shouldn't think you will.'

'Easy to say. If it's in the family – and in its later stages it's completely horrific. You're not human any more.'

'It must have been difficult, coping on your own.' Mags looked at her.

Linda shrugged. 'I was resentful that Beryl had gone off and got married, and left me to deal with her.'

'Your aunt didn't help, then?'

'She broke all ties, really. She married her boss; he lost his wife, you see. And then he got a promotion and they moved to Wigan. She got sort of uppity; so important to be there for Geoffrey, Geoffrey needed her to run the home, she had to entertain clients, all that sort of thing. She didn't work after they moved. Mind you, Beryl was always snobbish. She would make sneering remarks about my mother, and she thought I was a waste of space, I think.'

'Best to be rid of her, then.'

'Yes.'

Linda finished her tea and sat on the edge of the bed staring out of the window into the growing blackness of the evening.

Then she said 'It's true, I was glad to be rid of her, I don't feel guilty about that. Later on I had years and years of coping with Grandma, and I didn't even have good memories to fall back on. But when Beryl left, I – '

Mags waited.

'When Beryl left, I went off the rails a bit. I should have done a lot better at school, but in your mid teens, if you suddenly get a little bit of freedom, it goes to your head. Well, it went to mine. I found I could run rings round Grandma, where Beryl would have seen what I was up to.'

'What were you up to?'

Linda waved a hand dismissively. 'Oh, the usual. Pop music. Wimpy bars. Make up.'

'Boys?'

'Is my pill box on the table near you? I need to take three of them before dinner.'

Mags stood up and passed the box over, and then shut the balcony door and drew the curtains.

'I needed this afternoon; I really needed the rest' said Linda. 'I'm feeling better now. I'll have a shower and wash my hair and get ready for dinner – it's beginning to feel like a proper holiday.'

They were ready half an hour before they were due to meet the others, so Mags suggested that they have a drink in the bar first. When they got downstairs they found Celia there with a gin and tonic, reading her book. She saw them, put in a bookmark and closed it, lifting her drink in a toast.

'Chin chin!' she said cheerfully.

Linda sat heavily down on the sofa beside her, keeping hold of her stick. Mags went to the bar for their drinks.

'My, don't you look glamorous!' Celia said approvingly. 'Long skirt and that lovely pale blue top – it looks so good with your hair. I always admire the way your hair looks so well groomed.'

'Thank you' replied Linda.

Mags reappeared; she put the drinks on the table and sat down in a chair opposite. 'Cheers!' she smiled, lifting her Campari and soda. 'What have you been doing, Celia – emailing home?'

'Oh, I didn't know you could. Do you ask reception?'

'No, there's a computer for guests to use. I'll show you later – it's on the floor below ours.'

'I might try to email the children, just for fun.'

'Where are they?'

'Both in the Army. Justin's stationed in Washington, duties at the British Embassy.'

'That sounds exciting' said Linda.

'He's been there for over four years; he'll have another posting soon. He's married to an American girl, Meredith – they've got two children.'

'Lovely!' smiled Mags. Have you got pictures of them?'

Celia laughed. 'No!' she said. 'I always swore I wouldn't be one of those awful grandmothers who bore people they hardly know with photos of horrible children that nobody wants to look at. Mind you, Bryony and Wilbur are not horrible, they're the most gorgeous tots in the world.' She sipped her drink. 'Of course.'

'Of course!' Mags nodded. And your other son's in the Army too.'

'Daughter. Charlotte. She's a surgeon; she's in Afghanistan at the moment.'

'That must be a worry' said Mags.

Celia's face clouded. 'Of course, it is a worry. It's her third tour of duty. But you accept the risk, if you're an Army family, and Kenneth was – is so proud that they both joined up. He gave them a real talking-to when they were teenagers, trying to make sure that they knew what was involved. But they'd grown up with it, with the whole tradition and the culture of Army life. It's hard to explain to people who haven't experienced it.'

'I don't know anyone in the Army' frowned Linda, wincing as she tried to shift position.

'She's single, is she?' asked Mags.

'Yes' Celia put her empty glass down. 'I think she might be close to one of the other surgeons; she doesn't say much. She does mention him sometimes, though – a bit pinkly!' Celia gave a girlish grin.

'Pinkly!' Mags was delighted. 'I know exactly what you mean!'

'She's thirty-four now' ended Celia 'so I hope she hasn't missed the boat. But she loves the life. Now, let's go and find our table. Linda, are you taking your drink with you?'

They found Gwen and Gerrie already seated at the round table, but the rest of the dining room was surprisingly quiet. Win Burns was at a window table for two, with her book. She had dressed up, again, but gave out an almost tangible force field, rebuffing any attempt to strike up a conversation. Tabitha and Teresa were gliding towards the salad bar, and academic Simon Ryecart was just bearing two salads back to where Floral Patricia sat looking large and discontented.

The next ten minutes were taken up with checking that everyone in the Hennessey party had put in their choices that morning at breakfast, when a tick menu had been left on each table, and getting up and collecting a salad plate.

'Really good, this' said Gwen approvingly. 'There's such a variety, and it's all fresh. I like the sweet corn and the beetroot, and the pasta has a delicious sauce – mustn't have too much or I'll never get through the rest!'

'I had a bread roll and butter last night; it was delicious, but it made me too full' responded Celia.

Once they were all seated and the wine had been poured, Gerrie looked round and said 'Quite a few empty tables. Where is everyone?'

'Ah' nodded Mags 'we know that. There's another hotel, round the bend in the road, and some of them have gone there. Tonight's meal isn't included in the holiday, is it, so they thought they'd have a change.'

'Silly' sniffed Linda. 'There's nothing wrong with this, is there? And they've got to walk back afterwards. Still, it's a bit more peaceful.'

'Now' said Celia, with authority. 'Gwen. You were going to decide on a subject for us to talk about tonight. Tell us what you've come up with.' She put a forkful of salad and rice into her mouth.

Gwen's choice, and what it led to.....

Gwen sat back in her chair. 'Right' she said 'I want to ask a question. Is there anything your husband might do' she glanced at Gerrie 'or could have done' her gaze moved back to the rest of the table 'that would make you leave him?'

Gerrie's colour rose a little; she picked at a slice of tomato.

It was a moment before anyone spoke. Then Linda said 'Plenty! I bet we could come up with a list of ten things between us without even thinking.'

Gwen said seriously 'Ten things that would tempt you to leave him, but would you really? I bet you wouldn't. I'm not just talking about snoring, or not telling you when he's going to be late for dinner. I mean, what would honestly make you end your marriage. Honestly.'

Celia said 'Adultery. Being unfaithful. That's the cliché, isn't it – it's what most women say would destroy their trust.'

'Adultery doesn't always destroy a marriage' responded Gwen. 'If we're honest, I imagine there must be one or two people round this table who have either committed adultery or whose husbands have, but even if they've thought seriously about it, in the end they have continued with the marriage, haven't they?' she looked round.

Celia opened her mouth and then shut it. 'I – I've known people, in the army' she said, dabbing her mouth with a napkin 'who have made mistakes. It's hard not to when you're separated for a long time, and you're young and – um – lively.'

'Virile' said Mags.

'Well, yes. The men are virile. You have to make allowances, if they're away on a tour of duty for months – Kenneth spent a year and a half in Cyprus, with the UN.'

'So you turned a blind eye to what he got up to – '

'Oh, I wouldn't say that, exactly.' Celia was flustered. 'I didn't ask him. We didn't. It was a – a protocol, amongst the officers' wives.'

'What if he had come home with a dose?' Linda asked.

'On a charge. Self inflicted wound' snapped Celia briskly.

'No! Honestly?' Mags was amused. 'Is that true?'

'It was in our day. There was one famous time when our men came back from a training exercise in Belize and almost all of them had what was delicately called an infection. They told their wives that it had passed round their quarters via towels and showers and things; they were all on antibiotics for ages and had to practise abstinence. But they all had their pay docked; that annoyed their wives more than the possibility that they had been unfaithful.'

'So what did the wives do, when the men were away? Goose and gander and sauce come to mind' Gerrie sipped her wine.

Celia fiddled with a fork. 'Oh, it's all a long time ago. We need to think about Gwen's question. I mean, all marriages go through difficult times. And you read some very lurid stories; what about someone who lives a lie, says he goes off to work every day but really he's been sacked and can't tell his wife? How would you feel if that happened to you?'

Linda said 'I can never understand how that can happen for very long. Most wives run the family finances, don't they? I do, and I'm not the only one; though working at Sadler Samuel has made me really sharp about keeping an eye on our money. But how could he hide the fact that his pay wasn't going in any more? And you'd know something was wrong, wouldn't you, apart from the fact that in almost any town somebody would see him lurking furtively in a coffee place or something.'

'Perhaps he'd drive off to somewhere else for the day.'

'No, Celia, that's part of the same thing. He'd need to buy lots of petrol and she would see the mileage on the car had gone up –'

'Not necessarily. She might have her own car. They might have separate accounts. And a housekeeping one that he would still keep up.'

Linda sighed. 'Not everyone is Officer Class, you know.'

Celia didn't reply.

'So' offered Gerrie 'are we saying that even if we found out he had lost his job and not told us, we wouldn't leave him?'

'No, I wouldn't have thought so' Mags gestured that the dirndled and bodiced waitress was bringing the first of the main courses across the room. They abandoned the conversation until they all had their plates in front of them. At that moment Sandy materialised to tell them that it was Monty and Helen's Ruby Wedding Anniversary the next night, and there was a card at reception which it would be nice for them all to sign. Making Tracks liked to mark these occasions, and it helped to bring everyone together as a group.

'So, where were we?' asked Mags, picking up her knife and fork. 'Yes, this chap who got sacked and didn't tell his wife. Well, you'd have a lot of work to do wouldn't you? With the relationship. You'd feel let down and a bit betrayed, and you'd want to know why he felt he couldn't tell you. And he must be feeling diminished and emasculated and scared. So you would have to have lots of talks and it would take a while to rebuild things, but you wouldn't necessarily end the marriage. Would you?'

'All right' agreed Gwen 'So what would make you end the marriage, then?'

'Drink' said Celia, firmly. 'My father was the headmaster at a school in Wiltshire. He had a deputy who was an alcoholic. Absolutely irretrievable. I was only in my early teens, but I remember how awful it was; Daddy tried to keep it from the other staff, but he couldn't. I think they knew before he did; he was quite otherworldly. Then he tried to keep it from the parents. This man refused to admit there was anything wrong, but he hid bottles of whisky all over the place, in the cisterns in the changing rooms and in the music library – everywhere. I don't think we had breathalysers then, but he drove his car into a wall and then he borrowed someone else's and crashed that one, too. Daddy tried to get him to go for treatment, but he wouldn't. He used to get quite violent. I remember going into our kitchen and Mummy was looking after his wife; she had been hit, and she had bruises on her face and a cut on her forehead. She was crying. She left him in the holidays, and he was sacked. I've no idea what happened to either of them after that.'

'So – an alcoholic husband would make you end it?' Gwen wanted to know.

'Yes, I think so.' Celia sighed. 'Yes, I think in the end you would have to.'

'Absolutely' nodded Linda. 'There are some things nobody should have to put up with.'

Mags nodded too.

'So. Gwen continued. 'Is that the only thing?'

'Murder' suggested Gerrie. 'Could you live with someone who was capable of killing another human being?'

'You wouldn't be living with him' objected Linda 'he'd be in prison.'

'Not necessarily' said Mags. 'What if he confessed to you, but he hadn't been caught? Would you stay with him?'

'Good heavens. This is getting complicated.' Celia spoke briskly. 'Are we going to go into every eventuality?'

'Yes' said Gwen, her voice calm. 'that's the whole point. I want to know how the rest of you judge these things – sometimes it's hard to see the wood for the trees, and you don't know if your reactions are normal. I just want to try some possibilities out on you and hear your views. What other chance do I get?'

'So, if he confessed to you, would you be loyal and loving and keep his secret, or would you give him up to the long arm of the law?' Mags frowned. 'I'm not sure what I would do. It depends, I think.'

'I don't see how it can depend' said Celia. 'Depends on what?'

'On who he's killed, and why' answered Mags. 'If he knocked someone off their bike, and they died, you'd persuade him to go to the Police, wouldn't you? You'd probably go with him. He'd have to take his punishment, but it wasn't a deliberate act of killing. It would be manslaughter, followed by moral weakness, but I think I could cope with that. Now supposing he'd – say – murdered a prostitute, just think how that changes your whole mental landscape. It's not just the murder, is it?'

'No. Roy would never – I'm sure none of us would ever be in that situation.' Gwen looked uneasy. 'You'd have to cope with the fact that he's been using prostitutes, and that is so hurtful. And destructive.'

'I'd feel that he's opened the gap so wide between us that it can't be closed' said Linda. 'With one stroke he's destroyed so many levels of our life together that, yes, I'd probably leave him. If he gets off on doing unspeakable things with prostitutes, and gets off even more by killing them, I don't want to be anywhere near the inside of his head.' Her curls shook vigorously. 'Do you know, the more I think about that scenario, the worse it gets? Ugh! Horrible!' She shivered. 'Now, what did we order for dessert?'

There was silence round the table while they considered the conversation they had just had.

After a while Celia said 'I think it depends on what you consider marriage is.'

'What do you think it is?' asked Mags.

'Goodness me! Actually, it's either very simple indeed, or immensely complicated. Or both. Sociologically, it's evolved all over the world and it's very ancient, the pair bond, for bringing up children and knowing whose bloodline they belong to. So you don't get genetic mutations and so on. And later when people were settled it was also about wealth and security and succession and passing on assets. Against that background, a husband who is a philanderer or mentally unstable would not be a good source of DNA, would he?'

Desserts arrived, and the exchanges stopped for a few minutes.

Then Mags said 'I don't think you'd finished, Celia. That was very interesting about genetics and pair bonds. But we don't have that motivation nowadays, do we? Or perhaps we do? Does it operate at a subliminal level?'

'I'm sure it does' nodded Celia. 'But if you're religious, or even if you look at the words of a registry office wedding ceremony, you're making a promise. To stay with one woman or one man, for life, whatever gets thrown at you and wherever it's thrown from.'

'Yes, but if it's thrown from the other half, what do you do then?' Gwen asked.

'The point is that the marriage is a separate entity. It's more important than either of you, on your own. If you both use the wellbeing of the marriage as your compass point, then some of the problems which break a marriage up don't seem so catastrophic.'

'If you both. But I've always thought that it takes two to keep a marriage going, and only one to break it.' Gwen scraped the last of her ice cream from her plate.

'There are people who would disagree with you' said Celia, mildly. 'I've known people who take their vows, before God, so seriously that even if their spouse divorces them, and they remarry, the first partner still considers that they are married and should stay faithful. They never look for anyone else.'

'That's pretty rare, especially these days, and a bit over the top. Well, I think so, anyway' said Mags.

'Yes. But it's a valid point of view.'

'Gambling' said Linda, suddenly. 'What if your husband is a gambler? I knew someone at work whose husband was so hooked on gambling he even disappeared on their wedding night.'

'Heavens' said Gerrie. 'Didn't she know? Why did she marry him?'

'She was very young. It was at the end of the sixties; she was a bit naive. I think she thought she could change him – as usual, he made all the promises and kept saying it was no problem, all his friends did it. They played cards most of the night. He said some men went to the pub, some went horse racing, some went to football, it was only a hobby.'

'We didn't know much, in the sixties' mused Mags. 'At least I didn't.'

'So she divorced him?' asked Celia.

'No, she didn't. I would have, I can tell you' Linda insisted. 'On their wedding night, which was a Friday, he said he was going out for some cigarettes and he didn't show up again until the Monday. They went on to have two children; he was always in and out of work – she said that if he won, he was really generous. He bought lovely presents and toys and took her out. If he lost, he would gamble everything they had. They only ever lived in rented houses; Christine said she was glad of that because he couldn't gamble their home away. But she came through the door from work one day when they'd been married for about fifteen years – she worked much harder than he did – and there was nothing in any of the ground floor rooms except a lot of defrosting food on the kitchen floor. He'd gambled all their furniture, even the fridge freezer. All the chairs, the table, china, television, everything. I knew her quite well by then – we worked together, as I said. She rang me up, sobbing her heart out.'

'That's appalling. Truly appalling' Celia was outraged. 'There's something called Gamblers Anonymous, isn't there...'

'Oh, please, Celia' Linda said impatiently 'Things had got far beyond that. Christine had been to those meetings, they have them for the families, but there's nothing you can do if people won't admit they have a problem. That time after the fridge freezer Christine told me she cried for three days. But she had to keep going for the children. And – get this – she even thought she was lucky. Lucky! Because, she said, he didn't drink much, he'd never lifted a finger to her or the children, he kept himself clean and tidy and didn't smell. When he was at home, he was a good family man; he took the children to the circus and the seaside, he would sit and help them with their homework. It was just the gambling.' Linda gave an extravagant shrug. '*What?*' She paused. 'I ask you. If he was mine, he wouldn't have lasted five minutes. I may have my problems, but at least we've got some money behind us. If Stuart had behaved like that his feet wouldn't have touched the floor.'

'Co-dependency' commented Celia firmly.

'*What?*' shrugged Linda again, challenging.

'Well known. It's well known. Your friend Christine knew what she was getting into, or at least she recognised it once she was there. But she needed to be needed, so the relationship fed her vulnerabilities as well as his. Like these silly women who get engaged to people on death row that they've never met.'

'Hang on a minute' Gwen raised her hand. 'Wait a minute. All relationships involve a degree of needing each other, don't they? Every marriage does. If, say, she needs him but he doesn't need her, it'll never last. Will it?' she stared at Celia. 'It needs to be equal; otherwise there's a power thing going on, but you can't just say co-dependency and imply that there's something wrong with that.'

'Yes, you can. Co-dependency is about extremes. We all need each other – mothers need their children, children need their fathers, friends like us, we need each other. We bring equal qualities to the relationship. We each get something out of it as well. But in cases like Linda's friend Christine, it's spilled over into being something unhealthy. She's lost her autonomy, her self worth. Her purpose in life has morphed into being the wife of a gambler. Even her children get sacrificed for that. If her husband left her or he died, she'd be seriously at risk, mentally. My guess would be that she would volunteer as a counsellor for people with a gambling addiction, and then marry another one. She's addicted too.'

'Rubbish' Gwen's eyes flashed. 'You can't have it both ways. Either she's not taking her vows seriously because she's breaking up the marriage, or she's staying and she's mentally unstable. You tell me what she should do, then.' Gwen was trembling.

Celia was at her most imperious. 'Now, Gwen, I never said that she should or shouldn't do one thing or the other. I'm just examining the situation that someone like her finds herself in. In some of these cases there is no right course of action, it depends on the individual. But sometimes you can start from a moral standpoint, even if you have to modify it in a particular set of circumstances.'

Gwen snorted and sat back in her chair with her arms folded.

'The thing is' began Mags thoughtfully 'the thing is, life isn't perfect. People aren't perfect, and nor are their relationships. What's more they don't stay the same, they change as people change and some people learn to handle things better and others don't. Some people can see the bigger picture and some people can't. We can have ground rules and norms and ideals, but we'll never achieve them.'

'We can try' said Celia, apparently unpeturbed.

'Yes, we can try. 'We've always got to try. Otherwise we don't try, and things will be even worse.'

'Do you think women try more than men?' asked Gerrie.

'Oh, I think so.' Celia nodded. 'Yes. But not because we are better people, just because we're made differently. We spend a lot more time analysing and fine tuning relationships and talking about them. Just as we're doing now. I feel quite sad for men; not only is it really hard for them to articulate their feelings and so on, but if they talk to their friends it's seen as weakness.'

'I'm not sure I agree' Gwen unfolded her arms and rejoined the conversation. 'I've no idea what they talk about, but they spend enough time together. They've got their own form of bonding. It must be a support system or they wouldn't do it. How do we know what they talk about? Maybe they talk about us as much as we talk about them.'

Mags looked down at her hands. 'They don't all spend time with their mates' she said. 'Dudley doesn't.'

'Stuart doesn't, either' added Linda. 'He did a bit when he was younger; never very much, though, come to think of it. We did most things together when he had free time. We did the garden and we had a motor caravan; several, actually. We went travelling and camping with those for years – Wales, Scotland, Cornwall – in some places we met the same people every year and we sent them Christmas cards.' She bit her lip. 'Oh well, time moves on. We've got some good memories. But no, Stuart was never one for going off to the social club or the Masons or anything like that.'

'Leo had his Rotary' commented Gerrie.

'Ken must have had his Army mates' said Linda.

'Kenneth. Yes, of course, there was the Mess and various Regimental Dinners and occasions like that. I went with him if they were important. You have to remember, he's been retired nearly thirty years – his last tour of duty was in the Falklands.'

'That long?' Gerrie was amazed. 'Ah well, they retire young in the Army, don't they?'

'He was kept busy for years, after that, on various charities and voluntary organisations. I don't think he palled up with anyone particularly, though. His passion was music; we used to go to Glyndebourne, of course, being fairly close. And up to town to St John's Smiths Square and the Festival Hall. We went to Oberammagau once, with the church, and he's been to Bayreuth several times. Music was very meaningful for him; I think he had the feeling that he had to catch up and see all the performances he missed being away in the Army.'

'And what about Dudley?' Gerrie asked Mags. 'What are his hobbies? He's not retired yet though, is he?'

'No. No. We'll have to see, when the time comes.'

'Roy has his golf, doesn't he, and his horses?' Celia turned to Gwen.

She nodded. 'Yes. Lots of chaps for him to spend time with. He seems quite happy.'

There was a lull, and then they realised that the dining room had emptied and they ought to be thinking about preparing for the day ahead. Not to mention signing the card for Monty and Helen.

'Well, thank you all for a fascinating conversation' Celia brushed her front down lightly in case there were crumbs and pushed her chair back a little. 'That topic put the cat among the pigeons, Gwen! It's given us all something to think about.'

' "Can I thank our guest speaker..." muttered Linda. Mags dug her in the ribs.

Gerrie looked up. 'We need to decide whose turn it is tomorrow' she said. 'Gwen, you should pick the next person.'

Gwen's eyes narrowed. 'Right. Let me think. I'll choose Linda – Linda, you're on tomorrow night! Get thinking – come up with something really challenging.'

'I'll try' Linda fished for her stick. 'We've got Hallstadt tomorrow, so that will be a hectic day, but I'll think of a good subject to wake you all up over dinner.'

The light went out under the door of Room 308 at exactly half past ten.

In Room 315, Gwen and Gerrie had an animated conversation which went on a little longer than that.

'That was a bit dangerous, wasn't it?' Gerrie demanded as soon as they had closed their door.

'Why?'

'God knows what might have come to light. God knows who might have had wounds re-opened or some secret dragged out of them...'

'Rubbish.' Gwen seemed to have let loose a streak of truculence which took Gerrie by surprise. 'Nobody had to say anything they didn't want to. And you can't tell me that everybody who's ever been married – well, every woman, anyway – hasn't wondered at some time where the end of her rope is.'

Gerrie got her pot of cleansing cream and a cotton wool pad and sat on the edge of her bed.

'Maybe. But they haven't done it in public.'

'That wasn't in public. It was amongst friends. And we agreed that anything we discussed would stay inside our circle.'

Gerrie got up to look for her hand mirror. 'You can't be sure of that. I don't know your friends –'

'No, you don't' Gwen said vehemently as she pulled her top off over her head.

'But they might talk. You can't be sure.'

'I didn't say anything, though, did I?'

'No. I suppose that's true.'

'So stop being so patronising. Condescending.'

Gerrie sat down again sharply. 'Hey, now that's not fair! I'm only trying to make sure you don't open up too much, under the influence of being on holiday, and tell people things you might regret when you get home.'

'I didn't – say - anything.' Gwen said again, through gritted teeth. 'I'm not an idiot, Gerrie. Even when Linda went on about that woman with the fridge freezer, I kept my mouth shut. I do get fed up when you try and organise my life for me – it was the same when I was running the farm with Dad and Robert; whenever you and your precious Leo came to see us, I got the impression that we didn't come up to your standards.'

'That's not true' responded Gerrie equably as she took off her make up. 'And if we're going to bring it up again, there are things I could say about the way you all treated Mother. That was quite unforgiveable. I always thought of you three as 'the men', in contrast to us. You were rough and rude and domineering, just like Dad. Leo was cultured, at least.'

'Don't let's start that argument again.' Gwen buttoned up her pyjamas. 'Mother was a self-pitying wimp. And you encouraged her.'

'Mother was miserable, homesick, left out, and unwell. Without me, I think she would have just given up and faded away.' Gerrie reached for her nightdress and started to get undressed.

'Fading away was what she was best at' sniffed Gwen. 'It was the three of us who did all the work around the farm.'

'You wouldn't let me join in!' objected Gerrie.

'All Mother did, unless she was having an asthma attack or a migraine, was tinkle away on that old upright piano.'

Gerrie's shoulders dropped and she looked had a faraway look. 'So lovely, that music. The Welsh in her. She played beautifully, and sang; she had such a sweet voice.'

'I wouldn't know. I hardly heard it. I was always out with Dad and Robert, calving a heifer or baling the hay or collecting the silage or putting the sheep through the dip....you were always indoors, with the cushy jobs.'

'David of the White Rock is the one which stays with me the most. In Welsh, of course' Gerrie's voice had taken on a lilt; she smiled. 'And the Ash Grove.' She began to sing softly 'We'll keep a welcome in the hillsides, we'll keep a welcome in the vales....'

Gwen went into the bathroom and shut the door firmly.

Gerrie continued to hum to herself; when Gwen strode back into the room she was singing 'Guide Me O Thou Great Redeemer'; she stopped when her sister got into bed.

'You know I said I'd wondered about coming to live with you and Roy, at some stage? Maybe not yet, but sometime?' Gerrie said.

'Oh – you wouldn't think of asking us about that?' Gwen flashed back.

'But it wouldn't work. I didn't think it would before – we don't have the same housekeeping standards – but I know it wouldn't, now.'

Gwen sniffed. 'Housekeeping standards! What rot. You try being married to a vet – if you spent your time wiping skirting boards and arranging flowers and plumping up cushions, you'd go mad. You have to deal with injured animals and emergencies and abandoned birds and fox cubs and swans that have got run over or flown into high voltage cables – you haven't got a clue, you really haven't.'

'I think at the very least I'd have a separate fridge for the worms and the vaccines.'

'Well, it's my house, and I'm happy with the way things are.'

'So I think it would be a bad thing to suggest I come and live with you.'

'I agree. Anyway, I thought you were going to Italy?'

'I'm thinking about it.' Gerrie found her puzzle book and a pen and got into bed.

Gwen said nothing.

'But there's something else I've decided to tell you. I wasn't sure, but I think I will.'

'Good grief, you're full of secrets, aren't you?'

Gerrie looked at her sister evenly, unblinking. 'You know Leo was married before?'

'Yes. Of course.'

'He didn't tell me; he didn't have time, I suppose. But a few months before he died, his ex-wife died, too. Probate came through just before I lost Leo.' Gerrie turned to settling herself against her pillows. 'And she left him a lot of money.'

'Oh. How much?'

'That's a bit direct!'

'Sorry. Don't tell me if you don't want to.'

Gerrie sighed. 'Well; actually, after the tax and everything – and then it was part of his estate – it would be about half a million. Pounds.'

Gwen didn't move.

After a minute, Gerrie said 'It's a lot.'

'Ha! I should jolly well say it's a lot!' retorted Gwen. 'Money goes to money, so they say.'

'And I was wondering whether I should give it to you. If you're right about Roy.'

Two conversations before bed

Gwen paled. 'Give it to me? Why would you do that?'

Gerrie shrugged. 'I don't need it' she said. 'I didn't know about it, and Leo has left me very well provided for even without this windfall. I thought you and Roy were all right, and you had plenty behind you, but if he really has been gambling and you're heading for a council old people's home, I think I ought to help.'

'Oh. Thanks' said Gwen in a small voice.

'I also wondered about suggesting that with Roy retiring I could put in some money and we could buy somewhere else, for the three of us. Less land, maybe a large bungalow, somewhere with two sitting rooms, nearer the shops. But you've sounded the alarm bells. I don't want to get into any situation where Roy might drag me down, along with you.'

'I should be standing up for him, after a comment like that.'

'But you're not.'

'I think I'm beginning to see things more clearly by the minute. It must be the result of getting away, and having a bit of perspective.'

'Well. Exactly. I knew a woman once with an alcoholic husband. She left him and even got divorced, to secure her financial future, but she still loved him to hell and back. She looked after him and had him over for lunch every Sunday, but she took control of her life because she had to. She had two adult sons and she could see

Maslow's Hourglass

the family money disappearing down the drain. Eventually her husband died of liver failure in a bedsit, but she always said she felt she had done the right thing. No regrets. She was in her fifties and it was too late to start again. You're in your sixties, so – no chance. And you've got Gavin and Jen and little Rosie to think about, as well as your own old age.'

Gwen chewed her lip. 'When you put it like that....'

'So. I'm not going to suggest I live with you after all. But I am offering a large sum of money, if you want it, so that you can buy yourself somewhere to live and have a bit invested for the future. It's up to you what you do about Roy – stay married, divorce him, nothing to do with me. But at least now you won't have to stay with him just because you can't afford to do anything else.'

'No. Thank you, Gerrie.'

'I'm not going to throw the money away, though. I'm not just going to give you a cheque and let you muddle along and allow Roy to bamboozle you into losing it all. The deal is, you leave and buy your own house, and I'll give you five hundred thousand pounds to do it with. If you stay with Roy, though, no dice. It's your choice.'

'How long have I got to think about it?'

'As long as you like. If you move out, you get the money.'

Gwen was silent.

'Still think I'm condescending and patronising?'

Gwen turned her light out.

There was an air of resignation in Room 311 as Linda and Mags pottered about preparing for bed. Mags was looking forward to going to Hallstadt in the morning, getting there by train and a boat across the lake, and then walking up to the funicular railway and going up the mountain before the excitement of a couple of hours in the salt mine.

However, she knew she needed to curb her enthusiasm because Linda would find the whole day challenging and certainly wouldn't be able to manage the walking and the funicular. So she had to think of another topic of conversation while they were getting ready for bed.

'When you look at all the signatures on that card for Monty and Helen, you realise how many of us there are, don't you?

'Yes – quite a few of them were at the other hotel for dinner. I saw them coming back as we went through to the lift.'

'Do you think Monty is his real name? Monty Bewley sounds too good to be true!'

'Oh, it's not his real name!' Linda laughed. 'He's Stanley. Mind you, that's bad enough.'

'Stanley Bewley.' Mags savoured the name. 'His parents weren't very imaginative, were they?'

'I was talking to Helen earlier today. He's been called Monty ever since he was a young man, because he's mad on classic cars. In his day, that would be ancient Bull Nosed Morrises and things, I suppose, but now he's the secretary of their local MG club. Apparently Uncle Alan's got one, and he's really dangerous in it now, but he refuses to give it up.'

'I can just imagine him! Did I see Uncle Alan eating on his own this evening, in the corner of the dining room?'

'Yes, I saw him too. Actually, Sandy went and sat with him over his coffee. Monty and Helen were in the other hotel. Do you think they deliberately left him out?'

Mags looked doubtful. 'Bit naughty' she said 'if they did. But you can understand it, especially if it's almost their anniversary.'

'I have to say it's been nice not to have Duracell bellowing away in your ear. I wonder if they enjoyed their meal?'

'Don't suppose Pat did. She's one of those women who are never happy about anything. It's like a badge of honour with her to find something to complain about.'

Linda sighed. 'The proprietor stopped me this afternoon' she said. 'He's going to use the hotel minibus to run some of us up to the station in the morning.'

'Oh good!' Mags gave a relieved smile. 'I'm so glad. I wondered how you were going to walk up there – it's probably not far off a mile and some of it's very steep.'

'Maybe I shouldn't go at all.'

'Don't be daft! That's what we've come for, the chance to see all these places. Hallstadt is a World Heritage Site – it'll be really interesting! And people like the Ghastly Garsides and Floral Patricia will be just as glad of a lift as you are.'

'My hip is getting worse.'

'I can see that. Even since we left London. Is it arthritis?'

'Yes. Amongst other things – I've got arthritis in my hands and feet. And my back; and my neck. But the hip is a problem - it's crumbling now. The bone is giving way. I had a reconstruction after the accident, but I've got osteoporosis as well. Whenever I see the consultant it's sharp intake of breath time. He sucks his teeth and says I'd better go on as long as I can. I don't think they're quite sure what to do.'

'Oh. You might lose your mobility.'

'Ha! What mobility?'

'I mean, you might have to use a wheelchair.'

'I'm trying not to think about that. And I've got to go into hospital as soon as I get back; for something else.'

'What?'

'I had tests for bowel cancer and there's a bit of concern. I haven't told Stuart about that one, he's been in a bad enough state about his cholesterol and high blood pressure, and I knew he had diabetes. He wouldn't listen to me, but I'm not surprised.'

Mags changed the subject. 'What did you think of Gwen's outburst?' she asked.

'I wouldn't call it an outburst.'

'No, all right, although she was a bit prickly. Do you think it was a rhetorical question, or do you think she really does have a problem with Roy?'

'Problem, definitely' Linda's curls bobbed against her neck. 'The question is, which one?'

'As in, drinker or murderer or – '

'Gambler or adulterer – '

Mags giggled 'Tinker, tailor, soldier spy!'

'Perhaps it's domestic violence' suggested Linda.

Mags looked doubtful. 'Don't think so. I've never seen her with bruises or tearful or scared. I've met Roy quite a few times, and he always seems very affable.'

'Wife beaters do seem affable, to outsiders.'

'Yes, but they seem happy together. She's always been quite relaxed and normal when I've been with them, and there would be an undercurrent if he was thumping her. She's even been a bit off with him, like we all are sometimes, and you wouldn't dare to do that with a violent man.'

'And you would know.' Linda's eyes were sharp.

'Yes, actually. Yes, I would.'

There was a pause.

'All right' continued Linda 'So it's not domestic violence. Drink?'

'Could be. Roy does like a drink, and he's always at the golf club or the races. But I've never seen him drunk, not that that means anything. He doesn't look like a drunk though – puffy eyes, a bit bloodshot, shaking hands, a haystacky appearance. His clothes aren't always immaculate, but then again, when I've seen him he's usually been doing vet type things.'

'Adultery?'

'Definitely maybe. He's not bad looking, even in his sixties, and there must be plenty of opportunities where he hangs out. I bet that's it. He's got a floozy.'

Linda nodded slowly. 'Sounds the most likely' she agreed. 'Not a murderer, then?'

'Perhaps he murders koi carp or rabbits. Can't see him bumping off a human being.' Mags smiled. 'He's got quite nice manners, actually – '

'Don't tell me you fancy him?'

'Oh please. No, I don't. I just mean, unless he's gone up to some horse vaccine rep and said "Excuse me, you're charging far too much for this stuff, I think I'm going to kill you" I can't see him committing a capital offence.'

'So poor old Gwen has got a rival. Perhaps he's gone for a younger model. I expect if she just bides her time he'll come to his senses. Most men stray at some time, don't they?'

'Well, some do. And some don't.'

Linda read her book while Mags leafed through some information about the salt mine. Their lights were switched off almost at the same moment.

Hallstadt

There was time for a leisurely breakfast before the mid morning train left from the station above the village. The Hennessey party managed to miss each other; Celia had evidently been down first, her place at the table was used and empty. Gwen and Gerrie arrived next, planning to explore the village a little more until it was time to catch the train.

By the time Mags and Linda were in the dining room most of the guests had dispersed. The Quiet Americans were just finishing at a window table; they inclined their heads in greeting, dabbed their mouths with napkins, looked at each other and rose to leave. Mags was taken aback yet again at how tall they were, and how slender. Uncle Alan was leaning over a table and talking to Win Burns, his sunburnt nose only inches from her face. She looked furious.

One of the tall grey sisters was reading a book and eating a boiled egg and a croissant. As Mags walked past her with two portions of yoghurt and fruit, they smiled at each other.

'On your own this morning?' Mags asked.

'Yes' replied Tabitha or Teresa. 'My sister didn't sleep very well. I've left her in bed. I'll take her up something' she indicated a plate with a Danish pastry and a pear on it 'and I'm sure she'll be fine. Are you going to be adventurous, and go up to the salt mine? Or will you stay in Hallstadt and wander about? There's a charnel house full of painted skulls, and a couple of fascinating churches.'

'Oh, I'm going to the salt mine, definitely. Sandy says it takes several hours, so you have to make up your mind and go straight there. If you dawdle around first you'll never get back in time for the boat and the train home.'

'It'll be too much for your sister, though won't it – she'll have to stay in the town and look in the shops. There are plenty of cafes, I understand.'

'She's not my sister!' exclaimed Mags, looking at the two bowls she was carrying.

'Oh, I thought she was' said Tabitha or Teresa. 'You seem to be looking after her so well. I'm sure she couldn't cope without you' she smiled, thinking she had paid Mags a compliment.

Thin lipped, Mags reached the round table and plonked one of the bowls in front of Linda. 'Hope that's what you wanted' she said.

'What else is there, then?'

'Same as usual. Ham, cheese, rolls, muesli, cornflakes, all bran, bread, scrambled eggs, bacon, tomatoes, boiled eggs, fruit salad, fruit bowl, marmalade, honey – '

'All right, all right!' Linda raised a hand. 'Sorry I asked. What's the matter with you? Someone rattled your cage?'

Mags sighed and rubbed an eyebrow. 'No. Sorry. I don't know why I felt – I don't know what I felt, really. Sorry.' She looked at her watch. 'We've got about three quarters of an hour.'

'I'll go up and email Stuart. Just quickly, when we've had breakfast.'

'I'll see you at reception, then. Oh no, up at the station – you're getting a lift, aren't you?'

Linda pushed her empty bowl away.

Sandy counted heads and gave out slips of paper with the times and arrangements for the day. There was a reserved carriage on the train, and they had to be absolutely certain of catching the right one back again at the end of the day; only one in every six or seven stopped at the village.

The straggly line of the Making Tracks group set off through the little byways, along fences, past gates, beside gardens and tiny orchards, up the hill to the station. Uncle Alan was in front, his camera and binoculars thumping rhythmically against his chest as he walked. He was talking animatedly to Simon Ryecart, loping enthusiastically beside him; Floral Patricia being safely transported in the hotel minibus.

Tabitha and Teresa came next, each in Craghopper trousers and neat ankle socks and good quality walking shoes, with small back packs. Behind them were Colin and Wendy Harbottle, Gordon and Pat Garside and Mike and June Finch, who seemed to have formed a happy group of like minded holiday makers. They pointed things out and agreed with each other volubly as they walked, laughing from time to time.

Celia, Mags, Gwen and Gerrie were a little further back. 'Goodness' said Mags 'Just listen to the noise that lot in front are making. I bet the people who live here get totally sick of the arrogance of the tourists. Just imagine – they have groups like this coming past their gardens all year round. It must drive them mad.'

'They probably put up with it for the sake of their economy; tourism is the highest source of income in Austria' said Celia.

Gwen glanced behind her. 'I wonder where Duracell is?' she commented. 'Pat's there, look, with Donald and Maewin. They seem to get on quite well; I think Duracell has a business connection with Oregon, or a relative there, or something. I heard them talking about it.' She had another brief look. 'And Win Burns is there, with Adam Adamant. No sign of Iris, though.'

They reached the station, rather out of breath. Celia checked her watch. 'Twenty minutes still' she said. 'That's quite a long time. Sandy has over estimated the time it takes to get up here. There's no need for it – we could have left at least ten minutes later.'

Gwen, next to Mags on the platform, put her mouth to Mags' ear and whispered 'Do you think that's what she says to Kenneth?'

'What?' Mags whispered back.

'When he gets fruity. Do you think she says "Stop it Kenneth! There's no need for it!" Poor bloke.'

Mags giggled behind her hand. 'Yes, I bet she does!' she said quietly.

'Who?' Celia was suddenly beside her.

'Patricia. I bet she comes up in the minibus.' Mags recovered herself.

'Oh, she is. She was waiting with Linda, as we left.'

Eventually the sound of a labouring engine and tyres on grit heralded the arrival of the hotel minibus, driven by the proprietor himself. Amongst those disgorged was Duracell, who went straight over to his wife and said 'I'm all right, I'm all right love.' He scratched his scalp with a thumbnail, leaving a carroty plume of hair standing up.

Linda limped over to Mags, looked at him, and muttered 'Woody Woodpecker'.

'Oh, you're right! Brilliant! Why didn't he walk up, do you know?'

'Had a dizzy fit. So he said. Iris Harper's got a corn which is playing her up. Floral Patricia, of course, we knew she would need a lift.'

'I can't see Monty and Helen Bewley?' said Gwen, turning a circle.

'Haven't seen them at all today' replied Gerrie, standing next to her. 'Uncle Alan seems to have come on his own.'

The train was on time, naturally. As it drew to a halt and the doors hissed open, a metal step unfolded as part of the mechanism.

'Oh, look!' exclaimed Gwen. 'Isn't that clever? I wondered why it was such a steep drop, but they've got it all organised, haven't they?'

They found their reserved compartment and settled into their seats. The journey took them along the lake to its southern end, through the little town whose livelihood was provided by a salt processing plant. It was small, industrial, with warehouses and piping and fleets of lorries neatly parked in yards waiting for their loads, but there were also residential areas, with small blocks of flats and individual houses. The train stopped there, and all along the river valley at villages and towns on the route.

'We saw a lot of this from the coach, when we came from Salzburg' commented Celia 'but it's much more interesting to see it from the railway. You're in the real heart of the place, finding out what makes it tick, instead of cruising along the main roads and bypasses. That's what I like about trains!'

They continued; stopping and starting, local passengers getting on and off, some of them greeting each other. 'Gruss Gott!' 'Gruss Gott!' A polite nod. Desultory conversation in the carriage. Although the journey took over an hour there was constantly something to watch or listen to. Sandy swayed down the carriage in good time, telling the occupants of each pair of seats that they would be getting off at the stop after next.

There was much excitement as they approached their destination and saw the lake growing bigger and bigger as the track converged with the shore, and once they had all got off they could see that a boat was waiting at the end of a path, moored to a jetty, and immediately across the lake was Hallstadt reflected in the water, just like all the pictures in the holiday brochures.

There was a collective sigh of anticipation. Appreciation. Uncle Alan was stooping and stretching and clicking away immediately, letting out a 'Cor!' and a 'That's grand, that is' as he captured the view, the boat and the mountains from every angle.

The boat journey across the lake only took about fifteen minutes, and then they were clambering out into the busy hubbub of Hallstadt as it was being thoroughly explored by tourists from all over the world.

'Right, off you go' Linda was brusque. 'Go on, all of you – I'm going to stroll along and look at the shops and the churches.'

'We will have to go now, if we're going up to the salt mine' nodded Celia. 'We're all going, the rest of us, aren't we?' she looked around at Gwen and Gerrie, and Mags.

'Where shall we meet you?' asked Mags.

'You'll either find me somewhere when you come down, if you've got time for some sightseeing, or I'll see you at the jetty for the boat back. For goodness' sake, Hallstadt's not that big.'

The group split; the Americans, Donald and Maewin, strode off with a map, and Celia, Gwen, Gerrie and Mags found that they were the only other ones prepared to tackle the mine. Everyone else had decided to stay in the town.

Three hours later they stepped off the bottom of the funicular and turned to walk slowly back into the centre of the town. 'Aren't the flowers lovely?' commented Gerrie. 'Everywhere you look – window boxes and tubs. And hanging baskets. It looks so beautiful against the wood and stone.'

'We've just got time for a look round before the boat back' Celia quickened her step. 'I'd like to see the charnel house with the painted skulls. Who's coming with me?'

'I will' said Mags.

'Not bothered' Gwen shook her head. 'Gerrie?'

'No. I think I can live without looking at six hundred skulls and a whole lot of bones.'

Celia and Mags set off, leaving the other two wandering slowly along the street, stopping to look in shop windows and cafes. Eventually they reached the marketplace. 'Stunning!' breathed Gerrie. 'Such lovely buildings! Look at those pastel colours!' and outside one of the restaurants at a coffee table they found Linda, sitting with Floral Patricia.

There were two spare chairs, so they sat down. 'What have you been doing?' asked Gwen. 'Have you found lots to look at?'

'It's been completely boring' snapped Patricia. 'Simon's all right. He's interested in history and architecture; he's visited the churches and looked at the bones, he's spent hours in the World Heritage Museum, God knows where he hasn't been. I've had to find one coffee place after another, just to pass the time.' She quivered with fury. 'I shall say something to Sandy. They should have planned this better – two hours here would have been quite enough.' She smoothed down the floral material over her ample bosom. 'Quite enough' she repeated firmly.

Linda rolled her eyes at Gerrie. 'Actually, it has been a bit too long' she admitted 'if you can't move about easily. What was the mine like?'

The waitress came out and they all ordered coffees. Gwen and Gerrie wanted apfelstrudels as well.

'Absolutely amazing. Fantastic. Wouldn't have missed it for anything. And the view from the top of the funicular – it's all quite new, lots of Perspex and viewing platforms. It's breathtaking.' Gwen fumbled in her bag. 'Look at this photo – '

'You go down these slide rails' added Gerrie. 'To get into the lower chambers. Shiny wood. You put your legs either side, and lie back, like this, with your hands folded over your chest and you just go! Wheee! The best fun I've had for ages!'

'And they take these photos?' Linda passed it along to Floral Patricia.

'Yes, they take you as you go down the longest one, sixty four metres. And those numbers are the speed – I was clocked at more than thirty kilometres per hour! It was fantastic' said Gwen.

'What on earth are you wearing?' Patricia looked closely at the picture.

'Oh, that's a real surprise' explained Gerrie. 'You get up there – and it's quite a way from the top of the funicular, and very steep – and the first thing that happens is you're herded into a big room where they issue you with boiler suits. Jacket and trousers. And the trousers have leather reinforced seats in them. It's a good job they do, you go screaming down those slides and you'd have your – bottom – on fire if they didn't.'

Patricia handed the picture back. 'No good for me' she sniffed. 'I couldn't do it.'

'Well, you can walk down some steps if you don't like the slide, but nobody did' Gwen put the photo back in her bag and started to tackle her strudel.

'There was a super guide, a woman. Very good English and quite amusing' said Gerrie. 'She said St Barbara is the patron saint of miners, which I didn't know. She wore a jacket with twenty-nine buttons, because St Barbara was born on the twenty-ninth of September, and so that's the miners' lucky number.' She sipped her coffee.

Gerrie went on 'They did it all very well. There were laser displays and videos, and moving models of the miners with audio commentaries – for children, it would be something you'd never forget.'

'Incredible, when you think it was a thousand years BC, and they had such a thriving salt trade' added Gwen. 'They had these huge chambers where they dried out the lakes of brine. A bit like salt pans, but underground. They lit them with pine sticks, the ends were full of resin and they burned, like firebrands, so they could see what they were doing. And they carried the salt away, then, and it all went by river - first to what is Salzburg today, and then either up the Rhine to the Baltic, or down to the Mediterranean.'

Gerrie put down her coffee cup. 'And then they traded it, of course, for things from all over the world. They were amazingly civilised. They loved colour and painting things; their houses and textiles were decorated with lovely patterns. The graveyards outside have thousands of burials there – it was a long lived and prosperous community. The lower part of the mine is still worked, so we couldn't go there, but they gave us each a tiny pot of salt to take home.'

'So you come out at the bottom of the mountain, then?' Linda asked.

'Oh, no!' replied Gwen. 'No, you finally ride on a tiny train, with your legs over each side – they almost reach the ground – through a long, long tunnel. Very cramped, there's hardly any space round you. Very low ceiling. And then you come out about halfway down the mountainside, in the open air, and you have to climb all the way back up.'

'Wooden steps, wide and steep – it kills your thighs' nodded Gerrie. 'There are handrails, and sort of landings. I had to keep stopping to get my breath back, and oh! My muscles ached! They still do. I tell you what, I'm glad I did it because in a year or two I don't think I'd ever manage. Anyway you get back up to the top of the mine in the end, and go back through the changing area to take off your boiler suit and hand it back.'

'Then you go through a shop' finished Gwen 'where your photo is pinned up. You can buy it – it's five euros. We both did. Well, it's a nice souvenir, isn't it? And they've got other stuff there, mainly for children. And a coffee shop; 'kaffee und kuchen'. And then you have to walk all the way back down to the funicular.'

Patricia wrinkled her nose. 'It's not something that would interest me in the least' she commented. 'Each to their own.' She got up heavily, leaning on the table, which almost tipped up. Gwen pressed down on it hurriedly. 'I'm going to find the loo before Simon wants us to get down to the jetty.' She moved away.

'You wonder why people like her come at all, don't you?' Gerrie watched as Floral Patricia lumbered away.

'Sour grapes' responded Gwen. 'She'd like to do these things, but she can't. So she just rubbishes them.'

Linda opened her mouth, and then shut it again.

Celia strode up, her crisp snowy hair lit by the late afternoon sun.

'There you are!' she smiled. 'How are we all? Had a good day?'

'I've managed to pass the time' Linda said. 'Mostly I've read my book, or found someone to talk to.'

'How were the bones?' Gwen got to her feet.

'You have to pay. I thought you would, but a lot of people turned away when they saw that. The church beside it is very interesting – so are the graves. They are so ornate and decorated here, aren't they? Oh, the bones – yes, they were all right. They are what they are. The painting on the skulls was only done in the eighteenth century. We ought to be going. Where's Mags?' she turned a full circle.

'Isn't she with you?' Gwen asked.

'She went into a shop – oh, here she is!'

Mags joined them, a little breathlessly 'Sorry' she said 'I went to find a loo and it was quite a way up the square. Here now.'

Everyone converged in good time for the boat back; the train arrived ten minutes after they had disembarked and assembled on the platform. Sandy supervised the stragglers and made sure they got into the reserved carriage, and the return journey progressed uneventfully. They passed through Bad Goisern and Bad Ischl – 'we're going there aren't we? Tomorrow?' 'No, the next day' 'Oh.'

'A good job it's downhill on the way back' said Gwen, climbing down off the train.

'Oh, my muscles!' moaned Gerrie as she massaged her thigh. 'It was worth it, though. I don't think I've ever seen anywhere quite like that. How about that mine?'

'Rosie would have loved it. She'd have had a brilliant time on the slides. Actually, I think the rest of it would scare her stiff.'

'I have been to a salt mine before, in Poland, with Kenneth' said Celia 'it was very different, though. Big caverns, shiny walls – they'd carved an altar out of salt, and people would get married there. The world is such a fascinating place, isn't it?'

More people took the minibus back than had used it in the morning. They had to be squashed in, and as Celia, Gwen and Gerrie fetched up outside the hotel, two of the staff were still trying to extricate Floral Patricia, as Simon waited on the stone paving hopping from foot to foot like a heron and calling 'Don't worry dear! Take your time! I'm here!'

They made their way past him and into the hotel, and returned gratefully to their rooms for a rest before dinner.

Linda's choice

Celia immediately had a shower, put on her satin robe, and sat against her pillows with her legs out watching a BBC television programme about the crisis in the Eurozone.

Linda sat in a chair by the window, silently looking out of the balcony window at the darkening lake. Mags clambered on to her bed with her book, but fell asleep within minutes.

Gwen took herself off to the computer room and sent a long excitable email to her granddaughter Rosie, full of descriptions of the salt mine and the skulls of Hallstadt.

Gerrie decided to have a bath, something she hadn't done for years. She pulled back the shower curtain and searched in her sponge bag, hoping she had thought to put in a sachet of bath crystals. Luckily she had, and after a delicious twenty minutes luxuriating in the fragrant, silky water, she got out, smeared on a face mask, and while that was working sat on the loo and gave herself a pedicure. Thoroughly wrapped up in a huge towel, she thought 'That's better!' and emerged into the bedroom to hunt in the wardrobe for something to put on for dinner.

Gwen returned at that moment, full of smiles.

'Did you email Rosie?' asked Gerrie.

'Yes! And she'd already emailed me. Bless her. She said she hoped Nannie was having a lovely holiday, and that I must be careful not to fall down mountains or drown in the lake. Mummy has a cold but she has gone to work anyway. And Joan Dawson has been looking after her until Mummy comes home. Not tomorrow night, though, 'cos it's Brownies.'

'She's growing up so fast, isn't she?'

'Yes. I hope she'll like the history book I bought her in Hallstadt – it's a bit beyond her, I think.'

'Best to stretch her a bit. If it was too babyish she'd be bored.'

'That's true.'

By the time Gwen and Gerrie were down in reception ready for dinner the hotel was crowded. The absentees from last night were eating in this time, and those who had been on the excursion were hungry and anxious to sit down to their meal. Celia tapped Gwen on her shoulder 'It's no good trying to get into the bar for a pre-dinner drink. It's packed in there'. They pushed through and threaded their way between the tables to where Mags and Linda were waiting for them.

'We didn't want to go for our salads till we were all here' said Mags. 'It's a bit different tonight, isn't it?'

Duracell bore down on them with an overloaded plate; a bit of coleslaw fell off the edge, and he peered down and kicked it under the table. Then he leant over Linda and grinned at them 'Don't know what you girls are doing on a rail holiday! Eh? Eh? Not a female thing, I wouldn't have thought! What do you find to talk about every night? Fashion, I suppose. Recipes. What's happening on Eastenders, eh?'

Celia said indignantly 'How ridiculous! Do you really think that's the sort of thing we're interested in? As a matter of fact – '

Duracell wagged his free index finger at her. 'You should all be at home with your husbands. Want your bottoms smacked. Deserting your posts, that's what you're doing!'

Still grinning he wormed his way round to a corner table where Pat was waiting for him with the Garsides.

Celia was snorting. 'Ghastly man! That man really is ghastly. How rude. How – common! That's the only word I can think of...'

Linda grinned. 'I had to put up with him for ages in Hallstadt' she said. 'Lucky you, rocking your socks off inside a mountain. He came and sat with me while Pat and the other Pat – Garside – went shopping for presents for the grandchildren.' She sighed. 'God, he goes on, and on...'

'Duracell' nodded Mags.

'Well, that's absolutely accurate. And he doesn't like the bells.'

'What bells?' asked Gerrie.

'The church bells. The ones that chime every quarter of an hour; I got about ten minutes on that one; how they keep him awake, he's told Pat, they've complained to the management and they've moaned at Sandy, and when they get their feedback form they'll make a point of putting it down.'

'They stop at midnight' said Celia. 'They start again at six o'clock in the morning.'

'Are you sure?' Linda was doubtful. 'He says they go on all night, and he woke Pat to listen at four o'clock because he was still awake.'

'Rubbish' said Celia roundly. 'I'm – I have a problem with sleeping. I thought the mountain air and all the exercise might help. But I'm having some really bad nights. It doesn't matter, it can't be helped. It does mean, though, that I've been awake at two and three and four in the morning and the bells are silent. They really are.'

'Well' retorted Linda 'He's making a meal out of nothing, then.' She laughed. 'One funny thing – you know they all trooped off to the other hotel for dinner last night?'

'Yes' nodded Gwen 'Was it any good?'

'He said the food was just the same as here; they had exactly what we had. And he was spluttering about how the staff asked them for their room numbers, and they all waved wads of Euros and said they weren't staying there so they would be paying cash. But actually both hotels are owned by the same family, and you can eat in either and put it on your room bill.'

'That man is an oaf' muttered Celia, getting up to fetch her salad.

'He really is' agreed Linda. 'He told the whole story as if it was the eighth wonder of the world. He didn't seem to realise that it made him look a fool. God, I wouldn't swap places with Pat for anything.'

It took a while for everyone to settle down; each table was occupied, and there were comings and goings and greetings as people fetched their salads and began to calm down. Plates were stacked and removed; there were a lot of main courses for the staff to serve. Gwen poured wine for everyone on their table, and just as she put the bottle down there was the sound of a glass being hit with knife and some clapping.

'It's Sandy' said Celia, peering across the room.

Sandy was standing up. 'Can I have your attention, everyone? Thank you! I know you've all signed the card for Monty and Helen, and we're very pleased to be able to congratulate them on their Ruby Wedding today.'

Everyone cheered and stamped their feet.

'We're delighted that you've chosen to celebrate this happy occasion with Making Tracks' Sandy went on 'and here is a very small present from the company. Also – ' There was the scrape of a match and a sudden flare 'we would like you to enjoy these flowers; and may the rest of your day go with a bang!' There were cheers from nearby tables.

'What's going on?' Linda craned to see. 'What's happening?'

'They've got a rather pretty arrangement of flowers with a candle in the middle' said Mags. 'Isn't that nice? I think that's lovely!'

'Huh. In a couple of nights we've got the dubious pleasure of Duracell's birthday' said Linda. 'He'll want to trump the Bewleys, won't he? He told me all about it this afternoon. He's got Pat to tell Sandy, so he can look as if it's all a big surprise.' She mimed astonishment with her hands spread out.

'Ridiculous. Stupid man. There's no need for it' Celia turned to her plate and began to eat. 'Now, Linda' she continued 'We're waiting. What do you want us to talk about tonight?'

'Right' replied Linda briskly. 'A simple question: would any of you ever consider Dignitas?' she took a mouthful of fish and potato.

The others looked at each other. 'We all know what that is, don't we?' asked Gerrie. 'The Swiss place, where - '

'Yes, yes.' Celia nodded impatiently. 'Of course we do.'

There was a moment or two of silence.

'I've shut you up, have I?' Linda's voice held a note of sarcasm.

'I'm just thinking, that's all' soothed Mags. 'Of course you think about it. At least, I have. In principle I would consider it. But it's quite complicated.'

Gwen put her fork down. 'You know what?' she said 'I've always felt we treat animals better than people. I've seen people suffer terribly. When I do the hospital car service, it's not just about taking people to appointments. It's often taking someone old and frail to visit a relative in hospital who is in an awful state, and not going to get better, full of tubes and drips and catheters, with urinary infections and dementia – oh, it doesn't bear thinking about. They're suffering agonies.' She tapped her index finger on the table. 'But the nursing staff just keep them alive, and the old person is terribly distressed by what they've seen. Sometimes it's the last time they see their brother or spouse or whatever, and all they have to remember is what I would consider inhuman treatment. All in the name of medical progress. Awful. If it was a dog, we'd give it an injection. I just don't get it.'

'But we're not dogs, that's the point' Celia commented. 'We can't just put people down. That would be open to all sorts of abuse.'

'What about the abuse of shoving tubes down people's throats? We need some system that reduces suffering, not one that condones it.' Gwen's face was flushed. She cut savagely into her chicken escalope.

'God, this is a huge subject' sighed Gerrie. 'We might be all night on this one.'

'Doesn't matter. We've got all night' said Linda.

'I didn't get on with my mother' began Mags slowly. 'I don't know why I said that; it's not relevant.'

'Go on' encouraged Celia after a pause.

'My mother only died fairly recently' Mags tried again. 'I haven't quite – what would you say? Processed it. Yet. Anyway, the point is, she had a massive brain haemorrhage. She was in a coma for four days and then she died. But I still can't quite understand what I was told.'

'Who by?' asked Gwen.

'The nursing staff. The consultant. They kept saying they had to turn her, in the bed. To keep her comfortable. But they said she wasn't suffering, because her brain had sort of burst. Awful. Sorry, I don't mean to spoil your meal. I thought at the time – they can't both be true; that she's totally unconscious, as they told me, or that she would be uncomfortable, which means that she could feel something. And she had a horrible mask on; it made red marks on her face.'

'Oxygen' said Gwen.

'Yes. And from time to time a tear would run down each cheek. She was crying. They said, don't be silly; she can't cry, she isn't feeling anything. She's totally unconscious. They said the tears were a chemical reaction. I don't believe it. I still don't believe it. She was suffering, terribly, and I let it happen.' Mags looked anguished, but she wasn't in tears. 'Well, I'm going to tell you now something I've never told anyone else.'

She took a swig of wine. 'She was dying. They said she was; I suggested that I went home and came back later, but they thought it was only going to be an hour or so, maybe less. So it would be better if I stayed. And they left me alone with her. It was almost beyond my control – something outside me – I kept looking at the oxygen cylinder and the mask, and I saw this hand – my hand – reaching for the mask and taking it off. I couldn't take it right off, it was resting on the top of her head. And she only took maybe three breaths after that, and there was a big shudder. And then she died. I watched the blood drain out of her face like a tap being turned on. She was white and waxy, and still. And there were no tears. I'll never forget it. I sat and watched her for several minutes, but she was gone. She wasn't there. So I put the mask back on her face, and went and fetched a nurse.'

There was silence at the table. Around them the buzz of conversation ebbed and flowed, but it seemed miles away.

Celia said 'That was very brave of you. It was the right thing to do.'

'Oh, I know it was' Mags nodded. 'I've never been in any doubt. I'm not wracked with guilt or anything like that. I did for her what the medical people didn't. Either they didn't care enough, or they didn't think about it; or probably they didn't want the risk. But I'd do it again, tomorrow. Whatever they said, I'm sure she was suffering. And she wasn't going to recover. I'd want someone to do the same for me.'

'So – Dignitas, then' said Linda.

'I'd need to check them out' Gwen shook her head. 'Maybe they're all right, I don't know. Wasn't there a documentary on TV?'

'Yes, there was' Gerrie dabbed her mouth. 'I saw it. It was amazing. Moving. But I wouldn't say it was completely free of suffering. This chap had to drink some stuff, and he made some horrible noises before he died.'

'I still don't understand it' persisted Gwen. 'It's so easy to make it painless. If you put an animal down, you just give it an injection. It's dead almost before you pull the needle out. Even a large animal, a horse – all you need is one shot between the eyes, it's not expecting it and it drops down dead. Why is it so difficult to treat humans - well, humanely?'

'We shouldn't have to go to Switzerland, in any case' said Mags. 'That's just mad. We should have a proper system of our own. Somewhere you can go when you've had enough, and they'll put you out of your misery. You need all the safeguards, like a signed permission letter and things. You might want your family with you. That would be much easier if you didn't have to go abroad.'

'Yes, but supposing you changed your mind? At the last moment?' objected Celia.

'Then you'd tell them' Mags shrugged.

'You can't tell them, if you've got motor neurone, or you've had a stroke' Celia drank some of her wine 'or if you've got Alzheimers.'

'Isn't there a living will thing?' asked Mags. 'You work it all out in advance and get it witnessed, and then your wishes are carried out at the right time.'

'Sorry, but that's rubbish' objected Linda. 'Who's to say what is the right time? I know someone who's wheelchair bound with MS. But he has good days and bad days, and on a bad day he might ask someone to end it all for him, but on a good one he still has some quality of life and he would want to go on. I know he would. And what about people with learning disabilities? How can you make those choices for them?'

'Well, you're the one who chose the subject' retorted Gwen. 'What would you do?'

'What will I do.'

'Oh. What will you do, then?'

The plates were cleared and there was a pause for the desserts to be served.

'I love this ice cream – I could eat it every night!' enthused Gerrie.

Celia brought them back to the matter in hand. 'You were going to tell us what you will do' she said to Linda.

'It makes you evaluate your whole life' replied Linda, obliquely. 'What have you been living it for, anyway? What's been the point? Who are you there for? My life is empty, to be honest.'

'Don't be silly! We don't do self-pity' said Celia, bracingly. 'Everyone's life is of value.'

'Who says? Stuart and I have spent our whole life keeping our heads above water. I'm not saying we've been badly off; we haven't. Money has meant a lot to us. We've earned quite a lot and spent quite a lot. We moved house four or five times, always to somewhere better. We've driven nice cars, almost each one has been new. I've had everything I wanted, really; if I wanted nice clothes, I bought them. We have new furniture every few years, and I can have what I like. We've had three motorhomes, one after another, all new. And they're not cheap. We really have pleased ourselves.'

'You've only had yourselves to worry about' remarked Mags.

'Exactly. That's my point. And now the party's over, whatever the party was all about, if anything. Remember, I was brought up by my grandmother, and she had Alzheimers, for years and years' Linda nodded at Mags 'and I never, never want to live with it if I get it myself. Never. Anyway, that side of the family is all gone now. Stuart has a sister somewhere - she's married, got a couple of kids. But they fell out over their parents' will. I kept out of it; mind you, it was probably twenty years ago.' She waved a hand in the air. 'No, it's just us. And I've got these crumbling bones and probably bowel cancer. I'll be in a wheelchair soon; maybe by Christmas. Stuart's got diabetes and high blood pressure and very high cholesterol - they said the arteries in his neck are nearly blocked. He'll have to have an operation, and they want to do an angioplasty. But his diabetes is going make it all much more difficult. Life is only going to get worse, for both of us. Do you know what –' Linda gave a humourless laugh 'I used to have a saying. Money and booze' she raised her glass 'the two best things in the world. They never let you down. Well, it's true, they don't. But when you get older, they don't get you out of the mire, either. It's all irrelevant where your health is concerned; you can't drink any more and money won't buy you a new body.'

'It might in the future' smiled Gerrie 'the way things are going.'

'Too late for me' replied Linda equably. 'So at some stage I intend to do the world a favour and bow out with dignity. At a time of my own choosing.'

'With Stuart?' Mags wanted to know.

Linda shrugged. 'With him or without him, I've no intention of getting to the stage when it's too late, and I can't take control of my own death.' She reached across the table for the wine bottle, and tipped what was left into her glass.

'Should you be doing that, with the tablets you're taking?' frowned Mags.

'Sod it.' Linda took a gulp. 'I can't walk properly, I can't climb, I can't go up funiculars or down salt mines. Damned if I'm going to be dictated to about what I can drink.'

The others exchanged glances.

'So anyway' Linda continued. 'That's enough about me. My question was, would you ever consider Dignitas?'

'I'm not sure it's moral' Celia said. 'It's something I haven't worked out yet; it reminds me of the play "Who's Life is it Anyway?" Have we got the right to decide when to go?'

'Oh, really.' Gwen sighed. She fiddled with the salt shaker. 'Are we back to religion?'

'Yes, I think perhaps we are' replied Celia. 'If we have the right to decide, someone must give us that right.'

'If you take God out of it, you remove the question of rights. It becomes a matter of taking control.' Gwen was emphatic. 'I mean, who else does it affect except you, if you want to end your own suffering? Even your nearest and dearest shouldn't have a view, should they?'

'All right, look at it the other way round. What's wrong with suffering? Supposing it's a good thing?'

'No! No!' said Gerrie and Linda together. 'How can it be?' asked Linda. 'suffering is negative, painful, evil, bad. Nobody would want pain and misery, except a masochist.'

'There is an ancient and universal tradition of improvement through suffering' said Celia. 'Not just the Christian rituals, and fasting, and sackcloth and ashes, and those Roman Catholics who flagellate themselves. And hairshirts. There are the Indian aesthetes and lots of examples all over the world. Perhaps there's something in it.'

'Ah, but they choose to do it. It's a conscious effort of will' said Mags. 'If you're ill or blind or demented, it's not your choice. It's thrust upon you. That's when you need to take back control over your body, and what happens to it.'

Celia was silent.

'I had a car accident' said Linda, leaning back in her chair.

'We know you did' said Mags. 'It was a long time ago, though.'

'But you don't know why.'

'You had a row with Stuart, didn't you? We've all done that. I remember when I was married to my first husband – '

'I need to tell you this. It's my subject tonight, my turn to take the floor. I'm going to tell you something. It's important.' She was flushed; her forehead was shiny through her fringe.

'Linda, you've had quite a lot to drink. You may regret this' Celia reached out for Linda's empty glass.

'Take it! I don't care. I'm not drunk, and I'm not having any more, anyway. I just feel that this holiday is releasing something. I need to tell you something very important. We all said anything that came out would just be between ourselves, didn't we? Nothing said, to anyone, when we get home?'

Mags nodded. 'Yes, we did. We'll keep to that, don't worry. But please, don't say anything you might wish you hadn't'.

'I'd had a row with Stuart.'

'We know that' said Gerrie.

Mags reached out suddenly and gripped Linda's arm. 'Don't!' she said sharply. 'Don't, Linda. Really. Please don't. If you really want to tell us, wait till tomorrow night. You can tell us then, if you still want to. But you may change your mind, and then there's no harm done.'

Linda bit her lip. She began to speak; then she stopped. 'All right' she nodded, eventually. 'All right' she said again.

'Well, now - we should think about going up' said Celia, briskly. 'Tomorrow is Salzburg; I'm looking forward to that.' She pushed her chair back, reaching for her handbag on the floor. 'So it's about an hour and a half – maybe a bit less – on the coach. We have to be ready by a quarter to ten, in reception.' She stood up.

'We're going to Mondsee on the way back as well. It'll be quite a full-on day' added Gwen, also standing. 'Isn't Mondsee something to do with the Sound of Music?'

'The wedding scene' said Gerrie. 'The church from the wedding scene. I think that will be lovely, if the weather's good.'

On the way to Salzburg

Gwen, Gerrie and Celia moved off, slowly making for the lift and their rooms as they chatted happily.

'Come on' said Mags to Linda. 'Here's your stick. Let's go up to the room. I've eaten far too much; I need to lie down.'

Up in Room 311 Mags dropped into the armchair by the balcony window while Linda sat heavily on the edge of her bed. She sighed.

'You all right?' Mags turned her head.

'Oh, of course I am.' Linda was tetchy. 'Got to be. What else can I be? But I meant what I said. As soon as I think the time is coming when I'm not going to be independent any more, that's it.' Her lips were a thin line. 'I'm off. When I get home I'm going to look up Dignitas on the web and see what you have to do to register with them. I'd much rather there was somewhere in the UK, though. Wouldn't we all?' Mags noticed her breathing was slightly laboured; wheezy.

'It would mean a change in the law.'

'Of course it would! Why don't our politicians listen? There have been court cases, like that Mrs Pretty, to establish whether someone who helps you to die would be prosecuted. And every time they all agree that it's mercy killing, it's humane, it's what any of us would want if the chips were down. But they're too scared of – something – to actually draft the legislation.'

'The Church of England, maybe. The bishops.'

'I can't see that. They changed the law on abortions, didn't they? And divorce. Against some very entrenched views in the church. By the way - ' Linda struggled to take off her shoes and then stood up to start undressing.

Mags waited a moment. 'By the way, what?' she prompted.

'Thank you for stopping me, earlier on. I probably would have regretted what I was going to tell them.' Linda's face was expressionless.

'I was afraid you might' Mags smiled. 'Keep your own counsel. You go in the bathroom first, and I'll put the news on and nip in afterwards.'

Half an hour later they were both sitting up in bed. Mags was looking at a map of Salzburg, and working out where the places of interest were. She had passed a guide book over to Linda, who had flicked through it and was scanning the back cover. She put it down on the duvet.

'Could I say something?' she asked. 'Could I tell you what I was going to tell the others?'

Mags looked across; Linda's chin was high in the air as she gazed at a corner of the ceiling.

'Are you sure?' Mags frowned. 'I thought you'd decided....'

'I won't tell them. But – I don't know why, perhaps it's being away from home – it feels like a heavy lump inside me. Maybe it's being away from Stuart, as well. I've kept this hidden for so many years' Linda's voice broke; she dropped her head and her chin trembled until the tears could not be held back. She reached for several tissues from the box on the bedside table, covered her face with them using both hands, and sobbed quietly. Mags sprang up and was swiftly round beside her, sitting on the edge of the bed with her arm round Linda's shoulders.

'Oh, what is it? Hey, don't cry! I don't mind if you tell me, of course I don't, if it would help. What's the matter? You poor thing.'

Linda wiped her face and blew her nose. 'I'm not a poor thing. God, that's one thing I couldn't stand.'

'Sorry' shrugged Mags. 'But I hate to see you so upset, that's all.'

'We haven't any children' sniffed Linda, reaching for more tissues. Mags smoothed her pyjama top down and went back to her bed; she climbed in and pulled up the covers, turning to listen.

'So no future, nobody to leave anything to, no point to anything, really.' Linda blew her nose again. 'At least that's what Stuart thinks.'

Mags' eyes opened wide. She didn't say anything.

'I had a car accident' Linda almost chanted it, like a mantra. 'A long time ago. I had a row with Stuart. He thought I was having an affair. He had found out that a man had been ringing me, and I had met him. Twice. In town, in a hotel bar.'

Mags felt herself breathing in.

'That was probably silly' Linda wiped her eyes. 'Perhaps I should have suggested somewhere further away; but I was taken by surprise. The man I met was a private detective.'

'Goodness. I don't think I've ever come across one of those - in real life.'

'He'd been engaged by a young man who was trying to trace his birth mother. Me.' Linda said dully. 'He'd found the right person. I had a baby when I was seventeen; I went off the rails a bit, when Beryl moved out to get married and I was left with Grandma. It was a boy, a little boy.' The tears started again; Linda dabbed her eyes, and regained her composure.

Mags shifted position. 'How awful. How awful for you, I mean' she said quietly. 'And you had him adopted, I suppose.'

Linda nodded slowly.

'Did you see him? Did you meet him?' Mags watched carefully to see how far she could probe.

'No. We had these two meetings, me and the detective. We proved without any doubt that this young man, twenty-three years old, was my son. I had such a terrible decision to make. Another terrible decision. I'd pushed it all out of my mind and I thought that was that, there would be no more to worry about. But to know he wanted to see me....' Linda leaned her head back against the headboard. 'Oh, it was too tragic. Too difficult. I think I may have been wrong. I don't know. I had nobody to talk it over with.' She sniffed.

'So you said no. To a meeting.'

'Well, yes, I did. It was too painful; I thought it was best if we went on as if nothing had happened. Ian – they'd called him Ian – had his adoptive family. How would they feel? He was about to get married; that was why he wanted to find out about his origins. I thought he should forget about me and get on with his life. Draw a line. He might not have liked me, anyway; he might have been very disappointed. And then there was Stuart.'

'Did you tell Stuart?'

'No, I never have. And I never will. That's the only thing I can cling to, that I must be strong and keep this secret to the grave.'

'It must be hard.'

'Oh, it's awful' Linda's voice was trembling and she wiped her eyes again. 'Supposing I get dementia? Like Grandma? I might say something then. I always worry about talking in my sleep. I've done such a terrible thing. I thought I had put it right fifty years ago, but you never do, do you? Really bad sins are a stain on your soul forever. I'm such a bad person. I think I'm evil.....'

'No you're not!' Mags sat up straight. 'Of course not! You made a mistake in your teens, when you were looking for affection and you'd lost your mother, and your aunt – anyone could see how it happened. Lots of people do, it's life. You grow up, and learn, and move on. Of course you're not evil – don't be ridiculous!'

'Well, I can't accept your opinion on that. I know what I am. I've had nearly half a century to get used to it. And twenty-five years to come to terms with knowing that I have a son somewhere, who wanted to find me and I rejected him for a second time. Because I was afraid – I thought Stuart would leave me, and I'd have nobody. Nothing. Or at the very least he would know he was married to a woman who was capable of wicked things, and destructive actions. I couldn't have lived with his looking at me and knowing what I'd done. I would have taken an overdose.'

'I'm so sorry.'

'I've deprived Stuart of a family; he always wanted children, but we didn't get married until I was well into my thirties. He's accepted that he'll never be a father, but if he knew.... and perhaps I've got grandchildren somewhere. I must have. Every Christmas I look in toy shops and watch people buying things for their grandchildren, and I wonder about mine. Sometimes I've thought my mind has gone; in the past I used to look at children and wonder if it was them, if they'd come shopping in Canterbury – it's mad. Absolute madness. I've committed a sin which has overshadowed my whole life. And Stuart's. I don't deserve to live.'

Mags was silent.

'Some people would say I've already been punished. I've never had good health, never. Ever since I was a young woman. It's just gradually got worse. I almost embrace it, sometimes; it's all I deserve.'

'I don't think that's very logical.' Mags shook her head. 'Good people and bad people, there's no explanation for what happens. Bad things happen to good people; it's very hard to believe in natural justice sometimes.'

'Well, bad things have happened to me, and I'm not a good person. So that makes sense as far as I'm concerned.'

'I think it's more likely that you've tortured yourself all these years, and the stress hormones have damaged your immune system. That's really sad. Making yourself ill has had absolutely no impact on the situation, it hasn't put anything right. All it's done is to make you miserable. It probably hasn't helped your marriage, either. Or Stuart.'

'Oh, Stuart. Goodness knows. I don't think he thinks much about anything these days.'

'He must wonder why you've been – as you are, I suppose – throughout your marriage. He probably wonders why you've been unhappy, and whether it's his fault.'

Linda waved her hand in the air. 'He's given up trying to work me out. He did used to ask me, at one point, that's true. Whether he'd done something wrong. I used to get really irritated by that.'

'That must have puzzled him.'

'Perhaps it did. The time I got most annoyed was when he thought I was having an affair – he wouldn't leave it alone! God! And I couldn't tell him what was really going on. So when he said, that night, that he thought he must have done something wrong, well – red rag to a bull. I'd had a good deal to drink, and I just grabbed the car keys and drove off at a rate of knots. I couldn't deal with it, I really couldn't. And of course I crashed the car into a wall on a bend.' Linda shrugged. 'Another example of natural justice. Except that I should have been killed. I wish I had been.'

'You should have had counselling. You've been trying to deal with something far too big to handle on your own.'

'Ha! Counselling's rubbish. How could anyone else know how – desperate – I feel inside? Guilty, and full of hate. I couldn't have talked to anyone about it. I don't want to come to terms with it. I'm not supposed to; I've done something too unforgiveable.'

Mags sighed. 'I'm really sorry' she said quietly. 'I think you're torturing yourself quite unnecessarily, without achieving anything except damaging the life you're living now. For all you know, Ian might be a huge benefit to mankind – perhaps he's invented some wonderful machine, or he's found a cure for a deadly disease. Maybe you've had a hand in something much better than you're aware of.'

'That's about him, not about me. It doesn't alter the fact that I've done some terrible things.' Linda put out her light and pulled herself down into the bed, drawing up the duvet round her ears.

In Room 315 Gwen and Gerrie had a much shorter conversation. Once they were in bed, Gwen asked:

'Do you think Linda was tipsy?'

Gerrie shrugged 'Probably. She looks the type that likes a drink, and she's on medication.'

'Interesting discussion, though.'

'Mm. It's something we've all thought about. I don't think there's an easy answer. I've known people go into hospices; they seem to be wonderful, inspiring places. And the advantage is the high staffing levels and attention to food, and decor, and the care of visitors. And the relaxed rules. But there aren't enough of them, and they're expensive to run. You can't run hospitals like that.'

'No' agreed Gwen.

'What do you think Linda wanted to tell us?'

'Goodness knows. Nothing much, I should think. Probably about her health, but we can guess that it's getting worse. I expect that's why she chose the topic.'

'Good night'.

In Room 308 Celia had a file out of her suitcase; she spent ten minutes looking through some papers and letters before returning them and making sure she had padlocked the case and put the key in her handbag.

★★★

An ultra modern coach arrived on time in the morning; wonderfully comfortable accommodation, good views and an onboard WC. The steep steps defeated several members of the party, though, and Sandy and some others amongst the fitter ones had to push, pull and generally manhandle those who were less mobile up into their seats. Exhaustion and embarrassment silenced Floral Patricia, Linda and three of the men. Not Duracell, though, who could be heard saying 'What you want is exercise, Gordon, exercise. Like me. I play golf, and tennis – it shows, you know, it pays off, doesn't it Pat?' as the coach pulled away.

Gordon droned something in reply. The two grey sisters sat together, efficiently dressed in smart slacks and cotton floppy hats with their backpacks beside them. Donald and Maewin were at the back, immaculate in beige poplin and expensive pigskin jackets, one in rust and one in claret, lined in silk. The day was not a warm one.

Mags sat next to Celia. 'How on earth do they do it?' she mused. 'They always look like a page from an upmarket catalogue. I can't understand about their washing.'

Celia turned to her. 'What about their washing?'

'How do they get it done? They can't have an inexhaustible supply of shirts and slacks and cotton polo necks, can they? Apparently they spent three weeks touring England and Scotland before this, then they're going to fly to Venice for four days, and then they have ten days in Ireland visiting some relations before they go home to the States. You never see them doing anything practical, or getting flustered. I just don't know how they manage to be so – soigné? Is that the word?'

'Yes, if you mean well-groomed. The word that I always think of when I look at them is "languid". They just float through the world, don't they, without getting wound up about anything. Even when they were sharing a table with Reg and his wife, they were unfailingly courteous and patient.'

'Duracell, we call him.'

'Because he looks like a battery' Celia's brow was furrowed.

Mags laughed. 'Not exactly – it's because he has a copper coloured top, and he goes *on, and on*....' she looked at Celia 'The advert. On TV.'

'Oh, I see. Kenneth and I don't watch much television.'

'It's his birthday tomorrow. Sandy's left a card at reception for us all to sign.'

'Ghastly man.' Celia folded the jacket on her lap. 'Do you know, he actually stopped me this morning, and asked if I knew what he was having for supper tonight. Honestly! I said I'd no idea. He wouldn't let me pass, you know how he jabs your shoulder with his finger' she shuddered 'and then he said "two fried eggs and chips". I tried to look interested, but really....his wife started to lead him away, but he kept on "I've asked them to make me two fried eggs and chips for tonight, haven't I, Pat? And they've said they will". I feel for that woman. Well, at times – she's not somebody I would choose to spend time with.'

'You're getting as bad as the rest of us!' smiled Mags. 'Don't call him Duracell by mistake – I keep thinking I'm going to!'

'It's not good form to make personal remarks' replied Celia primly. Then she relaxed a little. 'Mind you, it's tempting. There are so many – *types* on this holiday, aren't there? And some who defy categorisation, like poor Win Burns. But really, the Garsides and Reg and Pat and the Bewleys – it would be easy to sink to their level, if you're not careful.'

'You mustn't do that' Mags hoped she sounded serious; she bit her lip.

'Oh, I shan't. There's no need for it.'

Salzburg

In Salzburg there was a repeat of the struggle to get on the coach, but in reverse. Floral Patricia almost fell down the steps from top to bottom; Sandy and the driver who were standing below managed to catch her, and if Donald Chisholm hadn't grabbed her from above by the collar of her raincoat, her weight would have knocked them to the ground. Simon had got off ahead of her and made a spirited, though sloping, bid for freedom; or at least for the public lavatory a few yards away.

Linda fumbled her way carefully, holding on to the handrail and freezing into position as she became frightened of the drop below her. She let her stick go; it clattered down and had to be hooked out from under the coach body. Uncle Alan's binocular strap caught on something, and nearly strangled him as he trotted happily down the steps. Luckily his crimson face with a fixed smile caught the attention of Sandy, who called up to Monty behind him to free the strap before there was a crisis.

The crocodile of English tourists, some a little shaken, wound its way across the road and round a corner to meet their guide for the day, a dapper little Austrian in a Tyrolean hat and with a manner which reminded Mags of someone. Next to Gwen at some traffic lights, she hissed 'That chap in 'Allo 'Allo with the little tank – Gruber, was it? He's got that precise way of speaking, with pursed lips - '

'Yes! Absolutely!' Gwen agreed. 'Even the tilt of his head.'

The guide turned out to be amusing and informative; the first place he took the party was to the Mirabelle Gardens. He apologised for the chilly turn the weather had taken, gave them an overview of the history of the city and the places they would be visiting, and then led them into the next part of their tour. Mags was amused to see the Quiet Americans striding to the front of the line with their long legs to ask him a question, and to hear two words in his reply. 'Sacher Hotel.' Maewin nodded seriously and asked him a little more. Having satisfied herself she turned to Donald; a smile passed between them, they nodded politely to the guide, and then quietly left the group and could be seen marching purposefully up the road.

The rest of the party were led skilfully up and down sidestreets, shown places of interest and museums, a puppet theatre and the house where Mozart grew up, and eventually the guide took them across a bridge to the Old Town.

Halfway across they all stopped, and the guide pointed out hundreds of padlocks fastened to wires on the bridge, on both sides. 'You have these in England, no?' he smiled. 'For love? They are very popular in here, in these days. You see? Big locks, little ones, tiny brass, all the colours – each with the message, the initial letters. You see?'

Duracell and Pat bent down and squinted. 'Oh, yes! See, Pat, see?' Duracell straightened up and waved an expansive hand at the others in the group. 'Never seen that before! I was looking for R and P, but I can't see one of those! Hey? Have to do one myself!'

'It ought to be RIP, not R and P,' muttered Linda.

Uncle Alan elbowed his way to the front and took some photos at rakish angles. 'Bit better than carving your initials in a tree trunk' he commented. 'Mind you, I wish I was a locksmith here, you'd clean up, wouldn't you?'

'What do they do with the keys?' asked the ever practical Celia. 'You'd need to come back and undo it if you split up, wouldn't you?'

The guide shook a forefinger from side to side. 'Nein, nein! The keys are thrown into the river! That is the whole thing! The padlock, it is for ever!'

Several of the women breathed 'Aaahh. Isn't that lovely!'

They set off again; Gwen said 'I wonder if they do that in London nowadays? I'll have to look next time I go up.'

Gerrie shook her head. 'I bet you can't do that at home. Too many regulations.' They both said together 'Elf and Safety!' and laughed.

Linda managed to keep up, but only just. She arrived, breathless, every time they stopped, joining the others just as the guide finished one of his explanations and the party were laughing at his witticisms before moving on again. Mags felt conscious stricken once or twice, but she wanted to get as much as she could out of the visit, and to find out more about Mozart and his connection with the city, and the rest of its history. They threaded their way through squares and markets, stopping to visit churches with important pictures and memorials in them.

The weather got worse and worse; standing listening to the guide the group were buffeted by increasingly strong winds, soaked by chilly showers of rain, and began to suffer the effects of freezing cold feet as the ice-cold pavements took effect. They looked up when examples of architecture were pointed out to them, only to receive a face full of rain or a poke in the eye from an umbrella. Mags peered through a crush of soggy shoulders to see Sandy going into a shop that sold Mozart chocolates – a rich combination of nougat, marzipan and chocolate that allegedly sprang from another secret recipe and were sold only by authorised outlets. It's the same at home, I suppose, she thought; Sally Lunn buns made in Bath to a secret recipe, those gingerbread shortcake things that you buy in Grasmere which are closely guarded by one family who make them. All part of the allure. All part of the tourist trap. But we fall into it, don't we? To take home. We might never come back.....

So it was a real relief when they all trooped into the warmth of the Salzburger Dom, to have their breath taken away partly by the sheer beauty of what was inside, but also by the five organs – four high up on corners of the chancel and one huge four-hundred-pipe main organ.

'I would love to hear all those organs in full throat, all being played together' said Celia quietly to Mags. 'Can you imagine? Did you hear the guide say that they have to start pieces at slightly different times to get the music to sound synchronised? Amazing. I want to see the huge font where Mozart was baptised.' She moved off.

Mags sat in a pew and took it all in. She gazed slowly round the cathedral, absorbing the paintings and gilding and the ornate memorials; little groups of their party were either sitting in quiet contemplation or gathered in front of something of interest, their raincoats dripping as they began to thaw out. Dudley would like this, she thought. I ought to feel guilty that he isn't here. But I mustn't weaken; if we're to go on, I must use this holiday as a safety valve, a space to work out my attitudes and strengthen my resolve. I must learn a new way of coping with him. I have to develop some sort of transparent layer, a carapace, so his barbs don't actually pierce me. It has to be clear, otherwise he will see it and pick away at it. That only makes things worse, because it starts the whole ritual again and we say the same things and have the same rows and I think it comforts him, in some unhealthy way. Even if we are saying upsetting things to each other, it somehow validates him. I've got to stop thinking about that. I've got to stop spending so much time trying to understand him and make excuses; I need to find myself again, before it's too late. And that's best for him, too, because he needs a strong external influence to counteract the needy, unstable person that he is. God, it's all so exhausting. She sighed and ran fingers through her windswept hair.

Over to one side she could see a group of people gathered round a tall, dark haired man with glasses. They seemed to be almost fawning on him, vying with each other to get near him and speak to him, quietly, and be granted an acknowledgment; a tilt of the head, or a smile. At the end of the pew she was sitting in, the Austrian guide, now without his hat, was standing motionless. She slid up the polished wooden bench and whispered 'Who is that? What's going on over there?'

'It is a sculptor; a name Stefan Knor – you know him?'

Mags shook her head.

'He has displayed, a Pieta. I don't know the English –'

'A Pieta, yes. We say the same.'

'Today is the last day of it is displayed. He is here to talk to people of his work, before it moves to another exhibition. It is his reworking of a Pieta by Balthasar Schmitt which was in St Paul's Church, in Munich. It was destroyed by fire – Stefan Knor has made it again in clay, from a model of the charred original, but used gold and black paint to make it seem burnt, as the original. It is very moving.' He nodded at Mags. She smiled back.

After a few minutes Mags slid her legs round the end of the pew and got up to join the throng of people round the sculptor. There was a low murmuring and a few camera flashes, and nobody noticed her as she made her way round to look at the Pieta. It made her catch her breath. So very stark, so serene, so beautiful. Larger than she had expected, lit in such a way as to enhance the mystery and accentuate the shadows. Mary, sitting with her almost featureless charred face, cradled the long body of her dead son across her lap. His lifeless arm dangled to the floor over the folds of her robe. Mary's hands – so full of meaning – one lost to sight under Christ's shoulders, the other one extended, almost to say to the world 'Here is my son. Look. He was given to me. I gave him to you. Feel for me. Feel for me.'

Mags had no idea how long she gazed on the figure. It seemed to be etching itself on her mind, and she hoped it was. The wordless, fathomless grief seemed to speak for all women, of every age. To suffer such agony and to keep one's dignity, that's the challenge facing us all, she thought. At last she let her eyes move away and down to the ground, and to her shock she saw the crumpled form of Linda, on her knees, her head almost on the floor in front of her, sobbing noiselessly. Her stick was thrown to one side, her bag still slung across her body; she had lost herself to emotion, her shoulders rising and falling with her gasps.

Mags' first impulse was to bend and touch Linda, a gesture of sympathy and comfort. But a moment later she realised that it would be intrusive even to show that she had seen her; Linda would need help to get to her feet, but that would be the role of strangers. Better to move quietly away.

The Austrian guide assembled the group inside the door of the cathedral, and they set off again outside in the cold to look at a graveyard under the walls of the fortress.

As they shivered outside, Gwen turned to Mags and Gerrie and asked 'Have you had enough? I think I have. We don't have to stay on this tour, you know – Sandy said we could peel off and do our own thing at any point.'

'I'm frozen' said Mags. 'I'd be happy to go and do something else. Preferably indoors.'

So Gwen ran up and told the guide that she and Gerrie and Mags had decided to leave the tour and take the funicular up to the fortress rather than go on to the catacombs. They walked away quickly and went to find the ticket office.

'There should be a fantastic view from the top' said Gerrie, shivering again. 'Oh, it's so good to be under cover, isn't it?'

'Well, I'm not sure the weather will be clear enough' frowned Mags. 'It might be all right. Anyway, it'll be interesting.'

As they reached the top and left the funicular to explore, Gwen looked at her watch. 'There are lots of things to look at' she said 'there's a chapel, and a big organ called the Bull' –

'Sounds good!' giggled Gerrie.

'Stop it! The point is, I don't know if we've got time to see any of the sights and have a hot drink as well. Didn't we say we wanted a coffee?'

'Oh, at least!' enthused Mags. 'Actually I want a hot chocolate, I think. God, I'm cold.' She stuck her hands in her pockets.

They went to look over the wall of the fortress to get a good view of the city, but it was overcast and very cloudy, and the mountains in the background were lost in a chilly mist.

'I think we've been educated enough for one day' said Mags firmly, turning away. 'Let's go and find the cafe'.

They spent a very happy half hour in the restaurant, beautifully furnished with light wooden panelling and comfortable chairs. Gerrie and Mags ordered hot chocolate and apfelstrudels, but Gwen wanted coffee and Sacher Torte. 'I'm not going to let the Americans get away with trying that if I'm not' she said.

They needed to hurry to get back in time, taking into account the wait for the funicular and the twenty minute walk back to the meeting point for the coach. That was assuming they didn't get lost. But Gwen wanted to stop quickly in the amber jewellery shop at the bottom of the funicular to buy a bracelet for Rosie, so after that they really had to stride out to get through the shopping areas, over the bridge, and back though the maze of side streets.

Mags hauled herself up the steep steps into the coach; everyone else was in their seats and as soon as the group was complete the doors hissed shut and the driver pulled away. Sandy weaved from side to side down the aisle, counting heads. Suddenly Mags wondered about Linda; she realised she hadn't given her a thought since the cathedral, and looked about her, eventually spotting her in a seat at the back where she was chatting to Tabitha or Teresa.

There was a stop at Mondsee on the way back to the hotel, to visit the church which was featured in the Sound of Music for the wedding of Maria and von Trapp. 'Too much' Pat shook her head at June Finch. 'I said to Reg, didn't I, Reg? I said, that's one thing too much. They shouldn't have planned it on the same day as Salzburg. It's too tiring. I'll have a word with Sandy – you'll write, won't you, Reg? You'll put it on their form.' She settled back.

'It's true, Mike? Isn't it? Too much on one day' June craned her neck to talk to her husband in the seat behind, but he was asleep with his head leaning on the window.

The visit to Mondsee was irritable, chilly and damp. There was quite a distance between the coach park and the centre of the town, and everyone was pulling on coats and jackets which were already wet. They had no appetite for any more sightseeing, but the prospect of probably an hour in an increasingly cold coach with nothing to do was even worse. The town was very attractive, and the approach to the delightfully ornate church, surrounded by wide paved spaces, would have been breathtaking on a sunny afternoon if one was rested and cheerful, but today it was darkening, windy and scudding with sleety rain.

Some people didn't even reach the church, herding instead into brightly lit coffee shops for kaffee und kuchen. Linda somehow hauled herself along at the back of the group, her raincoat trailing in the puddles; luckily Uncle Alan was stopping every few yards for photography, so that the rule of the convoy progressing at the rate of the slowest member did not mark her out as obviously as it might have done. The church itself was worth the effort of getting there; once again, little groups of dripping people gathered inside, to look up at the decorations and whisper to each other and point things out. Then they hurried outside to where Duracell had found a public loo and was dancing up and down and gesticulating to everyone he could recognise, pointing to the entrance. By the time those who wanted to use it had been inside and emerged again, and found each other, and decided which direction led to the coach park, another twenty minutes had passed. Sandy, under a Making Tracks umbrella, stood patiently on a prominent corner, directing the party across a soggy sports park and counting heads, yet again.

Another hour passed before the coach disgorged them, mostly silent and exhausted, in the darkness outside the hotel. Keys were collected and the group took themselves off to their rooms either via the lift or by struggling up the stairs, to prepare for the evening meal.

Preparing for Celia's.....

'I – am - knackered.' Gwen sat heavily on the bed, having taken her raincoat off.

'Technical term used by vets, is it?' Gerrie was pulling off her wet trainers.

'Yup. I actually feel like a horse that's going for glue.'

Gerrie wrinkled her nose. 'That's nice, I must say. Anyway, how do you know?'

'Well, I'm too worn out to gallop, or pull a cart, so I guess the next stop is the knacker's yard.'

'Oh, cheer up. You'll be all right when you've had a wash and got changed. Think about dinner and a couple of glasses of wine!'

'Give me a few minutes. That was really quite a hectic day. Incidentally, whose turn is it tonight? To choose the topic?'

Gerrie had peeled off her trousers and socks and was looking in the wardrobe for something to change into. 'Celia's' she said.

'Celia's turn? Oh, that'll be interesting. I wonder what she'll pick? How do you choose the right stockbroker. Or deciding the correct age to give a debutante her first pearls.'

'A guide to under-gardeners for the proletariat.....'

Gwen giggled. 'She does try, to be fair. I think she really does live a different life from the rest of us.'

'Noblesse oblige.'

'Something like that. I wish she would let her hair down; you never feel you've made contact with the real person, do you? I won't say she puts on an act; she's just very protective of – something. Guarded. Don't you think?'

Gerrie closed the wardrobe and turned round with a white pleated skirt and a dark pink top over her arm. 'I think it's just women of her type. Of her class. They're brought up to be well mannered but not to reveal any family matters.'

'Family secrets.'

'If you like. But she probably has friends, people from her background, that she's more open with.'

'Do you think so? I can't imagine that.' Gwen got up. 'You have the bathroom first, I'm not ready yet.'

'Actually, she probably does have to be pretty self contained' Gerrie headed across the room. 'If you think about the fact that her father was a head master, so they would have had to keep at arm's length from the other staff, and the pupils and their families. And then her husband was a senior Army Officer, so again you couldn't fraternise much, could you? I expect she'd had to learn to think for herself and stand by her own decisions. She's not had the opportunity to cultivate the sort of female friends that we have. I think that's a bit sad.' Gerrie went into the bathroom and closed the door.

Gwen nodded; 'Mmm' she said.

Downstairs the usual supper melee was in progress. The Hennessey party were about to tackle their salads when Duracell pressed in close to the table. He bent down with his mouth in Linda's face. 'Know what I'm having tonight?' he grinned. 'I bet you can't guess! It's not on the menu. If you don't ask, you don't get, I say.'

Celia, at the other side of the table, looked up. 'Egg and chips' she pronounced crisply.

Duracell looked taken aback, but quickly recovered. 'Double' he wagged a finger at her. 'Double egg and chips! How do you know?'

'You told me this morning' replied Celia evenly, forking some sweetcorn and spring onion into her mouth.

Duracell wagged his finger again. 'You women!' he shook his head teasingly. 'You ought to be at home, making egg and chips for your men! I wouldn't let my Pat have a holiday on her own, I can tell you!'

'I bet you wouldn't' said Mags.

'She wouldn't want to, she wouldn't want to!' Duracell was triumphant. 'There's nothing she can do on holiday that she can't do at home.'

'Except talk freely to her friends without being stifled' Mags' mouth was a thin line.

'Now that's where you're wrong. I know about you women and your conversations; it's all film stars and cooking and babies. You can talk about that any time.' He turned to leave. 'You just ask yourselves – what are your husbands doing while you're gadding about on holiday with their money, eh? Eating in a pub, or getting a takeaway. You should be ashamed. You cook your husband a jolly good square meal when you get home, and say you're sorry.'

'I'm a widow' said Gerrie loudly to his retreating back.

There was a short shocked silence, and then Mags and Gwen exploded with laughter.

'I didn't know men like him still existed!' said Gwen. 'Pat deserved a medal'.

'Ghastly man' commented Celia, finishing a buttered roll.

'If I could do one thing before I get on the plane for Switzerland I would put a hand grenade in his trousers' Linda winced as she tried to change position on her chair.

'Are you all right, Gerrie?' Mags put her hand on Gerrie's arm.

'Fine. No, really. He's just so boorish; I don't know whether he heard me or not, but it wouldn't make any difference. You can't get through to people like that.'

'We had someone like him in my choir' said Mags. 'I missed a rehearsal for a concert, and he came up to me the next week and gave me the third degree about why I hadn't been there. He wasn't even the director, he's only a bloody tenor.'

'Ah. A tenor. We all know about those' Gwen was amused.

'And I said I wasn't there because it was the night my mother died. I had been at the hospital. He just glared at me, for quite a long time, and then turned away. He never spoke to me again. Weird.'

'Interesting psychology' Celia pushed her plate away. She tapped her finger on the table cloth in time with her words. '*He* committed a social gaffe. *You* brought it to his attention. So *you* insulted *him*. You were the one at fault.'

'Is he married?' asked Linda.

'Yes.'

'What's his wife like?'

'Surprisingly normal. He behaves like this a lot, actually. I think he's got some sort of problem. He puts a lot of people's backs up.'

'He's not in the choir now, you said.' Linda poured some wine.

'No. He's been through a lot of them. Apparently he's very bright; he runs some sort of specialised scientific website. He works from home.'

'He'd have to' sniffed Linda.

'His wife is the deputy head teacher at a special school. She's quite glamorous and incredibly patient with him. They haven't any children as far as I know.'

'Co-dependency?' Gwen looked quizzically at Celia.

Celia shrugged. 'Could well be.'

Once the main course was served, Linda said: 'Now, Celia. Your turn tonight. What shall we talk about?'

Celia finished eating a mouthful of fresh lake fish, took a sip of wine, and said 'Maslow.'

A roar of laughter from a neighbouring table silenced them for a minute, then Gwen said:

'Sorry, Celia, couldn't hear. Say that again?'

'Maslow. Maslow's hierarchy – have you heard of that?'

'Vaguely' said Mags doubtfully. 'I'm not sure. What is it?'

'Maslow was a psychologist. I think it was in the Second World War, round about that time, that he published his paper on the hierarchy of needs. It's very well known, now. It's a pyramid, with five levels. The widest one, at the bottom, is physiological needs – it means that the first things humans need are the ones that keep them alive; food, water, sleep. Sex, interestingly enough. Air to breathe. The basic, obvious things.'

Celia parted the next piece of fish delicately with her knife and ate a mouthful. Then she went on 'The second level up is a bit narrower, of course. That one is about security. So you need to be safe from things like natural disasters, poverty, ill health. And you need financial security. The third level is about love and belonging. In order to function, a human being needs family ties, friendships, sexual intimacy with a partner. They need to be accepted and loved, and to love. We all know that, really, don't we?'

The others said nothing, listening as they ate.

Celia drank some wine. She put the glass down and continued:

'The fourth level is called esteem. When the other levels are in place, you need to go on and have self esteem, self respect, and to respect others. It includes confidence, and achievement.'

'I can understand that' nodded Gerrie. 'I know Leo felt that his business meant an awful lot to him. I don't think he would have ever retired. He felt proud of how he had built it all up, and he liked to think that people at the Rotary and lots of other people respected him. And admired him.'

Celia drew a triangle in the air. 'So the top of the hierarchy is quite narrow, and pointed, and it's called self-actualisation. It means that when you have all the other building blocks, you're free to make of yourself what you really would like to be. For us, that would mean learning to play a musical instrument, or travelling, or painting, or collecting vintage cars. Anything that fulfils you, as a person.' She cut the last piece of fish in two and ate one small piece. She left the other one.

'Using your talents' commented Mags.

'Yes' Celia laid her knife and fork neatly on the plate and dabbed her mouth with a napkin.

'But you have to have all the other layers in place first – is that what you're saying?' asked Gwen.

'Absolutely. You have to be well, safe, assimilated into a family and a community, provided for financially, all of that, and then you can start to put your most personal plans in place.'

There was another, longer silence.

'So, are you just telling us about all this?' Linda frowned. 'I mean, it's interesting. I need to think about it a bit. Or are you asking us something?'

Celia smiled. 'I'll tell you in a minute' she said, as the cheerful dirndled waitress carried some of the plates away.

Between the courses Sandy arrived at the table to tell them about Duracell's birthday. 'We know' nodded Mags. 'I expect there will be a card at reception for us all to sign?'

'Yes, there will' agreed Sandy. 'Did you enjoy your day? How did you find Salzburg?'

'I'm worn out' said Linda flatly. 'It's a lovely place, but I really found it hard going. And Mondsee was just too much. I'll have to take extra painkillers tonight.'

'You look pale' replied Sandy. 'It probably was a bit much, especially with the bad weather. But when you get home I expect you'll just remember the interesting sights, and the guided tour.'

'And the Pieta in the cathedral' added Mags, with a sideways look in Linda's direction. Linda slumped, very slightly, in her chair.

'Oh, the Pieta was incredible' Sandy smiled. 'Weren't we lucky to see it? Today was the last day!'

The waitresses bringing the desserts were the opportunity for Sandy to move on to the next table. Celia and Gwen had ordered a selection of Austrian cheeses and biscuits to share between them.

'Look at that!' exclaimed Gerrie. 'Heaps for two of you! I might pinch a bit, it looks lovely. Here, I'll take a couple of grapes, anyway' and she leant across the table.

'What have we got?' asked Linda, peering at her glass bowl.

'It's a sponge base, with apricot conserve on it, and a creamy sauce on top of that. And something else – nuts, I think. And a dusting of chocolate on top. And look, a jug of cream' Mags blew her cheeks out. 'I'll go home the size of a house. Pass the cream over here, what the hell!'

'So anyway' said Gwen 'about this pyramid. You said you had a question.'

.....Subject

'Yes' said Celia, biting the end off a small stick of celery. 'I've got one thing to say, and one thing to ask. I want to say that I think Maslow was wrong.'

'Oh, I don't' objected Mags. 'You explained it very well. It makes good sense.'

'But it isn't a pyramid, I don't think. I think it's an hourglass. The way I see it, Maslow was absolutely right, but he only half thought it through. You get to the tip of the pyramid, and you have a few years – if you're lucky – for the self-actualisation. Then the whole thing goes into reverse; slowly you begin to lose the respect of others, and your sense of achievement, and your confidence. Then you lose intimacy, and your place in society, and even your place in the family. As time goes on, you lose your health, and probably your financial security, and you start to have accidents and not to be safe in many ways.'

'Vulnerable' nodded Gwen. 'I know a lot of elderly people like that.'

'Exactly. And if you live long enough you end up exactly where you began, on the widest level of the hierarchy where even your physical well being is compromised. You may not be able to breathe, or to eat, or drink, or manage your bodily functions. So, you see, I think it's an hourglass, not a pyramid, and I think we'

Celia gestured round the table 'all of us – women like us, in our sixties and still more or less able bodied and in our right minds – we are in the waist of the hourglass. It won't last long. It'll be different periods of time for each one of us; and we won't get any warning when we're jolted up to the next level. We might lose our investments, or our husbands, or we might have a stroke or develop some awful disease. We don't know. So we absolutely must make the most of the time we have now, at this time of life. We'll never get it again. We only get each day once.' Celia's face was as tight as whipcord, the skin on her jaw drawn and shiny, the tendons in her neck standing out.

'Life is not a dress rehearsal' said Linda quietly. 'I've got that on a fridge magnet. I think I've only just fully understood what it means.'

'No, it isn't a dress rehearsal' Celia was vehement. 'So that's what I wanted to say. And what I wanted to ask was, given that we are in Maslow's waist, if you see what I mean, what are you all going to do that you've been wanting to do all your life? Before it's too late?'

'What would we like to do....' mused Mags.

'No. What are you *going* to do.' Celia cut violently into a wedge of cheese.

A different silence this time. Something had changed. Each of them felt that they would never look at life in quite the same way again, and they needed time to adjust to the new landscape.

'I think I may move to Italy' ventured Gerrie. 'It's been on my mind for a little while now.'

'So what's stopping you?' Celia asked, with a penetrating look.

'Nothing, really. I mean, I have a flat in Tuscany anyway, and lots of friends Leo and I made when we went there several times a year. I – I have some arrangements to make. To decide on.' She looked at Gwen, whose expression was unreadable. 'I've got the business on the market, and I'm trying to sell my house.'

'And when you've done that, you can afford to go' nodded Mags.

'I can afford to go, anyway. I'm very lucky. I could go whenever I wanted, and buy a nice villa there without selling my property in the UK.'

'Well, why don't you?'

Gerrie picked at a fingernail. 'I don't know, really. Maybe I should. Maybe I will.'

'What about you, Gwen?' asked Celia.

'I love travel; not like Gerrie, I don't want to move abroad. Apart from anything else there's my daughter and Rosie, I wouldn't want to leave them.'

'And Roy' said Mags.

'And Roy. But I always thought when I retired there would be lots of foreign holidays, walking tours and things like that. Bird watching.'

'Don't end up like Uncle Alan' laughed Mags.

'No. But I would hate to think I might have a stroke in six months time and never do any of it.'

'Then do something about it as soon as you get home' insisted Celia. 'Are these things that Roy would like to do as well?'

'I don't know, really.' Gwen fiddled with a spoon.

'Well, ask him. If so, shake yourselves up and start organising next year, go to places you both like, plan the year out.'

'Roy's got his own fixed things, like races – '

'Then either work round him or book up on your own account. Just think how many years you've planned everything around your parents, your job, your husband, your children – can't you see that? When have you ever said *I'm* going to do this? This is what *I* need to do? Never.'

'No. Well, you can't, can you? You have obligations – '

Celia was tapping the tablecloth again. 'Sorry, but listen; it's your turn now. You need to get back control over your own life. It's the only little sliver of time when you can.'

Gwen gave a heavy sigh and looked out of the window.

Celia turned her head. 'Linda?'

'I'm thinking.'

'All right, what are you thinking?'

'I'm thinking that my situation is different from all of yours.'

'Why?'

Linda smoothed her auburn fringe. 'I think I feel a bit guilty.'

Mags looked up sharply.

'I don't need to do this' Linda went on. 'I've pretty much always pleased myself anyway; no children, no parents now. Stuart and I have always done what we liked. I think I've used up my self-actualisation already, quite honestly; I reckon I'm ahead of you.' She smiled and looked round the table.

'Isn't there something you still have in your head – a dream, some ambition?' asked Celia.

'Well. I've told you all before, but I don't think you've really understood. You haven't got it. What I really want is a good death.'

Nobody said anything.

Linda went on 'That really is an ambition, you know. I don't think any of you have really thought about it properly, but I've had to. It takes a lot of planning and preparation. There are so many possible variations; I might die under the knife, having a hip operation or because of my bowel cancer.'

Gwen and Gerrie looked shocked.

'If that happened the whole thing is wrapped up, and I needn't worry about it. But I might have to undergo horrible treatment, and I might not want to die until I was far too damaged to tell anyone. So it's probably better to take control soon and arrange a dignified death before that stage. You all know I dread losing my mind; I've had some indications already that my marbles are going – it's not a smooth curve, a lot of the time I'm functioning, then I get periods when I'm definitely not right in my mind. The trouble is, I only realise that when I'm coming out of it again. I'm frightened of seriously deteriorating in a hurry and then it's too late.'

Mags rubbed her nose. 'Well, I suppose if we all got morbid, we could say that the only thing everyone wants, ultimately, is a good death.'

'Of course! That's obvious!' Linda said impatiently 'But can't you see that it's all academic while you've got a busy life and you're doing things you enjoy? You say airily, oh, I hope I die in my sleep. And the person next to you says the same thing. And then you have another Martini or you go and do some gardening. You still haven't grasped that I'm already staring the reality of this in the face.'

'I think that makes my point even more strongly' said Celia. 'You're right, you are a step further along than the rest of us – '

'As far as you know!' Linda wagged a finger.

'As far as we know. Yes. Well, exactly. It comes back to what I said earlier, any one of us could drop down tomorrow with a stroke or get a brain tumour. All bets off, all chances gone. We'd be dependent and sick and miserable, and if we could speak at all, we'd be bemoaning all the things we thought we were going to do.'

'Life is what happens to us while we're making other plans' said Mags.

'Death, or at least disability, is more like it' said Celia firmly. 'So we must go for it, girls. We really must.'

Dessert plates were cleared and the coffee arrived.

'We haven't heard from Mags' commented Gwen.

'I've had a bit of a funny life' said Mags. 'What I mean is – well, for one thing, I think I'm the only one on this table who's been married twice.'

Nods greeted this remark. 'My husband was married before' offered Gerrie. 'I know that's not the same. Otherwise' she looked round at the others 'You're right, aren't you?'

'I'm not sure what you mean' frowned Gwen. 'Does that make a difference?'

Mags chose her words carefully. 'It does. Rather. Because you've put your head in the noose twice. No, that sounds wrong. What I mean is, if your first marriage failed, you work much harder at the second. Too hard, sometimes.'

'So you would worry that Dudley would be neglected if you found something absorbing that you wanted to do?' asked Celia.

'That's putting it mildly, as far as Dudley's concerned' said Mags grimly. 'He wouldn't stop me doing anything, but he'd manage to make me so uncomfortable it wouldn't be worth it.'

'Selfish bugger, is he?' sniffed Linda. 'Most of them are.'

'Whenever I've come across Dudley at the office he seems delightful' said Celia. 'He's very efficient and polite; he's got a real charm about him.'

'Yes.' Mags said flatly.

'But I do accept that people can be very different in a domestic context' conceded Celia. 'And men are children, really. They like routine and comfort and to have their women at home.'

'Roy's not like that' shrugged Gwen. 'He likes me to be there, of course, but he never makes a fuss or comments if I'm out. Even at meal times. If I come home late he just asks a few quick questions about where I've been and if I'm all right. He's usually got himself a snack and he just gets on with it. No drama. Maybe it's because he's never been a nine to five sort of person, office routine and all that. Perhaps I've been lucky.'

'Yes, you have' Mags was firm. 'I envy you.'

Celia put down her coffee cup. 'What would you do, if Dudley said to you – go on, find something you've always wanted to do, and do it. What have you always had on the back burner?'

'Writing, actually' replied Mags. 'I've got several ideas for stories; short stories or novels. From things that have happened. I lived a hippy life with my first husband; we were in a commune for several years and there were some real characters there. Then we worked in a zoo, and that's a subculture you wouldn't have any idea about, really. People who work in zoos and wildlife parks have a sort of circuit of their own; they all know each other and they move around from job to job.'

'That sounds really interesting!' Gerrie enthused. 'I'd love to read about that!'

'Would your stories be for grown-ups or children?' asked Celia.

'I've always assumed they would be for grown-ups' said Mags 'But now you mention it, I think I could write something quite meaty for older children. For instance, one of our neighbours reared a lion cub at home. That was quite an adventure.'

'Terrifying, I should think' commented Linda.

Gwen leant forward. 'I had no idea about all this! You've never talked about it before. You are a dark horse!'

'Everyone's a dark horse, aren't they?' Mags smiled. 'Actually, the neighbour was more terrifying than the cub. She and her husband were alcoholics. We had to put them to bed most nights. We left Drusilla in the living room with the door tightly shut, but we could hear her tearing the furniture up with her claws and knocking over the coal scuttle.'

'I assume Drusilla was the lion cub, not the neighbour?' Gerrie giggled.

Celia wrinkled her nose. 'Awful, the way things go when people drink too much.'

'You reminded me about it when you said one of the teachers at your father's school was alcoholic. Betty and Rankin used to hide bottles from each other all over the house. Rankin hid his export strength gin in the spin dryer. He said Betty would never find it because she never did any housework.'

'Rankin?' queried Celia. 'How extraordinary!'

'Rankin Parsloe!' laughed Mags. 'Isn't that a brilliant name? He was a Lieutenant Commander in the Navy. Had been.'

'Oh, you really must write!' Celia said. 'It's too good to be true!'

They suddenly noticed that most of the other tables were empty and the waiting staff were standing about anxiously waiting to collect the last coffee cups and lay up for the morning.

Celia stood up. 'Long day' she yawned. 'Time we went to bed.'

'Just a minute!' Mags raised a finger. 'You haven't told us what *you* are going to do, that you've always had in mind. You can't get away without fessing up! Go on.'

'Academia. A University course, something to really stretch my mind. I don't want to sound conceited, but it's only in the last few years that I've realised I'm actually quite bright. There are so many things I'm interested in – I might go back to art history and the history of textile design, which I studied in my teens. That would be lovely; I could really immerse myself. Perhaps progress to a doctorate and teach, or run a museum, or write wonderful books with gorgeous illustrations.'

They waited for Linda to struggle to her feet; Mags handed her her stick and let her walk in front through the empty tables and out into the foyer. Mags and Linda got into the lift, and Celia and Gwen and Gerrie moved to the foot of the stairs.

'But actually' said Celia, as the lift doors began to close 'it will be psychology. I'm desperate to go on with that.'

In Room 311 Mags was thoughtful, and Linda in pain and exhausted; they hardly exchanged a word as they went about preparing for bed and dropped their heads on to their pillows with utter relief. The only conversation consisted of Mags asking 'Have you emailed Stuart today?' and when Linda shook her head she sighed 'I ought to contact Dudley tomorrow.'

Gwen and Gerrie, in 315, pottered about for a few minutes.

'I took our wet things to reception for washing' said Gwen. 'They'll be ready tomorrow night.'

'Costs quite a bit. I looked in the literature on the table' replied Gerrie, taking off her nail polish with a cotton wool pad 'but it's worth it. I want to wear those trousers again to travel back to Cologne.'

'Hah! Says someone who doesn't exactly have to worry about paying for things like that.'

'I'll foot the bill, don't worry.'

'I'll let you'. Gwen ran a brush through her thinning hair. 'What's tomorrow? I can't remember.'

'Bad Ischl'.

'Oh yes. We go on the coach, don't we?'

'No, on the local bus. Public transport. Goes at ten to eleven from the stop in the square.'

'Brilliant; we can have a lie in. Whose turn is it for tomorrow night's conversation stopper?'

'Mine.' Gerrie was repainting her nails a frosted coral pink.

'What are you going to come up with?'

'Shan't tell you. Wait and see.'

Gwen shrugged and got into bed. 'Night' she said.

Interlude

Mags woke up not much later than usual; she lay looking at the suffused curtains which indicated that there was sunlight outside and therefore it might be a better day than yesterday. She wondered about going back to sleep, but determined not to miss any of the holiday in brutish slumber, she slid out of bed quietly and opened the curtains a couple of inches.

It was indeed a better day. There must have been more rain in the night; the roofs and the square, and the balcony just beyond her nose, were full of bright puddles. Some of the colourful flowers in the window boxes had clearly taken a bashing and were a rather battered, but already they were starting to recover and seemed the better for a soaking.

There were wreaths of thick mist over the mountains so that the vista was like a film set which only went just over head height; just enough for the cameras to capture. And the lake was a stunning milky love-in-a-mist blue, hazy as if it coloured with pastels and then smoothed with damp muslin. A small boat was out in the centre, fishing. The little red train had stopped at the village station to let commuters on, to go and work at the salt processing village and further on in other small towns along the valley.

Mags let the curtains close again and picked up her watch from beside the bed. A quarter to eight. Perfect. She glanced across at

Linda's sleeping mound under the bedclothes; a deep rhythmic breathing told her that she was the only one awake.

Ten minutes later Mags had showered, dressed, picked up her handbag and quietly clicked the room door shut as she made for the stairs. One floor down she passed the opening to the computer room; she hesitated and put a foot across the threshold, but saw Sandy engrossed in the screen with several sheets of paper on the desk so she withdrew and went down to breakfast.

Celia was at the table, with her book open as she ate some yoghurt and muesli. 'Mags!' she smiled, and shut the book. 'Early bird!'

'You too' nodded Mags, slipping into her place with a croissant and some butter and jam.

'Oh, I try not to waste a minute when I'm away' said Celia. 'You need to squeeze every drop out of times like this, don't you? To sustain you when you get home.'

'Yes, you do' agreed Mags. She held up her knife with a pat of butter on it. 'Don't you just love these little flower shaped portions? They pay so much attention to detail, don't they – you imagine some lovely girl in a bodice and dirndl up all night pressing the butter into flowers and arranging them on the little white dishes.'

'They really do seem to have got things right here; things that we've lost. And the prices are much lower than I expected. Have you noticed?'

Mags spread some raspberry jam on her croissant. 'Oh, absolutely. Do you know I had a large mug of hot chocolate and a simply delicious apfelstrudel in the fortress restaurant yesterday, and it was only just over six Euros.'

'Euro. That is one thing I get cross about; in the Eurozone you don't use a plural. If you listen, you'll hear people always say three Euro, or ten Euro forty, they never say Euros.'

Mags thought about this. 'I think you're right.' She ate some of her croissant.

Celia got up and went to fetch a boiled egg and some ham. When she had settled herself back in her seat, she asked 'How's Linda today?'

'Still asleep. I crept out, I'm afraid. She will need to rest, after yesterday. I'm not sure if she's coming on the bus; she might be better off having a quiet day.'

'Oh, she told me yesterday that she wants to come. She wants to see Bad Ischl; she's a fan of Franz Lehar.'

Mags left the table to get a glass of orange juice and a small breakfast roll with two slices of cheese.

'We do eat funny things when we're away, don't we?' she smiled. 'Well, funny to us. It seems perfectly natural though, here. It's nice to be let off the leash.'

Celia nodded. One of the tall grey sisters moved by with a plate of toast and a bowl of fruit salad. Celia caught her eye and asked 'How's Iris? I didn't see her at all yesterday?'

'Still very upset, but there's nothing she can do. She might as well finish her holiday. Sandy's been great, liaising over the arrangements and keeping in touch with the family on the internet.'

Celia gave a sympathetic look and went back to her breakfast.

'What's happened?' asked Mags.

'It's Iris Harper – you know Gerald and Iris – '

'Yes, of course.' Mags thought she wouldn't add 'we call Gerald Adam Adamant'; too complicated.

'Iris's sister has died. I think it was the day after we left home. She's trying to arrange things from here; Sandy's being marvellous – otherwise she would have had to break off and go back, I'm absolutely certain. It's even more difficult because the sister's husband has Parkinson's.'

'Do you know, I thought I hadn't seen Gerald or Iris for a while, but there's so many of us. Was it sudden?'

'Totally unexpected. I understand she'd been watching the Antiques Roadshow, got up to make a cup of tea, and dropped down dead on the carpet with a heart attack.'

'Gosh. Not much of Maslow's Hourglass for her, then.'

'Well, it only emphasises the point, doesn't it?' said Celia. 'You've got to put all you can into each day in case you don't get any more. You know, after last night's conversation I had a thought which made me even more determined. My mother died at eighty.'

'That's not bad. That's a good innings' smiled Mags. She drained her glass and put it back on the table.

Celia looked horrified. 'Yes, but that's less than fourteen years away, for me! That's nothing! I'll tell you what I think; I think the quickest part of your life goes by between your parents dying, if they lived a full life, and you getting doddery. My mother died at eighty, but she'd been past her best for a long time.'

An image sprang into Mags' mind of a curling ham sandwich. She shook her head to get rid of it, and also in case she giggled, and asked 'So when did she start going downhill?' Even that provoked the possibility of unseemly mirth, so she scrubbed her mouth hard with the napkin until she regained her composure.

'She had heart trouble' explained Celia. 'She couldn't do very much for a long time. Ten years at least. She had plenty of friends but she couldn't get out, they had to visit her; so as they got too frail, or fell off the perch, she got very lonely. She was in a wheelchair most of that time. And she had several spells in hospital. She got MRSA during one of those and she was much worse after that. She died of pneumonia, through not being able to move about. It was quite awful.'

'So if you say that she started losing control over her life at the ten year point before she died, you've only got four years before you catch her up.'

'Less than four years.' Celia set her mouth firmly.

'God. No wonder you don't want to waste time.'

'There's no need for it. Do things while you can.'

'Going back to Iris' said Mags 'I wonder what'll happen with the brother-in-law, then, if he's got Parkinson's?'

'I spoke to her yesterday about that. It looks like he'll have to go and live with them, now his wife's died. She was his carer.'

'Poor woman. No other family, then.'

'Yes, there's a niece, but she's in Australia. She's got her own family. That's what's making it difficult; Iris is having to deal with the funeral director and all the official people from here, so Sandy's helping with all that. The niece – the sister's daughter - is making arrangements to get back to England for the funeral, and I think she's going to stay for a month or so, but Iris and Gerald will never have their lives back, will they?'

Mags sighed. 'No.'

'See what I mean?' asked Celia with a slight smile, tilting her head to one side.

They decided to meet in twenty minutes to go to the monastery and look at the Fisher Pulpit before the bus came. Mags found Linda awake when she got back to the room, determined to go to Bad Ischl, but stiff and in a lot of pain.

'Tell you what' suggested Mags 'Why don't you get room service to bring you some breakfast up here? Then you can get ready slowly and enjoy your meal on the balcony, really give yourself the best chance to get the most out of the day.'

'That's a very good idea. Bugger it. Yes, I will' agreed Linda.

'Well, here's the information folder with the menu in it' said Mags, bringing it over to the bed. 'The phone's there. You get on with that. I'm meeting Celia downstairs and we're going to visit the monastery and see the Fisher Pulpit before the bus goes. See you downstairs at half past ten. Ish.'

She turned at the door. 'It will be ish' said Linda grimly. 'But I'll be there. I've been looking forward to Bad Ischl. No pun intended.'

'Good' said Mags, closing the door.

As she reached the foyer she saw Duracell's back framed in the main doorway, moving quickly to catch up with Pat, and Mike and June Finch who were already in the square, looking around them in the sunshine. They were all wearing sunglasses and floppy white cotton hats.

Celia was beside her immediately, following her gaze. 'That man! Honestly! He's so – so – *sub prime.*'

Mags was delighted. 'That's exactly what he is!' she said. 'What's he done now?'

Celia wiped her mouth with the back of her hand and then wiped her hand with a tissue. 'Ugh!' she grimaced 'He came up and said "It's the Birthday Boy! Give the Birthday Boy a kiss! I'm getting all the pretty ladies to kiss me today, aren't I Pat? Eh? Eh? It's my birthday, give me a kiss then!" Ugh!' she said again, screwing her face up.

'Well, he'd better watch out!' Mags grinned. 'I've got my not-your-daughter's-jeans on, and my designer top, and a splash of Chanel – he'll be putty in my hands!'

'I'd use him to stick the glass in windows if I could, I must say' Celia was reapplying her lipstick.

'Celia! I've never heard you make a joke like that. Well, a pun, anyway. This holiday must be doing you good.'

Celia looked down at her, eyes twinkling behind her glasses. 'I think it is. You begin to see things a bit more clearly, don't you?'

The Fisher Pulpit

They followed the Ghastly Garsides and Uncle Alan out of the main door and into the square; Gordon Garside could be heard droning on about the synchronicity or otherwise of Austrian public transport in general, vis a vis the local buses and the trains, and the seasonal variations in timetables. Uncle Alan nodded enthusiastically but was looking up at the now cloudless mountains, where he spotted the two eagles circling again. He stopped and pointed his binoculars up to get a better look.

'The shop's open' remarked Celia. 'Shall we take a look in on the way to the pulpit?'

'Oh, let's' agreed Mags. 'I'm out of milk to make tea in our room. I've been surreptitiously filling the little plastic bottle from the buffet at breakfast time.'

'Have you got teamaking facilities?' Celia was puzzled. 'I haven't. Mind you it took me a day and a half to find the little fridge. It's very well disguised.'

'No, I always bring a travelling kettle and everything with me when Dudley and I go anywhere. If we think we'll need it.'

'Your voice changes, just slightly, when you mention Dudley' Celia was pushing the shop door open and not looking at Mags. 'Did you know?'

'Oh'.

The shop was small but absolutely filled with a surprisingly large selection of goods. On the way in were tiers of wicker baskets containing fruit and vegetables, including herbs and salads, everything fresh and appetising and in top condition. Celia picked up a hand basket and peered at the bananas. 'These look delicious' she said 'and I'm fussy about bananas. Shall we take one each for the bus?'

Mags picked up a basket, too, and put a banana in it. Then she went off and found a fridge containing milk, and browsed the shelves of biscuits and lebkuchen and packets of nuts. By the time she had rejoined Celia her basket contained more than she had planned to buy.

Celia's eyes were shining. 'There's a wonderful deli counter at the back' she said. 'I've just bumped into Tabitha Amherst-Smith, and she says they will make up a lunchtime roll for you with whatever filling you like, and it's very reasonable. Shall we get some for Bad Ischl?'

Mags followed her down the shop where a little gaggle of Making Tracks people were waiting to be served. Luckily there was no sign of Duracell and Pat, but Win Burns was at the top of the queue collecting a huge figure-of-eight roll with poppy seeds on it, full of fresh ham and tomato. It was carefully wrapped in stiff cellophane.

'Two Euro fifty' smiled the deli girl, and Win paid her without acknowledgment before turning round to walk away.

'That's such good value!' said Tabitha to Celia. 'I always thought Austria would be really expensive. It was years ago, when we used to come skiing.'

'And you were right about the non-plural Euro' said Mags.

Sandy was next in the queue, buying two similar rolls, but without poppy seeds, and some sliced salami.

Colin Harbottle and Simon Ryecart were next, having clearly had their orders from Wendy and Floral Patricia. Mags heard Colin passing the time by telling Simon all about the waste collection in the area where he lived, which coloured bin took which waste, and how often it was collected. Simon's rather world-weary shoulders seemed to bow a little more.

Before long Celia and Mags were outside the shop in the sunlight with their purchases. 'Bother' said Mags, crossly. 'I should have bought something for Linda, shouldn't I?'

'You're not your sister's keeper' responded Celia. 'She can buy something in Bad Ischl, anyway, and that gives her an excuse to sit in a cafe. You've done her a favour.'

'It's half past nine' Celia looked at her watch. 'Why don't we nip upstairs and get ready, and just bring what we want for lunch, and meet down here in a quarter of an hour? Then we can go to look at the pulpit and not have to go back into the hotel again before the bus comes. Don't forget your passport and your bus pass; we get half price tickets as oldies!'

Mags found no sign of Linda in their room; a rather catastrophic breakfast tray had been left on the bed, and the bathroom door was open with the light left on. She almost had a quick tidy up, but checked herself. 'No!' she thought. 'I've got to stop this pathological need to run round after people. I need to get out of here as soon as I can, otherwise I'll start picking up Linda's towels'. She put the milk in the fridge and shut the door. Within minutes she was out of their room again; but she did turn off the bathroom light.

As Celia and Mags turned towards the door of the monastery Tabitha and Teresa marched purposefully past them; both in knee length cotton shorts with their neat backpacks. 'We're off to see the Russian House before the bus leaves' they called.

'Going to see the Fisher Pulpit' Mags replied.

'Beautiful' nodded Tabitha 'You'll love it!'

And they did. Sitting in a beautifully carved pew, utterly absorbed, Mags whispered to Celia 'I don't know what I was expecting. But this is astonishing. Completely spellbinding. Just imagine a priest standing in the pulpit, preaching the word of God as if he were on a fishing boat in the middle of the Sea of Galilee. It's the most amazing sight.'

'I will make you fishers of men' whispered Celia. 'Look at the figures in the boat at each end, pulling up the nets. The fishermen apostles, James and John.'

Mags could feel her own breathing.

'All Jesuit stuff, of course' Celia's voice held a brittle edge. 'They had two fires in the monastery, and the Jesuits rebuilt it in the seventeen hundreds. This dates from 1753.'

'Who carved it?'

'Nobody knows. The figure on the top of the sounding board is St Francis Xavier, the mission saint of the Jesuits who was sent to India and Japan. He lived in the early fifteen hundreds. His right forearm, the one he used to bless people, was detached after he died and it's on display in Rome, apparently. See those four brown and black figures? They represent the far east.'

'Not very politically correct nowadays. The large figure with all the gold is Christ, I suppose.'

'Mm. With St Peter.'

Mags was silent again. She heard a faint clicking sound, and turned round to see Uncle Alan taking photographs of some of the other Baroque artworks and sculptures that filled the building. Then she stood up. 'Shall we go?'

When they were both outside, she turned to Celia and said 'I suddenly felt claustrophobic. Wonderful stuff, all that gold and silver and passionate carvings, but I can only take so much of it, I'm afraid.'

'I quite agree. And when you contrast it with the clean, uncluttered, almost aesthetic purity of the surroundings and the lake and the mountains, it seems almost polluting to the brain if you stay in there too long.'

'It messes with your head.'

'Is that the expression now? Yes, it does.'

They went and sat on a bench by the lake to wait for the bus; there was still half an hour in hand and only a few yards to walk to the stop. They would be able to see when people started to congregate.

'I'm sorry about Gwen' remarked Celia. 'It's a shame. I do hope she'll be able to come through this – well, and Roy of course, but it's Gwen who's suffering.'

Mags nodded. 'She didn't really say anything, though, did she? But I don't think she would have set us that subject unless there was something wrong.'

'Oh, there's something wrong. Definitely. She said it was the only chance she had to get other people's views, didn't she? And she said she couldn't see the wood for the trees, and wanted to know if her reactions were normal.'

Mags nodded.

'And anyway, the problem is that Roy's got a lover. A mistress.'

'Really?' Mags turned her head. 'How do you know?'

'Linda told me. She seemed quite certain.'

Mags studied Celia's profile against the light coming from the lake. Celia's so lucky, she thought. Her skin will always be that translucent alabaster texture even when she's very old. She's getting the usual neck and very slightly emphasised jowls, like creamy chicken breasts, but she has that poise and bearing that will always mark her out. I'm just a short woman with dark hair who tries to keep her figure. You couldn't describe my face; nothing memorable about it. It's just a face. Celia has a delicate nose, as if it was sculptured out of wax; she must have been a beautiful child.

'My hair's always a mess' Mags said. 'It's not that it's thin, it just won't hold a cut or a style. I have to brush it all the time and it still looks as if it's been cut too much or it needs cutting again. Drives me mad. You're so lucky with your crisp white waves. You always look groomed.'

Celia smiled. 'Thank you' she said. 'It looks all right usually. I can't do anything with it, of course. I can't grow it, or put it up. My hairdresser is an excellent cutter, so as long as it's taken in hand every three or four weeks I can forget about it. Mind you, I look a fright in a fascinator!'

'I'd have thought one of those would absolutely suit you! I just look as if I have a dead bird on an abandoned nest on my head. Can't wear them.'

'Well, nor can I. No - a well shaped hat is all I can get away with.'

They watched as the little fishing boat pulled alongside the jetty; two muscled young men vaulted out and tied it up. Tourists were taking pictures and speaking to them. The fishermen were cheerful and responsive, but carried on briskly with their work.

'You can't always have had white hair' ventured Mags. 'What colour was it before?'

'Chestnut brown, my mother used to call it.'

'Oh. It's usually jet black hair which turns so completely white, isn't it. Unless you've gone white overnight with shock, like someone in a Victorian Penny Dreadful.'

'Mine took eight weeks.'

'Good heavens! Were you ill?'

'Not ill, no. Long story.'

Mags knew better than to prod any further.

After a minute or two Celia continued 'I was really interested to hear you talk about writing last night. You should do it; we are all at the age when we have lots to say, but most people either haven't the talent or they continually talk about it and never actually start anything.'

'Mm. I have other – matters – to deal with; to cope with first. I think I will write, one day, but – ' She stopped.

Celia turned to look at her. 'Dudley?' she asked.

Mags sighed. 'Well. Yes.'

'Would he try to stop you?'

'It's not that simple. No, he wouldn't, in bald terms like that. But he wouldn't understand it, and he rubbishes everything he doesn't understand, so I would lose my confidence and then it really would be rubbish. So he would be right, but I would be – there must be a word for it.'

'Diminished.'

'More than that. Something more permanent, more visceral. I tell you what, Celia, I think the best way to put it is that my husband lives his life in black and white, and I live mine in colour.'

Celia thought about this. Then she said 'I had a dream last night. Early this morning, actually. I don't think I went back to sleep afterwards; I may have dozed.'

'What was it about?'

'It was about my mother. She was as I remember her best, in her prime – about fifty, I suppose. She was glad to see me.' Celia's eyes lost their focus. 'She came towards me, smiling her smile-for-me.

But she was enigmatic. Cool. Slightly distant. I cried, and cried, and cried' her voice cracked 'and she gradually faded away, still smiling her smile-for-me.'

Mags was quiet. Neither of them spoke for several minutes.

It was nearly time for the bus. Mags looked across the square and saw a knot of people waiting at the stop, including Linda who was talking to Gerrie. 'Time to move' she said, slinging her bag across her chest and checking for her purse and bottle of water and ham roll.

Iris opens up

The bus was spot on time. Sandy counted heads and talked in German to the driver. Not everyone was coming today, but it was important that those who wanted to were not left behind.

'Four Euro for tickets' said Sandy to everyone as they passed up the steps. 'If you've got proof that you're over sixty, it's only four Euro.'

Celia and Mags separated, Mags finding herself next to Win Burns while Celia was on the back seat with the tall grey sisters and the Quiet Americans. She craned her head as the bus moved off and found Linda and Gerrie sitting one row in front and on the nearside. She couldn't see Gwen.

The journey to Bad Ischl was a glimpse into rural Austrian life, and Mags was mesmerised. It was obviously going to take quite a while since they stopped every half mile or so; the passengers getting on and off were mostly local inhabitants. 'Gruss Gott!' they greeted the driver, and 'Gruss Gott!' was returned politely. One or two elderly men; otherwise mostly women, including an amazingly ancient crone at one stop on the main road which didn't seem to be near any habitations at all. The driver put his flashing lights on and leapt out of the bus to help the old woman up the steps; she wore inch-thick pebble glasses and greeted everyone who came into her field of vision as she slowly climbed up, both feet on each step before she could start feeling for the next one. She started to talk to all the passengers in German, asking questions which nobody understood. They smiled and nodded and one or two of them managed a 'Gruss Gott!' as taught in their guide books. The driver nipped off again and picked up a white plastic clothes horse, still in its polythene, which the old lady was taking to the next town. He propped it against a seat, and settled the passenger in another one. Then, bracing himself against the rail at the top of the steps he looked up something in a printed book he'd pulled from a shelf in the cab, his finger moving up and down several pages and going back and forth until he found what he was looking for. Mags smiled to herself; I bet it's a while since he's had to look up the fare for a clothes horse, she thought.

The driver collected some cash from the old lady, jumped back into his seat, closed the door with a hiss, checked his mirrors, switched off his hazard lights and clanked the bus into gear rapidly as he made up for lost time.

The bus route was quite different from either the main roads taken by the huge modern coach or the winding railway track which mostly followed the line of the river. It felt like being allowed behind the scenes of a silent drama. As the journey continued it wound back and forth over the single track of the railway, crossing and re-crossing the train route with only a couple of red wooden crosses on white posts to warn you to be careful. But this was a community on a level not seen at home, certainly since the nineteen fifties, perhaps since before the war. The driver knew the train timetable and was confident in its reliability, so that he knew when to check for danger and when he could bowl happily across the judder of the tracks. The road was narrow; it had no pavement, zigzagging past the corners of houses and little stacks of winter firewood so closely that you could see into the tidy homes and study the flawless lawns, raised vegetable beds and spotless garden furniture. Beside some railway crossings there were little gates leading down a path, with hand painted wooden signs tacked to them in the shape of school satchels. Oh, how charming! thought Mags – they're just at child height so that they know which way to go to school. And the Dads must have made the satchels. So in this country children are allowed to use the train, get off and find their way to school without anyone screaming about abduction and paedophiles, even when they are only six or seven; everyone looks out for each other.

Mags lost herself in a reverie as she half registered the departure of the old lady, again helped down by the driver and followed by his carrying her parcel for her. She absorbed all the minutiae of life in the string of villages - the little shops, the traffic which sometimes gave way to the bus on the narrow road and sometimes pushed through; the rules about that were unclear, but the drivers seemed to know what they were doing and there was no road rage. Even the smallest lanes were well metalled and free of potholes. She marvelled at the self sufficiency of each little household; every plot had a walnut tree, an apple tree, an apricot or a pear, or one of each if it was big enough. Once or twice she saw people carefully picking some of the fruit and putting it in baskets. Modern people, well dressed, with BMW and Audi cars in the drive, but living the traditional life.

They were dropped at the station car park in Bad Ischl; not a long way to walk into town, perhaps half a mile, but Mags immediately started to worry about Linda. She got off the bus and stood back, watching as passengers appeared and looking for Celia, Gwen, Gerrie, Linda. Once again the Quiet Americans seemed hardly to touch the ground as they moved off towards the centre of the town, tall and elegant, patrician and unreachable. Or so it seemed to Mags. Simon emerged and waited at the foot of the steps for Floral Patricia, who staggered, puffing, to the ground. Gordon and Pat Garside. Colin and Wendy Harbottle. Tabitha and Teresa. Win Burns, immediately setting her jaw and walking briskly away. Monty and Helen and Uncle Alan. Oddly, Iris Harper but no sign of Adam Adamant. Sandy was counting heads, giving out maps and timetables, explaining about the return journey.

The party began to make its way along the pavement, split into subgroups. Mags found she was walking abreast with Iris Harper, whom she had hardly spoken to so far.

'I'm so sorry to hear about your sister' she said, to open the conversation. 'I only heard this morning. How sad for you.'

'We've had that sort of year' sighed Iris, colourless and, as far as Mags could tell, rather lacking in personality. 'You get them sometimes, don't you?'

'Yes, you do' agreed Mags.

'It started in January when our Martha died. Tragic, that were.'

Yorkshire? Mags asked herself.

'Oh, I'm so sorry.' She was slightly non-plussed.

'Eighteen and a 'alf.'

Mags tutted and shook her head.

'Upset Gerald something awful.'

'Of course. Well, it would.'

'Run over, right outside our 'ouse.'

Mags began to see a light.

'Deaf' stated Iris.

'Oh.'

'Had her since six weeks.'

'Such a long time, then.'

'Oh aye. Aye. Used to fit in Gerald's hand, she did.'

Mags shook her head.

'Grandchildren loved her.'

Mags nodded. 'Bad start to the year' she said.

'Oh, it were. And then his knees.'

'Whose knees?'

'Gerald's. He had one done, come February, that went all right, that did.'

'Good.'

'Come May they did the other one. New budget, you see.'

'Yes, of course.'

Iris shook her head sadly. 'Went all wrong, that did. Infected, bit of bone come loose, two more operations. Had to live downstairs till August.'

'That must have been difficult. Good job he was fit enough for the holiday.'

Iris looked even more lugubrious. 'Flooded' she said. 'Flooded in July.'

'What was flooded?'

'Us and next door. Water main up the road collapsed. It all seeped upwards, came through our floors.'

'At least it wasn't sewage.'

'It were water. From the mains. We're still talking to officials. Gerald doesn't want to use our insurance. It's the water board's fault, you see.'

Isn't it funny how people still think there are water boards? thought Mags. It's a generation since everything was privatised. Longer than that. I wonder if I can provoke something –

'Sometimes you can claim benefits, can't you – grants – if you lose things like carpets and cookers in a flood.'

Iris shook her head again. 'Gerald tried that. He rang up the DHSS but he weren't eligible.'

Bingo! thought Mags. Good game, this.

'Gerald's not with you today, then?'

'Fell.' Iris said palely.

'He fell? Good grief, is he all right?'

'Oh aye, he's all right. Sandy were very good. Very good. Got the hotel doctor to him. He's twisted his new knee very bad, but it's the first one, not the second.'

'The February one' nodded Mags seriously.

'Aye, that one. Got to have it up all of today. We'll see tomorrow. Last day, tomorrow.'

'I know' agreed Mags 'I can't believe how quickly the time has gone. I'm just beginning to enjoy it.'

'Well enjoy it while you can, lass' Iris turned her washed out eyes to Mags 'You don't know what's next.' She shook her head. 'You really don't.'

God, that was a cheerful conversation, thought Mags, making her way to where Gwen and Linda were standing on the pavement looking vaguely around at the shops. I think I'll shoot myself now, save time later.

'Ah, there you are!' Gwen smiled at her. 'How's Iris today?'

'Some people are radiators, some are drains' said Mags firmly.

'I haven't heard that one before' said Linda. 'Rather good, actually.'

'Iris is a burst water main' giggled Mags 'she seeps up under your floorboards and' she put on an exaggerated Yorkshire accent 'floods ya'.

'Well let's go and flood ourselves with coffee' said Gwen. She looked at her watch. 'It's lunch time, really. Let's go to Zauner's – look, it's just down there. You remember Sandy said it was world famous for pastries and confectionary, a bit like Fortnum and Mason.'

'Tell you what, I'll come in for a coffee but that's all; I bought a ham roll from the shop by the hotel. Linda, I'm really sorry, I should have thought to get one for you, too; but at least it gives you a chance for a long sit down if you need to have lunch in Zauner's, doesn't it?'

'It's all right, Sandy bought me a delicious looking huge roll with ham and tomato in it. It's in a figure of eight, enough for an army.'

'That was kind' said Mags. 'What about you, Gwen?'

'Gerrie bought something for us to eat. She's gone off to find Franz Lehar's house; we'll have to meet up soon, anyway.'

'Come on then' said Mags 'let's go and have a look at Zauner's, at least, and then we can split up. I want to see the river and the Kongresshaus and the park – there's just never enough time, is there?'

They walked briskly down the road to Zauner's and paused to look in the windows, totally unprepared for the gloriously hedonistic sight of pastries and fruits and cakes that were beyond imagination. The building itself was pink and white and gold, with ornate display windows and a riot of pink and white geraniums peeping over a wrought iron balcony at first floor level. But in the windows – complicated chocolate confections with fresh raspberries and Chinese gooseberries nestling in piped cream with little tiles of chocolate on top, jauntily perched at an angle, with edible gold leaf decorating the corners. Wonderful things called marmorgugelhupf, marbled cakes that looked as if they had been made in tall Victorian jelly moulds, some left dusted with icing sugar, some smothered in the glossiest bitter chocolate.

'Look, the little ones are only three Euros!' exclaimed Linda.

'Euro. You don't use the plural' Mags felt smug, and hoped she didn't sound it.

'Stollen!' Gwen pointed 'but not like the ones you get in England. Oh boy.'

'Truffles! Pralines!' Mags was afraid she was dribbling; she wiped her mouth discreetly.

'Nougat! I love nougat!' Linda leant on her stick and stroked the window with the forefinger of her other hand. 'What's that there? Linzertorte. Looks really delicious, it seems to have jam and nuts in it. It looks a bit like those fat rascals I used to have as a child.'

Gwen had crossed to the window on the other side of the entrance. 'Look on this side' she beckoned 'florentines, like you've never seen before. And little bears made of chocolate – aren't they sweet? I must get a box of those for Rosie.'

'Tell you what' said Mags 'I love the porcelain things; they're not expensive, really – a tall hot chocolate cup with the shop's name on it, and dear little swags of pink and gold flowers, and the cup's filled with a bag of chocolates as well. They'd make fabulous souvenirs; coffee cups and saucers, little dishes with lids, full of chocolates. I think I've died and gone to heaven!' She draped herself in a mock swoon against the wall.

'Now, now girlies! You'll spoil your figures, won't they Pat? I said they won't want to go home all fat and puffy! Your husbands won't let you in!'

Oh no; not Duracell, thought Mags. Talk about a rude awakening.

'Just been in there, haven't we, Pat? You should go in, they've got our tea and tea with lemon and all sorts of coffee, and if you don't want that you can have beer, or apple juice – we had apple juice, didn't we, Pat? And lots of things to eat with cheese and spicy sausage and eggs and pasta – spoilt for choice. I say, we were spoilt for choice.'

'I didn't see you on the bus?' asked Gwen icily.

'No, no – we came on the train! What's the point of a rail holiday if you go everywhere by bus or coach, eh? We came here to go on trains. Not that it would mean much to you, I know. Girlies out on the razzle, having your gossip – trains won't mean much to you.'

'I like trains' protested Linda. 'We all do. That's why we chose – '

'Now, I understand why you wouldn't want to fly. Pat doesn't like to fly, do you Pat?'

'No' Pat emerged from behind Duracell, shaking her head. 'No, I don't like flying these days. Too many delays. Too many regulations, can't take this in the cabin, can't take that. Not enough room. Horrible food. Surcharges, taxes, extra to pay all the time. Can't be doing with it. And we know two people who've caught awful things – '

'Awful things on planes' Duracell cut in. 'Bugs. From the air conditioning. You wouldn't understand how that works, but – '

'Recycled air' said Mags crisply. 'But that's a bit of a myth, actually. The air in the cabin of a plane is completely changed and filtered more times an hour than in, say, a hospital or an office block. Typically fifteen to thirty times an hour. The filters are very sophisticated; they screen out bacteria and viruses. Over ninety-nine percent of them. The prevailing opinion now is that it's the close proximity to someone sitting next to you which passes on these bugs, not the air filtration system.'

Duracell looked at Pat for help, but didn't get any. 'You're a clever girl, you know that?' he poked Mags on the shoulder. 'No flies on you!'

As he and Pat turned away, Mags said 'Happy Birthday, by the way! Hope you're enjoying it!' She smiled.

Duracell took a step towards her. 'Thank you. Thank you very much. You wait till tonight at the hotel, you might be surprised. I've got a surprise for them, haven't I, Pat?'

Pat merely nodded, waved, and moved off up the street.

'Well done, Mags!' approved Gwen. 'Is all that true? What you said?'

'Oddly enough I read it in the paper a couple of days ago. For some reason it stuck in my mind, but I didn't think I would suddenly have to dredge it up like that. Listen, you two do what you like now, but time is getting on and there's lots I want to see. I've got my roll and some water, so I'll be fine – and I saw Gerrie crossing the road up there' she pointed 'she's spotted you. So I'll see you later. All right?'

Twenty minutes later Mags found herself sitting on a bench in the park surrounding the Kongresshaus, next to Celia, who had been examining the colourful planting in the large beds and borders, and had seen Mags walking along the path. They ate their lunches in silence for a little while, then Celia wiped a poppy seed from the corner of her mouth with a tissue and asked:

'Do you really think Linda has got bowel cancer?'

Mags had her mouth full; she nodded. When she could speak, she said 'Yes, I do. I do think she has – or at least, I think she thinks she has.'

'She rather prone to the dramatics, don't you think? I've got to know her a bit better on this holiday.'

Mags considered this. 'I can see why you would say that' she replied 'but drama queen type people have outbursts, don't they? Moments of high emotion, when they rather exaggerate things. Linda is consistently – oh; I was going to say bitter and miserable, but that isn't fair. She is doggedly aware of her situation. She seems to have thought about it thoroughly, and quite dispassionately, really. I think perhaps she's made up her mind, and almost feels it's out of her hands now.'

'Made up her mind about what? Dignitas?'

'Yes'.

'That's a shame, if it's true.' Celia applied a little peachy lipstick with the aid of a compact mirror.

'It's up to her. Isn't it?'

'Oh, I know. I wonder what Stuart is like, really. I wonder what he thinks about it. Do you think she's discussed it with him?'

Mags shrugged. 'No idea. Other people's marriages are closed books. But she got an email from him this morning, and he's got more problems now.'

'What, health problems?'

'His diabetes' nodded Mags. 'He went for an eye examination yesterday and apparently he's on the way to losing his sight, which has shaken him rather.'

'I'm not surprised!'

Bad Ischl

'Let's go and do a bit more exploring' suggested Mags, standing up and looking round for a bin to throw her rubbish away.

They went into the Kongresshaus, entering via some outside steps which led into a long restaurant running along the length of the building with French windows opening at intervals on to a balcony terrace.

'The food looks lovely!' approved Celia. 'Home made tomato and herb soup, in that hotpot – it smells wonderful!'

'Too late, now' said Mags 'We've had our lunch'.

They walked through the restaurant on to a landing, where delegates to a conference were gathering at a large desk before going in to their afternoon session. Polished marble floors everywhere, chandeliers, the afternoon sun washing the walls with a primrose glow. They descended the wide staircase to the hall area where there were publicity stands advertising forthcoming drama productions, opera, ballet, exhibitions and conferences.

'They certainly use their facilities to the full, don't they?' commented Celia. 'Even our hotel, in a tiny place, has conferences booked all the time, some of them with accommodation as well.'

Having visited a palatial ladies' washroom downstairs they ventured out into the sunlight to enjoy the gardens.

'Have you seen the bust of Franz Lehar?' asked Celia, turning a half circle. 'It's over there, near the exit into the town.'

'No, let me look on the way back' said Mags 'See those gorgeous huge houses over there? It looks as if there are two roads of them at least – I want to go and investigate.'

They found impressive residences from the nineteenth century, when the well-to-do from all over Europe would congregate for the health spa benefits of Bad Ischl and hold balls and performances during the season.

'Like Bath' said Mags 'and Jane Austen, and all that. Instead of the Pump Room they had a Trinkhalle, I was reading about it last night. If there's time it would be nice to go and look at it.'

'But these houses are absolutely enormous' said Celia, craning her neck upwards. 'such careful wood carving, look at those decorations! And three or four storeys – presumably the servants slept up in the attics, look up there!'

They walked slowly along, admiring the architecture and noticing that most of them were now offices for high flying companies of one sort or another. They had very expensive cars parked outside on gravelled or pavioured drives which must have once held carriages and horses.

'Shame' said Mags. 'Posh offices are never a substitute for a rambling family home.'

'No, but don't forget' said Celia 'that these businesses mean the buildings are still being used and maintained. Otherwise they would be peeling and neglected, wouldn't they?'

'That's true' Mags agreed. 'At home the big houses have mostly been carved up into flats or student accommodation, and they look like bomb sites. Anyway, it's lovely to enjoy them; the pine carvings and the pastel shades of the stucco – pale pink and yellow and blue and white – you can't help being cheered up.'

'Now, this is interesting.' Celia had walked on a few yards. 'Look at this shop!'

Stretching from the corner of one little side street to the next was an outfitters which filled its tall windows with Austrian costume; the men's displays were full of Loden capes and coats and knee breeches, hiking boots and hats with feathers and badger brushes in the bands. For the women there were dirndls in sprigged fabrics which reminded Mags of the Kate Greenway illustrations that she had loved as a child; willow green and plum red and sky blue. Scoop necked drawstring blouses with big sleeves, velvet bodices in rich colours which laced at the back. Polished shoes with silver buckles and hunting costumes with fur collars.

Celia and Mags lingered at each window, taking in the skilful displays and peeping in further to where shiny chrome racks were carefully placed on the waxed wooden floors and one or two wealthy customers were trying things on in front of floor length mirrors.

'Extraordinary!' commented Celia. 'People obviously still buy these clothes; I had vaguely wondered about the girls in our hotel, and the proprietor, but I thought it was the theatrical side of the hospitality trade. Actually, of course, it's their national costume, and they're proud of it.'

'We haven't got a national costume' replied Mags. 'I've often thought we should have. I had a friend at school whose father worked for Shell. He went all over the world and he brought her back dolls from Japan and India and Hungary, gorgeous things full of colour and individuality. Even the dolls themselves had proud expressions! But there was nothing for England.'

'There's a Welsh national costume.'

'I know, and she had one of those, and a Scottish piper in a kilt with a tartan bonnet and a lace jabot on his front. But nothing for England.'

They moved on up the street, and on the other side they found a toyshop, everything in it made of wood.

They climbed the three steps to the door, glanced at the windows each side, and went in; it was much deeper than it looked and was a treasure house of trains, dolls houses, rocking horses – all in numerous sizes – and Noah's Arks and zoos, puppets and clocks, wooden garages for wooden cars. Everywhere they looked were more enticing creations, even wooden Christmas decorations, and naturally, nativity scenes.

'I'm so tempted!' smiled Celia. 'It's ridiculous. I haven't any grandchildren at home, I shouldn't even think about it. Wilbur and Bryony are too far away. It would be very expensive to send them anything, and we can't carry much in our luggage in any case. I've got to control myself. Don't let me buy anything.'

'Look at these painted letters!' Mags had unhooked two capital letters about six inches high, hand coloured in red and blue and white. 'I'm going to get two for my grandchildren, Tom and Sophie. They're so small, I can get them in my case, and they're only three Euro each. Unbelievable.'

As they descended the steps, Celia said 'You hardly ever mention your grandchildren. Do you see much of them?'

Mags sighed. 'Not as much as I would like. It's all part of – oh, never mind.'

'All part of the Dudley scenario?'

'Yes. Not to worry – let's start back, because I want you to show me Franz Lehar and it would be nice to see the Trinkhalle, though I don't think there's time for the museum or the river.'

'I wouldn't mind coming back for another holiday and staying here' mused Celia, looking round thoroughly as they walked briskly back through the park.

Sandy had arranged to meet them all on a corner in the centre of the town ready to walk back to the station to catch the bus. When Mags and Celia arrived only Iris, the Harbottles and the Ryecarts had appeared. Floral Patricia was sitting on a bench a little way away; Mags heard Simon explaining to Sandy that Patricia simply could not walk so far, and he would like to order a taxi to take them.

'Excuse me' Mags stuck her head between Simon and Sandy 'Sorry, I wasn't eavesdropping, I just wondered whether you could include Linda as well? She'll be exhausted by now –' Mags looked around for her 'and if you're getting a taxi anyway, she could share the fare.'

Simon was readily agreeable. Eventually Linda limped out of a souvenir shop and went to sit next to Floral Patricia; Mags went over to her to explain about the taxi while Sandy disappeared to find one. Gwen and Gerrie come into view from the opposite direction, and ten minutes later Sandy was back and the headcount revealed that everyone was accounted for.

They walked crocodile fashion back to the station, but took a different route; this time they passed a large secondary school where teenagers were kicking footballs and generally messing about in the playground after school, and the area seemed at odds with the glossy tourist spots they had just visited. The housing was shabbier, many of the people seemed to be immigrants and the shops were full of cheap things and wilting produce. 'I suppose it's the same anywhere' said Gwen 'there's always an underbelly.'

Sandy got them all back on the bus which was fuller than it had been in the morning. There were housewives with shopping bags, people who had finished work and were heading for home, and several pensioners. Mags found herself wondering if they would see the ancient woman with the clothes horse on the way back, but they didn't. She was sitting next to Iris Harper, who silently looked out of the window. To make conversation Mags asked her if she had enjoyed her day.

'Oh, it were not too bad. I shall tell Gerald, it were not too bad. Reminded me of Harrogate, except for some things.'

Except for the scenery, the mountainous setting, the colour of the stone, the architecture, the history, the language.....thought Mags.

'Did you buy owt?' Iris turned her pale eyes to Mags. 'I didn't. Nowt to buy. That's like Harrogate, that is.'

'I only bought two wooden letters for my grandchildren' smiled Mags, delving into her bag to pull out a brown paper package. She unwrapped the letters and showed Iris. 'T and S' she said 'for Tom and Sophie'.

'Oh, they're nice, them' Iris approved, fingering them. 'They were a good find.'

Mags examined them again before putting them back in their brown paper. There was a tiny label on the back of each of them. It said 'Made in China.' She felt annoyed all the way back to the hotel.

Another interlude, and Celia confides a little more

When everyone had been disgorged from the bus and Sandy had briefly thanked the driver, in German, most of the group ambled into the hotel to have a rest before the evening meal. They were earlier than usual today, after a day out; it was only just after five o'clock, so there would be time for a snooze, or to read a book, or to get in touch with the family at home. Mags, however, didn't feel like going in just yet. She crossed the square to stand by the lake and take in the scenery again, glad of some time to herself. Then she walked a few yards along the shore to the cafe where she bought an ice cream and sat on a bench to eat it; there was an evening breeze starting up over the water, and she tucked her hair behind her ear on one side and zipped up her fleece.

She found herself consciously hoping that nobody came to make conversation, revelling in the sense of invisibility as she watched the actions of others who were unaware that they were being observed. An enormous motorhome lumbered into the square; it had Spanish plates, so Mags couldn't tell whether it was new, but it certainly looked it. A hatchet faced man and woman sat in the front seats, unsmiling, assessing the scene through narrowed eyes. They backed the vehicle between two parking lines, but left the engine running. Having slowly surveyed the lake, the hotel, the square, the little shop, the promontory with the onion-domed church on it, and the miniature town hall with the Salzkammergut regional insignia over its door, which ran along one side the car park, they exchanged a disdainful expression and slowly drove away again.

'Good!' thought Mags, smiling to herself. 'Don't want you here if you're not going to enjoy it. Take yourselves off and be miserable somewhere else.' She took another lick of her ice cream.

Two parents with lively children, boy and girl, came round a corner. The youngsters laughed and teased each other, running happily round their parents and hiding before jumping out and pretending to be startled. As they came nearer the father took each child by the hand, stooping to speak briefly to them, and still hand-in-hand led them to a shiny Audi estate car which was parked at the edge of the lake. The children obediently climbed into the back seats and the mother and father leant in each side to fasten their seatbelts before getting into the front to drive away. Mags finished her ice cream and felt her eyes pricking. 'What on earth is the matter with me?' she wondered as she got a tissue out of her pocket. 'Such a lovely family, they looked. Happy children, unbowed but properly disciplined. Parents working together to bring them up, father fully engaged. Authority figure but relaxed enough to let them play. It just seems such a rare sight these days. At home, anyway.'

As she watched, four or five employees of the Town Hall came out at the end of their working day. Smartly dressed women, two men in suits finishing a conversation by their cars before going home; after a couple of minutes they both laughed heartily and one slapped the other on the back before they waved farewell and drove their cars out of the square and away in different directions. It's all an illusion, said Mags to herself. What strikes you is such a sense of order here; people contented, well off, driving nice cars, getting on with each other. The buses well-run and on time, the villages full of functioning institutions and families, the roads beautifully maintained, the tourist economy working well and benefitting both the visitors and the local people. It's like a holiday romance, but with the way of life instead of with someone you've just met. There's no point in worrying about the contrast between what you see here and what you know is so dysfunctional at home. Just enjoy it and add it to your holiday memories.

She shivered suddenly; time to go back to the hotel. She stood up and walked slowly across the square, hanging back as she saw first the Quiet Americans on their way in, and then Win Burns trotting along sharply, her force field repelling even from twenty yards away. Mags didn't feel like talking to anybody; she waited until the coast was clear and then slipped into the foyer.

Passing the reception desk she saw a familiar Hermes scarf on the counter, carefully folded in a square. She stopped and asked 'Has this been found? It belongs to Celia Hennessey'.

'Ah, Madam!' the genial proprietor was there as usual. 'It was found on the bus. You know the owner?'

'I'll take it up to her' smiled Mags, picking up the scarf. 'It belongs to my friend – she'll be pleased to have it back.'

She went straight to Room 308 and tapped softly on the door.

'Coming.' Celia had heard her, so she wasn't resting. She unlocked the door.

'Oh, my scarf! Lovely! Come in, Mags!'

'I don't want to disturb you....'

'No, no, don't be silly. Do you know, I hadn't even missed it. Did I drop it somewhere?'

'It was at reception; somebody found it on the bus and handed it in.'

'I'm so glad. Charlotte gave it to me for my birthday, and I really would hate to lose it.' Celia took the scarf and opened the wardrobe to reveal her clothes beautifully hung in order of height, her shoes neatly ranged below them, and the shelves organised into tops, underwear, jumpers; she put the scarf on a shelf with other ones and handkerchiefs, a jewellery roll and a pair of navy leather gloves.

'Do sit down' Celia closed the wardrobe and crossed the room to the sliding balcony doors, which were open. She closed them almost completely, leaving a gap of a couple of inches. 'It's getting chilly now, with the wind off the lake. But I do love fresh air.' She smiled and gestured to the easy chairs. Mags took one and Celia sat on the other.

'You have a different view from us. Slightly. We have some roofs in the way on one side, so we can see the lake but not as well as this. It's a super room. You're nearer the church, too.'

'It is lovely' agreed Celia, softly. 'It's just what I need. You can think, and dream, and salve your soul.'

'Does your soul need salving?'

'Doesn't everybody's?'

'A vale of tears.'

They sat quietly, watching the light changing outside.

Eventually, Celia roused herself and said 'Oh, Mags – actually, I've just remembered. I need to ask you something.'

'Go on.'

'Sandy had a word with me on the bus. There's a problem with the hotel we use for that night in Cologne on the way back.'

'Oh?'

'It affects Linda. They've started their renovation of part of the building, you remember where they already had dustsheets up, near our rooms?'

'I did notice that, yes.'

'So that part of the hotel is out of action now, and it includes the lift. Linda can't manage the stairs, so they've changed our allocation and she now has a room on the ground floor.'

'Oh, that's all right, then.'

'But it's a single. I've got a twin upstairs, the same as before, so would you terribly mind sharing with me, just for one night?'

'Of course not! Heavens, why would I mind? You're the one who will have to put up with sharing. I don't think I snore.'

'I think I may do!' smiled Celia. 'You'll have to tell me.'

Mags noticed the photo on the bedside table. 'Is that Kenneth?' she asked.

Celia got up and fetched it, running the tip of her finger down the glass before handing it to Mags.

'He was at the height of his career, then' she said. 'He was fifty-four. Working closely with the Chief of General Staff and his office, heavily engaged with strategic planning and bringing a lifetime of military experience to bear in all sorts of ways. Much of what he did at that stage was concerned with security; top secret. He couldn't tell me about it. He would be away for weeks at a time, and I was supposed to think that he was abroad, but I don't think he was. I'll never know, now, exactly what he did do, but I'm sure he played an important part in keeping us all safe.'

'If he was fifty-four, you must have been – '

'Thirty six. Completely taken up with the children; Justin would have been seven, and Charlotte – four, I suppose.'

Mags was silent, studying the photograph. Here was a typically strong jawed, clean cut Army man with a facial expression which at once spoke of complete self-effacement, and of a depth of experience which a woman like Mags could never imagine.

'There must have been a lot you couldn't discuss with him' ventured Mags at last, handing the photograph back.

'It worked both ways' replied Celia. 'We were apart for so long, sometimes, that we were like strangers when he came home. That's quite apart from the age gap, which would have made it hard enough in any case. And once the children got into the popular culture at that time, the films and the music they listened to with their friends, all the television programmes and that sort of thing, Kenneth was completely out of his depth. It became really difficult to find things they could do together. Things they had in common – well, they didn't have any, really.'

'What did Kenneth do with them, then?'

'He took them to the Imperial War Museum' Celia pressed her lips together. 'And once they went to the Henley Regatta, and he had a friend who had a yacht at Cowes so he took them down there, but I think they were all just baffled by each other.'

'What a shame.'

'They got on with their uncle better, which was a bit tricky.'

'The uncle in Norfolk?'

'Alistair, yes. He was only two years older than me, rather than Kenneth's eighteen. He could relate to us much more easily.'

'That's understandable.'

'I used to take the children to Norfolk for the summer holidays, to Kenneth's parents. We had an idyllic time. Alistair would come whenever he could; he was in Chambers in Norwich. But he would always be there at weekends, and we had a tradition of really enjoying the August Bank Holiday weekend, just before we went home to Wiltshire and the children went back to school.' Celia's smile was full of nostalgia. 'The village they lived in always put on a show that weekend, a glorified fete. Of course, the Hennesseys were held in very great regard, almost like the lords of the manor. They opened the show on the Saturday afternoon, and Kenneth's mother would be presented with a huge bouquet of flowers. She used to judge the children's fancy dress parade and the produce and the home made cakes. Justin and Charlotte would dress up too, with the things in the Hennessey family dressing up chest, but they were always told they couldn't win. That would be very poor form. Their grandmother must encourage the other children, not give prizes to members of her own family.'

'Noblesse oblige.'

'I suppose so, yes. But their Uncle Alistair always found something to make up for it. He took Justin out in his boat to look for seals, or taught him to fish. He used to take them both bird watching. I remember he made a tree house for them one summer, and a wonderful tented pavilion thing for Charlotte when she was little, all brocade curtains and silk underskirts his forbears had worn in India during the Raj. He built it in the Dutch barn, which was a good thing because that summer was a very wet one. He was very good with them.'

'You must have appreciated that, being separated so much from Kenneth.'

'I – I was very fond of Alistair. We came to be extremely close, actually.' Celia's smile held a formality and the hint of something else that intrigued Mags but warned her not to probe too far.

She rose from the chair. 'I'd better go' she said 'have you told Linda about the arrangements for Cologne?'

Celia shook her head. 'Not yet' she answered. 'I haven't seen her, for one thing, but anyway I'm not sure how she'll take it. What do you think?'

Mags was at the door. She shrugged: 'I can't see that she'll mind. It's one of those things, isn't it? See you at dinner.'

Duracell's surprise, and Gerrie's turn

Linda was in an odd mood when Mags found her in Room 311.

'Don't mind me' she waved her hand dismissively. 'I'll probably say things I shouldn't. It's not you; I feel angry and out of sorts today. Better leave me alone.'

'Anything in particular – '

'Don't! You've been warned!'

'Fair enough.' Mags thought better of mentioning the change of plan at Cologne, and set about freshening up and changing for the evening. She was ready long before Linda, so she simply opened the door, stepped into the corridor and called over her shoulder 'See you downstairs, then.' Linda made no reply.

Mags dawdled a little on her way down to the restaurant. She could hear the sound of a hubbub of voices behind some of the conference room doors, and surprisingly there was nobody using the internet as she passed the archway. It crossed her mind to sit down and email Dudley, but she decided against it. Trying to rationalise the reason, she had the feeling that she was developing an extra layer of emotional skin, a strength, being away from him. If she could maintain that and even make it stronger she would be able to cope better when she was back home in the middle of all the stresses. But if she contacted him now, even by email, she would be stripping away her new-found defences. And after all, he didn't know about the computer in the hotel, did he?

She found an air of hectic activity downstairs. The staff in reception were efficient and busy, but when the swing doors to the kitchens were open the frenzy was almost palpable. The bar was packed, so she walked into the restaurant where the tables had been rearranged so that half of the area was divided off from the rest. The Making Tracks tables were still in the other half but they were much closer together.

Mags heard a puffing behind her; Floral Patricia was trying to get through. 'They've got conferences in, staying the night and booked for the day tomorrow as well' she complained. 'They've packed far too many people in. No wonder there aren't enough staff behind the bar, and the menu is smaller tonight. Shocking.'

Oh, well that explains it, thought Mags. I wouldn't call it shocking, though; I know shocking, and it isn't this.

Aloud she said 'How was your day? Did you enjoy Bad Ischl?'

'We've been before' Floral Patricia was dismissive. 'We went to a light opera festival there years ago, and we went with the children before that. There was nothing new for us to see.' She plonked herself in her seat and puffed out her cheeks.

Mags sat at the Hennessey table just as Gwen and Gerrie arrived, looking round them in surprise. 'Bit of a squash tonight!' commented Gwen. 'Hope we'll be able to hear ourselves think.'

By the time all the Making Tracks guests had assembled and found their seats, and the conference delegates had gathered at the other end of the restaurant, a degree of peace was restored.

Sandy squeezed from table to table to tell everybody that there was no going to the salad bar tonight, everything would be brought to the table.

'Just as well' commented Celia crisply 'Can you imagine the chaos if all these people got up together to go and get their first course?'

'Do you know, I really don't care' said Linda. Her right hand had a tremor, and her forehead glistened behind her long fringe. 'I'm not hungry.' Mags shot her a glance, but decided discretion was the better part of valour.

All the dirndled waitresses had been called into action, as well as a number of young men who were new to the scene; the proprietor and his son patrolled in the distance, casting eagle eyes over the proceedings and whispering the occasional instruction into somebody's ear.

At some stage during the salad course there was the most almighty crash from the kitchen; long drawn out, as if several piles of dishes had toppled off a counter on to the floor, one after another. It took so long that as the proprietor strode urgently along the back wall of the restaurant it was still spasmodically in evidence, and when he opened the kitchen door there was another loud explosion of shattering crockery. The diners exchanged looks; anything less serious would have prompted shrugs and laughter and jokes, but this was too major to be amusing. There was silence; then people cleared their throats and resumed their conversations.

Soon the level of noise reached its usual height and the incident was forgotten. Just as the Hennessey table were finishing their salads, the sound of a knife tapping on a glass pierced the general cacophony.

Sandy was standing in front of Duracell's table. 'Oh, heavens' breathed Celia 'I'd forgotten it's that ghastly man's birthday today.'

Sandy gave the glass another brief tap, smiled round at everyone, and then spoke. 'As you all know, many of our clients enjoy booking a Making Tracks holiday as a special occasion, to mark a wedding anniversary or a birthday, and we are delighted when you share your happy times with the rest of the group. We've already had a Ruby Wedding, and now it's my pleasure to announce that it's Reg's birthday today – I think you've all signed the card. Here you are, Reg, with our best wishes, and here is a box of Mozart chocolates with the company's compliments. I know you want to say a few words, so, – Reg – over to you!'

Everyone except Linda clapped.

Duracell rose to his feet, a little wobbly as he reached his full height so he leant on Pat's shoulder for a moment. Once he was perpendicular, he scratched his carroty scalp with a thumbnail, and began:

'I'm allowed to speak on my birthday, aren't I, Pat?' he turned briefly to look down at her. 'And what I want to say won't take long. I would like to say thank you. Thank you, to all of you, for being so friendly on this holiday. Thank you for this nice card, which we'll look at properly later. And I want to put you in the picture, you might say. Things you may not know. Like the lottery.'

Duracell stared down at the table, gathering his thoughts. Looking up again he continued:

'Pat and I won the lottery this spring.'

'March' nodded Pat.

'In March' said Duracell. 'We won over three quarters of a million pounds, and that's a lot of money, that is.'

A ripple of applause ran round the tables.

'So we thought, what shall we do? We'll go on holiday, that's one thing. And this holiday is what we booked. And it's all right, isn't it Pat? We're enjoying it, and enjoying your company. You're all nice people, good people, and we're pleased to have met you.' He cleared his throat. 'Now, most of you would say, well, all that money – you could see your family right with that. Couldn't you? Make sure your children and grandchildren were provided for. Look after the future, a bit. But for us, well – I'm going to tell them, Pat. They're our friends, now. They ought to know.' He looked round at the faces at the other tables. 'We had twin sons, we did. Scott and Darren. Lovely lads, good boys. You never worry, do you? You think you've got them for ever. Well, Scott was only sixteen; he was in a car that one of his friends was driving, his friend was seventeen, he'd only just passed his test. There were five of them packed into a Mini, wet road late one November night, I won't go into it. Two lads survived, one crippled for life. We don't bear a grudge, do we, Pat? What's the good of bearing a grudge? The driver died, his parents are in the same boat as us. And it won't bring him back. Nothing will bring our Scott back. So there we are.' Duracell blew his nose on a rather ancient handkerchief.

'Darren took it badly. He went off the rails, you can see why. He didn't stay on at school, got in with the wrong crowd, happens all the time, I know. We wore ourselves out with Darren. Pat did, didn't you, Pat? It's cruel for a mother, to have to see your boy get into trouble, he went to prison for a while. We weren't the sort of family to know what that's like, were we? We do now, though. We hoped he'd come to his senses and settle down, find a nice girl, get a job – we held out hope. All the time, we held out hope. But it was the drugs, in the end. He started smoking stuff, and then he got on to the hard ones, we had to learn all about that, didn't we, Pat? Went to the family sessions, the support groups. It did no good.' Duracell shook his head, and sighed; there was utter silence as the diners listened to him. 'Pat used to say, we can't reach him. He's out of reach. And then one day there's that knock on the door, the one you know is the blackest news coming. Policeman on the step, sorry, Darren's been found in a derelict factory, dead of an overdose. Two of them there, one got taken to hospital but he died too. Bad heroin, apparently. The scum that sell it on the streets, they put all sorts in it. Don't care, don't give a tuppenny damn about the poor sods that use it. That batch killed a girl in Cardiff apparently and put two people in hospital in Glasgow. So, anyway, I'm not making a song and dance, not going for the sympathy vote!' he looked round at the other tables, his face reddened and his eyes glistening. 'I'm just telling you, we've won the lottery, but I'd give it all back for – you know what I'm saying.' He looked at the table and swallowed twice.

'Now, we want to be jolly, that's the point! It's my birthday, and I can do what I want, can't I? Eh?' There was a whoop and a cheer from Mike and June Finch, but everyone else stayed quiet. 'So listen, I'm telling you that tonight's drinks are on me.' He raised a glass high in the air, and then took a gulp of wine. At each table people struggled to their feet and raised glasses too, calling out 'To Reg! Happy birthday, Reg! Here's to you!'

Duracell clapped loudly until he could make himself heard again. 'Folks, folks, one more thing' he held up a restraining hand 'Listen. Now. It's not just tonight's drinks, I'm picking up the tab for the whole holiday, all the drinks for the whole trip. The bar bill is on me' he tapped his chest 'and it's my pleasure. Thank you very much.' He sat down.

Several people including Gerald and Iris Harper, the Garsides, Colin and Wendy Harbottle and Simon Ryecart started singing 'For he's a jolly good fellow' and most of the others joined in.

There was a settling down after that as the main course was brought and people regained their composure. Nobody spoke at the Hennessey table for quite a long time.

Eventually Celia put her fork down and said 'It just goes to show. One shouldn't judge, should one?'

'Oh, that's just sentiment' said Linda crossly, shaking her fringe out of her eyes. 'I still don't like him. I'm sorry to hear about the tragedies they've had, but why should that change my opinion of him? That would be giving in to moral blackmail.' She cut a slice off her schnitzel.

'Hate to say it, but I agree. A bit, anyway' nodded Gwen. 'I don't like being manipulated. I'd rather buy my own drinks, thank you.'

'I think you're being rather ungracious' Celia frowned. 'Let him buy the drinks, if that's what he wants to do. Imagine, if you had lost twin sons like that.'

'Well, I'm sorry, but I don't see the connection' persisted Linda. 'We've all got things to deal with. Nobody goes through life unscathed. Unless you're born with a silver spoon and you have a successful life and exemplary children' she looked pointedly at Celia 'otherwise you just grit your teeth and get on with it. What on earth does paying a drinks bill do to help you cope? I feel I've been bought.'

'Don't be silly, you haven't been bought!' Gerrie put out a calming hand, but Linda pushed it away.

'I've got to be nice to him now, though, haven't I? I've got to be grateful. Let him leer all over me or make fatuous remarks about the fact that he thinks we should be at home, tied to the kitchen sink. Grotty man.'

'Hey, hey now!' Mags objected. 'You don't have to do anything! He's like most men, at sea in a chaotic storm of emotions he can't cope with and doesn't understand, and his instinct is to be kind and generous to us, because he can't do anything for his sons now. Let him alone. Be big enough just to accept his gesture graciously.'

Linda angrily finished her plateful and clattered the knife and fork down.

'Oh, look!' Gerrie had noticed a movement in the other part of the restaurant. 'All those delegates are getting up and leaving! Just as well, perhaps it will be a bit quieter now.'

When the waitress came to collect the plates they asked her what was happening. 'They go to the other hotel. Our hotel by lake' she gestured 'for present – present – certificates.'

'Presentation?' queried Mags.

'Ja, ja, presentation. In there, hotel, a bigger room for that.' She nodded.

When the desserts were on the table, Mags said 'Right, Gerrie – come on! Your turn tonight. Thanks to Duracell we haven't got as long as usual. What's your subject, then?'

'This is one that concerns us all, really' Gerrie began. Gwen shot her a questioning look. 'I want to know if you would ever consider moving in with a member of your family, when you get old and frail? Or whether you would go into a residential home instead. When you can't look after yourself any more.'

'That lets me out, straight away' snapped Linda. 'I haven't any family. End of conversation.'

'Sorry, Linda' Gerrie looked rather shocked. 'I didn't mean to say anything that would upset you – '

'I'm not upset' shrugged Linda. 'Honestly. Things are as they are. I haven't got the choice of moving in with a family member, but I bet when you've all had your say I'll be the one who feels the luckiest.' She sat back in her chair. 'Go on, I'm looking forward to this!'

Mags bit her lip. She looked as if she wanted to start the discussion but wasn't sure what to say to begin with.

'It's crossed my mind, I must say' Celia said with her usual precision. 'I suppose if you have a daughter you automatically have this assumption that you would go to her if you had to. Not that I feel anywhere near ready for that yet. Let's say, another fifteen years and I might.' She drank some wine.

'That's Charlotte?' Gwen was checking. 'She's not married, though, is she?'

'No. But I'm not sure that's relevant actually. In fifteen years she will be fifty. Awful thought. But she will be thinking about retirement, I suppose, if she's still in the army.'

'She'll have a good pension' put in Linda. 'And so will you. You could buy a palatial place for the two of you and still afford to have care coming in.'

Celia didn't respond to this. She continued 'There's Justin and Meredith. I can't see Meredith wanting to retire to England. She had lots of family in the States and the children will be grown up and in careers by then, so I'd have to go over the pond if I wanted to live with them.'

'Would you want to?' asked Gerrie.

Celia thought for a moment. 'No' she said.

'What about you, Gwen?' asked Mags. 'Would you want to live with Jenny?'

Gwen half closed her eyes and said nothing for a few seconds. Then she opened them wide and said 'No, I don't think so. I'd want to be near, but in the same house – no, it wouldn't work.'

'Why not?'

'When Jenny broke up with Mark she came to live with us for a few months. Rosie was very small. You gloss over things, in your memory, don't you? I like to think that we had a wonderful time while she was with us, but when I really think back, we had some epic rows. She can be difficult and moody and possessive. Over all sorts of things – she criticised the way I organise the kitchen, and we never could agree over the central heating. I like to put the washing outside, although I forget it's there sometimes and it gets left out for a day or two. She uses the tumble drier and it drove me mad. We didn't agree over what television programmes Rosie could watch or whether she could have sweets or what time she should go to bed. Jenny used to go into white rages sometimes and refuse to be in the room with me, and I remember telling her once that I wasn't surprised Mark had left her, I didn't blame him.'

'Goodness, that was rather harsh!' Celia raised her eyebrows.

Gwen shrugged. 'Well, it was true' she said. 'I liked Mark. I really missed him. These kids, they don't realise that we get fond of their partners and it's nearly as hard on us as it is on them, when they split up.'

Gerrie said sadly 'I expect you all know that I do have a son. Steven. And technically a grandson.'

'I didn't know' said Celia. 'What do you mean, technically?'

'Anton. He's six. But I'll never see him again; he lives in France with his mother – she was lovely, we got on well. But she's remarried, she's already got one child with her new husband and she's expecting another. He's adopted Anton, so it would only confuse him if I pushed in now. You're right, Gwen, it's really painful. I try not to think about it.'

'Doesn't Steven see him?' asked Linda.

'No. He lives in Quebec, with a new partner.'

Celia said 'You've got a son as well as Jenny, haven't you, Gwen?'

'Gavin. He's married to Ruth. They live in Dubai with their two children. We don't fit in with their lifestyle – there's no way on earth I could live with them!' Gwen laughed. 'I mean, don't get me wrong – they come over here on paid flights from his firm, and we see them and have a lovely time, put on our glad rags and go out for meals, but they're in a different world. I ask Gavin things and I watch him think – how can I make this simple so Mum will understand? And of course I don't understand it. I love them to bits, but we're like chalk and cheese. The children are coming back next year to go to boarding school in Scotland, where Ruth comes from. Her father is a retired oil company executive.'

'Hmmm.' Celia digested all this information.

'Mags' she said, looking up 'You've got two, haven't you? What about them?'

'Sally and Will are fine' she smiled. 'They've got Sophie and Tom, eight and six – do you know' she said, leaning forward 'Celia knows this – I bought them two beautiful painted wooden letters from a shop in Bad Ischl today – such a gorgeous toyshop, everything made of wood, a sort of Tyrolean paradise. I bought an S for Sophie and a T for Tom, hand painted, lovely – and on the bus I had a second look, and they've got Made in China on the back! Would you believe it! I was furious.'

Gerrie shook her head and tutted 'Terrible, everything is from China these days. You have to be careful with a lot of the things they sell in antique shops and at these fairs, you know. Porcelain, brass figures, pictures, you name it – a lot of it is fake, and made in China.'

'So would you consider living with them?' Celia asked.

'They live in Oxford – Will's a GP. They live a very busy life.'

'That's a no, then' commented Linda.

'I might if – the trouble is, things have gone too – I'm assuming you mean, if something had happened to Dudley? We are talking about whether we would move in with a family member if we were left on our own, aren't we?'

'Yes, I think so' nodded Gerrie. 'Definitely, yes.'

'What about your son?' continued Celia. 'It is a son, isn't it?'

'Raph. Raphael. He's in India at the moment. He's doing a PhD in ancient Indian languages. He's spent several years in Thailand and also he's been to Tibet – he's attached to a university, he doesn't have a base here.'

Linda smoothed her fringe. 'So that's another no. Looks like we'll all end up in residential homes, doesn't it? So much for the Big Society' she mimed quotation marks.

'Have we covered everything?' Gerrie looked round the table. 'Mags, two children; me, one; Gwen, two; Celia two.'

Celia studied the salt shaker, running a finger up and down it. She didn't look up.

Mulling things over

'So that's it!' Gerrie sat back. 'It didn't take long, tonight, did it? Unless any of us are suggesting that we live with our own siblings, if we have any – shut up, Gwen! – we need to go home and put our names down for a rave of a nursing home, where they play cards and golf and serve steak and chips and Eton mess and generally treat us in the way we are accustomed to.'

'And has its own still' added Linda. 'Illicit hooch. Bugger Switzerland, we'll just drink ourselves to death on moonshine.'

Gwen's face looked strained. 'It'll cost' she said. 'Even now it's a thousand a week they say, in some homes.'

'You must read the Daily Mail' sniffed Linda. 'Scaremongering.'

Gwen went on 'So in, let's say, ten years time – what will it cost then? Supposing we can't afford it?'

'I think we're all lucky enough to be in a fairly comfortable position' soothed Celia. 'I wouldn't worry too much.'

'Oh, come on!' Gwen sounded brittle. 'Fifty thousand a year? Supposing we linger on for another ten years after that – that's half a million! It scares me to death.'

Linda fished for her stick on the floor; then she leant on the table with one hand to get to her feet. 'You'd better cosy up to Duracell' she said grimly. 'He's got half a million.'

The others picked up handbags and cardigans and made their way out of the restaurant.

'Steinmunden tomorrow' smiled Mags. 'Boat trip and sightseeing and mountain railway and little train. Brilliant. I think the weather's picking up for our last day.'

Gerrie turned as she went upstairs 'And your choice of topic for dinner' she said. 'Think of something really contentious to go out on!'

Gwen and Gerrie sat in their room chatting for quite a while before getting ready for bed.

'It's interesting' said Gwen 'When you started the conversation tonight, I thought, well – we just need to go back to the old days. Everybody's full of it, in the papers and on TV, saying that two or three generations ago you'd always have a Gran or Grandad propped up in the corner. It's part of the austerity thing, make do and mend, digging for victory. We should be more self sufficient, looking after our own relatives when they get old, and not relying on the state.'

'Go back to the fifties, you mean.'

'Well, yes. You didn't have everybody shoved into homes then, did you? Remember all the families back home in Devon with the elderly folk living there, old ladies podding the peas and ironing the shirts, the old gents doing – well, not much, actually. Once they couldn't dig the vegetable plot they were usually in the pub, in the snug, puffing on a briar pipe.'

'That could be looking back through rose tinted glasses.'

'The economy is different now, though. Mum has to go out to work, not babysit the elderly. And the kids have to be taken everywhere, after school clubs and swimming and off to the pictures with their friends. Late night shopping. There was none of that when we were young.'

'That's a social change' commented Gerrie 'not an economic one.'

'No, it is. Mum needs a car, so she has to go out to work to earn the money for it; there's the mortgage, the computers for the kids, all the latest clothes and gadgets. And have you seen the cost of extra things for school? Even at Rosie's age they have educational outings and trips that cost forty or fifty pounds, and there's subscriptions for Brownies, and uniforms. And don't even start me about birthday parties these days, you can say goodbye to at least a hundred quid on those. Even taking a present to someone else's is twenty, at least.'

'Really?' Gerrie was wide eyed. 'Good grief.'

'But if our group is representative, and it may be, none of us will end up being cared for by our children. Not one of us. All for different reasons, but all the same, really.'

'They don't want us.'

'No, they don't; we don't fit in with their lifestyles. And they don't fit in with ours – can you imagine Steven, or Jenny, or one of Celia's on this holiday with us? It would be crazy! We'd all drive each other mad in half a day. Time has moved on, and families aren't what they used to be.'

'Also' said Gerrie 'We're a lot older before we need support, these days. Some of those geriatrics we remember from our childhood were probably only seventy.'

'If that.'

'We wouldn't be prepared to sit in the corner of someone's kitchen and do nothing but darn socks, would we? We still want to go on holidays and live in our own houses and do our gardens and see our friends.'

'Well, absolutely' Gwen agreed. 'There must be a whole lot of reasons for all this. But some cultures seem to manage things all right. Asian families pool all their money and buy several businesses and several houses, and they all work together to grow their capital. So do Italians, and Greeks.'

'Would you want to live in a big house with Roy and Jenny and maybe Jenny's new partner, and Rosie, and Gavin and Ruth, and the children, all of you under one roof? All working in the family business? Maybe with your widowed sister there as well?' Gerrie looked mischievous.

'Huh!' Gwen threw her head back. 'I'd give it a week before there was murder in the air. Mind you' she said thoughtfully 'there is a bit of a safety valve in all that, isn't there?'

'What do you mean?'

'Well, Roy would find it much harder to hide his gambling, wouldn't he?'

'Now that is very true.' Gerrie got up to find her nightdress. 'Maybe that's why some cultures have such big families – much harder to keep secrets.'

'Exactly.'

In Room 311 Linda and Mags were also having a conversation.

'There are lots of things that worry us all, aren't there?' mused Mags. 'Things we don't talk about, but they're universal, really.'

'Such as?' Linda was fiddling with her cellphone.

'Well, we've covered quite a lot of them. Illness and being left on your own. Partners who misbehave. The fear of not having enough money for your old age. That's a big one, isn't it? Once you retire, that's it – you can't make any more. You do your sums and buy your annuities and your ISA's and sort out your tax liabilities as much as you can; you buy your bonds and insurances. All you can do after that is cross your fingers.'

'We always said our house was part of our pension' nodded Linda. 'You could always be sure that bricks and mortar were a good bet. Move upmarket when you could, and you'd have something to sell if you fell on hard times. But I'm not so sure about that now.'

'That's another whole subject.'

'You could choose that for tomorrow night' Linda looked up, and put her phone on the bedside table.

'I've got another idea for tomorrow night!' smiled Mags. 'Going back to this one, though – you're right, it's a biggie. We keep hearing that young people aren't saving for their pensions, but they're not buying houses either, are they? The ones a bit below ours; in their twenties and early thirties. That may be another timebomb even bigger than the baby boomers.'

'They're not buying houses partly because of the credit crunch' said Linda. 'The banks used to have money sloshing around they didn't know what to do with – they'd lend it to practically anybody. Now it's all restricted.'

'And the youngsters can't be sure of their jobs, can they? So that's scary. And they have to save up a whacking great deposit first. That must be really hard if they're renting, how can you save up twenty or thirty thousand for a deposit if you're paying out a grand a month in rent already?'

'But renting is more flexible' said Linda, removing her watch and earrings. 'If you lose your job you need to be able to move around the country, don't you?'

'That's true; if you're renting you just up sticks and go. I wonder what all this means, in the end? Maybe it's a good thing. I'm not sure.'

'You'd need to be an economist to answer that one. But it seems to me that today's generation will amass far less wealth than we have tried to do. Perhaps they will be happier, less burdened. Maybe we've overcomplicated things, and they will go back to the basics.'

'Yes, but what does that mean for the country? Less tax to collect, so how do we pay for things like hospitals and pensions?'

Linda managed to stand upright, took her stick and made for the bathroom. 'I have absolutely no idea' she said. 'It won't affect me, and I'm too knackered to think about it any more. Over and out.'

Mags smiled and began to undress.

Holidays do you good!

The last day of the holiday began in a leisurely way; there was no particular rush for breakfast since the boat would collect them from the jetty by the monastery at ten o'clock, for the journey down the lake to Steinmunden. As usual Mags woke up before the alarm, and as usual Linda was still sound asleep. The weather seemed to be the best it had been all week, warm sunshine and very little wind.

By just after eight, Mags was dressed and downstairs, heading out of the hotel for a walk round on her own. She felt energetic, invigorated; wanting to explore the little lanes and paths she had missed, before it was too late. There was a gap in the stone retaining wall opposite the second hotel, with steps leading up to higher ground and clearly up a mountain if you ventured far enough. She climbed steadily, passing the back entrances of some large houses which seemed to belong to out-of-towners. Upmarket holiday homes. The historic Russian House which the grey sisters had found was at the edge of a stony path; it was shut up, with heavy padlocks on the ornate wrought iron gates which stretched way above her, but inside the grounds there was a curious array of garden statuary dotted about, some stone, some cast in bronze, some of other metals. Fascinated, Mags stood squinting through the iron scrolls for quite some time, intrigued by the sights and occasionally looking up at the windows of the house with a vague feeling that someone was there. Or had been. Or would be. There were faded blinds at some of the windows, patchy and threadbare at the corners where the sun had beaten down on them. The sort of house I could write a story about, she thought. Celia is right; I must do this. When I get home, I really will, this time.

A memory suddenly came into her mind of a visit with Dudley to some stately pile in the Lake District at home, not unlike this house They had arrived at lunch time, and had a look round. Mags had been hungry, and she knew that Dudley got ratty if his meals were late, so she had suggested they had something to eat before they left. There was a converted stable which sold delicious looking food, and it was after two o'clock by then, but it was busy and the only seats were at tables which already had other people sitting at them. Mags had gone in and already chosen something off the blackboard, but Dudley seized her arm and frogmarched her outside. 'Why?' she spluttered 'Aren't we going to have something to eat? Aren't you hungry?' 'I'm not going to sit at a table with people I don't know' he'd said grimly. 'We'll go somewhere else.'

There wasn't anywhere, of course. They were miles from any towns, and although they passed one or two country hotels, Dudley found something wrong with each of them and drove away again. Knowing how tricky he could be, she had got into the habit of always taking something edible out with them, so this time she reached into the back of the car for a box of Mr Kipling cakes she had packed, just in case. He had three of those and became human again. But it made her cross for the umpteenth time that it was she who had to think ahead, she who had to plan and take corrective action all the time when it was he who behaved like a spoilt child.

She walked a little further up the path, a tiny track with grassy crags on one side and brambles and a fence on the other, which overlooked the church on the promontory and the lake. A local man with a dachshund approached her, coming back from his walk. He lifted his hat: 'Gruss Gott!' 'Gruss Gott!' Mags smiled broadly. I'm getting the hang of this, she thought. She walked a little way along, where the man had come from, but realised that eventually the path would meet the railway and then continue up the mountain and she would only have to come back again. As she turned to retrace her steps she saw Uncle Alan teetering amongst the scrub and grass high up above the back of the Russian House garden. Taking his photographs, his camera pointed this way and that, and his feet nearly missing their hold at times as he hopped from foot to foot and stretched out and squatted down.

'Lethal' thought Mags. 'He could career down those crags any minute. I hope he doesn't see me – if he waves at me and falls base over apex I'll feel really guilty.' She kept her head down and retraced her steps to the village. It was getting surprisingly hot; she had taken off her fleece and tied it round her waist, but now she thought that jeans were probably not a good idea, and that when she went into the hotel for breakfast it might be better to change into light cotton chinos instead.

Her mood became increasingly happier as she drank in the atmosphere, the views, the weather; she sauntered back to the hotel with such a wide grin on her face that even the sight of Win Burns bursting out of the door of the grocery shop like a small stream of volcanic larva couldn't bring her down. 'Morning!' she waved. She got no reply.

'Breakfast next!' thought Mags. 'I'm starving, now. A good breakfast, then I'll go upstairs and change out of my jeans, and see how Linda is. I wish I could bottle this feeling and take it home – life can be so good!'

Celia was at the table, reading a guide to Steinmunden. Gwen and Gerrie had been down, but had gone again.

'Good morning!' greeted Celia, closing her book. 'What a lovely day, don't you think?'

'Oh, it's glorious!' agreed Mags happily. 'I've been out for a ramble; I got quite high up, and you could see the village set out below, and the lake and the mountains – it's getting hot already! Too hot for jeans, I'll have to change. I want orange juice and eggs and coffee and a croissant with jam – I'm really hungry now.' She left her bag and fleece by her chair and went off to pick up a tray and fill it with goodies.

'I've finished' said Celia when she returned 'but I'll have another cup of coffee and keep you company.' She giggled, a sound Mags had never heard before.

'What are you laughing at?' asked Mags, her mouth full of scrambled egg.

'People watching, I think you call it. There's been a conference taking place quietly in that end of the restaurant, where those delegates had their breakfast. The man who runs the hotel, and his son, and the head waiter, and two people from the kitchen. I don't speak German – well, only schoolgirl stuff, and they were talking very quietly – but it was obvious they were talking about all those crashes last night.'

'Oh, yes! I forgot about that' Mags was buttering some toast.

'Bad, bad' Celia shook her head theatrically. 'They don't like things going wrong. You must not stack so high, so high as this' she put on a thick accent and raised one hand to shoulder height 'you must stack like this' she lowered it towards the table 'and you must have more piles, one, two three, four, five. You must move the preparation area like this; like this. You must peel the potatoes over here; over here. We must have no more bad smashes, upsetting the guests and costing all these Euro. You see? You understand? It must not happen again.' Celia nodded three times very firmly. Then she giggled again.

Mags drank some orange juice.

'And then there was Monty and Helen Bewley; they tiptoed in here, one behind the other, like Inspector Clouseau and that man in the film.'

'Really?'

'I think they were trying to avoid Uncle Alan. Helen's chins were quivering in all directions and Monty kept peeping round the pillars and looking at Helen and shaking his head and smiling.'

'Uncle Alan's halfway up a mountain, taking photographs' said Mags, reaching for the raspberry jam. 'I saw him while I was out. I was afraid he was going to tumble head over heels into the Russian House garden. So I tried to keep out of sight, like a burglar in a silent movie.'

'Isn't life fun?' smiled Celia merrily. 'There's so much to see, when you have time to enjoy it.'

'I know! You forget, don't you? I'm sure I'll sink back into the whole dull routine when I get home. But at least we've had these few days. We know life can be different, all things being equal.'

'Oh, and one other thing I spotted – nothing to do with us, but the son of the proprietor, you know – '

'I know' nodded Mags.

'As he went out into the foyer, the receptionist looked up from the desk with a big smile and he stopped and gave her a kiss. A lovely big lingering one. They didn't know I was watching. They make a very attractive couple.'

'The receptionist has a diamond ring. On her right hand, not her left. I noticed that when I picked up your scarf – I spoke to the owner, but she was on the phone. It looked like a solitaire, very pretty.'

'Well I hope she's engaged to him and not somebody else, because it was an exceptionally passionate kiss!' Celia gave another giggle.

Mags wiped her mouth and stood up. 'See you at the boat, if not before' she said. 'I'm going upstairs.'

Passing reception Mags looked carefully at the girl busy typing at the computer; she sported both a solitaire ring and a bashful smile. Mags continued on her way, climbing the stairs to the first floor; she stopped at the archway and wondered whether to email Dudley, but decided against it. 'We've been away six days' she thought 'and I've spoken to him once and sent two emails. Is that enough? I suppose it is. I'll send him a text from Cologne.'

Heading down the lake

Linda was dressed and about to go down for something to eat. 'You'll have to hurry up' said Mags, looking at her watch 'and they may have cleared the breakfast away by now.'

'I'm not hungry' said Linda as she limped out into the corridor. 'If there's no breakfast I can always go into the shop for something. They've got a coffee machine there, that's all I really feel like.'

Mags changed into her chinos; she sat on the edge of her bed, thinking. Then she collected sunglasses, a floppy hat and her lighter weight fleece and checked her bag for bottled water and some Euro notes.

She spotted Sandy once or twice, in the hotel foyer talking to Adam Adamant and Iris, coming out of the shop, standing over by the fishing boat jetty using a cellphone. Always on duty, she thought; unobtrusive, but available. That's the sign of a good holiday guide. I wonder if I would like to do that? I don't think I would, actually. Anyway, Dudley would have a fit. That's a good reason to do it, then.

'If I said there was more of a holiday atmosphere today, would you understand what I mean?' Mags had joined Gwen and Linda as they sauntered into the little park by the monastery.

'I think we're all just getting into the swing of it, now it's the last proper day' said Gwen. 'It always takes a while.'

'No, it's more than that' Mags looked round at the flower beds and saw that all the seats were occupied. 'I think we're shedding emotional loads. I had breakfast with Celia, and she actually giggled. Twice.'

'I don't believe it' said Linda, leaning heavily on her stick. 'That's like saying you heard a – oh, I don't know - a Persian cat singing a rugby song.'

'Good grief, Linda, you can be quite poetic sometimes!' Gwen put her sunglasses on and looked out over the lake.

'And it's only us, going a bit doolally' added Mags. 'Look at everyone else. They've made allowances for the better weather, but they're the same old sour characters, some of them. Win Burns hasn't changed, she's sitting right at the end of that bench with a face like a slapped arse.'

'That's true.' Gwen followed her gaze. 'Pat's squeezed up the other end, as far as she can get away from her, and Duracell's standing up. Floral Paticia's still whingeing, I heard her going on at poor old Simon outside the shop.'

Linda pointed with her stick-free hand. 'Look!' she said 'Gerrie and Celia – they're walking on to the landing stage. I think Celia's found the timetable for the boats.'

'That doesn't apply' said Mags. 'Sandy was telling the Quiet Americans, we've got a chartered one. It starts from the top of the lake, and picks pre-booked parties up from the hotels at various stops on the way. I think this is it, now – '

Sandy leaped forward as members of the group converged on the landing stage, facing them against the steps to the deck and raising both hands for attention. 'Please wait, all together. I've got a block ticket, which the captain needs to see, and then I'll count you all aboard. Just wait, please.'

Eventually everybody had got themselves on to the boat, which was large and hung with bunting along the railings. International flags fluttered from the wires; there were curved seats all round the white painted prow and at the stern, and varnished benches, athwart the deck, with extra seating below amidships where there was a bar selling snacks and drinks. They were the last pick up point, and from there on the boat took a stately course out into the centre of the lake and then chugged in a straight line down to the far shore, where Steinmunden was spread out before them.

Celia, sitting on the front deck next to Gerrie, had a map spread out on her lap. It flapped around disconcertingly in the wind, so she held on to it grimly with navy-gloved hands, and then turned it through ninety degrees. 'I find this really confusing' she frowned. 'I keep thinking the boat has come from the top of the lake, and – look up ahead – there's Steinmunden bathed in sunshine, so you think this is north/south, don't you? It feels as if we're heading south. But Steinmunden is at the north end of the lake, looking south. That's why the sun is full on it. I'm usually good at maps.'

Gerrie patted her on the arm. 'Put it away' she smiled. 'It really doesn't matter. Stop using your grey cells for once, and just absorb the experience'. She closed her eyes.

Celia looked slightly surprised. Then she smiled, too, and folded up the map as best she could before stuffing it in the outer pocket of her bag. 'Perhaps you're right' she said. 'Perhaps I work too hard at things.'

Gerrie, her eyes still shut, nodded. Then she opened them and looked about her. 'It's all so beautiful' she said. 'The light on the lake, the mountains, the little villages perched halfway up with their pretty churches. Look, there's the train!'

'The pleasure boats are out today' observed Celia. 'See that little group of them by the shore, there – delicate white sails. I think they're getting ready to race.'

'Perhaps they are. Remind me, what is there to see in Steinmunden? I know we can go on the mountain railway if we want to. And isn't there something about a tram?'

'Oh, it's a fascinating town' nodded Celia. 'There's lots to see, actually. Medieval buildings, an interesting bridge. The town hall is hung with a peal of ceramic bells, very unusual – they play folk songs on the hour. I'd like to hear those. I think they're big on ceramics; there's a very good museum, apparently.'

'It won't take long to get there' said Gerrie, twisting round on the bench 'we've come a long way already.' Facing forward again, she added 'Lovely castle things over there, to the left of the town. One looks as if it sticks out into the lake.'

'There's the land castle and the lake castle' explained Celia. 'I read the guide this morning. The lake castle goes back over a thousand years.'

'Wow.'

'The courtyard is built in a triangle. It all burnt down once, in the sixteen hundreds. Most old buildings have to be rebuilt after fires, don't they? All that wood and roasting of suckling pigs and whole oxen. Nowadays I think they film some TV soap there, and it's licensed for weddings.'

'Wouldn't it be fantastic to be married there?' said Gerrie dreamily. 'How romantic! Sometimes I really miss Leo, so much. He would have loved all this. He was especially interested in ceramics; that's why we first went to Italy. Perugia.'

'Would you ever consider marrying again?' asked Celia. 'I'm so sorry, that was most impertinent. I seem to be losing my manners on this holiday. I do apologise.'

'It's not impertinent at all!' Gerrie turned her bright blue eyes on Celia's face. 'Please don't apologise. It's a perfectly fair question. No, I wouldn't. I've been very happy, once, with a good man. We were married for forty years and seven months. And three days. He was my best friend. What a cliché, I know, but he was. He was kind, and funny, and he left me very comfortably off. I have such happy memories – no, why would I want to take a risk with someone else?'

'An emotional risk.'

'Well, obviously. But financial, too. I could be the target of a con man, I'm well aware of that. There are men that prey on wealthy widows; they can be very plausible indeed. I can think of several examples, in Italy, where I know a lot of people. A lot of women on their own. One or two have suffered very badly, coming out of relationships they've made late in life. Impoverished, made a fool of. One lost her home and all her savings, and she didn't even marry the man. Actually it can be worse if you don't, sometimes. I have no intention of getting involved with anyone else.'

'We're almost there' Celia tied the Hermes scarf tighter at her neck, gathered up her bag and put her gloves in her jacket pocket. People were beginning to stand up and preparing to disembark.

Steinmunden, and a near miss

The warmth of the sun-soaked stone hit them as soon as they got on to dry land; it was tempered with the light southern breeze to provide a perfect climate for the day. Ragged groups of people wandered off, occasionally standing in open spaces to wait for their companions or to discuss their itinerary. After about twenty minutes they were mostly dispersed into the town, and the Hennessey Five found themselves standing in the main square with their backs to a fountain, looking up at the Town Hall with its twenty four ceramic bells hung on six rods, three each side of a central supporting pillar.

'We've missed the chime' commented Mags 'and we can't wait for the next one and waste all that time. We must try and be sure to get back here on the hour, before we go.'

'It's such an elegant building' said Celia, gazing at it with her arms folded. 'The sage green and cream and white, and all the delicate embellishments, like Wedgwood, isn't it?'

'When you look all round' said Gwen, turning slowly in a circle 'it reminds me of a packet of Refreshers – remember those? It's the slightly fizzy pastel colours, the yellow and the apricot and the pink, and the apple green – I just love it. I really do. They haven't let the modernisers spoil it, have they?'

'No, and I don't think it can have been bombed in the war. So they had a head start.' Linda sat down on a bench beside the fountain.

The day passed like a dream; like something unreal. The group split up, came together again, passed each other on street corners, and took solitary walks. Gwen and Gerrie met the Quiet Americans coming the other way, who showed them the pairs of feet painted on the pavements in various places. 'They tell you which way to go' explained Donald. 'Go the way the feet are pointing – it's a town trail, and you find the most fabulous old buildings.'

'Be sure to look up, wherever you go' Maewin's muted contralto added, as she nodded wisely. 'there's so much to see. And where the feet are painted standing together, like so, there is a plaque – right there – with information.' She nodded again, and smiled.

'That was useful' said Gerrie. 'We've already done some of this trail, the wrong way round because we didn't know about the feet, so let's start again and do it properly.' When they met Celia a little way up a crooked alley, like something out of a fairy tale, she knew about it because the Harbottles had told her, but Mags didn't, when they saw her coming out of a ceramics museum. Mags told the Garsides when she met them, later, in the square. Mags had found a general goods store, clearly used by the resident population, and bought herself a suitcase on wheels.

Duracell and Pat had discovered a very good cafe which sold a local beer and excellent food; they told Simon Ryecart when they rounded a corner, and he told Gerrie when she bumped into him as he waited outside a public loo for Floral Patricia.

'Are you going on the mountain railway?' Mags asked Simon a little later, when she came across him looking at a ceramic statue of a man carrying a lump of salt; marking the history of the area. 'No, you have to catch it a little way out of the main area, over the bridge. Patricia can't walk that far. But the Bewleys and Alan are going, and so are the Garsides – look, they're on their way, now – if you run, you'll catch them up.' He stared after her as she sped along the pavement, pulling her new black case behind her. It bumped and bounced rather because, being empty, it was so light.

Mags did catch the others up. They walked past the town museum, under the ancient gateway buildings which guarded the bridge in days gone by. Along the lake edge, past some lime trees. In the lake there was a metal sculpture of a long legged bird, perhaps a stork, so real that they stopped for a moment to see if it moved. Then they cut through some houses, past a scrubby piece of derelict land, and there was the train. No station, no ticket office, no shop. No loo. Linda would never mange this.

Once everyone was assembled, it was clear that most of the party had decided to take the train trip. Mags looked round and could only see that Linda, Gerrie and the Ryecarts were missing. And Sandy. Otherwise most of the familiar faces were there.

It seemed very casually run, compared to the highly organised transport they had experienced so far. There was no timetable on view; after about ten minutes a young man appeared in appropriate uniform, walking towards them between the tracks before stepping on to the platform and solemnly unlocking the door to each carriage. He returned to the front of the train and climbed into the cab. The cab connected with the first carriage – the seats were of slatted wood – but none of the other carriages linked so you would have to get out and in again if you wanted to move between them.

Celia, Mags and Gwen sat together. 'Sandy said this goes to Lambach; that's at the top' said Celia. 'There's not much there, apparently. It's just worth going up for the views and then coming down again. But it takes quite a while. About an hour, to do the return trip.'

'It's used a lot by the local people, I think' said Gwen. 'It's not really a tourist thing, it's what the villages up the mountain use, to get to work and to school, and to go shopping.'

Away from the theatrical splendour of Steinmunden the little train took them through real communities; children got on from schools, and got off again several stops later to go the few yards to their homes. Higher and higher they climbed, passing small farms with herds of cattle looking so clean that they were almost like toys, grazing the bright green fields or sheltering under perfectly symmetrical trees that looked as if they belonged in a child's farm set. At one point they crossed a wide river; at another there seemed to be a link road to a motorway.

A conductor had sprung into the cab at the first stop – a boy who looked about sixteen – and at each one after that he jumped down on to the platform and walked along, tapping at the windows until the passengers pulled them open with leather straps and paid for their fares. He kept an eagle eye on everyone, and knew exactly who had stumped up and who hadn't.

Unfortunately the Ghastly Garsides were in the same carriage as Mags, who was finding her case rather a nuisance now, plus Celia and Gwen. They were accompanied by Uncle Alan, and Gordon Garside had taken it upon himself to drone to Uncle Alan all the way up the mountain about the statistics of the railway. 'Fifteen kilometres, approximately' he intoned 'built in nineteen-o-three, well I say built in nineteen-o-three, but I should really say it was opened in nineteen-o-three, and it was electrified in nineteen thirty one – seven hundred and fifty volts at the time, the maximum speed being now, today, as we speak fifty kilometres per hour and it can draw seven hundred tons, that's the maximum draw weight seven hundred tons which when you think about it is quite impressive, isn't it, with the gradient we have here and when you think the train has a maximum length of one hundred and fifteen meters or thereabouts, when I say one hundred and fifteen of course.....'

'Great Bores of Today' whispered Mags in Gwen's ear.

Gwen laughed out loud. 'You read the Oldie too, then?' she said.

A little later, Gwen nudged Mags in the ribs: 'Look at Celia!'

Celia had put her gloves on again and was looking out of the window with great interest, the tips of her forefingers in her ears.

After a quarter of an hour Gordon seemed to be running out of steam.

Uncle Alan seized his chance. 'Are you getting off at Eggenberg?' he asked chirpily.

'Eggenberg? No, I don't think so. What's at Eggenberg?'

'A brewery!' Uncle Alan nodded like a Churchill dog in a car going over a cattle grid. A huge grin spread over his face. 'A brewery! Pilsner beer, they tell me. Reg is getting off to go and look for it. My nephew Monty was coming too, but he says his ankle's gammy. We're going to get off, and then we have twenty five minutes to go and find it and get back before the train goes down again. Yes. Ten minutes while you go up to the top of the mountain, five minute turn around, ten minutes back down to Eggenberger. That's right. Twenty five minutes. Eggenberger. Yes.'

Gordon shrugged. 'Go on then' he said. He looked at his watch. 'When's Eggenberger, then?'

'Next stop!'

'Oh.'

Gwen and Mags watched as Uncle Alan, swathed in cameras and binoculars, climbed out of the carriage and looked around him. Duracell had got down too from another carriage, and the two of them turned circles on the spot as they surveyed the bucolic scene and wondered which way was Brewery.

The child-conductor slammed both carriage doors and clambered up into the cab, and the train set off again. It was true, there was nothing much at the top. The Making Tracks group climbed out raggedly, muttering to each other 'Can we leave things in there, then?' 'Well, the train's not going anywhere, is it?' 'Yes, but we might miss it.' 'Huh! Doing what? Staring at a tree?' 'They said there was a cafe.' 'I don't care what they said, can you see a cafe? If you can see a cafe I'm a Dutchman.' 'You mean I'm a banana.' 'Now what are you on about?' 'Ian Hislop.' 'Oh, that's it, you've finally cracked.'

Mags stood on the platform and listened to the grumbling. She thought 'from now on I'll have to have a notebook with me, like a proper writer. It's all there, you don't have to invent a thing.'

There was a bit more aimless wandering about and ill-tempered banter; Mags wondered whether people were affected more by altitude as they got older, or perhaps they were just feeling crotchety after all the activity during the day. The driver and conductor had vanished, but eventually they appeared again round the end of a farmhouse; perhaps there had been more to discover after all.

The train simply drove in reverse down the mountain; the advantage of the wooden benches was that you sat the other way round, and you were still facing the front. After a little time, they drew to a halt at the Eggenberg stop; but there was no sign of Duracell and Uncle Alan. Celia took charge, suddenly. She stood up, pulled down the window with its leather strap, and called to the guard on the pavement. 'Don't go! Stop! Stop! We have two passengers missing – two! Two people! Hang on – '

She opened the carriage door and stepped carefully down, keeping hold of the handle, and Gwen and Mags could see by craning their necks that she had her work cut out. The child-conductor shrugged extravagantly and said something in German. Celia wagged a finger at him and pointed up a lane that ran at right angles to the railway track. The conductor drew back his cuff, looked at his watch and then held his wrist out to Celia, tapping the watch face. Celia shook her head, looked up the lane again, opened her mouth and began making come-here-quick gestures with increasing irritation. She pointed up the lane, said something to the conductor, nodded, and got back into the carriage; she left the door open and stood in the gap with her arms folded. Eventually she came and sat down, a little breathless, and there was the sound of a carriage door being slammed. The train pulled away.

'They're back' she said 'they're all right, but God knows what they've been up to. They were trying to run, both as red as beetroots, and Uncle Alan seems to have broken at least one of his straps.'

'Where is he?' asked Gwen, looking round.

'Got into the carriage with Reg.'

Mags whispered to Gwen 'Couldn't cope with any more of the Great Bore of Today.'

Back in Steinmunden everyone got carefully off the train and dusted themselves down; they all needed a loo. The Quiet Americans, ever graceful, receded in the direction of the bridge at speed. Most other people looked round uncomfortably before taking off down the pavement. The only facilities seemed to be in the back of a cake shop where you could sit and have a coffee as well; the Garsides, the Harbottles and several others invaded en masse and sat down at tables. More hardened travellers, such as Win Burns, simply marched through the cafe to the washroom at the back, used it, and marched out again. Gwen did the same, but Mags and Celia decided to make it to the museum on the bridge and used the loo there.

Eventually they were back in the town square, looking once again at the ceramic bells. 'It's nearly a quarter past four' said Mags.

'Great, isn't it? We've got to meet Sandy at five o'clock at Franz Josef Platz for the tram, so we won't be able to hear the bells after all. What a pain.'

'I did want to' Celia looked disappointed. 'Never mind, I always seem to miss something, wherever we go. I didn't get to the fortress in Salzburg, I didn't see the World Heritage museum in Hallstadt either.'

'Well if you had, you'd have missed something else. Like the salt mine' said Gwen 'You can't do it all.'

'Perhaps it's an incentive to come back' smiled Mags. 'It would be nice to think we might come again, and there would still be new things to see.'

By the time they had wandered a little way down the esplanade, looked at some boats, admired the colourful civic planters full of marguerite daisies and marigolds, bought an ice cream and wandered back again, it was time to walk the few hundred yards to the tram stop which would take them to the railway station. Opposite the tram stop was a small park with shady trees and flower beds and some benches, and there they found Linda, Gerrie, Floral Patricia and Simon chatting happily to each other.

'Ah, there's Linda' said Celia, relieved. 'I hope she's had a good afternoon.'

'I wonder if Gerrie's been with her all the time, or whether they've each done their own thing?' mused Gwen.

'You'll find out' said Mags. 'It's nice when we all have different things to tell each other.'

'It hasn't felt real, today' murmured Celia. 'I can't tell you why. I haven't felt as if any of it has really happened, I've been one step removed from reality.'

'Light headed?' suggested Gwen.

'Yes, in a way. Dreamlike.'

Gwen nodded.

'Too much contrast with life back home' she said. 'The brain can't take it.'

'Actually you may be right' agreed Celia. 'This sort of dislocation is interesting, psychologically.' Gwen rolled her eyes at Mags.

Gradually everyone appeared round corners, out of shops, along the esplanade. Sandy stood unobtrusively near the tram stop, watching the group assemble and mentally counting them all. They took the tram up to the station, and then the red train carried them along the lake and home; it took less than half an hour, in spite of several stops. 'It seemed a long leisurely trip on the lake, didn't it?' commented Gwen 'and so quick, to get back on the train.'

There was a slight hiatus at the station at the top of the hill; the minibus had been supposed to collect those who couldn't manage the walk back to the hotel, but it didn't materialise. The majority who were fit strode out down the hill and through the little lanes and gardens, but Sandy had to phone the hotel and wait for nearly half an hour before the transport arrived. There was considerable complaining, especially from Floral Patricia and Duracell's Pat. Gerald Harper, who had gamely got the most he could out of the day, sat on a bench and looked deadly pale. Linda told Mags all about it later in their room; it eclipsed even her own sufferings, and she said his knee was so bad he could hardly get into the bus. Several of the passengers and the proprietor's son who was driving gave him a fireman's lift into the hotel.

'Was Iris with him? I don't think she came with us' asked Mags.

'Yes – she's like a wet weekend, isn't she?' sighed Linda.

'Sure is. Like a wet weekend in Harrogate, wi' nowt to buy.'

They sat looking out of the balcony window. A slight breeze was getting up, flapping the edge of the curtains, and the last of the sun lit the mountain tops.

'You know, I really feel like a strong gin and tonic. It's our last night, apart from Cologne' said Mags, getting up 'and the bar is always packed later on. Why don't I go down and get us both a pre-dinner drink?'

'Lovely!' agreed Linda, a rare smile creasing her face. 'I'll have a gin and tonic too. Let me pay for them....'

Mags wagged a finger. 'Uh uh; it's all on Duracell, isn't it? Actually, though – '

'Actually, I don't want to put it on his bill.'

'Actually, I don't, either. We'll pay our own way.'

'Take my purse with you – it's by the bed.'

Mags was back before long, so they sat and enjoyed their drinks quietly.

'We've got three quarters of an hour' said Linda. 'Are you going to change?'

'Oh yes; and I've got to pack my new case tonight, the one with wheels.'

'You wouldn't believe the comments I heard' laughed Linda. 'Some people just stared at you walking along with it, some people made what they thought were witty remarks – '

'Who? Who did?'

'Duracell, for one. He made some awful quip about how your husband had summoned you home and you were jumping to attention, and quite right too. Somebody else, Wendy Harbottle I think, said it was probably full of duty free booze. They forget, don't they, that you don't have duty free any more, in Europe. They're in a time warp.'

Mags nodded. 'Iris thinks there are still Water Boards, and the DHSS.'

'We'll be the same' Linda sipped her drink 'before long. Perhaps we are already, and we don't know it. Can you close the window, now? I'm getting cold.'

Mags stood up to pull the glass door shut, and then she made for the wardrobe. 'Bathroom' she said 'and change. See you in ten minutes.'

The Eggberger Incident

Meanwhile Gwen and Gerrie were starting to pack in their room, stopping to talk and look through piles of tourist leaflets from time to time.

'People seem to have catchphrases, don't they?' said Gwen. 'Their own phrases, sort of mantras. Do I have one? I don't think you realise, yourself.'

'What do you mean? What phrases?'

'Celia says "there's no need for it", doesn't she. That's her stock answer to anything irritating.'

'I expect that's her upbringing. Her mother probably stood no nonsense, and the pupils at their school had to be jollied along. If they were homesick, or if they hurt themselves, or got bullied.'

'Yes, but it says a lot about her, too. That's what I mean. Unconsciously she's refusing to engage with things that are uncomfortable, or unpleasant. Don't think about it. Move on. Get over it.'

Gerrie looked at her with a broad smile. 'It sounds as if you're interested in psychology, too!'

'Isn't everyone?'

'I suppose they are. They might not call it that.'

'People watching is psychology.'

'Mm. Who else has these phrases, then?'

'Mags says "I didn't get on with my mother". I've noticed that several times, not just with us – someone asked her where she was brought up, and that sentence just popped out. I don't think Mags even realised she had said it.'

'Oh. That's interesting.'

'Linda, of course. "I had a car accident. I had a row with my husband". Like Meryl Streep in that film – ' she put on a heavy accent ' "I had a *farm......in Aaaafrica......*"'

'That's easy to understand. It was the defining moment in her life, wasn't it? The injuries she got are the root of her problems today. It's probably some sort of post traumatic thing, flashbacks and all that.'

'Possibly.'

'I haven't got a stock phrase, though, have I?'

'You say "I'm a widow".'

'Well, I am a widow! That's not the same.'

'I don't agree; I've heard you say it when it's not really relevant. It's as if you're trying to get used to the idea.'

'That's pretty shabby, Gwen. I am trying to get used to the idea. You can't imagine – honestly, I could get really angry about that. You just think what you would feel like, if you lost Roy!'

'I have lost him' said Gwen, her face grim. She tore up some leaflets and dropped them in the bin. 'I know now what he's been doing. What's happened. When you've spent that night with us, after the holiday – '

'I've got to stay! We get in so late, I can't get back to Winchester the same day – '

'I know that! It's fine! I'm saying, when you've gone the next morning, I shall tell him I know all about it. I shall tell him I've been to the bank, and they haven't got the deeds or the jewellery, and that I know he's sold the things from the farm and used my pension pot. I won't ask him any questions, I shall just tell him I know all about it. And I'm leaving him. I want a divorce.' She sat down on the bed and started folding some socks.

'You'd better be sure of your facts.'

'I am sure. All sorts of things fit into place now; I haven't told you about all of them. One of his friends tried to drop me a hint; more than once, actually. Anyway, if I'm wrong, he'll soon tell me.'

'You'd better get a good solicitor' Gerrie laid her case on a chair and opened it. 'That's really important. Doesn't Mags's Dudley work for a firm of solicitors?'

Gwen sighed. 'How horrible. I hate to think our dirty linen will be all over the town. But - yes. And they are a good firm; good reputation. Celia Hennessey uses them.'

'You need to make careful plans, then. And get good advice.'

Down in the restaurant the atmosphere was unsettled; there were undercurrents. The hotel had found a wheelchair for Adam Adamant; the Harpers had moved tables to accommodate it, and were sitting with the Quiet Americans and Win Burns, who actually seemed to be responding to Maewin's gentle approaches.

Monty and Helen Bewley were with Uncle Alan and the grey sisters, but the Bewleys did not appear to be speaking to Uncle Alan, who sat red faced looking straight in front of him. He looked dishevelled and seemed to have a cut on his bald head.

Mike and June Finch were talking a little too loudly, laughing with Pat Cooper, but Duracell was redfaced and almost silent, sitting with his arms folded across his chest and his chin in the air.

'What's going on?' asked Mags. 'Does anyone know?'

'I think it was the Eggberger Incident' replied Celia crisply, enunciating with great care.

'The what?' laughed Mags. 'You mean, when they were late back for the train?'

'I understand it was more serious than that' Celia unfolded her napkin. 'I was reading my book in the bar, and unfortunately one of those pillars keeps you completely hidden from people sitting in the window.'

Mags looked up sharply, but Celia still looked stony faced.

'Go on' encouraged Gwen. 'What did you hear? Don't keep us in suspense.'

'Duracell's Pat was talking to Sandy. And, credit where it's due, Sandy persuaded Pat that it wasn't worth putting in an official complaint.'

'About what?' Mags leant forward impatiently. 'Celia, for heaven's sake! You make it sound like an international incident – '

'It was, almost' Celia nodded. 'Uncle Alan and Reg went to find the brewery. And they did find it, but it was shut; it's closed down. But it's a beautiful building, apparently, with some interesting paintings of sheaves of corn and baskets of hops and things on the stucco, on the outside walls. And a very well tended garden round it, with pleached pears on wires and immaculate beech hedges. Anyway, Uncle Alan decided to take lots of photos, you know what he's like – '

They all listened intently.

'And suddenly up jumped a security guard from behind a hedge, demanding to know what they were doing on the site. He didn't speak any English, and those two don't speak German, and you know how crass Reg is, grinning and poking people and invading their personal space – '

'Oh, God' groaned Mags, her face in her hands.

'And it ended in a punch up.' Celia suddenly threw her head back and laughed, giggling until she had to catch her breath. 'One guard against the two of them' she giggled again 'but he's young and fit, and trained, and doing his job, and Laurel and Hardy over there had no chance. One of Uncle Alan's cameras got broken, and the strap of his binoculars, and he got a thump on the head. Duracell got kicked in the - '

'Goolies' said Gwen, laughing.

'Yes, well, I was going to say crotch' said Celia, trying to sound prim, but collapsing again.

'Oh, there is a God!' Gerrie clapped her hands.

'They look really sheepish!' said Linda, looking round happily. 'I bet they've both had a good telling off from their families. Well, it's embarrassing, isn't it?'

'I wondered why Duracell had to take the minibus back!' Mags put her hand over her mouth. ''E ain't 'arf walking funny....!'

'You know, some people really shouldn't be allowed out on their own.' Celia regained her composure. 'It makes you think, doesn't it? All these baby boomers with money to burn, lots of them in their second childhoods, we won't need holiday guides, will we? We'll need career diplomats – '

'And nannies for the elderly' grinned Mags. 'now there's a new industry, isn't there? Norland Nannies for pampered children, and Mogadon Minders for pampered pensioners who've lost their marbles.'

'I really don't want to think about that' said Gwen seriously. 'The thought of a whole generation of mad old biddies and senile potty Uncle Alans on the loose in Europe, or anywhere else, is too scary to contemplate.'

'No salad tonight. Soup.' Celia brought them back to the matter in hand.

'Is it?' Linda was surprised.

'Don't you remember?' asked Mags 'the menu choice we filled in this morning? Soup or pate and bread.'

'I didn't have any breakfast.'

'Oh no, you didn't. Well, pot luck then, for you.'

Once they had been served, Gerrie said 'Right then, Mags. Big responsibility. You have the floor for the last night of the holiday – or at least, the last as we know it. What shall we talk about?'

Where there's a will there's a relative

Mags bit the end of her finger. 'Hm' she said. Then: 'All right. Here's one for you. It might not work. It might be a bit too personal.'

'Go for it' Linda had been assigned bread and pate; she spread a slice and cut it in half. But she didn't eat any.

Mags asked brightly 'Have you made a will? And how did you decide who to leave what to?'

There was an audible exhaling of breath; Gerrie changed position on her chair.

'You know, that's a tricky one' said Gwen. 'Gosh. It really is.' She took a spoonful of soup.

Mags shrugged. 'I'll think of something else, then' she said.

'No, don't – it's something I've always wanted to talk to someone about, and you can't, can you?' said Linda. 'You wonder how other people approach the whole thing, but it's not a subject that's ever talked about.'

'Dudley must deal with these things all the time, doesn't he, Mags? Wills and trusts and inheritance, all that, at Pierce Wiggin Fry?' Gwen looked up.

'Yes he does, but that is absolutely no help at all when you have to think about it for yourself. Each case is different.'

'And doesn't Sadler Samuel advise about writing wills to avoid Inheritance Tax and things like that? You must have quite a lot of experience, Linda.'

'Mm. That's where solicitors and financial advisers cross over. But it opens another whole can of worms. Do you tie up your money, in something like a trust? That can take you out of liability for Inheritance Tax. But then what happens if you need it – it's back to the cost-of-nursing-homes thing again. If you do tie it up, they tell you it's all under your control, but it isn't. Not really. Who manages it? Who do you trust? How much does it all cost, and what if the charges shoot up in years to come? What happens if you suddenly have new members of the family to provide for, like orphaned grandchildren?' Linda spread her hands.

'But you have made a will? You and Stuart?' Mags dabbed her mouth.

'I suppose we've made two or three, over the years. One when we got married. One after the break up with his sister. We ought to look at it again, really.'

'They say you should go over a will once a year, don't they, in case things have changed' said Gwen. 'We've left everything to each other, and then to Gavin and Jenny. Mind you, I suppose now – ' she stopped suddenly.

'Now what?' asked Linda.

'Oh. I was just going to say, now that Roy is retiring, and we've paid off the mortgage, we ought to look at it again.'

'I don't see what difference that makes' sniffed Linda. 'But some people fine tune it a bit more, don't they – you could say that Gavin and Ruth ought to have more because they've got two children to bring up and Jenny's only got one.'

'Yes, but there are two incomes in Gavin's case, and those children will inherit from Ruth's parents. Jenny only has one income and Rosie will get sod all from her father.'

'You simply can't be fair to everyone' said Celia as the waitresses cleared the table. 'Meredith and Justin are doing very well. Meredith's father is a State Governor and the director of a bank. Her mother was a cotton heiress, going way back, there's lots of money in that family. Her mother's dead now.'

'Well, that opens up some dangerous possibilities' said Gerrie.

'How do you mean?'

'Supposing her father marries again?'

'All straightforward, I should think' Celia leant back as a main course was put in front of her.

'Not if he marries someone with children' Gerrie took her plate from the waitress. 'Or if he marries someone younger and they have children of their own.'

'Oh, I simply refuse to worry about the possibility of my daughter-in-law's father having more children half way round the world from here. There is a limit.'

'I'm just saying, these situations can be complicated, that's all' replied Gerrie.

'Absolutely' agreed Mags. 'That's why I brought the subject up. When you're a second wife, it's difficult.'

'Why?' asked Linda, toying with some pork in tomato sauce.

''Do you pool all your money, or do you keep it separate? I've got children and Dudley hasn't. Supposing I die first?'

'That's what mirror wills are for' said Linda.

'But how do I know he won't change his mind when I'm dead, and leave all the money that's meant for my children to a cat's home?'

'You've got to trust him' said Gerrie.

'And what if he remarries? And then dies, and all my money goes to some new woman he's taken up with? He wouldn't even have to marry her, co-habitees can hit the jackpot, can't they?' Mags was wide-eyed.

Celia patted the tablecloth. 'That's what I meant the other night when I talked about the pair bond, and protecting succession and family wealth. In some ways it was much easier in the old days.'

'No it wasn't – look at Dickens! All those court cases that went on for generations' exclaimed Mags. 'I think he was saying that the only people to get rich out of these situations are the lawyers. And so many women died young in the past, men had a succession of wives and lots of children. That's why women weren't allowed to own property themselves, and why rich men were so careful with a daughter's dowry. They had to be sure she married a man with similar means, so he didn't squander it all.'

'What have you and Kenneth done, Celia?' asked Gwen 'if you don't mind saying.'

Celia considered carefully how she was going to answer. Then she looked up:

'As a matter of fact, I'm going to our solicitor in London the day after we get back' she smiled. 'I'm staying in the hotel we usually go to, and then I've got an appointment in the morning to discuss all our family legal matters including our will. Sadly, it's because I have to arrange a Lasting Power of Attorney for Kenneth. Because of his dementia.'

A slightly awkward silence followed.

Linda broke it: 'Gerrie – I presume your beneficiary is Steven.'

'Um – I'm in the middle of various arrangements, actually – '

'But what about your little grandson in France?'

Gerrie looked stricken. 'I feel awful about him' she said. 'Of course I'll leave him something, but it's so hard to judge what's the right amount. If I leave him a lot it will single him out from his brothers and sisters, it might cause a real rift in that family.'

'You wouldn't be leaving him enough for that, surely?'

Gerrie exchanged a glance with Gwen. 'Who knows?' she sighed 'I might have had to spend thousands on care for myself by then. But Anton is the only blood descendant of my late husband. And the money came from him, so I know he would want his grandson properly taken care of. It's hard, it really is.'

Over dessert, Mags said 'One more aspect to this will business; what are you all going to do about leaving some to charity?'

Gerrie said firmly 'Leo left a sum of money to the National Trust, and some more to the Guide Dogs for the Blind. I shall do the same.'

'How does that work, then?' asked Linda. 'Is it a fixed sum, or a fraction of the estate? Some people leave, say, ten percent to the charity of their choice.'

'A fixed sum' said Gerrie.

'Because it's so hard to know how big the estate will be when you die' Linda persisted. 'If you leave, say, twenty thousand to charity when you think your estate is a hundred thousand, and then in the end you only leave thirty five thousand, you are depriving your heirs of rather a lot. Not that we've got any heirs.'

'Well, we decided on a fixed sum' Gerrie indicated that she wasn't going to pursue the matter any further.

'Linda, if you haven't got any heirs, what are you going to do on the second death?' asked Mags. 'Leave it all to charity? You don't want the government to get it, do you? At least, I assume you don't.'

'Good God, no.' Linda's curls shook fiercely. 'It depends how much it costs to go to Dignitas. I'm going to find out as soon as I get home, and start the ball rolling. Obviously, Stuart will have all the rest, and who knows what he will need to do with it in years to come. He may follow me to Switzerland. His future looks less and less appealing.' She sniffed. 'We've already decided that any estate left when we've both gone will be bequeathed to the local hospice. But it may not be much, in the end.'

'I've always supported children's charities' said Mags. 'My parents and grandparents did, so you just continue it, don't you? I remember my mother having coffee mornings in aid of Great Ormond Street. I think that was about the time that there was so much polio, wasn't there? Children on iron lungs and in callipers. It's like another age. Oh, and do you remember those Dr Barnardo's houses we used get given each term at school? To bring home? They were little thatched cottage houses that you put coins in, through the chimney. Did any of you have those?'

'We did!' Gwen and Gerrie spoke together. Gwen went on 'I'd forgotten all about them. I don't know what they were made of, some sort of varnished pulpy cardboard stuff, but they were like miniature dolls houses. You brought them back at the end of term and the money was counted, and you had a certificate to say how much you'd collected.'

'There was a round disc in the bottom, sealed over with paper' smiled Mags 'so you couldn't get at it. They would know straight away if you'd tampered with it!'

'Did you have those, Linda?' asked Gerrie.

'I went to a Catholic school. We raised money for Catholic missions in India and Africa; it was a big thing. People came once a year to show us slides and tell us all about the little native children and how we had to lead them to God.'

'You don't support those charities now, though?' asked Gwen.

'Not likely! Poor little sods. Who did they think they were, these white people sweeping in with their terrifying stories of hell fire and avenging angels?'

'They thought they were saving young souls' said Celia equably. 'You can't judge these things out of their time. It was how people thought in those days. They just accepted it.'

'Well, I think it was no better than the religion the natives had in the first place. All of them bloodthirsty.'

'So now you support the hospice' continued Celia.

'Yes. No religion involved, no far flung people that we don't understand, and don't understand us. Just helping to make people comfortable in their last days, and supporting their families. What's wrong with that?'

'Nothing' agreed Celia. 'It's a worthy cause.'

Linda shot her a sharp glance. 'What charities do you support, then?' she asked.

'My parents were great church goers. Church of England, of course. They always gave to the British and Foreign Bible Society, and Christian Aid. But for the past twenty odd years, we've given to the National Autism Society. We know someone who has a profoundly autistic son, and it really opened our eyes. We're leaving quite a substantial sum in our will.'

'It's good to have a reason' said Gwen. 'Something you feel connected to. I have a friend who runs marathons for Breast Cancer; she raises masses of money doing all sorts of things, because she lost her daughter from it at the age of thirty one. It was a terrible, terrible thing. The girl was engaged. All those dreams coming to nothing. The only way Carol can cope is to focus on raising money, doggedly, nothing else matters to her. In memory of Gemma. She has a lovely big picture of her in the living room - you know – one that was a studio photograph but it's made to look like a painting. And she talks to Gemma all the time, telling her about the fund raising and the latest research. It's the reason she gets up each day.'

There was silence for a moment.

Then Celia said 'I imagine it's animal charities for you and Roy, isn't it, Gwen?'

'Oh, yes. We like the National Canine Defence League as was, it's the Dogs' Trust now, and Riding for the Disabled. They use our paddock, now that Jenny hasn't got her pony any more.'

Celia looked at her watch. 'Well, time's getting on' she said, standing up and shrugging a cashmere cardigan over her shoulders. 'I need to go and pack. Tomorrow will be a long day.'

Preparing to leave

On her way up to the room, Mags stopped at the archway and saw that the computer was free. 'You'd think it would be in use much more' she mused. 'you'd expect a queue of people most of the time, waiting for it. But I suppose most of the guests, the younger ones, have iPads and iPhones and all those things, and most of our lot are too old. I can't imagine the Garsides or the Harbottles or Uncle Alan using the internet. Not here, anyway.'

She sat down and logged into Hotmail, to send a message to Dudley. Her fingers hovered over the keyboard as she tried to compose something suitable. She sighed and leant back in the chair, her head lolling back and her hands over her face. She breathed regularly, ten deep breaths, and then sat upright again and put her hands back on the desk. 'I don't feel any better' she said to herself. 'That did no good.' She sighed. 'What on earth am I going to say to Dudley?'

Letting herself back into Room 311 she found Linda fiddling with her cellphone. 'I'm not sure why this won't work' said Linda. 'I've recharged the battery but there may be something wrong with it. Or I can't get a signal.'

'Do you want to use mine?' asked Mags. 'I think it's all right; it was working a couple of days ago.'

Linda shook her head. 'Don't worry' she said. 'We'll be home in a couple of days. Stuart won't be expecting me to call him any more. Where have you been?'

'Sending an email to Dudley.'

'Celia had a word with me after dinner' said Linda. 'She said you already know – they've changed our rooms for tomorrow night.'

'Yes, I'll be sharing with her. You need to be on the ground floor, but it's a single.'

'I'm a bit miffed, actually' Linda screwed up her mouth.

'It can't be helped. The lift isn't working.'

'No, not about the room. I don't mind about that. I just don't see why Celia made such a drama about it, taking me on one side and talking to me as if I was a simple minded toddler. Did she think I would make a scene? Why couldn't she just mention it at the table, normally?'

'Maybe she thought you would be upset.'

'I'm more upset over the way she told me. I felt quite insulted, to be honest.'

There's no pleasing some people, thought Mags.

They got on with their packing; it took longer than they expected, but eventually they got into bed with just washing things and clothes for the next day still out in the room. Mags had rinsed and dried her kettle and scrubbed the mugs and packed them away in her new case, and found a plastic bag to wrap round the remains of the McVitie's biscuits. She smiled ruefully as she fitted the wooden letters in their brown paper bag safely inside a pair of shoes. Never mind, Sophie and Tom would love them. Normal life will be resuming far too quickly.

The next morning, after breakfast, Mags stood on the bottom step of the hotel staircase watching the Making Tracks group milling about. All the cases had been stacked in a lobby beside the reception area, and the sight of familiar figures in their travelling clothes almost brought a lump to her throat. Whether she liked them or not, they had become a temporary family; and they had all been affected by their experiences one way or another. Only a week had passed, but so much had happened.

Iris stood near the reception desk, looking sombre and quiet. She must be thinking about her sister's funeral when she gets home, thought Mags, and about the brother-in-law with Parkinson's. It must suddenly have hit her; now it's much more real. Gerald was beside her in a wheelchair provided by the hotel; diminished, shocked, a little frightened.

Floral Patricia was sitting on a chair just inside the restaurant area, puffing out her cheeks and distractedly running fingers through her hair. No sign of Simon. The Quiet Americans were side by side, standing, looking at the shelf of leaflets and guide books next to the reception desk. Mags stepped down into the foyer and made her way through the throng and out through the door.

In the square the sun was beginning to warm up the tables and chairs. The two grey sisters were sitting chatting to Monty and Helen Bewley; no Uncle Alan. At another table were Mike and June Finch and Duracell and Pat. Mags surveyed them all, noticing that Duracell's ginger hair was contrasting even more strongly with the grey roots in the sunshine; it had grown out noticeably in the week they had all been together.

Gerrie came hurrying out behind her. 'Bit of a flap!' she told Mags. 'We'd got all packed and they'd brought our cases down, and then the girl on reception reminded me that we'd had our wet clothes laundered. You know, from Salzburg, that bad day. I'd completely forgotten! So we settled up and we had to find our cases and unlock them and get the things in, isn't it odd how you can't get the same amount in that you started out with?'

'Especially if you've bought anything!' answered Mags.

'Well, we haven't bought much, really. Anyway it all took time, and we were so calm and organised one minute and panicking the next!'

'I'd like to leave a tip, for the staff' said Mags. 'Although they say in the literature that you don't need to. I think Making Tracks build it into the holiday charges. But I would like to, they've been really good. It's a bit embarrassing, though – '

'There's a china pig on the counter' replied Gerrie. 'I'm not sure it hasn't just been put there, I didn't notice it before. But anyway, people are putting little bits of money in it. It's discreet.'

'Oh, I'll go and do that, then' Mags turned and went back into the hotel.

When she came out again she saw Win Burns and the Garsides coming out of the shop; Sandy was across the square talking on a cellphone again. Linda fetched up beside her, breathing heavily and leaning on her stick. 'Sorting out assistance for Adam Adamant' she wheezed. 'He's going to need help changing trains and things.'

'You know, looking at us all, we've aged quite a bit in a week' Mags cast her gaze round the members of the group.

'I have, I know that' Linda said grimly.

'Duracell looks chastened and he's still walking badly; Floral Patricia seems as if she's on her last legs as well.'

Linda nodded. 'I think it's just dawned on Iris that reality bites when she gets home.'

'It does for all of us' said Mags reflectively.

'Have you seen Uncle Alan, though?' Linda cracked a smile.

'No?'

'He's got a whacking great plaster on his dome and he's tried to mend his binocular strap with sellotape!'

'Oh, poor old Uncle Alan! He's a game bird, you've got to give him that.'

'I reckon the only person who's going home in the same frame of mind that she came in is Win Burns' observed Linda.

'I think she's softened, slightly' said Mags.

'Huh! Not likely. Look, she's over there on a bench, reading that damn book again.'

'Maybe she's got several books.'

'Maybe'.

Gradually everyone assembled and stood or sat in the square waiting for the coach, which arrived on time. The hotel proprietor came out and shook hands, beaming and wishing them all a safe journey. There will be a new intake tonight, thought Mags; it'll start all over again. I wonder what those people are like? All grist to the mill for the hotel management, though. Just theatre, really.

Mags opens up, at last

There was very little conversation on the journey to Salzburg, most people taking in their last memories of the scenery and thinking their own thoughts. Almost mechanically they collected their cases as they were unloaded from the bowels of the coach and trundled them in a crocodile across the pavement and into the station concourse. Sandy was preoccupied with checking that everyone knew which platform they wanted, and which compartment they were booked into, and collecting the wheelchair which had been prebooked for Gerald Harper.

Eventually the group were settled in their seats, cases stowed in luggage racks, and the train moved out of Salzburg on the way to Munich. Gwen and Gerrie were opposite the Quiet Americans with a table between them; Maewin took out her book and began to read while Donald closed his eyes. Linda, who had been seated next to Win Burns, sat grim faced looking out of the window. Celia and Mags sat together, Celia in the window seat.

'Sandy is very good, you know' said Celia. 'We've been put together on the train because we're sharing tonight.'

'Do you think so?'

'Oh yes, definitely' Celia nodded 'For every train journey Sandy does a seating plan, I've been watching. People are put together either because they are travelling companions, or they've made friends, or because they haven't actually made contact with each other yet. It's quite an art, like working out the settings for a week long dinner party.'

Mags was impressed. 'I suppose you're right. There's a lot more to being a holiday guide than you think.'

'Psychology, again' Celia smiled. 'It affects every aspect of life. The more you know about it, the better you understand things.'

'I wish you could help me understand Dudley' Mags sighed.

'He can't be so very hard to fathom' said Celia firmly. 'There are only so many types of people, with variations of course, and if you start with the premise that men are children, you're halfway there.'

'I don't want to be married to a child' Mags replied miserably 'especially a needy, self referencing child. And anyway, you can teach a child, train them out of bad habits. See them making progress. It's far too late with Dudley.'

'You've probably got into behavioural patterns with him. If you went to counselling, you would be shown how to break those patterns and make progress with your relationship.'

Mags stared at her. 'Celia, with the best will in the world, you simply don't understand. You don't get it. Dudley is damaged, inconsistent, unpredictable – he makes me feel physically ill sometimes, and he is causing emotional pain to me, and hurting my relationship with my children. Irreparably, as time goes on. Do you know' she shifted in her seat 'sometimes I wake in the night with a feeling like a punch in the stomach. I feel as if I've been kicked - a huge, sudden contraction of all my stomach muscles so that my knees shoot up to my chest. And I think – what have I done? What have I done? I've married a man who is mentally ill.'

'Why did you marry him?'

'It was a gradual thing. We met; and for quite a few months we saw a lot of each other. He was coming to me for meals. He wouldn't stay the night, though; he said it was immoral, and that impressed me.'

'So where was he living?'

'He'd inherited his father's house. He was living there.'

'I suppose he moved in with you, in the end, so perhaps he feels he's on your territory and it's challenging his masculinity.'

'No, it wasn't like that. I sold my house and he sold his father's, and we bought this one together. As a new start for both of us.'

'Oh, well that should have augured well. So it must be something in his background. Tell me his story.'

'What, all of it?'

'If you'd like to. We've got a couple of hours on this train!'

'Well, it might help you understand what a problem I've got with him.' Mags stopped to assemble her thoughts.

'I suppose the first thing to say is that Dudley is an only child, but there was another boy before him. He died when he was twelve, he was drowned in a water pit, one summer, swimming with his friends. His name was Dudley, too.'

'That's already rather significant' Celia's eyes gleamed behind her glasses.

'I know. The first Dudley was the apple of his parents' eye; good looking lad, very clever, expected to go to university. He was good at everything – music, science, maths, sport. His parents were totally wrapped up in him and they were devastated when he died. Their reaction was to have another son and call him Dudley, and start again. Of course, his mother was almost forty by then.'

'A recipe for disaster.' Celia tutted.

'It was for Dudley. Almost from the word go, he didn't live up to the sacred memory of his older brother. The spectre of this perfect boy that he was meant to be was held out before him, something he could never achieve. His father used to beat him; but the odd thing is that it's his mother he blames, for standing by and not coming to his rescue.'

'Did you meet his parents?'

'No. His mother died quite a few years ago, and when Dudley's first marriage broke up, he went to live with his father. He'd died, too, by the time we met.'

'Tell me about his first marriage.'

'That was partly why I told myself everything would be all right. I thought, well, here's a man who's been married for nearly ten years, so he knows the score. He knows how a relationship works. He must be domesticated, if you see what I mean – he'll do his share of the chores and there'll be give and take, we'll both make a new start.'

'You didn't think that if he had a failed marriage already, there might be problems?'

Mags shrugged. 'I've had a failed marriage too; people must be allowed a second chance.'

Celia nodded. 'No children?'

'No children. I don't know why. I have asked him, but he just smiles and says "well, there we are." It's a stock phrase of his. If he doesn't want to open up any more, he says "well, there we are" and smiles and changes the subject.'

'At least you can work out what are the subjects he doesn't want to address, I suppose.'

'That's true' agreed Mags 'but there's an awful lot of them.'

'Which partner ended the first marriage?' asked Celia.

'Oh, she did. Their next door neighbour was a widower with two small daughters, and she struck up a relationship with him. Dudley says he was made a fool of; she was always popping next door to help with the girls, especially with baths and things like that. He says he didn't suspect a thing until she said she wanted a divorce. He says he had been proud of her, showing such kindness.'

'On the face of it, he sounds like the innocent party there.'

'Push-pull, isn't it? According to Dudley his father never tired of saying that if she had been happy, she wouldn't have left. It must have been his fault. Anyway, he found it too painful to stay in the house with her and this man and his children living next door. He stuck it for a few months but then he sold up and went to live with his father. Which was out of the frying pan and into the fire, from what he says.'

'Don't forget, you only have Dudley's analysis of all this. Only his version. If you haven't met his parents, and who knows what his ex-wife's perspective is on it all – well, it may all be factually correct, but the interpretation of it tells you more about Dudley's thought processes than anything else.'

'I know. I try to keep that in mind, but he's my husband. I must take his side. And after all, I've made my own mistakes.' She paused. Then she continued 'Dudley says he's moved on, now, but he hasn't. For instance, whenever anyone has a wedding anniversary like a ruby one, or golden, or whatever, he goes all wistful and melancholy, and says they're so lucky. Aren't they lucky? Isn't that man lucky to have a loyal wife who stays by him all those years? And when I say it upsets me because it sounds as if he's still hankering after Karen, he asks me if I don't wish the same thing? That my marriage had lasted so long? Surely that's not wrong? I can't say it is wrong, can I – but I feel it's wrong to keep on about it to me; I really do. If I say yes, I wish I had had such a long marriage too, it feels as if we're reducing our own to second best. Worse than that, actually – as if it should never have happened.'

'Well in that case, I don't think he has moved on, no. He's got to deal with this and put his energies into what he's got now. If he values it.'

'He says he has put the divorce behind him. But it was a pivotal moment in his life, he says. It changed him.'

'I don't think that's very likely. He's seized on this event where he can so clearly play the victim, as a sort of displacement activity so he doesn't have to face anything unpleasant, where he might find he's to blame.'

'I rather thought something like that, but not in those words. I'm not a psychologist.'

'Generally speaking, upsetting events like that don't change people, not at the age he was. If they have matured emotionally by then, they go through a recognised pattern of reactions, rather like grief, and eventually process it and move on. They go on feeling upset and betrayed if they think about it, but their response to life is pretty normal otherwise.'

'Dudley's responses aren't normal. At least I don't think so. He always turns it back on to me, very subtly. Implying that I'm the one with a problem.'

'Give me an example' said Celia. She took two bananas out of a paper bag. 'I bought these from the little shop. Would you like one?'

'Yes please.' Mags took a banana and began to peel it. 'An example. When we first met we used to have days out together at the weekend. He would nearly always take me to places where he and Karen had been.' She bit off a piece of banana and ate it.

Then she said 'We went to the house they lived in, the shops they had shopped in, the restaurants they had eaten in. He took me out to the coast during the summer, but always to places they had gone on holiday. He wouldn't tell me till we got there. The worst thing was one weekend when we ended up at a swanky hotel where he'd booked dinner and he insisted on showing me the room they had had on their honeymoon.'

'Good God.'

'I mean, we didn't go into it. We stood outside in the corridor and he stared at it, saying the number over and over again and shaking his head.'

'I'm assuming you didn't stay there on *your* honeymoon?'

Mags gave a short laugh. 'No. We didn't have a honeymoon.' She finished her banana and put the skin in a rubbish container by the seat.

'What did you say to him? Did you tell him it upset you?

'Well, I had lost a lot of confidence. In one way. I mean, I had been on my own with the children for a long time and started my own business; I had plenty of confidence about running our lives efficiently and making financial decisions and things like that. But I'd made a mistake with one man, and I thought, well this must be what they do. How they think. I need to learn this all over again. So I didn't say anything for a while, but in the end I said I don't want to go to all your old haunts, Dudley, I really don't. It would be much better if we started to build some memories of our own. We need to go to new places and enjoy them together.'

'Quite right. How did he react?'

'He stared at me. He said we would do whatever I wanted, he only wanted me to be happy. But how could we understand each other if we didn't share everything? His life with Karen was so much a part of him, he needed to share it with me. Wasn't a successful relationship all about sharing? That's what I had always said;

he quoted it back at me. Then he said maybe I wasn't ready for a new man.'

'Clever.'

'I know. I immediately felt I had overreacted. So maybe there was something wrong with me, then?' Mags shrugged. 'Dudley said he wouldn't mind going to places that featured in my own marriage, if I wanted to do that. But I didn't; that was over and done with, I was thinking of the present and the future, not the past.'

'Much healthier; unless you're blanking things out.'

'Oh, I'm not doing that. And if he's been particularly moody and negative and horrible, he'll come and apologise in the end. But then he gradually turns it round and says he's been really tired lately; and so have I. We've both been a bit edgy. I've been bad tempered too; and I'm not always easy to live with – he doesn't blame me, of course, but I can be difficult, and before I know it, he's implying that I'm the one with a problem, and I'm not really cut out for relationships am I? Not that he's blaming me, of course, and with the greatest respect, and so on. Sometimes I end up apologising just to move things on, and he gets a horrible smug look which makes me think he knows exactly what he's doing.'

'I expect he does' Celia commented, tight lipped.

'But that devalues both apologies, if you see what I mean. His because it's only a ruse to attack me, or the children, in a subtle way. And mine because I don't feel sorry at all, I don't feel responsible. I don't start these horrible atmospheres, he does. I never had them when I was alone with the children, or with anyone else. I think I'm pretty easy going, on the whole. I just hate being manipulated into confrontations.'

'Of course you do!'

'Dudley says 'you don't do confrontation, do you? You don't like having to stand up for yourself. You should do, you should say what you think.' But if I do stand up for myself, he says he doesn't want a row, why do I want a row? And off he goes to bed and I won't see him till the next day.'

'Well, goodness me' Celia breathed heavily 'I don't think I could live with someone as difficult as that. It's verging on a personality disorder. I'm not sure what to suggest. You certainly needed this week away – has it made you feel better?'

'It has, yes – day by day I've felt more liberated and full of life. Now we're on our way back, I'm beginning to get a niggling feeling of dread.'

'You shouldn't dread going back to your husband; that's appalling. Mind you, I'm trying not to think about what's going to happen with Kenneth........'

'Sorry to go on, but you did ask!' Mags gave a bleak smile.

'I had no idea things had reached this point. He doesn't seem as if he has a care in the world when I see him at PWF – always keen to help and quietly efficient. You never know how people are when they close their own front door.'

'I'll just tell you one other aspect of all this, and then I'll shut up, I promise. But it's a rather crucial one, to me. When my children – you know what I mean; they're adults, but we still say the children, don't we? – come over, we sometimes reminisce a bit. They talk about memories we have of when their father and I were still together, and afterwards when it was just the three of us, and have a giggle at some of the things that happened.'

'Naturally'.

'We try to include Dudley, and explain the context to him. If the roles were reversed I would love to get to know my stepfamily and be told all their funny little stories. But Dudley goes off into a terrible mood. He takes himself off to his study and won't come out. He says we're all talking about things that are nothing to do with him, and he might as well be out of the way, since he can't join in. It ends up with the kids asking where he is, and I go to fetch him, and he's just really, really nasty to me.' Mags looked up at the ceiling and bit her bottom lip.

'What does he say?'

'Oh, horrible things about how rude it is to talk about things that someone can't participate in, how he will never be part of my family, how men are belittled and ridiculed – '

'Wait, wait' Celia held up a hand. 'What's that about men being belittled?'

'He thinks that men are held in very low esteem by society today, and that's proved by all the sitcoms showing fathers as incompetent buffoons. And courts award all the benefits to mothers, and fathers are left out in the cold and have to pay exorbitant maintenance and hardly ever see their children.'

'I suppose he sees a lot of that at PWF.'

'I'm sure he does. And how most divorces are started by women, so women are the ones who destabilise the family, but they move another man into the home and the real father has to live in poverty in a bedsit.'

The rail steward brought coffee on a tray, and Celia and Mags each took a cup.

'I thought there were no refreshments provided on this train?' queried Mags.

'Oh well, perhaps Sandy's worked some magic. Just enjoy it!' smiled Celia.

'And he says that when the chips are down, and she has to make a choice, a mother will always be loyal to her children over anyone else.'

'That's true.' Celia sipped her coffee. 'We know that.'

'But it's as if he's testing me. He says quite nasty things about Raph and Sally, and then watches to see if I stand up for them. When is Raph going to stop indulging his interests and start doing a proper job? And he'll never find a wife if he stays in his ivory tower, or had I thought that he might not want a wife? Perhaps he's not the marrying kind? That sort of thing. Raph's had several girlfriends, and he's close to a girl in Delhi; another student. Her photo is on his screensaver and he Skypes her most days. Not that I'd mind if he was gay – I only want him to be happy.'

'Do you react?'

'Huh. My instinct is to react, and stand up for them, and then he either smiles and says, you see? You'd stand up for them against me, wouldn't you? So your love for them is the strongest. Or he says he was only saying what he thought, and isn't he allowed to do that?'

'Allowed. That's an interesting word.'

'And then you're left with two choices. Yes he is allowed, but I don't like what he's thinking, which makes me out to be a controlling witch. Or no he isn't allowed, which is just as bad. So I've been trying simply not to retaliate, and bite my tongue. On the principle that if he gets no response he'll give up, like a bully.'

'Well I think it is bullying. Emotionally.'

'So do I. But he doesn't give up, anyway, he keeps pricking and digging until I have to say something. He said he is suspicious of women who don't buy their husband's clothes for them; it seems to him that they don't care and aren't totally committed to the marriage. Sally doesn't buy Will's stuff, he's perfectly capable of doing it himself. He knows what he likes. Dudley was getting at Sally, that's what he was doing. He has digs at the fact that Will is good round the house, he often gets the evening meal if he's home, if he's off duty. Dudley hints that Sally doesn't look after him properly. That daughter of yours, he says. I asked him not to say that, and he went all innocent and puzzled, and said "Isn't she your daughter, then? I thought she was?" so of course I said, you know she's my daughter. "So what am I supposed to say, then?" he wanted to know. "If I've said something wrong, tell me what I should say. I only want to make you happy, I don't want to upset you". He's very good at saying 'I'm not being critical' or 'with the greatest of respect' before saying something totally critical and disrespectful'.

'Passive-aggressive.'

'Is that what it is?'

Celia nodded firmly. 'But I accept everything you say; and as I said before, Dudley puts on a good front in public.'

'Oh, I know. And in the room with Sally and Raph he's conversational and perfectly behaved, asks them questions, seems really interested. He's even chatty with Sophie and Tom. But the minute they're out of the house he starts to pull them apart, little by little. Lots of mean little character assassinations that make me feel utterly wretched. Last time as they drove away, he said "can I have my house back now, please?" I gave him a look and he grinned and said "Joke! Only a joke!" But it wasn't. He went off and moved everything slightly as if a hurricane had gone through the house, pretending to straighten pictures and correcting the positions of vases and ornaments. Shaking his head and huffing.'

'What do they think of him? Do they like him?'

'They made a real effort when we first got together, but they've discovered he can be moody. He goes off to another room. Or he goes up to bed, draws the curtains and goes to sleep. Once it was his own birthday and I went up to see what was the matter and he was out like a light. Sally and Will were a bit taken aback, but they packed the car up quietly and left. The minute they'd gone he was up, within seconds, and downstairs smiling and giving me a hug. When I said we'd missed him he said he'd had a headache, but I don't believe that. I said I wished he'd told us he was going upstairs because he didn't feel well, but he said he couldn't get a word in edgeways and he thought he wouldn't be missed. But then he took the opposite tack - for months afterwards he insisted that my children were rude because they'd left, on his birthday, after a good lunch, without even the courtesy of saying goodbye to him.'

'I don't suppose he tackled them about that.'

'No. It wasn't true, anyway! Besides, he's always nice as pie to them. He makes these withering remarks to me, and I just have to try and ignore them.'

'But I still wonder, what do your children really think of Dudley?'

'You know, it's never come up. They get tight-lipped sometimes and look a bit cross but they never say anything to me. I think they just accept now that their mother's married a rather difficult man, but she must love him. They have never, once, commented on it, which I think is pretty remarkable. They may talk to each other, of course. I suppose they don't want to put me in the position of being disloyal to Dudley. But he doesn't seem to mind me being disloyal to them, although if I don't stand up for them he gives me the impression he thinks I'm being a bad mother. And if I do, I get pilloried. I really don't know what to do, Celia.'

There was silence for a little while. Then Mags continued 'It's coming between us, between me and my family. They don't ring up much now. Dudley never answers the phone without checking the caller display anyway, and if it's one of them he passes the phone to me and says "It's your lot. Must want something." He hangs about listening – pretending not to, of course. So I usually go into another room. Then he sulks for hours after that because he thinks we've cold shouldered him.'

'I'm going to give it some serious thought' Celia finished her coffee. 'I hope there's a way forward. You can't go on like this.'

'Don't!' exclaimed Mags, reaching into a pocket for a tissue. 'You'll make me cry. I don't want to cry, I want to make my marriage work. That's all I want.' She blew her nose. 'And' she sniffed 'I want to get rid of this awful feeling that I'm losing my children. And my friends.'

Celia touched her on the arm. 'Oh, you're not losing your friends, don't think that for a moment.' She smiled warmly.

Mags gave a deep sigh. 'Well, but I am, by the back door. It's like wading through treacle' she said. 'You know we've got a double garage?'

'I didn't, actually.'

'My car is kept inside, next to Dudley's. There's enough room if you're careful. But if Dudley knows I'm going out after he comes home, or on a Saturday or something, he parks his car so close to mine I can't get into the driving door. If he doesn't think I'm going out, he parks it further over. I've tested it out.'

'That's bad' Celia frowned.

'I know. I couldn't quite believe it, so I started not telling him if I was going to the book club, or something like a film with a girlfriend, and if I didn't, I could get into my car easily. But if I let him know in advance, I had to go back in the house and ask him to move his car so I could get into mine. And of course he would delay, and say he couldn't find his keys, and eventually do it and be in a bad mood for hours.'

'That man has some real issues, I think' commented Celia.

'So if possible, I get in through the passenger door and slide over, but it's really difficult with the handbrake and everything, especially if I've got a skirt on – '

'Stop!' interrupted Celia. 'Just listen to yourself. This is crazy behaviour! He'll drive you mad at this rate!'

'I know. This is only the tip of the iceberg, Celia.' Mags said in a small voice.

'Good grief. What on earth else is there? Is he violent?'

'Oh, no. Not physically violent. Just difficult. That's the only word I can think of. I did manage one small victory, though. Dudley doesn't drink, much. He has the occasional glass of wine, but I like a glass when I'm cooking the evening meal. I've always done it; it's my way of dividing the rest of the working day off, starting the down time if you like.'

'Kenneth and I always had a gin and tonic at six o'clock. Whatever else had happened during the day, we met in the kitchen at six and had our G and T. It was the start of the evening.'

'Exactly. Well, Dudley doesn't like me doing that. He never stops me – that's the thing, he never tries to stop me doing anything. He just makes it seriously uncomfortable until it's not worth it. If I try and arrange any social events he keeps saying he's got something one evening, for work, but he's not sure when it is. It goes on for weeks and weeks, and in the end he tells me to go ahead and book it anyway. And then a couple of days before, he claps a hand to his forehead and says "Thursday? Did you ask them for dinner on Thursday? I've got to go to a Chamber of Commerce meeting, so sorry. I forgot. You'll have to go ahead without me." I usually cancel things; you can't entertain friends as a couple, if one of you is out. That's what I mean about losing my friends.'

'Difficult. You may have to call his bluff.'

'Anyway, one day he hovered in front of me as I poured a glass of Merlot and watched the potatoes boiling. He grinned and said "My name's Mags, and I'm an alcoholic!" I don't know what came over me, but I shot back "My name's Dudley, and I drive my wife to drink!" I said it smiling, and lifted the glass and said "Cheers!" and I don't think he knew what to do. He's never mentioned it since. But he did have one of his heart to hearts a couple of days later, wanting me to promise I would tell him if he did anything that upset me, and saying that he only wanted me to be happy. And he loved me very much. And if I left him it would be the end, for him; the only reason he has for living is to look after me, that's all he's ever trying to do.'

'Manipulative.'

'Well, but aren't we all?'

'Not like that.'

'And whatever he says, I think I understand men pretty well, actually. They want to be comfortable, they want approval, they want praise. They don't like their routine upset, especially as they get older. I'm talking about men like Dudley, of course, who've been brought up pretty much middle England, with middle class values and mores and conventional role models – '

'I have to say, public schools do much the same to boys from further up the social scale. Kenneth is incredibly repressed in some ways. I don't think we've ever had a conversation about emotions or feelings, or – ' Celia shook her head vigorously 'no, we're talking about you, not me. Go on.'

'And honestly, he is looking after me. He's in total control of our money, he checks our statements and investments every day and makes sure we're getting good deals on things. He'll change our gas and electricity and internet providers and negotiate with them – he does the same with our car insurance and house insurance and everything else. He's really good at giving me a lovely holiday every year. He won't choose where to go, I'm always supposed to do that.'

'You've been to some wonderful places.'

'I know. I feel awful saying all these things; he can be really kind. And generous. And nobody's perfect – I'm certainly not.'

'Do you love him?'

'You have to remember no relationship is perfect. I was probably expecting too much – I thought this marriage would put right all the things that went wrong with the last one. You pin too much on to it.'

'But do you love him?'

'Makes you think of that interview with Charles and Diana when they got engaged. When they were asked "Are you in love?" and he said "Whatever being in love means". At the time I could have thrown a brick at the television screen, it was so humiliating for the poor girl. She went scarlet. It was a real indication of what was to come.'

'You still haven't answered!' smiled Celia.

'I tell him all the time that I love him. He's so fragile about that; he says that one woman left him, so why not me? I tell him every day I love him.'

'Do you think you'll convince him?'

Mags was silent for a moment. 'It's me I'm trying to convince' she answered quietly.

Cologne, again – and Celia has been thinking

They spent most of the last part of the journey dozing, reading, queuing for the WC and chatting to Sandy about the next train and to other members of the group as they passed up and down the carriage.

One would think, mused Mags, that the beginning of these holidays would be the most challenging for the leader, with everyone out of their comfort zone and not knowing each other, and liable to get lost, and unused to their luggage and where they had stowed important documents. But in fact it's the journey home which is the most unsettling. All the build-up and preparations are accelerating into the past, and the memories of the holiday itself are already losing their sharpness. The train journey across Europe is no longer an adventure but an endurance test, and the best you can hope for when you get home is a mountain of washing, a pile of post, an overgrown garden and a sense of anticlimax. For some people, the long trek back to Blighty heralded the beginning of a discomfort zone, and the start of a much more challenging era. And so the Making Tracks group were ragged, irritable and unreliable. Sandy began to look a little strained.

Somehow everyone was disgorged from the train at Munich station and they and their cases were safely loaded just over an hour later on to their connection for Cologne. Another Making Tracks group joined them, on their way home from a holiday in Vienna, so the carriage was crammed with people who ought to have been on friendly terms but weren't. Sandy and the other tour leader had several quiet chats in the little area between the carriages; Mags watched the body language and was amused to see shrugs, folded arms and open handed gestures of dismay, followed by a lot of serious nodding.

One or two people were still cheerful enough to attempt a conversation with members of the other tour. How was Vienna? Palaces – how lovely. Salzburg was wet and cold, unfortunately. A river trip? That sounds nice. We had several lake voyages, smashing, they were. Desultory, and apart from two brothers on the Viennese holiday who found they lived in the next village to the Harbottles, the interaction soon petered out.

Oddly, Cologne station didn't look nearly so interesting this time in spite of the ornate wrought iron advertisement for Eau de Cologne suspended from the vast canopy over all the tracks. The temporary wooden slopes and walkways were scuffed and crowded; the concourse was dirty, the other passengers had a frayed and unfriendly look. Once again the cases were rattled away in cages to the hotel, in the rapidly falling darkness, and Sandy's wobbly crocodile made its way across two lanes of a road full of cones and diggers to the side street and the familiar lighted reception area. This time it seemed much more utilitarian, and the small foyer irritated the guests as they jabbed each other with impatient elbows, dropped cases on sore toes, or snatched room cards from the desk clerk.

Celia was keen to make sure that Linda's ground floor room was suitable. She gave her room card to Mags and said 'You go on up – I'll just see Linda inside. Be there in a few minutes.'

Mags made for the lift, but remembered it was out of action just before she saw the sign. She pulled her new wheeled case up the stairs and nodded to herself; much better. Her twin room with Celia overlooked a well tended garden area at the back; it was bigger than the one she had shared with Linda and was better equipped. Lovely. On the pillows were two small packets of 'schlaf-schafe' – sleep sheep. Like tiny jelly babies in the shape of sheep, they were a little joke – in the slightly heavy handed German manner – and she thought she would ask Celia if she could have them both to take home to Tom and Sophie.

It was only a few minutes before Celia tapped on the door. She tucked her Samsonite neatly in an alcove by the bathroom and hung up her jacket in the wardrobe before turning to say 'we're expected downstairs as soon as possible for a buffet supper. They're bursting at the seams tonight, so we have to go in shifts. Are you ready?'

'Give me a minute just to freshen up and brush my hair. It's driving me mad!'

There was no choosing between free tables this time; an Asian couple rose from their seats and Celia and Mags dived for their places. The two grey sisters and Win Burns were standing in a corner, looking about them vaguely as they tried to find somewhere to sit down. No sign of Sandy, or the other tour leader. The buffet food was adequate; good, even. But already the counters were untidy, the soup bowls had all been used and there was a wait while more were brought, still hot from the dishwasher. The casseroled chicken ran out as Celia and Mags waited in the queue, so they had a hot fish dish in a dill sauce instead, with breadcrumbed mushrooms and a side salad.

'I don't want any dessert' said Mags, taking off her glasses and passing a hand over her eyes. 'There's that cheesecake again or some fruit, but they've put some bananas and apples in a wire holder on the reception desk; I think I'll grab one of those and go back to the room.'

Celia rose: 'Good idea.' They shouldered their way through the waiting queue and each chose an apple from reception.

Celia paused at a rack full of tourist leaflets. 'We've got a couple of hours tomorrow morning' she said, picking out two or three 'so I'd like a brisk walk down to the old town, to see the cathedral and the river. It's not worth going now, it's dark. I've been before, but not for about thirty years I should think. Coming with me?'

'Yes, I'd love to' nodded Mags. 'I haven't been to Cologne before. Apart from our stopover on the way.'

They turned and started up the stairs. 'Good. I've got two information leaflets and a town map. We can have an early breakfast and then an hour and a half or so to explore.'

Mags was in a thoughtful mood. She sat in an armchair watching Celia as she glided elegantly round the room, setting out her photograph and travelling clock and neatly positioning a book on the bedside table. She had packed overnight things separately, so her silk nightdress came out and was folded at the foot of her bed, and a rather splendid coral brocade sponge bag went into the bathroom. Mags noticed for the first time that she was developing a very slight hump at the top of her back, and that she had the beginning of bunions. Sad.

Eventually Celia finished her routine and came and sat in the other chair, with a slight sigh. 'I've been thinking about you and Dudley' she said in her clear tones. 'I have one or two suggestions, if you want to hear them. Perhaps you'd rather not.'

Mags turned her head. 'No, I would like to hear them. I keep thinking I've made my mind up, and then I'm not sure. You know a lot about what goes on in people's minds; tell me what you think.'

'You might not like some of it.'

'Celia, I don't know you very well, but I know you a bit better now than I did. I know you'll be honest, and I can take that. Honestly.' She smiled.

'Well then. I think you've got a whole number of things going on here, and it would help you to tease out what's what. Some of it's about you, and some of it's about him, and some it is just life. You won't be able to change that part of it – you don't get a handbook with a nice convenient index, to look up the problem and get a shiny glib solution. And you don't get a lifetime guarantee. That's a lesson we all have to learn.'

'No, I know that' Mags was serious again. 'I'm not expecting miracles, I know nobody's life is perfect. I know I'm very lucky, I keep telling myself so. I've been through all those thought processes. But, to use another cliché – you only get each day once. It really isn't a dress rehearsal, and surely you can't be blamed for wanting each day to be as fulfilling as possible, not exhausting and unsatisfying, and – well, painful.'

'Of course not. But you can choose whether to be hurt or not. You can choose your reaction. That's how you can change your patterns of behaviour, and your partner's pattern of behaviour as well.'

'Celia, that's all very well. But he goads me, he goads me!' Mags threw up her hands. 'I've tried not reacting, but he keeps on until I say something. He says, tell me what you think? Tell me what you're feeling? If you won't tell me what you're feeling, then we haven't got the close relationship I thought we had. I don't mind if you tell me I'm upsetting you, because how can I make sure I don't do it again if you don't tell me what I'm doing wrong?'

'That's quite a healthy approach.'

'No, but it isn't. Because however diplomatic I am, he can't take criticism. He twists it all round bit by bit until it's my fault; I'm too sensitive, I don't understand men, I've been damaged by a failed marriage, I didn't get on with my mother, so I'm not good at family relationships. I end up feeling so wretched and useless that I really don't care any more what happens.'

'He didn't get on with his father, though, did he?'

'No, his father beat him for not being the first Dudley. That's how he puts it. So he says we're both broken human beings and that's why we should stay together. I don't want to be a broken human being; I don't believe I am, and it's a mindset I've never had and I don't want to develop now. I've always been an optimist. I've always been strong.'

'Good. Stay strong.'

'I used to think Dudley was – difficult, as he is – because his marriage failed. Now I think, in fact I'm sure, that it's the other way round. His marriage broke down because he's difficult. I sometimes find myself sympathising with Karen. Lucky you! I think; you escaped and found a nice family man and you've got a happy home now. I've got the prickly bundle of barbed wire you left behind.'

'That's a very unproductive line of thought. I should stop doing that. You can't possibly know about Karen's motivation and point of view.'

'I sometimes think he's slightly autistic. Or Aspergers, is it?'

Celia leant her head back on her chair and looked at the ceiling; she tapped the padded arm with two fingers of her right hand. After a moment or two she turned to Mags and said 'I'm going to tell you something, I think. You've trusted me with some very personal concerns, and I feel honoured for that.'

Mags looked at her, surprised.

'You think he may be autistic; that's a wide spectrum. A huge number of people are mildly autistic, in that they have trouble reading other people's emotions, and they relate everything to themselves. They have difficulty in company and are very uncomfortable in social situations. You may well be right about Dudley.' Celia stood up. 'I think I'd like a drink – would you?'

'What sort of drink?'

'Alcoholic' nodded Celia firmly. 'We could have something sent up, a bottle of wine perhaps, but they're run off their feet downstairs. It might take forever. Let's see what's in the minibar.'

They found the minibar well stocked; they could have had a small beer each and a miniature of whisky, but they chose two small bottles of wine and two eighth bottles of brandy.

Celia fetched glasses from the bathroom. 'Last night of the holiday. Back to the real world tomorrow, and the waters will close over our heads again. I think we should have a heart to heart and drink to the future.'

'Good idea' nodded Mags. 'The future is all we've got – that's my point!'

They clinked glasses and sat down again. Celia took a sip of wine and said:

'Autism. It's something I know much more about than I would choose to.'

Celia drops a bombshell. Two, actually.

'You said you and Kenneth were leaving money to the Autism Society, because you knew someone – '

'It's my son, Adrian.'

'I thought his name was Justin? No, hang on, that can't – '

'I have three children. Adrian is the youngest; by quite a few years. He's severely autistic, and it's utterly devastating. Totally destroying. It's terrible for the person with the condition – it's not an illness, it's not a disease, it's a condition. When you first have it diagnosed, you have no idea what it means, for the whole family. And it only gets worse, and Adrian got big and heavy and out of control. His tantrums were terrifying.'

'I had no idea.'

'It affected Justin and Charlotte so much that it became unacceptable. We couldn't go anywhere with Adrian once he was out of his buggy or reins, which went on until he was about eight, I suppose. Their friends wouldn't come and play, because Adrian scared them. He smashed up their toys and threw food everywhere. I couldn't leave Adrian at home to take the others to their tennis lessons or swimming and I couldn't take him with me. We did engage an au pair, three actually, two of whom were supposed to be used to children with behavioural problems, but they couldn't cope with him.'

'I'm not surprised.'

'Water held a fascination for him – he couldn't leave it alone, but he didn't understand the dangers. We lived in officers' quarters then and I just couldn't keep him in our garden. He would run off in any direction, towards rivers or ponds or pools, over roads, across the firing range or the drill square, anywhere he wanted.'

'What a nightmare.'

Celia sighed. 'Kenneth's career was threatened. Nobody actually spelt it out, but he was nearly at the top of the tree and he was expected to have his wife with him on postings. We would have found it impossible to travel, and represent the Queen and the Head of the Armed Forces at various functions abroad, and on board official yachts, and formal occasions like that, with Adrian to look after. So, very sadly, I chose to put him in a residential home.'

'That must have been a really tough decision.' Mags shook her head.

Celia sniffed. 'I don't think you can imagine. Just because your child is severely affected by a wicked, wicked condition, it doesn't mean you stop loving him.'

'Of course not! You must love him even more, in some ways.'

'You have a lot to work through' said Celia slowly. 'You feel angry – incredibly angry, as you would with anything that damages your child. And you feel guilty that you've brought him into the world with such a handicap; you feel protective of him, and protective of the other children, and your husband, against him. And then you feel guilty about that. I found studying psychology was helpful, I must say. It didn't change anything, but it helped me to understand the dynamics of what was going on.'

There was silence. Celia broke it: 'My hair went white in eight weeks when I had to surrender Adrian to an institution. Eight weeks. It's surprising what psychological trauma can do to the body.'

Mags was quiet, thinking. Then she asked 'Kenneth is developing Alzheimer's, you say; could there be any genetic connection? Between that and autism?'

Celia drained her glass and broke open the top of one of the brandy bottles.

'Adrian isn't Kenneth's son' she said matter of factly.

Mags drew a sharp breath. 'Oh. Oh, I see.' She finished her wine, too.

'Well, you don't. Because Adrian's father is Kenneth's brother, Alistair.'

'Good God. Oh.'

Celia poured half the brandy into her glass, but put it down again without drinking any.

'Do you remember that first morning at Ischlkirchen, when we sat on a bench and waited for the boat trip?'

'Yes, you told me about Alistair and Kate, and Burnham Staithe, and how Alistair was only two years older than you – oh, I see.'

'Quite.'

'He used to come and help you with Justin and Charlotte in the summer, while Kenneth was away. It must have been easy to....I can quite see how....oh dear.'

'Oh dear is rather mild, really. So you can imagine that another dimension was added to the whole problem with Adrian; perhaps I was being punished for committing adultery with my brother-in-law. Or worse, Adrian was being punished for my misdeeds, and what sort of God does that? Only an Old Testament one.'

After a pause, Mags said slowly 'I don't want to speak out of turn, but I think....I think people have the wrong idea about you. Oh, that sounds awful; I mean they have an image of you which is not – it doesn't reflect the life you've lived. The things you've had to come to terms with, to cope with.'

'I know people think I'm starchy and privileged and don't live in the real world.'

'Well, yes. But everyone has a skeleton in their cupboard, haven't they? Of some sort. Something that bothers them, or keeps them awake at night, or makes them feel guilty.'

'I wanted to tell you about mine because I thought you might understand; and it might help you put things with Dudley in perspective.'

Mags thought 'What a holiday! Now I'm privy to two people's secrets about their sons who were conceived when they shouldn't have been. I'll never need to read another novel in my life.'

Aloud, she said 'Does Kenneth know?' a pause, then 'What about Alistair?'

Celia shook her head. 'Didn't tell anybody. There's no need for it. It would only have made things far worse. But I do sometimes feel I want to punch Alistair – he's had such a smooth life, everything's gone well for him; and he can be insufferably smug. That's why I've sent Kenneth off to Norfolk, so that he and Kate can finally take on board the fact that Kenneth is losing his mind. I've coped with bloody Alistair's son all these years, and made sure that bloody Kate was spared the pain of knowing about his parentage, I think I'm entitled to a certain amount of sympathy.' Celia took a swig of her brandy. The she smiled. 'I did have to resort to one piece of subterfuge, though' she said.

'What? Why?'

'Well, Kenneth was away; we were in Norfolk, for the summer holidays when Adrian was conceived. Even Kenneth would have been able to – do the math? Is that what they say nowadays?'

Mags nodded.

'So as soon as I knew I was pregnant, back home in Wiltshire, I pretended there had been a burglary and that I was traumatised and needed Kenneth at home. He got compassionate leave for a fortnight.'

'I can't imagine you traumatised, Celia!'

'Hm. We all have our Achilles heel. Anyway, it was all right. I bundled up my jewellery and some money and some family silver, and Kenneth's medals, and stuck it in a sack, and hid it under a hedge behind the NCO's Mess.'

'I'm surprised the Police didn't look for fingerprints....'

'It was the MP – the Military Police. It was all on MoD territory, so the civilian police weren't involved. One of their trained dogs found the sack and we got it back within three days. I had the vapours for a fortnight, though, and Kenneth jolly well had to comfort me. A lot.' Celia grinned.

'Well, well.' Mags poured some of her brandy.

'Well, well. Exactly. So perhaps you can see that I might be able to help you improve things a little with Dudley. I do know something about human nature, although perhaps for the wrong reasons.'

'So what do you suggest?'

'I think you have to separate some of the strands. Some of what you worry about with Dudley is just men. It's how they are. They have the emotions of children, and you coped with your children all right, didn't you?'

'Yes, but as I said, I don't want to be married to a child!'

'Tough. I didn't want to be married to an Alzheimer's sufferer.'

'You married a man eighteen years older than you, so you must have known that would kick in one day.'

'I think that's rather a facile remark. I thought I might be a widow quite young, that's true. You can try and second guess everything bad that might be ahead of you, but you'll never succeed. Supposing I had died in an accident and Kenneth was left with young children to bring up? Supposing Kenneth was killed on manoeuvres? Supposing I had fallen in love with his ADC and run off to Borneo? You can sit on your hands all your life, or you can get on with it and see what happens.' She paused. 'And cope with it.'

Mags digested this. 'Forrest Gump's chocolate box' she commented.

'Who?'

'Oh, a film. Never mind.' Mags sighed. 'Well. I think perhaps I was on my own too long. I did cope with it. Life. Bringing up the children, running a business, making all the decisions. My mother.' She grimaced. 'Now I feel that I could do all that again if I had to – not the mother bit, thankfully, and not gainful employment. Unless there was no alternative. But being Dudley's wife has to be worth it. It has to add value, if you see what I mean, life has to be better with him than without him, and more often than not it isn't.'

'Have you ever wondered if he feels the same?'

'He certainly doesn't! He can't do a thing for himself. He can't bear being on his own. He needs constant reassurance and support and approval. I've stopped doing so much of that – it's never ending, it's never enough. I have to look at every little thing he's done and tell him how grateful I am and how clever he is. I tried being the same with him – look! I've ironed your shirts, I hope they're all right! I hope they're how you like them! I thought he would see that I was teasing him and he would connect it with his own behaviour, but he didn't. So I don't do it any more, and I only give him the minimal amount of praise for things like checking the bank statements or booking the cars in for service. And that means the gap between us is widening.'

Celia frowned. 'This is a man whose emotional development was interrupted. Arrested. His basic emotion is fear; that you will leave him, that he's not loveable, that he will fail. He knows he isn't his sainted older brother, so he's already failed in a deeply existentialist way, and that's just how it is. It's too late to put that right, in some ways – I should spend about ten minutes loudly cursing his parents, if I were you, and hoping they can hear you. And then never give it another thought.'

'So it's hopeless.'

'No, it isn't hopeless. He's still talking to you, even if you have to pick your moment. He's desperate to make you happy, but he doesn't know how.'

'He wants me to be happy so that he feels better, not for my sake.'

'We can explore that one, if you like, but there's not much point. You wanted your children to be happy, didn't you, but I imagine part of it was so that you could describe yourself as a good mother.'

'Mmm. Oh. Well, I can see that, I suppose.'

'So Dudley, being a child, needs a framework to reassure him. He's quite typical, really, although a bit more extreme than most. You find a lot of these types in the armed forces, especially amongst the officers, where they've been sent off to prep school very early by absent fathers and mothers devoted to serving the needs of the regiment. Or the Chambers. Or the University, or the Church, or the Government Department or whatever. It's how the Establishment continuum works. We're all broken on the wheel, unless we drop out altogether and go and live in a yurt in Wales.'

'How do other people cope, then? With men like this? How do other wives manage?' Mags took her glasses off and polished them on the bottom of her blouse.

'You just have to develop ways to work round them, to create some modus vivendi that you can accept, but you can't change the fact that they're children. Well, boys. If they thought and acted and spoke like us, they'd be women, wouldn't they?'

'Oh. Yes. I hadn't thought of it like that.'

'How often have you heard a woman say "It was my idea, but he wouldn't do it. In the end he came round, but he thinks it's his idea now. He tells everyone it was his idea, and I just keep quiet". Does that sound familiar?'

Mags laughed. 'Certainly does!'

'Well, there you are then. And how often do you decide to tell him something he doesn't want to hear after he's had something to eat? Or when he's just done something awful so that he wants to please you?'

'Oh God. That's true as well.'

'Well, we all have to do these things. It's the skill of the partnership; except all the skill and the intuition and the finesse is on one side. But it's the only way to make it work. Think of the problems I had when Kenneth retired and was around much more. All the time now, of course. I had to learn all this very late on – up to then, we had months on end when I ran everything, and short bursts of unrealistic idyll when he was home on leave. I think everyone ought to learn a bit about psychology; you need it more and more as your life goes on.'

'Yes, you do. You're right.'

'So, yes, I do think Dudley's got a whole heap of problems. They go back to his parenting, and you can't alter that now. You might help him understand it, though, and he'll enjoy the sensation of the two of you trying to unravel it together. It'll make him feel important, and also he'll feel more confident that you really do love him.'

'If I do.'

'Can't answer that one for you; only you know if you love him.'

'He won't go to counselling. I suggested it, but he's completely rock solid on that.'

'So you'll have to do it. But you'll have to keep slightly detached; every time he tries to draw you in, to include you in his skewed emotional situation, you have to be absolutely firm. Don't let him superimpose unstable states on you. Don't get cross, just tell him he doesn't understand, you are well adjusted, thank you, and from that position you can help him. If he wants to put you in a fictional position where you are as wobbly as he is, you'll have to tread a path without him.'

'Tough love.'

'Exactly.' Celia finished her brandy. 'That was fantastic. I don't want any more, but that was just what the doctor ordered.'

'I don't suppose Duracell will foot the bill here!' smiled Mags. 'He must have paid a huge amount at Ischlkirchen. We all had wine every night and the men had beer and schnapps and the women had gin and tonics and Camparis – I hope he knew what he was doing!'

'Oh, I think he did. And just imagine; twin sons, and both dead. It makes us take another look, doesn't it? How would you ever get over that? I can imagine that winning all that money would mean nothing, really.'

'You know, I think everyone's life is a drama. A fascinating story. All the people we've met have had a tale to tell. I think I'll do a writing course and have a go, there's so much out there. You don't need to invent it.'

'No. And one more thing I wanted to say about Dudley. Or suggest, really.'

'Go on' Mags tipped the rest of the brandy into her mouth straight out of the bottle, not bothering with the glass.

'There must be some things he does and says which make you happy.'

'Oh, there are. I've said that. He does try.'

'So you need to use positive instead of negative reinforcement. Think of, say five, or ten – certainly not more than ten – things you appreciate about him.'

'What sort of things?'

'A mixture would be best. You can even manipulate things and train him that way.'

'You make him sound like a dog!'

'I love dogs. And a well trained one is admired wherever he goes. So there's nothing wrong with that.'

Mags smiled. 'All right. What do mean, manipulate things?'

'Write a list for him of things he does that make you happy, and they could be the opposite of what he's really been doing. So you could say – Number One, it makes me happy when you welcome my children into our house.'

'He doesn't, though.'

'But he's a man; he won't understand that. It just turns into accusations and defensiveness; he'll be thinking about his own pride, and not what's really going on here. But he may understand it if you put it the other way round; he'll think, next time they come – I'll welcome Sally and Will and the children, and Raph, because when I do, it makes Mags happy.'

Mags nodded.

'You have to remember' Celia was at her most didactic 'men are at a perpetual disadvantage. They're an open book to us, but to them we're a complete mystery. What else bothers you a lot?'

'Seeing my friends; having a bit of a social life. He doesn't seem to want one.'

'So you say – Number Four, or whatever – it makes me happy to know that I have a lovely home to come back to when I've been out with friends, and that you're waiting for me.'

'Ah.'

'And you could say something like: Number Five – it makes me happy when you buy me flowers for no reason at all. It makes me feel that you're thinking of me even when you're at work, and then when you come home I can give you a loving kiss!'

'Yuk!'

'All right, use your own words, but do you see what I'm getting at?'

'I do, actually. I wish he would make me a cup of tea more often. And I wish he would put his coat and keys and briefcase and scarf and all that stuff away, instead of leaving them all over the kitchen table.'

'So you say it makes me happy when you make me a cup of tea; and when you put your coat away without being asked. And you need to include things he already does, like – it makes me happy that you manage our money so well and I don't have to worry about it. Don't do more than ten, and sprinkle them about a bit, so when he reads it he thinks aha, I do that already! And she appreciates it!' Celia held a forefinger in the air.

Mags looked doubtful. 'I think it's a really good idea' she said. 'If anything works, I think this might. I just worry that it might be too late, and he might be too locked into his behaviour patterns to change.'

'You say he is on edge, because he only wants to make you happy. And he's afraid he isn't achieving that, and you're going to leave him?'

'That's what he says, yes.'

'So this will give him something tangible to measure himself against, and as long as you keep a copy of the list and praise him and smile a lot when he's acting on it, he'll be more relaxed. And so will you. It's worth a try, surely?'

'Oh, it's worth a try. More than that. It's a really good idea, Celia – thank you, I'm very grateful. Honestly. I'll think hard about what's best to put down and I'll do it. Unless I get home and realise that there really isn't any point in going on. I was almost at that stage when I left.' Mags got to her feet. 'I'll just go down and check that Linda's all right, I think. Be back before long' and she made her way to the door.

Celia drummed her fingers on the arm of the chair and took a long look at her photograph of Kenneth.

Conversations

Downstairs Mags had to knock three times, increasingly loudly, before Linda heard her and struggled to the door.

'Oh!' she said, surprised. She looked dishevelled and hot. 'Do you want to come in?'

Mags hesitated. 'I don't want to disturb you' she said. 'I needn't come in, I just wanted to check that you're all right.'

Linda opened the door wider. 'Come on, then' she said. 'Bit of a mess, sorry – but then if you will bugger off and share with Celia....' she closed the door and leant on the furniture until she could collapse on the edge of the bed. Mags perched on the corner of the dressing table.

'So you're okay then? I must say the room is very poky, but it's only for one night.'

Linda stuck her chin out. 'Huh. And you should see the bathroom; it's back to a strip wash until I get home. Does your mobile work?'

'It does in our room, but we're higher up and there's a clearer view outside. I haven't got it with me – do you want me to go and fetch it?'

Linda shook her head. 'Don't bother. I think there's something wrong with mine – I keep charging it but I haven't been able to get a signal since the day before yesterday. Or before that. I can't really remember, the time has gone all odd on this holiday.'

'You want to contact Stuart, is that it? Shall I see if they have internet here for guests to use?'

'No, no, it'll wait. I emailed him this morning from Ischlkirchen and we'll be home tomorrow. I told him I would do as I said – get off at Ashford. I can get a train to Canterbury and a taxi home from there, although it'll be ever so late.'

'We can all do that together; Gerrie is staying the night with Gwen and going home to Winchester the day after tomorrow, and I'll be going the same way. We can share a taxi, at least for part of the journey at the end.'

'I suppose Celia has Parker coming with the pink Rolls Royce' sniffed Linda. 'Yus, Milady' she said mockingly, tugging her fringe 'though I don't suppose she'd know what Thunderbirds was. They don't show it on BBC Four.'

Mags felt colour rush into her cheeks. 'That's not very nice' she objected. 'There's more to Celia than you think. She's had – more to put up with – well, a more normal life – not that you'd exactly call it normal, I suppose – '

'Oh, stop trying to suck up to your new best friend' Linda shook her head impatiently 'I'm sure you've been having cosy girly chats in your room. I don't care whether she comes with us or not, quite honestly.'

'She's going on to St Pancras; she's got an appointment the next morning with their bank and the solicitor.'

'I thought they were with Pierce Wiggin Fry?'

'I think this is a bit too complicated for the Canterbury branch, to do with Power of Attorney for Kenneth because of his Alzheimer's. So she has to go to the big office in town.'

'Big fleas have little fleas' dismissed Linda, reaching for her pill box. 'Well, thanks for coming to check on the old crock. I'm still alive.'

I'm not reacting to that, thought Mags. She pulled herself away from her perch and said 'I expect I'll see you at breakfast. Although Celia and I thought we would get up early and have a quick look-see round the old town since we don't have to catch the train till twelve. She's been before but I haven't; I'd like to see the cathedral and the river, the part where the old buildings are.'

She let herself out of the room, thinking that Linda was increasingly reminding her of a female Eeyore. She began to climb the four flights of stairs. A grin spread over her face as she took her thoughts further – so who were the others in their little band? Celia was definitely Kanga. Gerrie was sort of Piglet – pink and slightly plump and fluffy, but a much stronger personality; she had a core of steel that Piglet lacked, and, rather than trying to please, would speak her mind. Gwen might be Rabbit; long and skinny and a bit battered, trying to do the best thing but rather out of her depth. An air of slight panic. You could imagine her leading an expedition and getting lost in the fog, like Rabbit. Look at the near disaster in Brussels, when they had got lost and found the Mannequin Pis but nearly missed the connection and had to practically run at the double back to the station.

She fetched up, only slightly out of breath, outside the door of their room; encouraging – it showed she was still in condition. Dog walking was good for you in so many ways. She was just about to tap for Celia to let her in when she realised she hadn't decided which A A Milne character she was herself. Perhaps she was Pooh; puzzled, kindly, getting into scrapes while trying to help other people. A bear of very little brain. It would be nice to be Owl, able to read and spell and someone that people went to for advice. Only Owl was actually punching way above his weight and was, to be honest, not nearly as clever as he thought he was.

She had better try to be Tigger.

In their room, Gwen and Gerrie were operating in an atmosphere of tight lipped tension.

Gwen sat at the dressing table brushing her thinnish gingery hair and trying to ignore freckles and age spots and rather more lines, both under her eyes and on her neck, than she had been aware of. This was one of the refurbished rooms and the light above the mirror was merciless.

She turned to Gerrie. 'The moment of truth, tomorrow' she said. 'I really don't know what I'm going to say to Roy. Or when.'

'Is he meeting us at the station?'

'I told him I'd let him know which train we'd be on from Ashford, but I don't want him to come. I don't. I'd rather get a taxi. It'll be so late, anyhow.'

'Are you going to say something straight away, or wait until I've gone?'

'Hah! I expect you'd like to be well out of range before the excrement hits the air conditioning. Just like at home. You and Mother always managed to be miles away from the seat of the fire.' Gwen put her brush down and sighed. She turned off the light above the mirror.

Gerrie had taken an earring off and was twiddling it in her fingers. 'Now' she said 'I think that's enough. I didn't know about any of this until you told me – '

'You dragged it out of me!' Gwen exclaimed, bridling. 'I kept saying I didn't want to be disloyal, but you – '

'Well, I could see something was wrong. You couldn't have kept it from me for the whole holiday, and it was much better to get it off your chest right at the beginning. Besides, who else can you confide in? You needed to talk about it.'

'I still have the hurdle ahead of me, though. It's starting to make me really nervous; how can I act normally when I get home? When I know I've got to sit him down and say that I've been checking up on him, and I think he's just ruined our family.'

'Natural justice says that he ought to feel a lot more awkward than you do. He ought to feel hugely guilty and embarrassed and ashamed.'

'Whatever he's going to feel, when I get back he won't know what's coming, he'll think it's like any other homecoming. I've got to pretend everything's coming up roses to start with. And then I've got to go for the jugular. I'd rather do anything else.'

'The anything else would be kidding yourself that you've made a mistake and there's really a perfectly sensible explanation for empty bank accounts, disappearing deeds, missing jewellery and antiques, non-existent Premium Bonds……'

Gwen raised a hand. 'All right! All right! I know what I've got to do, you don't need to tell me. It doesn't mean I'm not dreading it.

But if I do turn out to be wrong, I'll have wrecked our relationship in any case.'

After a moment, Gerrie replied 'So – do you think you're wrong?'

Gwen got up, picked up her sponge bag and made for the bathroom. 'No' she said shortly.

Celia had undressed while Mags was with Linda; she let Mags in to the room and then went and sat in the armchair in the window. Mags went to the loo and when she came out Celia asked:

'Was Linda all right?'

'Yes, she was, really. Her phone seems to be on the blink, but she doesn't need it. She's not worried. I think she's a bit miffed that we're sharing and she's on her own, but she'll have to put up with it.'

'You've gone above and beyond the call of duty, you know. While we've been away. Getting things for her and generally keeping an eye – she ought to be grateful.'

'Yes, she ought – but the people who ought to be grateful are often the ones who aren't!'

'You're learning.'

'Psychology?'

Celia nodded. Mags looked at her, and suddenly realised that Celia was in a long silk nightdress with thin straps, and it was obvious that she only had one breast. Her right breast was small but perfectly normal; but on the left side the shaped material hung empty and loose, and there was a white threadlike scar reaching up and under Celia's arm. By the time this had registered, Mags was aware that her face must be giving her away.

Celia smiled. 'Hope you aren't squeamish' she said. 'During the daytime I wear a prosthetic, but at night I'm as nature didn't intend, but has had to adjust to.'

Mags shook her head quickly. 'No, no, not squeamish. Of course not. Sorry, I'm really sorry – did I look horrified?'

'You did a bit' admitted Celia.

'Just shock. Surprise. I had no idea. Was it cancer?'

'Yes. One of those things; it happens to so many people, doesn't it? Still, it's not something one would choose.'

'No.'

Mags decided she could either feel awkward or take her cue from Celia; and if Celia could take such a breezy attitude, she could.

'Did they get it all?'

'They think so. I'm still going for six month check ups; it was only two years ago. Nearly two and a half, I suppose.'

'You didn't lose your hair. That must have been some comfort.'

'I had some chemo, but not enough for that. It meant nobody knew about it, which is what I wanted. I was diagnosed early.'

'It must have worried Kenneth, and your children....'

'Hah!' Celia gave a short laugh. 'As I said, nobody knew! You must think I'm a very secretive person, but I'm not really. At least I've never thought I was. All I've ever done it try to minimise the damage of things.' She suddenly looked very pale, almost transparent, with the light shining through her white hair, the pearly night-creamed skin, the glint of her frameless glasses, the oyster silk nightdress. And that telltale white thread emerging and travelling across the taut white skin.

Mags had a sudden rush of emotion; pity was too simplistic a word, and sympathy made you think of arum lilies and incense. Empathy, perhaps, and a deep admiration for the quiet courage of this woman, her refusal to let events grind her down, her sheer persistence.

'How did you keep it from them?'

'Another subterfuge, I'm afraid.' Celia uses words you don't often hear nowadays, but they're often absolutely appropriate. 'I pretended I was going on holiday with a group of friends. A rail holiday.' She caught Mags' eye with a mischievous smile.

Mags nodded slowly. 'Oh! Tricky, I should think.'

'It was. Kenneth was easy to deal with; he was already pretty bad and he wouldn't ask any questions. Charlotte was due back in the UK for some leave, so I told her I was exhausted from looking after her father and needed a couple of weeks off, and she said she would Fathersit as she called it. I was tempted to talk to her about my operation because she's a surgeon, of course – '

'Of course.'

' – but I resisted it. I'm glad I didn't tell her. No need for it. Why worry her? It turned out that it's probably been caught in time and it hasn't spread. I went off to a private hospital; it cost a considerable amount but it was worth it. The trouble was I had created a bit of a three volume novel. Oh what a tangled web we weave, when first we practise to deceive!'

'It sounds to me as if you'd thought of something very plausible.'

'Not really. I had to invent the people I was going with, the holiday company, whether I was going abroad, all sorts of things. I decided we were going to Scotland because if I used the mobile telephone it would look odd if the call came from this country and I was supposed to be in Switzerland!' Celia yawned 'and I wouldn't be coming home with a tan!'

'Mmm.'

'I thought about my passport, too. If I was supposed to be abroad and there was an emergency at home, the family might contact the foreign office if they couldn't get hold of me. So fictionally I needed to be near enough to cut short the holiday if something happened. Oh dear. After I got home I had to make up so many stories! Even about the weather. I'll never forget being all woozy from the anaesthetic and saying please, please can you find out for me if it's raining in the Highlands. Please. I need to know. They thought I was delirious, I think!'

'Goodness! You wouldn't think it would be so complicated.'

'And the friends I was going with – to start with I thought I would just ring two or three and ask if they could back up my story if anyone ever asked. But I couldn't, when it came to it. I couldn't ask people to tell lies, and anyway they would have had to be doing things that would fit in. My friend Eileen told me she was off to Australia for six months to see her grandchildren, and she was going to be my fallback in case I needed corroboration. So it was no good, I had to invent three friends from the U3A, including one whose husband was a rail buff. He was coming with us, and organising the whole thing. So I could honestly say I didn't know, if I was asked about the itinerary beforehand. No idea, I would say. Randolph is in charge.'

'Randolph!' Mags giggled.

Celia shrugged. 'Randolph Scott' she yawned again. 'Sorry, tired. Travel and wine and brandy' she stood up 'So this time it had to be all above board and genuine. A real holiday with real friends. No fibs. I'm going to bed'.

A quick look at Cologne

Mags went into the bathroom to undress and wash. 'Randolph Scott' she thought. 'Strange. Not sure I understand that; Celia must have had a reason, I suppose.'

Mags didn't wake up until eight o'clock in the morning; shocking, and most unlike her. It took a couple of moments to orientate herself. Not in Ischlkirchen. No Linda. Twin beds. Unfamiliar room. Woolly head. Brandy; ah yes, and Celia. Long conversation. Oh, they were going sightseeing, and she had to get moving! She sat up and pushed her hair off her face, trying to focus. Celia was sitting in one of the armchairs looking immaculate, beautifully made up, with her pale linen travel suit on and wearing her expensive low-heeled court shoes. Her Samsonite was perkily upright near the door, clearly packed and locked, with the labels properly attached to the handle.

Celia smiled. 'Good morning, Mags!' she said in her cut glass tones. 'I'm sorry, but I've already been down for breakfast. I've brought you some yoghurt and a little fruit puree, and a Danish pastry.' She stood up 'I can make you some tea, or would you rather have coffee?'

Mags threw aside the duvet and swung her legs over the edge of the bed. 'Oh, that would be great – thank you. Tea. Please. I'm very thirsty.'

'I expect you are. Alcohol in those quantities at bedtime can be dehydrating. Never mind, it was our last night. We deserved to push the boat out.'

Mags showered and put on some makeup, and was back in the bedroom in under ten minutes, tightly wrapped in a bath towel. Fronds of damp hair trailed over her forehead. She shook them out of her eyes and drank all of her cup of tea in one go.

'That's better' she nodded. 'I think the brain cell is flickering into life.'

'Shall I make you another?'

'No' Mags shook her head 'One's enough. Maybe we'll have a coffee somewhere while we're out. Give me five minutes and I'll be ready.'

And she was. By twenty-five past eight they were locking the room door behind them, Mags having dressed and eaten the breakfast that Celia had brought while she packed and brushed her hair. The last thing she was about to do was to fasten the Swarovski necklace chain behind her neck, but today she hesitated, looking at the glittering coil cupped in her hand. Then she dropped it into her sponge bag and zipped her case up.

Downstairs there was an air of disorganisation. Some little groups of Sandy's Making Tracks guests were sitting or standing in knots looking aimless, while two or three of the sister group were clearly ready to set off into Cologne and looked disparagingly at Sandy's. They were better dressed and seemed better educated. 'The Palaces lot; Vienna and Dresden' observed Mags. 'They think they're a cut above us.'

'Well if so, it says more about them' replied Celia as they swung through the revolving doors and out into the street.

They spent an hour roaming around the vicinity of the Cathedral, including going inside to have a look, but were disappointed.

'I remember it as much more impressive' sniffed Celia in the semi darkness. 'They say you should never go back.'

'There's a lot you can't see' commented Mags 'with all the work that's going on. Ladders and scaffolding and things. But quite honestly, I don't think I'd warm to it anyway.'

'Fourteen bombs hit it during the war. This information sheet calls it a perpetual construction site; they haven't finished repairing it yet. I'm not quite sure why they saw fit to make it a World Heritage Site in nineteen ninety six, but some things are inexplicable. There's a rather lovely triptych which dates from fourteen forty two which we ought to look at.'

They saw what they could; a floor mosaic from eighteen eighty seven was covered up, and a tenth century crucifix and twelfth century Magi shrine didn't move them as much as they would have liked. 'There's so much of this gilt stuff' Mags said 'we've seen a lot of these reliquaries and Madonnas in Austria, haven't we? All very ornate and overblown. I feel I've reached my limit, rather.'

'Quite honestly' said Celia as they left by the West Door, 'In spite of the scaffolding and the discoloured stone, I like the outside better than the inside.'

They stood a little way away and tilted their heads back, studying the crennellated spires standing out against the clear blue sky. 'There's something marvellous about things that reach up to the heavens' breathed Mags 'like mountains....'

'Yes, that's all very well' replied Celia crisply 'But this one was only finished in the nineteenth century. Those spires are Victorian. And I do find Catholic architecture a bit unnecessary.' She turned to start down the steps towards the shopping area.

Mags and Celia had already decided to buy some *4711 Echt Kolnisch Wasser* – Mags wanted some for Sally, and Celia for her sister in law Kate, always hard to buy for apparently, but she ought to have something as a thank you from Kenneth. However, although it was nearly a quarter to ten by the time they found the two hundred year old shop in the Glockengasse, it was closed. No notice seemed to give any information about opening hours, so they gave up and walked on.

'I'll buy some in another shop' said Celia. 'Kate won't know where I got it, will she?'

'I think quite honestly it's a bit old ladyish for Sally. If I can't get it in the famous shop I'll forget it and find something else. Maybe in Brussels.'

'It was owned by Proctor and Gamble for a while.'

'Oh, no!' Mags looked horrified. 'Really? What a shame. That takes all the romance out of it. I've gone right off it now!'

They made their way to the Rhine frontage and the old town buildings, set back from the quayside.

'Very pretty' approved Mags. 'I love the tall narrow houses and the pastel colours. A bit like Amsterdam.'

They found somewhere for a cup of coffee and a piece of ginger kuchen at a pavement table. But although the sun was out it was surprisingly cold, and they soon got up and walked on.

'Those are the river cruisers' pointed Mags. 'You see them in the brochures, don't you, but they really are just like floating hotels.'

'Floating Travel Lodges' sniffed Celia. 'You wouldn't catch me on one. They're like battery hens, all cooped up in there – it's not much better than a line of containers bolted to the hull of a barge. All the windows the same, all the net curtains, floor after floor. No thanks.'

Wandering along the quayside they found several places where the river cruisers were moored while their occupants took guided excursions ashore. Mags was shocked to see that the top of the steps were guarded with padlocked iron gates and barbed wire. She shivered. 'You know, the atmosphere here is quite different from Austria; almost menacing. There's much more rubbish around, and people walk about with hard faces. The stations are the same. There was something more human about Austria – the part we were in, anyway.'

From time to time they caught sight of some of their group; Simon and Floral Patricia were on the steps outside the cathedral talking to Iris Harper. Gerald seemed to be immobile; he must have been left in the hotel. The quiet Americans came loping back from a purposeful walk further down the quayside and turned up a side street.

'They're going to visit the Museum Ludwig' said Celia. 'I spoke to them at breakfast; they're very keen on British and European modern art.' She looked at her watch. 'Shall we make our leisurely way back? We can walk up the main shopping street and get back to the hotel in about twenty minutes. That'll be about right.'

On the way they spotted Gwen and Gerrie coming out of an upmarket clothes shop with the two grey sisters. None of them were carrying a bag, so no sale there.

'I feel sort of spaced out' said Mags as they rounded a corner and began to skirt the cathedral steps. 'It's a bit of a dream. You see people you recognise amongst all the strangers, but they're nothing to do with you, really. I've had some very entertaining conversations with some of them, but I'll never see them again. Like the sort of dreams you have just before you wake up, or when you've got flu.'

'To me, it's like an impressionist painting' answered Celia. 'I was good at art when I was young. I went to art school, but it was fabrics I was attracted by, the history of fabric design and manufacture. But you know, what I would like to do now is to paint again, seriously. This whole scene lends itself to a dreamy impressionist water colour, with just a dab of paint here and there to show that a few people are depicted more clearly; the ones we know. Everyone else is watery and unclear, out of focus.'

'That sounds amazing – I'd buy that painting!' laughed Mags. 'So that's one of the things you want to do before Maslow closes in on you?'

'Yes, one of the things. There are so many. I feel that time is running out; but I've got to banish that feeling and stay positive, and energetic, and make sure I actually do things rather than just talking about them.'

'You go, girlfriend! Turn the hourglass upside down!'

Celia shot her a frown. Then her brow cleared: she said 'I have got a rough timetable. I think I can more or less stick to it. Tomorrow I'll be in town to see the solicitor and the bank; there's a lot to do concerning wills, and Power of Attorney for Kenneth, and I want to set up a trust fund for Adrian so that he'll always be looked after. Then I've got to get Kenneth home and think about proper care for him – we can have people living in, but I need to interview agencies and get some references, to make sure that he only has the best. After that, towards the winter, I can start to think about myself. I might do an Open University course to study more about psychology, and I definitely will paint. And our U3A branch has asked me to stand for the steering committee. The AGM is in the spring. I haven't decided about that yet, but I might do it. I think they could do with some fresh ideas, and someone with a bit of organising ability, apart from the fact that they could run a lot more courses than they do.'

They were within sight of the hotel. Mags felt caught up in Celia's enthusiasm and determination to be in control of her life. It's infectious, she thought; I hope I can remember this feeling when I get home, and not go back to feeling flattened by what's been happening to me. She smiled.

Celia glanced at her, and smiled back. 'You look a bit happier today!' she said. Mags couldn't tell her that she had been thinking about A A Milne again, and wondering whether Celia was actually less of a Kanga, and more like Rabbit, who never waited for things to come to him, but always went and fetched them.

So she said 'Oh, I'm all right' and pushed open the revolving door. Inside, sitting on leather chairs in reception or a little further away in the bar were almost all the Making Tracks party.

Nearly home, and good news for Gerrie

Linda had found a seat quite a long way in, and was talking to Floral Patricia. In the bar at a table for four were Duracell and Pat, with Mike and June Finch. Gordon Garside was talking to Uncle Alan, who still had a plaster on his head and now a purple and green bruise was beginning to creep out from underneath it. He was nodding, his head bobbing up and down, as Gordon droned on about the trains they would be taking that day. He had already been over to the station and made rounds of all the platforms on various levels, so he reported on every engine he had seen and what he had found out about it. Uncle Alan continued to bob, but his eyes were glazing over.

The next hour was rather fraught. Two Making Tracks groups were coming together, with two tour leaders, going on the same train, but in adjacent carriages. Drinks bills and room cards had to be dealt with at the counter, where it was difficult to queue because of all the cases waiting to be caged and trundled to the station. People got up, sat down, looked for their coats and handbags, tripped over walking sticks, went to find toilets. Mags did what she could to help Linda, but kept losing her in the melee. She saw Sloping Simon launching himself above the scrum like an anxious giraffe, hunting for Floral Patricia who seemed to have disappeared. In the end Mags gave up and decided Linda would have to fend for herself.

Eventually everyone was in the station, corralled on an upper platform under the correct letter for their carriage number, and Sandy and the other tour leader counted heads for the umpteenth time. Adam Adamant sat forlornly in a very battered wheelchair belonging to the station, with Iris resigned and pale beside him. By now everyone knew the drill, and they waited patiently for the cages to arrive with their cases. 'Probably got all ours mixed up with the Vienna lot' Duracell said to nobody in particular, rocking back on his heels with his hands in his pockets. But to their credit, the hotel had stacked all the luggage very efficiently, room by room, even keeping couples together.

Pat, looking resigned, hauled two tartan ones off and put them down beside a sheepish Duracell who had limped to a bench for a sit down.

Cologne to Brussels; Mags found when she got home that she couldn't remember that part of the journey at all. She, along with many of the others, had spent most of it deep in thought and processing all that she had seen and heard and the conversations she had taken part in. At Brussels they had a fifty minute time lag before the Eurostar would take them to Paris and on under the channel to Ashford International and St Pancras. Celia had been right, though, all those days earlier; fifty minutes is nothing like fifty once you have managed to get your luggage off the train – no porterage this time – and struggled to join the others in your group while you are counted, yet again, and try to keep up and follow the Making Tracks sign through hundreds of people of all nationalities going in different directions down escalators and across concourses and up other stairs to the next platform. And all this in a noisy environment where echoing announcements are being made in an incomprehensible language, and you are trying not to get your pocket picked or your bag snatched. Not to mention finding a loo, if you need one, and waiting for Sandy to chase up the wheelchair that has been ordered.

Gerald and Iris had to take the lift, so Sandy got them in, carried their cases, took the others up the escalator and assembled them at the top, collected the Harpers, rejoined the group and did another head count. There was one heart stopping moment when Uncle Alan couldn't be found; Monty and Helen looked blank – they had been talking to the Ryecarts and hadn't noticed where he had gone – and four or five minutes went by before he wandered back through the crowds. He had spotted a news stall and wanted to see if they had a birdwatching magazine. They hadn't. Sandy grew pale.

They were only settled on the Eurostar just in time; under ten minutes before departure, and once the ticket inspector had spoken to Sandy and the other tour leader, checked group tickets and counted heads, the doors slammed and they were on their way. An attendant tweaked the wall of cases at the end of the carriage so that they weren't leaning at drunken angles ready to fall on someone when the train accelerated round a bend.

Gwen and Gerrie were in adjacent seats on the train. Gerrie got her mobile phone out and switched it on. 'Oh' she said 'there's a message. Two messages.' She thumbed the screen. 'They've made an offer on the house.'

'Which house?'

Gerrie looked irritated. 'My house in Winchester. What do you mean, which house?'

Gwen shrugged. 'Could have been the one in Italy.'

'That's not on the market yet. And it's an apartment.'

'Oh, don't be so picky. Is it the Italian chap?'

'Mmm. And the second message is about the shops; he wants those too. All part of his plan.'

'Is he offering a good price?'

'He's being very clever. He's only twenty grand below my asking price for the house; I could live with that, if that's all he was interested in. But he's way below on the shops – I'll have to negotiate hard on those.'

'Why not just let him have the house?'

'Don't be silly! He knows and I know – and he knows I know – that the house isn't the issue. I could sell that any time, or wait till the market picks up and sell it then. The shops are a liability, to me anyway. Most of the stock was bought before Leo died; turnover is right down, and if the managers leave I'm in real trouble.' Gerrie scratched her nose. 'In the current climate people aren't exactly falling over themselves to buy antiques. And the agent says – and I believe him – that he's had no other interest at all, either in one shop or all of them. This Italian chap, Vincenzo, has been over three times now. He's gone through the books. It fits in with his business plan, I can see that, but any house would do. He doesn't have to buy mine. He does want the shops, though. But he knows I'm pretty keen to offload them, so he's sweetened his offer with a good one on the house.'

'What do you think you'll do?' Gwen sounded anxious.

'Oh, I'll sell. I'll do a deal with him; I wouldn't cut off my nose to spite my face. I think the best way would be to negotiate on the shops and then accept his offer on the house. But the agent wants a sale, of course, so he'll play both sides to the middle. I shan't know what he says to Vincenzo Thingy, and he won't know what the agent says to me. We'll have to work out something we're all happy with in the end.'

'You must miss Leo at times like this.'

Gerrie gave a short laugh. 'Ironic, isn't it? I really wish Leo was here to deal with it all, but if he was, we wouldn't be dealing with it, would we?'

'Do you think they're sneering at you for being a fluffy little blonde? Perhaps they think they can wipe the floor with you.'

'Oh, they can't do that. I think the agent is clued up; I'm no fool, and Leo taught me a lot about negotiating. Never accept the first figure, for one thing. I know I can raise him a bit – his offer is laughably low, and he must see that I am aware of that. I'll have to tell the agent I'm quite insulted that he thinks he can even relay such an amount to me. But the bottom line is, there's nobody else lined up, I want to sell, and Vincenzo wants to buy. So we'll get there in the end.'

'Perhaps it's all a front for something shady. Perhaps Vincenzo is Mafia.'

'Perhaps he is. I don't care, that chapter of my life is over and I'm moving on. Anyway, his wife is English.'

'So you've been told.'

'No, I've met her. I didn't like her, but I've met her. She came to look at the house and pretended to like my cat.' Gerrie put her phone back in her bag. 'Anyway, don't worry' she said 'Your half million is safe. It's there if you want it.'

Gwen settled in her seat and looked glumly out of the window.

Linda had been allocated a single seat opposite Win Burns. They glowered at each other periodically all the way, first of all to Lille while there was a twenty minute wait and considerable comings and goings through the carriages, and then the entire way to Ashford. Neither spoke. Once again the Harbottles and the Garsides were sitting together just behind, so Linda was treated to an unwanted series of anecdotes about Ruby and Titus and their irresistibly cute escapades, while Gordon and Colin droned on about the relative merits of Tomorite and a homemade equivalent on greenhouse tomatoes. When they had exhausted that topic, well the on other side of Lille, they embarked upon the history of tomato and potato growing on the Isle of Wight. Win read a book. Linda had run out of reading matter so she closed her eyes and tried to blot out the sound.

Food and drink were served; a welcome if short lived respite for Linda, although she ate next to nothing. Most of the travellers had wine, and were brought a second little plastic bottle just before the tunnel. The conversation rose to a buzz, and people began to get up and go over to each other to say goodbye. Celia left her seat and went to lean over Mags'.

'I'm just trying to work out who's going on to St Pancras and who's getting off at Ashford' she said. 'I particularly want to say goodbye to the Chisholms, they're charming people, and Tabitha and Teresa, but they're going on.'

'The northerners are' said Mags. 'I think they're staying over again and going up by train in the morning. Good idea – it's far too late to try and go another two or three hundred miles. I don't know about the Bewleys and Alan, but I expect they'll do the same. Win Burns goes on to Cambridge, so she'll probably get home late tonight.'

'I'm not saying goodbye to her' snapped Celia 'ghastly woman. She ought to go inside her front door, turn round and come out again with a different attitude.'

'I need to find Sandy before we get to Ashford' Mags changed the subject swiftly. 'Don't they suggest about a pound a day for a tip?'

'I've got an envelope ready in my pocket.'

'Now' smiled Mags 'Last chance. Is Sandy a chap or a lass?' She looked up at Celia.

Dispersal....and for some - shocks

'You know what? It really doesn't matter.' Celia's eyes shone merrily behind her glasses. She shrugged. 'Who cares? We've had a brilliant time, Sandy has been all that a tour leader should be, informative, helpful and self effacing. That's what matters.'

'You're quite right' nodded Mags.

'Such a shame about the mishaps, but it all got smoothed over, even Patricia Ryecart'.

'Floral Patricia?' said Mags, alarmed. She half rose and looked about her. 'Where is she? What happened?'

'She fell, getting on to the train. In Brussels. Didn't you hear?'

'No! Good grief, is she all right?'

'Oh, I imagine she's all right. Sandy thinks she broke her arm – it was all strapped up by the paramedics at the station. It looked bad, though, and she was in a lot of pain. They carted her off to hospital. She and Simon will have to come home later on.'

'My God. We have been an accident prone lot.'

Celia went on, making her way to say goodbye to Linda and Gwen and Gerrie. As she swayed back up the train the lights of England pierced the darkness, and there were a series of bleeps as mobiles were switched on and cell networks veered back from continental to British connections. Celia paused at Mags' seat. 'Well, goodbye dear' she said. 'We'll keep in touch; I'll be back in a couple of days, and perhaps we can meet sometimes in town for a cup of coffee, or lunch. Thank you for being such a good travelling companion. I do hope you manage to work things out at home.' She touched Mags on the shoulder and turned away.

'Thank you, Celia!' Mags called after her. 'Thank you so much. You've been wonderful....' Well, fancy that, she thought. Celia called me dear – I don't suppose she does that very often.

Mags had an almost physical clicking feeling in her brain, as it switched from freedom and adventure to the familiar and prosaic. She sighed. Have to go shopping tomorrow. Wonder what Dudley will have done about meals? Rubbish day tomorrow, too. Good thing. Or not; Dudley won't have put out last week's and I'm certainly not staying up all night to tidy up before the binmen come at seven o'clock in the morning. So this one will get missed as well. Have to go to the tip later in the week. Dudley said he would try to find time to cut the lawn. That means he won't have done it; and he has his built in riposte 'I said I would try. I've been very busy.' Huh! Busy on the computer in his study. Supposing he got no evening meal one night, and I said 'Sorry about that. I said I would try, but I've been so busy.' She smiled ruefully to herself. In her present frame of mind she almost thought she might try that; Celia would probably advise it. Call his bluff, she said. Actually, that's not a bad attitude to have – lots of bluffs to choose from. Maybe I will pick one, and see what happens. Or try Celia's list. Oh God.

She got up and went to talk to Linda. 'My phone's working' Linda said 'It suddenly started just after Lille, which was odd. I've texted Stuart, and left a voice message as well. He must be out somewhere, but he knows roughly what time I'll be back – I've told him I'll get a taxi from the station.'

Mags nodded. 'Good.' She moved on and spoke to Gwen and Gerrie. 'So we'll stick together, the four of us – get the train from Ashford to Canterbury and then a taxi. That all right?' Nods of agreement.

Sandy was propped against a stanchion at the end of the carriage, a folder of paperwork in one hand and in the middle of a conversation on the mobile. Mags made eye contact and handed over a folded ten pound note. She mouthed 'Thank you. Wonderful holiday! Thank you, Sandy!' and was acknowledged with a nod and a smile, and a silent thank you in return.

They were fortunate to make a connection with the Canterbury train within twenty minutes. 'Perhaps it's all worked out' said Gerrie 'on purpose. So the Eurostar passengers have time to get off and buy tickets.'

'Probably'. Mags was pulling two cases, her own and Linda's. They settled themselves on the train and noticed three of the Vienna crowd a little further along the carriage. The journey was far from smooth, and it reminded them that they were back in England: no more high speed trains and modern, jazzy stations. No more tidy platforms with spotless bins divided into three – no bins at all. Terrorism, presumably. The train stopped at almost every station; Wye. Chilham. Chartham. Horrible lurid yellow light that made everything look dirty. At last they were coming into Canterbury West, weary, in need of a good wash, and bracing themselves for one last effort. Grabbing the cases yet again, hauling coats and bags and counting bits of luggage, wondering whether to leave plastic carriers full of half eaten sandwiches and empty water bottles in the train, or whether they would find that they had ditched something important by mistake. A book or a souvenir. Better take everything and sort it all out at home tomorrow. It nearly is tomorrow. Bloody hell.

In silence they gathered themselves on the platform, slinging shoulder bags over heads and pulling the handles of wheeled cases round in order to trundle them across the concourse to the taxi rank. Under a light near the opening to the street a man was standing with a bunch of flowers – more than that, a bouquet; a huge riot of gorgeous blooms tenderly displayed in tissue paper with a thick length of raffia wound round the stems and a big bow. Definitely not off the shelf; definitely created by a florist, to order.

Mags was several paces behind the others; she had her head down and didn't notice, but Gwen did. She stopped. 'Isn't that Dudley?' she called to Mags. 'Look – it's Dudley! He's come to meet you!'

Mags looked up; it was Dudley. He came and took the handle of the case from her. He kissed her on the cheek. A lingering kiss. 'I'm so sorry' he said quietly. 'I know I'm a mess; I know I make you miserable sometimes, but I love you so much. I can't tell you how much I've missed you. The house is dead without you, awful. Thank you for coming home.' He paused, and cleared his throat. 'I'll try to be better. You have to help me, though, I don't understand what I do wrong and what I do that makes you happy. If you'll tell me, I'll do my best to be easier to live with.'

Mags began to shake. 'I'm so tired' she said. 'It's been an incredibly long journey – wonderful holiday, I'll tell you all about it, but it took two days to get back. I just want to go home.' She looked up at him and smiled.

Linda leaned heavily on her stick, finding it difficult to breathe. Gwen and Gerrie had stopped to see what was happening with Mags; now they smiled and waved 'Bye! Talk to you soon! We'll get a taxi – come on, Linda – bye, Mags! Bye, Dudley!'

'For God's sake' grumbled Linda 'I'm coming. Just grab the taxi, you know I can't rush'. She gathered her strength and pushed her right leg forward, concentrating on the co-ordination between pulling the case and using the walking stick. Which was why she didn't notice the headline poster for the local paper, clipped into an 'A' board just inside the station. It read 'Body of Local Man is Found on Track.'

The End